On the run from his former allies in 1943, Janos Nagy's life is turned upside down when he stumbles through a mysterious doorway and finds himself in the hands of the Temporal Research Institute, a covert organization that verifies historical events through time travel.

The year, he is told, is 2041. Wounded, exhausted, and helpless, he's in a time he doesn't know and a world that has changed beyond his wildest imagination. Dieter Schmidt, one of the TRI linguists and historians, offers his aid in making sense of this strange new existence.

But Janos's arrival has broken the TRI's prime rule of non-interference. It's not long until someone in the TRI decides that if the rule can be broken once...well, why not break it again?

TIME WAITS

Out of Time, Book One

C.B. Lewis

A NineStar Press Publication

Published by NineStar Press
P.O. Box 91792,
Albuquerque, New Mexico, 87199 USA.
www.ninestarpress.com

Time Waits

Printed in the USA
NineStar Press Edition
April, 2020

Print ISBN: 978-1-951880-95-8

Also available in eBook, ISBN: 978-1-951880-92-7

Warning: This book contains sexually explicit content, which may only be suitable for mature readers, wartime bloodshed, and gore.

*To everyone who had to make a new home through
no fault of their own.*

Chapter One

The heavy rain had lightened, which was a small mercy.

The moonlight, thin and sickly, barely broke through the clouds. The trees shone a dull grey in the darkness. Only the rustle of leaves in the wind and the cries of some small creatures out in the darkness broke the silence.

A soldier broke cover from beneath the undergrowth. He stumbled and slithered down a muddy slope towards the track. Grass and dirt tore beneath his boots, and he caught himself against the trunk of a tree to keep from falling, his breath coming in ragged gasps.

In the distance, he was sure he could hear the howl of the dogs, the hunting party. He gulped down a breath before running onward.

He was armed, it was true, but what was one shot against a legion of men? He could turn it on himself, but he had escaped death once. He had no wish to face it again.

Though rough and little used, the narrow track was easier than breaching the undergrowth again. He had to get as far ahead as he could. They wouldn't continue the hunt much longer, not with the chill of night setting in, but they might follow just long enough.

So he ran.

His legs shook with each step, but terror drove him onward. If he stopped, even to catch his breath, he didn't think he would be able to start again. If he stopped, he would die. If he rested, he would die. If he did anything but run, he would die.

Something howled in the night, and his heart slammed against his ribs.

It might have been a dog, but it could have been a wolf.

The wind was picking up, whirling around him, the icy rain lashing his face cut through with scalding tears on his cheeks. Running and weeping. No honour. No dignity. All he knew was that he wanted to live.

Ahead of him, the track broadened, which meant it was coming closer to civilization, to people.

He hesitated a moment before plunging off the path and back into the forest, branches whipping at his face and limbs. His foot caught on a root, and he fell, rolling down the slope. He crashed into a stream at the bottom, breaking through a film of ice and plunging into the frigid water below. The cold cut to the bone, so sharp he couldn't even draw breath to cry out.

Blindly, he tried to find purchase on the bank. He fell forward heavily onto the ground, a thin keen of pain escaping him as he crushed his left arm beneath him. Warmth spread from the limb. The wound was open again.

"Ángele Dei," he whispered desperately, "qui custos es mei, me, tib..."

A shout cut him off.

Lights glowed, flickering lanterns visible, like fireflies between the trees.

He pushed himself onto his knees, keening in pain, and grabbed at the low branches of a tree to pull himself upright. Splinters of bark dug into his skin, fresh blood warm on his hands. His legs were numb with cold and pain, but he ran.

The bitter wind cut into his throat and chest. He pushed deeper into the thicker, denser undergrowth—somewhere to hide, somewhere safe, somewhere unseen. Thorns tore at his face and hand, and he tasted blood in his mouth.

He was scrambling over a fallen tree trunk when it gave way beneath him. His ankle folded under him, and he yelped, falling onto his knee. It was only when he fell that he saw the hollow beneath the fallen tree. A hiding place.

Breathing hard, he squirmed through the gap, the tree and ground tearing at him, at his clothing. It was a small space, tight and narrow, but enough to shield him. He pushed dirt up to block the opening, his nose and mouth full of the taste of moss and mud, and lay still and silent as the grave.

Chapter Two

A bell rang out.

Dieter glanced up from the desk, his pen caught between his teeth. The team had been gone close to an hour already. The chime of the bell meant they should be on their way back, which meant he was another minute closer to getting his weekend off.

Still, no good counting chickens until everyone was through the gate, and he knew he wasn't needed. The communication through the temporal gate was spotty at best, but just in case they had a good connection, he had to be on hand to provide information.

There was always someone in the team who thought they knew better, who would not have caught all the nuanccs of the briefing. When it happened, it could cause all manner of problems, given the time zone they had walked into.

He chewed on the end of his pen, studying the crossword in front of him.

One of the other linguists constructed a new one each day and left it on top of his briefing notes. The clues were always in English, but the answers could be in any one of the six languages he was fluent in. It made it more of a challenge, and Mei Xiao Cheung was a cunning witch when it came to cryptic word puzzles.

They took time, but any distraction was useful.

In the Temporal Research Institution, linguists and historians often found themselves sitting on the edge of a mission, waiting. Their role was to prepare the team for the historical period they were about to enter. They had to ensure the agents had all available knowledge and resources, and then debrief and make sense of the information the agents collected. They also had to be on hand throughout the mission, in case of emergencies.

Dieter tapped the pen against the ring in his lower lip.

No one would ever think scholar when they saw him. Scholar sounded dull and dusty. Being stuck in an office didn't help, so he made them look twice. From the piercing in his lip to the streak of blue in his bleached-blond hair, from the peacock-coloured eye shadow to the fitted shirts and braces, he made himself interesting.

He filled in one of the words, snickering. In Latin, it was more than a little rude.

It was a challenge. Unnecessary, but for someone who usually ended up stuck in dry conversations with tedious people in a similar line of work, a crossword littered with puns and lewd jokes was the height of stimulation.

He had half of the clues solved when the door dividing the monitoring station from the office opened.

Tom Sanders beckoned. "We have a problem."

Dieter scrambled up. He didn't bother slipping his feet into his shoes, hurrying after Sanders. The other techs retreated. From Sanders's expression, shit was about to hit the fan, and none of them wanted to be in the way.

The monitoring station had a direct video link down into the temporal chamber, which was little more than a steel-walled room with a metal doorframe connected to God only knew how many cables and connections. Time travel took a hell of a lot of power. Despite all appearances, it was a formidable piece of technology.

One of the team was standing in the room, his contemporary uniform—dirty and stained—and weapon out of place in such a clean and sterile chamber.

"What am I looking at?" Dieter asked. "One of the boys came back early?"

Sanders shook his head, zooming the camera.

The face wasn't one Dieter recognised, and he'd been responsible for briefing the team for the weeks before their departure.

"Fucking hell."

"We don't know which side he's from," Sanders said. He wasn't an agent himself, not anymore, but he was one of the pioneers of the time-travel technology they used. He always kept an eye on every temporal jump. "I've been telling them for bloody months to get the proximity sensor in place before they open the doorway."

Dieter pushed him to one side and sat down, touching the screen to drag in the close-up, studying their intruder. He might have been in his late thirties, but it was likely he was younger, though hard to tell from under the matted beard on his chin. Bone-thin, pale, ragged, and wary, he stared around at the chamber suspiciously.

"Could be a refugee," Dieter said.

"But?" Sanders prompted.

"He's military," Dieter replied. "He was quick enough to get the weapon off one of our people when they split up. You can tell from the way he's holding the gun—that's not a civilian." He scaled up the image and then hissed between his teeth. "Shit. It's not one of our prop guns either. He's got a live one." He called up the maps on the consoles. "Where did the doorway open?"

Sanders touched the screen. "Here."

Dieter pushed his hands through his hair. "Jesus fucking Christ," he groaned. "It wasn't meant to be anywhere near any combat zones. He could be Allied or renegade. Hell, he might even be a rebel or refugee with a grudge."

"And while he's in there, no one else can come through," Sanders said. "For all we know, he might shoot anyone who walks in through either of the doors. He might have already taken down more than one of the team."

Dieter leaned back in the chair and watched as the man in the chamber laid his hand against the doorframe, examining it. The intruder didn't realise he was being watched. Of course he didn't. He came from a world before security cameras and video relays.

"We can't send the big guns in," Dieter said. "They charge in, he might go off. We can't risk it. If there's a gun fight, it could take out the connection to the door, and we could lose the whole team."

Sanders nodded grimly. "Can you talk to him? We have the speaker down there."

"And tell him what?" Dieter asked. "Hello, friend, you're in the future. Would you mind going back wherever the hell you came from?"

"I was thinking about getting him to lower the weapon," Sanders snapped. "We need him either disarmed or out of the temporal chamber."

Dieter rubbed his forehead. He was right. If the man severed the connection to the past, the team could be lost. They still couldn't establish a link directly to a place they had been before, no matter how many times they tried.

There were backup plans in place, but they were only theoretical so far. If the door was closed, the team would be stuck. There was always a set rendezvous, just in case, but it could be days in the past before they could be picked up. Every moment spent in the past was a moment when something could be irreversibly fucked up.

And if they didn't get the room clear, and the man felt threatened when they tried to return, he might well attack them too.

"We can't demand anything," Dieter said. He motioned to the screen. "That's not a man who will make himself defenceless in an unknown place with an unknown enemy." He got up from the stool, steeling himself to do the stupidest thing he had ever done in his life. "Open the door into the corridor. Let me go in and talk to him."

"I don't think..."

Dieter shook his head. "We send any armed people in there, he'll go off like a bomb. Some people have fight or flight all over them." He tapped the screen. "This man's dangerous because he's desperate. How desperate would you need to be to jump through a portal into God knows where?"

"He might just shoot you."

Dieter gazed at the screen. "He might, but we don't have much of a choice now, do we?"

Sanders stared at him, then nodded. "You can get a vest..."

"No." Dieter got up from the desk. His hands were shaking. Fucking ridiculous. He'd spent his whole life wanting to meet people from the past, and now he was going to and he felt like he was about to shit himself.

Sanders stared at him. "Do you have some kind of death wish?"

"We have less than an hour before the doorway needs shut down," Dieter reminded him. "I can do this."

Sanders ran a hand over his stubbled chin. "We have an armed security team on standby. Get to the corridor. The first door is open. It'll close once you're inside."

Dieter nodded.

The walk down the stairs seemed like the longest in his life. The metal grid of the staircase pressed against his feet through his socks, and he wondered if maybe he should have stopped and taken off his makeup and jewellery.

There was no time.

The whole place was metal-cold, making him shiver, as he approached the corridor.

There were four heavyweight doors between the temporal chamber and the staircase, and even more on the levels above. If anyone came through, like their new intruder, they would never get out of the agency, but they could cause a hell of a lot of problems.

The armed squad were waiting. They always were, in case something got through that wasn't meant to.

"You sure you don't want a vest?"

Dieter wasn't, but he wasn't about to play chicken in front of one of the uniforms. It wasn't as if he didn't like the security teams. He liked them well enough. He just hated the arrogant pricks who thought he was helpless because he wasn't big and built like a fucking wall.

"I need to look harmless," he said, surprised how steady his voice was. "That means no sign of anything military. No vest."

The leader tapped a code into the console and then offered Dieter an earpiece. "If you can get him out of the transport chamber and into the layover room, it'll be enough," he said. "We just need to make sure the connection to the door isn't threatened."

"Is that all?" Dieter said with a snort.

His hands were still shaking, but he clenched them into fists as the door slid open. He stepped into the corridor for the first time. It was little more than a long metal tunnel with doors at each end and another chamber between them where returning teams would disarm. He padded towards it. It was empty, cold, like a cell.

The doors hissed closed behind him. He swallowed hard as he approached the last door, which led into the temporal chamber.

"I'm here," he said, sending up a prayer to any God who might be listening. He wasn't a religious guy, but sometimes it didn't hurt to try for a little bit of divine backup.

The locks shot open, and the door slid aside.

Dieter stepped through and damn near pissed his pants when the barrel of the gun pressed against his forehead. The smell made him gag. The man stank of rotten blood and dirt and stale sweat.

He didn't say a word, and Dieter found he had inconveniently forgotten every one of his languages. He scrambled desperately for something to say, something useful.

All he could think to do was kneel and raise his hands to his head. If he was passive and submissive, he wouldn't be seen as a threat, and maybe it would be enough to get the man's attention. He lifted his eyes to the man's face. Green eyes stared warily at him.

It was enough to make the intruder take a step back, but the gun remained trained on him.

Well, he wasn't fucking dead. Good start.

His dad's language was the first to come back to him, and thank fucking Christ it was the right one.

"I'm not your enemy," he said in German. He modulated the pronunciation and the accent to a more southern dialect, one of the lesser cities. Not strong enough to be misunderstood, but strong enough to make it clear he wasn't a high-ranking person.

"No? You speak. Who you are?"

It wasn't much to go on, but the man's accent was thick and his German basic. A Magyar. Hungarian.

Dieter kept his eyes on the man's face. He looked even gaunter up close. His eyes were ringed by shadow, his skin pale and sallow. "Someone who tries to save your life," he said. "You came to a dangerous place, friend."

The Hungarian's pale lips curled away from his teeth. "I am not your friend."

Another piece of the puzzle.

Dieter drew a quiet breath. "I am not an enemy." He spread his hands—empty—by his sides. "Ask your questions. If I can, I will answer them."

The man shifted the gun. He was holding it with his right hand, supported against his hip. His left arm was folded in against his gut, his hand hidden in the overlong sleeve. Dieter's eyes flicked to his torso. He could see no sign of blood, but that didn't mean there wasn't some hidden injury.

"This is a military facility?"

Dieter shook his head. "Scientific facility."

The man's expression darkened. "I hear of science. You think this is comfort?"

Dieter wet his lips with the tip of his tongue. "A different kind of science. It is not made to harm people."

The man snorted, shifting the weight of his gun. "Your people, they wear uniform. They carry weapon. But they are not soldiers, and they are not made to harm people?" He leaned over Dieter. "You lie badly."

Dieter met his eyes. "I do not lie." Fuck was whirling around in his brain. Over and over. "My people need to move unnoticed. They wear the clothing and carry the weapons to allow them to do so."

"I know these people," the man said, his voice sharp, clipped with barely contained anger. "They watch. They listen. They take words you do not say, put bullet in your head."

"No."

"Yes. I have seen it."

Dieter got to his feet, keeping his hands on his head. "No. This place has laws and rules. We cannot kill. We cannot harm. We watch and learn, but we do not hurt anyone."

The man sneered, but there was exhaustion in his stance, in the pallor of his face. "And what is this place? This special scientific place? Where are we?"

Dieter glanced at the camera and then at the man. If he failed, the man would be dead. If he succeeded, the man would be sent to his own time with one hell of a story to tell. What did it matter if he knew the truth? No one would believe him.

"We are in your future," Dieter said. "More than a century."

The gun was pressed to his brow, hard enough to break the skin. The man swore savagely in Hungarian, some of the words unfamiliar but easy to guess from their explosiveness.

Dieter closed his eyes. Blood was trickling down and matting his lashes. The metal was fucking cold against his skin, and piss soaked into his trousers.

"I do not lie," he said in Hungarian. He heard the man catch his breath. It wasn't Dieter's strongest language, but he could make himself understood. "Science is advanced here." He forced himself to open his eyes to meet the man's. "Maybe enough to heal your wound."

The green eyes stared at him. "Heal?"

Dieter could have bitten his tongue. It was against all the rules, but they needed to get the team home. They were running out of time. "Through this door. I can take you to a doctor who can tend your wound."

The barrel of the gun slid down his temple and pressed to his neck. "You will stay with me," the man said. "My finger is on the trigger. If anyone attacks me, I will kill you. Do you understand?"

Dieter jerked his chin in a tight nod. "I will call for the doctor." He slipped into English, the lingua franca of the agency. "Sanders, I need you to get a medic down to the layover room. He's willing to come that far in exchange for medical treatment."

Sanders cursed explosively in his ear.

"Who do you speak to?" his captor demanded.

Dieter put his hand to his ear and withdrew the small earpiece. "It's like a radio. We use them to communicate."

The man stared at the device. "It's so small." For a moment, he seemed fascinated, curious. He tore his eyes from it, back to Dieter, drawing on the mask of hostile indifference. "You asked for a physician?"

Dieter nodded, putting the earpiece back in. Sanders was barking orders on the other end.

"Three minutes," Dieter said. "There is a chamber through this door. Will you come with me to it? They will meet us there."

"Not here?"

Dieter shook his head. "They want a clean chamber." It was sort of true. "Many people come through here."

The man shifted the weight of the gun in his arm. "You go first."

Dieter put his hands on his head and led the way through the door. The next door was closed, but he knew it could be opened by the monitoring station. Dieter's mouth went dry as a bone, and his trousers were sodden.

"Medical team is in place," Sanders said. "Door will open in three."

Dieter paused, waiting for it to open. The cold weight of the gun against the base of his skull a terrifying reminder that one twitch of an unpredictable man's finger could kill him.

"This way," he croaked in Hungarian.

Doctor Bellevue was waiting, her case of equipment on one of the metal benches lining the wall. A silver-haired lady with a stern look, her long-fingered hands were folded in front of her, and she glanced at Dieter, then beyond him, at their guest.

"Injury?" she demanded.

"I don't know," Dieter replied. "Either torso or left arm." A jab to the side of his head reminded him that the intruder didn't appear to know any English.

Dieter tilted his head and spoke to the man behind him. "This is the doctor. She needs to know how you are hurt."

"A woman?"

Dieter snorted. "Times change. Do you want to be tended or not?"

The man shoved him farther into the room, and Dieter stumbled.

"Kneel," the man said.

Dieter knew he had to cooperate. He sank onto his knees, his head down.

Out of the corner of his eye, he saw the door to the temporal chamber slide closed. He breathed out with relief. The team would be able to come through. They might be stuck in the temporal chamber for a short time, but it was better than being stuck in the past.

The doctor approached as if she didn't notice the gun pressing to the back of Dieter's head. "Well?" she demanded.

"Your injury," Dieter said. "She needs to know."

"Arm," the man said. "And chest."

Dieter murmured a translation.

In the metal walls, he could see the reflection of the doctor unbuttoning the soldier's filthy jacket and shirt, pushing them open. He heard the way her breath hissed between her teeth. The soldier made no sound. He only bit out a tight curse when she drew the coat and shirt down over his arm.

Something pattered on the floor close to Dieter, and he glanced sidelong. Dark drops of blood fell from the soldier's arm. A pile of soiled and bloody cloth fell too. Makeshift bandages? A tattered shirt? Dieter couldn't tell.

"How long has it been like this?" the doctor demanded.

Dieter asked through dry lips. On the polished wall, the reflection of his captor swayed alarmingly. He kept imagining the gun going off in the man's unsteady hand, and his brains splattering all over the floor like the soldier's blood.

"Weeks?" The Hungarian's voice was raw with pain. "I forget."

"He doesn't know," Dieter said. In a war zone, who could be sure of anything?

The doctor was silent for a long moment. "Tell him to sit down, before he falls. If I'm going to tend him, I won't have him on his feet."

Dieter shivered. It was tempting to yell that if she wanted to tell the nice man with a gun to her head what to do, she was welcome to do so. But he had one job in the place, and he was going to fucking do it.

"She needs you to sit down," he said, forcing his voice to remain steady.

The soldier was silent for a long moment.

"I will sit," he agreed, "but you will turn, and you will kneel. If I am betrayed, I will look at you when I kill you."

Dieter nodded, shivering. He rose on his knees and turned as the soldier took one step, then another. He sat down stiffly on the edge of the metal bench that ran the length of the wall. The shirt and coat hung from his right shoulder, and the gun was still trained on Dieter.

"Closer," he snapped.

Dieter forced himself across the floor, a little closer to the man, close enough so the soldier could rest the muzzle of the gun against his forehead. It was shaking, which wasn't any comfort at all.

Dieter tore his eyes away from the gun, trying to look anywhere else but the potential end of his life.

The only choice views he had were the doctor—no, thank you very fucking much—or the soldier himself. The man was a ribcage on legs, his stomach a concave hollow beneath his chest. He was ashen, and his torso was a mess of blood and pus.

Dieter's throat tightened. A slash curved up from the man's right side, across his ribs. Dieter's gaze flicked to the soldier's left arm, then he wished it hadn't. The wounds the doctor uncovered had been left for too long; even he could tell that. The bone-thin upper arm connected to a mess of swollen and pulpy tissue. It was blackened at the fingertips, shading through purples and reds to the elbow.

He tore his eyes away and looked at the soldier instead, to find the green eyes gazing at him.

"What happened?" Dieter asked quietly.

The soldier lifted his right shoulder. "War."

The doctor prevented Dieter from asking more. She was taking out tools and syringes, and all the things guaranteed to make him feel unsteady on his knees. He wasn't squeamish, but the smell was making him gag. The thought of pus and blood everywhere was worse.

"What is that?" the soldier demanded sharply when the doctor leaned closer with a sterilizing aerosol.

"It will clean the wound and reduce the pain," Dieter replied, keeping his eyes on the soldier's face. "It may hurt at first. It's cold."

The man hesitated and then nodded, holding out his arm.

He was already pale, but when the icy spray touched the inflamed flesh of his arm, the soldier's face went grey. The muscles in his jaw twitched as he clenched his teeth, but he didn't make a sound. His pupils seemed to expand, dark and black and full of pain.

The muzzle of the gun shuddered against Dieter's head. He put all thought of it aside and touched the soldier on the knee, trying to offer some comfort.

"Breathe deeply," he said. "It helps."

The muzzle jabbed hard against his head, and the man bared his teeth. "Do not touch me," he snarled.

Dieter flinched as a fresh trickle of blood ran down from his brow.

"Breathe," he said again, subsiding to sit on his heels. He held his hands up, empty and nonthreatening. "I promise it will help."

The soldier watched him with suspicion, but the soldier breathed in, ragged, gulping breaths. The doctor glanced at Dieter.

"You told him to do that?" she murmured.

Dieter kept his eyes on the man. "I thought it would help. How does it look?"

"Not good." She circled around to the man's right side to clean the chest wounds. Her patient didn't make a sound, but Dieter saw the way he shuddered in pain. His head rocked against the wall behind him. "Severe malnutrition, dehydration, and septic wounds are the most obvious problems." She glanced at Dieter. "His doesn't have much time left."

It was one of the great injustices of the institution.

They had all the facilities and technology money could buy, but they were bound by a code of noninterference in the past. They could observe, collect information, lost artifacts, and missing scientific discoveries, but the people who had lived and died were not to be touched. Their timelines were to be maintained. The TRI was not allowed to save anyone. They were not allowed to change what had already happened.

The man would go back to his time. The door would close. He would die. That would be the end of it.

"What is she saying?" The soldier's voice was hoarse with pain. He winced as swabs, thick with antiseptics, were dragged over the seeping gash on his chest.

"Listing your symptoms," Dieter replied. "She will treat what she can."

The man nodded, drawing unsteady breaths through flared nostrils. His face was hollowed beneath his cheekbones, and every drop of blood had drained from his skin. The gun shook more by the moment.

"And then?" he asked, his voice raw. "Then you send me back? To nothing? To death?"

Dieter couldn't reply. The man in front of him had taken him hostage, threatened to kill him more than once. All the same, no one deserved to be put in a situation where they knew they had days, maybe hours left.

The soldier nodded, slowly, as if the silence was the answer.

Dieter maintained eye contact. "Boss," he murmured, "any sign of the team?"

Sanders's voice came at once. "On their way. They found Llewelyn. He's unconscious, but alive. The doorway is stable for the moment, but not for long."

Dieter eyed the soldier. "You didn't kill our man."

The man swallowed hard, his Adam's apple bobbing convulsively.

"He did not need to die," he said. The gun sank an inch, then two, as if he couldn't bear the weight anymore. His face was still ashen, but there was a blue tinge around his lips.

"Doc," Dieter whispered.

Bellevue raised her head. She moved faster than Dieter thought possible, brushing aside the gun. Just in time too. The man's hand tensed as he went into shuddering convulsions. The blast echoed deafeningly off the walls, and pain ripped through Dieter as the bullet plunged through his sleeve, tearing a ragged chunk out of his arm.

If the gun had still been pointing at him, it would have gone through his throat.

"Christ…" he whispered. His stomach clenched, folding him over. He was sick on the floor, shaking.

"Enough of that!" The doctor had her patient supported in one arm. The soldier's eyes had rolled up in his head, and he was shaking. "Help me lay him down. He's going into shock."

Dieter staggered upright. Blood streamed down his right arm, but no pain.

Strange, he thought distantly. He slid one arm under the man's legs to lift them up onto the bench, as the doctor set the soldier's head down on the other side. Dieter met her eyes. "You know we can't save him. They won't let you."

Doctor Bellevue gazed over the edge of her glasses, her expression hard as steel. "To hell with them," she snarled. "We can't save them in their time, but he isn't in his time. He's in our time, and no one dies in my care."

Dieter giggled. He actually fucking giggled. He didn't know if it was terror or adrenaline or shock or some heady cocktail of all the emotions he'd been smothered by in the last half hour, but he giggled like a schoolgirl in a fucking anime.

"They're going to be pissed," he said.

Doctor Bellevue scanned her patient's vital signs and placed a syringe module against his throat. "Let them be." She laid her fingers against the other side of the man's throat, checking against a palm console in her other hand. "You might want to lock the doors. If you want this man to live, we can't let them throw him back."

Sanders was listening. Sanders could hear every word and could stop them doing anything. But he was silent, even as Dieter stumbled to the doors like a drunk Bambi. He didn't stop them from slamming the manual locks in place. He didn't even stop them when Dieter heard the announcement that the team was home and the doorway was about to shut down.

The second it shut, the man was in their care for the rest of his life, however long that was.

Dieter leaned back against the locked door, staring down at the unconscious soldier.

It was one hell of a fucking day.

He was sodden in his own piss, blood, and vomit. He had a chunk knocked out of his forehead and a bloody great hole in his arm. He'd just broken one of the cardinal rules of the TRI, on camera, in front of one of the top people in the institute.

"I," he declared, "am fucked."

Chapter Three

It was warm, and it was quiet.

It had been a long time since Nagy Janos had experienced either of those things.

He did not open his eyes, not quite yet. Instead, he lay still and took in what he could from his surroundings. There was a chemical scent in filled the air, sharp, clean. The smell of blood and filth which had clung to him was gone.

Machinery whirred close by, so quiet he had to strain to hear it. Soft mechanical chirps repeated with the steady rhythm of a heartbeat. Beyond it, he could hear distant footsteps coming and going.

It was only after he had catalogued his surroundings that he realised, for the first time in weeks, he had not been woken by pain. The wounds on his chest ached, but it was dull, tolerable, not the tight agony it had been before.

And his arm...

Janos forced his eyes open a crack. It was more of a struggle than he anticipated, his eyelids heavy and thick with sleep. The room was lit gently, and the light didn't hurt his eyes, but it still took him a moment to focus.

He stared down, and acid boiled in his throat.

His left arm was gone, severed beneath the elbow. Fine bandages wrapped the stump, but it did not change the fact that his arm was gone.

You knew it would be, he chastised himself. He had seen the rot often enough in the field. He watched men hide it until it was too late, consuming them and leaving their blood thick and black and stinking. Buying a life with a lost limb was a price some would consider too high. But Janos lived. He knew to be grateful for it.

He dragged his other hand across his body to close shaking fingers around the bandages, as if it would somehow make it more real, tangible. His fingers recoiled at once. It felt wrong. He knew it would for a long time to come, if he lived.

He looked at his other hand, weariness slowing his thoughts. A spike of metal threaded into his skin. A tube, thin and transparent, connected to it. He followed it with his bleary eyes and found it attached to a clear bag of water. Stranger and stranger still.

He examined the room. It was big, white, and clean, the bed he lay on the same: big, with clean white linens. Even the nightshirt they had dressed him in was the same. It seemed he was in a very big, very white, very clean place.

A chair sat beside the shaded window. The person on it had their feet propped up on the window ledge. He couldn't see their face, and they didn't seem to know he was awake.

Janos carefully moved his left arm over his body to tug the metal spike from his hand, then flinched when his stump knocked against the spike. No fingers, he thought foolishly. He lifted his right hand to his mouth instead and tugged at it with his teeth.

The tube fell away, but the spike remained where it was. He watched curiously as a ruby-dark drop of blood welled out onto his hand and dribbled down between his fingers. It fell, spotting the clean white sheet with dark rosettes.

He blinked hard, trying to clear his head. There was a basin – also white and big – on the wall with a metal tap above it. Water. Cold water would help.

He managed to shove the sheets down, swung his legs from the bed, and rose. His legs shook beneath him, and he stumbled, taking the stand with the clear bag with him. His knees cracked against the tiled floor, but the pain seemed a long way off. He swore more in surprise than anything else.

The person in the chair must have been sleeping because they jumped at the noise, scrambling up from the chair.

Janos propped himself on his left elbow, his right forearm on the floor. He watched the growing pool of blood spreading from the spike in his hand.

The person from the chair swore, and Janos recalled the voice.

He stared as the person dropped to his knees in front of him and reached for Janos's wounded hand. Ah. The whimpering youth who had knelt and quivered in front of him. He was no doubt a pathetic young soldier who bartered safe passage on looks alone.

And now, here he was, kneeling in front of him once more.

He glared at the boy, who ignored him. Instead, the boy lifted Janos's hand and pulled out the spike. He set it aside and covered the wound with a handkerchief from his pocket, pressing down on it. Blood soaked through the fabric, but soon it slowed, and stopped.

"You should have left it." the boy said. He looked younger. His whore's paint was gone, his face clean and pale. He wasn't dressed up like an officer anymore, just wearing loose trousers and a long-sleeved vest. Janos couldn't miss the black bruise and gash he'd left on the boy's brow with his gun. "It was there to help you."

Janos stared at him for a moment. "You cut my arm off."

"The doctors did," the boy murmured, uncovering and examining Janos's hand. "It saved your life."

His passiveness made Janos scowl even more. He had spent every day of the past four years fighting: for his country, for respect, for dignity, for his commanders, for food, for his life. The pretty boy in front of him was well fed, clean, respectable, but he was pathetic, keeping his eyes down and not even raising his chin.

The boy put his hand under Janos's right arm. "You need to get back into bed."

Janos jerked his arm free. "I told you not to touch me." No pretty boy with soft hands and big eyes had any reason to pander to him.

He managed to struggle to his feet but slipped again. The boy caught his arm, ignoring his cursing, to help him to the bed.

It was humiliating how exhausting it was.

"Get me a drink," he growled.

The boy didn't argue, hurrying over to the basin. He filled a glass with water and returned, holding it out to Janos as if he expected to be struck. Janos snorted at the boy's wariness. What could he do, half-conscious and unarmed?

He took the glass, cursing again when it started to slip.

The boy's hand was under it, supporting it, all but holding it.

He helped Janos drink, which was even more humiliating.

"I don't need you to tend me like a cripple," Janos snarled, knocking the boy's hand and the glass aside. The glass hit the wall and shattered, adding a pool of water to the puddle of blood and fluid already smeared on the floor.

The boy raised his eyes to him. "We saved your life," he said quietly. "We want to help you."

Janos drew ragged gulping breaths. "I am not a cripple," he rasped, reaching out and grabbing the boy by the front of his shirt.

He dragged him closer and hissed, "Save my life all you like, but never treat me as if I cannot kill you one-handed if I want to."

The boy was silent, but he nodded. He reached up to the wall and pressed a small, round button and stepped back.

"The doctor will come in and see how you are," he said, his voice bland and flat. "I will translate any questions you have or any explanations she gives."

Janos turned away from him when the door slid open. The same doctor entered. She was an imposing woman with a face like a battleaxe. Disapproval filled her eyes when she took in the blood on the bedding and the floor. She made a gesture with one hand that was clear enough, so Janos drew his legs up onto the bed and sat against the pillows, watching her guardedly.

She inquired of his name through the boy, noted it down. That done, she checked his hand, which had stopped bleeding, then examined him from head to toe. The one small mercy was that the boy turned away to stand by the window, his back to them both.

Despite being a woman, she seemed to know what she was doing. His wounds were uncovered, examined, and in the case of his arm, she used the strange spray on the flesh again. It felt painless and refreshingly cool against the warm flesh.

Janos looked blankly at the blunt limb. The neat stump was sealed at the end with a thick, opaque white paste, and the shades of red and purple which had stained his flesh for days and weeks were gone, along with his forearm and his blackened hand.

She spoke in a language Janos didn't recognise.

"Doctor Bellevue would like to know if you are in any pain," the boy by the window said.

Janos took a moment to consider it. Compared to the agony of a festering arm, and knife wounds to his ribs tearing every time he walked, he felt light and free of pain.

"None," he said in surprise.

The boy turned, his expression grave, and spoke to the doctor, who sighed. When she spoke, it was directed at Janos, and her expression stern, but he had to wait until the boy translated for him.

"The needle in your hand was to provide medicine to ease the pain and reduce the infection," he said, folding his arms over his chest. "She would like to put another line in, but you would have to leave it in this time, and not remove it."

Janos curled his fingers into a fist. "Do I need it?"

The boy glanced at the doctor, who nodded and said something brisk.

"She says your current dose will wear off soon. There may be a lot of pain when it does."

Janos snorted. It explained a lot if they had been dosing him with opiates to keep him quiet and docile. "No."

The boy's brow creased. "What?"

"I will not have any needles in my skin," Janos said flatly.

"Even if it causes you pain?"

Janos lifted one shoulder. "I have had worse. No needles."

Reluctantly, the boy translated the words for the doctor, who rolled her eyes towards the ceiling in an international expression of frustration. She returned to her examination, and the boy turned away again. Janos didn't really know or care why. He fixed his eyes on the ceiling and let the doctor examine as she wished.

It didn't take long, and she drew the sheet over him to give him back something like modesty.

"Dieter," she said, calling the attention of the boy.

Janos took note of the name. He *was* a German, it seemed, this tall, slender blond boy.

The boy turned, his arms still folded across his chest. He listened to what she had to say and then approached the bed. "She says you still need to rest to recover. You are to remain here and stay in bed to let your wounds heal. She says you can try some food as well, but only a little to begin with because it might make you ill."

"And then what?" Janos said curtly. "I am put in a prison camp?"

Dieter started in surprise. "You're not a prisoner."

Janos looked towards the door. He had caught a glimpse of a pale corridor when the doctor entered. "There are men guarding this room."

Dieter's expression tensed. "You are not a prisoner, but you are not a guest yet."

Janos inclined his head. "So I might become one or the other?"

Blue eyes met his. "Better than dead," he said.

"So," Janos agreed. He had a habit of tapping his fingers together when thinking, and looked down when his fingers met nothing. His hand. Of course. For a moment, he thought it was still there. He looked at the doctor, who was touching a strange box in her palm.

"Doctor," Dieter said.

They exchanged a few words, and Dieter nodded, and then the doctor made her way out of the room. The German remained standing where he was, his arms still folded across his narrow chest, his face expressionless.

Janos ignored him, closing his eyes.

When the door opened again a moment later, he hoped the damned boy was leaving. But when he cracked open one of his eyelids, Dieter was back by the window in his seat, which he had turned around to face the bed. They had new visitors, it seemed.

Two people in matching blue uniforms had entered, one male, one female. They started cleaning up the blood and liquid spilled on the floor. They glanced up at him, as if they expected him to leap from the bed and attack them.

One of them approached and lifted away the bloody blanket to replace it with another, just as white and soft. Task completed, he and his companion departed in silence, but the boy lingered.

"What do you want?" Janos finally asked.

Dieter shook his head. "Nothing. But I'm the only person in the building who can speak any Hungarian."

"And I am expected to speak?"

"If you're in pain or you need something." He shrugged. "The doctor gets...annoyed if her patients can't ask for help."

Janos curled his fingers against his palm. "And I seem helpless to you?"

Dieter's hands were laced together over his belly, and the balls of his thumbs pressed together. He was gazing at his hands but looked up again.

"You're in a world you don't know with facilities you don't know and surrounded by people you don't know who speak a language you don't know in an agency you don't know. You've been unconscious for two days, you've had major surgery, you've not eaten in God knows how long." Dieter bared his teeth like an angry cat. "Yes. Right now, I think you're as helpless as a fucking child."

Janos stared at him.

Dieter glared back, but there was a flicker of terror in his eyes.

Still afraid, even of the half-starved cripple, Janos thought bitterly. He wished he had the strength to grab the boy, shake him, make him see it was not bravery to torment a man when he was weak, because a weak man could get strong again.

There would be time enough.

He laid his head against the pillows and closed his eyes again. He knew he wouldn't sleep, but it was easier than trying to talk to some foolish pretty boy with more looks than sense and no instinct for self-preservation.

The doors opened again to let another person in another uniform enter. Janos deigned to open one eye, watching as the man—a darker-skinned one this time—put the tray on a table which slid out of the foot of the bed frame. Like the doctor, the man had some kind of box in his hand, and he tapped on it before pushing the table within Janos's reach.

He said something, which Dieter translated.

"Take your time with the food and don't push your body." Dieter seemed half-asleep, his eyes shut. "You haven't eaten in some time, so you won't be able to eat as much as you might like to."

Janos said nothing, pulling the tray towards him with the one hand he had left. He didn't recognise any of the food, but it looked filling, and steam was rising from it. The bowl nearest him seemed to have some kind of porridge in it. It smelled sweet. His stomach gurgled, and he clumsily picked up the spoon.

Maybe it was the drugs in his system or maybe it was exhaustion, but it seemed an impossible task to scoop anything up. The bowl tipped and shifted precariously. Janos set his teeth, blinking hard to focus.

He'd barely managed two spoonfuls when a second hand slipped into his line of sight and took a hold of the edge of the bowl. The damned boy again. Janos flashed a glare at him, but the boy remained, his fingertips white against the edge of the bowl.

"Eat," he said.

A muscle in Janos's cheek twitched. He wanted the boy gone. He wanted to be left alone to deal with his infirmity. He didn't want to be humiliated by a man with two arms standing there, forcing him to acknowledge how much he was damaged. But he was hungry, and he was tired, and as the doctor had promised, the pain was returning to his body.

Mechanically, he shoved the spoon into the oat-filled mess and scooped it up. He tried not to think about the boy holding his dish for him as if he needed someone to tend him. He focused on the spoon. It was white like the room and wasn't made of metal. It clicked against his teeth with every careful mouthful.

At one point, the boy moved as if to withdraw the bowl, but Janos glowered at him, eyes blazing, and shook his head. He'd be damned if some child was going to instruct him.

Finally, he set the spoon down when his belly ached. He was so full the food seemed like it might crawl back up his throat. Too much, he realised, clutching his hand over his gut. He drew slow breaths, trying to keep the nausea at bay.

The boy was wandering about, and Janos didn't understand why until a round basin was set beside him on the bed.

"In case you weren't listening to the nurse," the boy said acidly before retreating to his chair.

Mercifully, the boy didn't say anything when Janos brought up part of what he had eaten. He just fetched another glass of water, half-filled, and left it on the table in front of Janos with a soft square of paper.

Janos used the paper to wipe his mouth. With effort, he managed to hold the glass and drink from it.

His throat burned, and his stomach still roiled, but the water helped.

Dieter leaned back in his chair, his legs stretched out in front of him, crossed at the ankle. His eyes were fixed on a point on the ceiling, and he was paying no attention to Janos at all.

Janos looked at the basin beside him, the water, the bowl on the table. The boy wasn't laughing at him or mocking him. He had every right to torment the man who had threatened him, who was now a cripple, who couldn't obey a direct instruction from a physician.

Janos stared into the glass, which trembled in his hand.

All the idiot boy had done was help him.

He drained the glass and set it down on the edge of the table.

"Thank you," he said, turning his face away, ashamed of himself.

Dieter was silent for a long moment, then said, "You're welcome."

Chapter Four

The soldier was asleep.

Dieter ran a hand over his face as he slipped out of the room into the corridor. He was fucking exhausted, but the thought of sleep made him recoil. He needed food, at least, and a shower. Both of those things were why he had left the room.

There were two new guards at the door, and they nodded in silent greeting to him.

Dieter tried to smile, but it was too much effort.

They were still within the complex that made up the Temporal Research Institute. The building had twenty stories above ground and half as many below. The secure medical bay was on the fifteenth level, far away from the training floors and the temporal chambers. It was separate from the standard med bay and not used a lot because they tried not to do any damage or get in the way in the past. But sometimes, accidents happened.

In a room several doors down from the one the Hungarian soldier occupied, a woman was still in a coma from an injury inflicted on a foray into the Middle Ages. They didn't expect her to wake, but they also were adamant she would be cared for, for the rest of her life.

Dieter padded down the corridor towards the room he'd been allocated before everything went to hell. He hadn't seen it in the nearly twenty-four hours that he'd watched over their...guest. He needed a shower and a shave, and to beat the shit out of something. Probably a pillow in the privacy of his own room.

"Hey! Dieter!"

Dieter paused. He didn't want to talk to anyone, but he recognised the voice. Llewelyn. The poor fuck was the one who had crossed the Hungarian's path and ended up unconscious in the middle of the woods.

Reluctantly, Dieter turned to face him.

For some reason, he expected the man to be beaten bloody. How else would a fully trained temporal agent be disabled by some deranged

Hungarian bastard, if they hadn't fought? He should have been all marked up and scarred like Dieter, but he wasn't.

Dieter folded his arms over his middle. "Mike."

Llewelyn strode towards him. He wasn't tall, which was why he made a good agent. He was stocky, shorter than Dieter, and no matter how much he shaved, he always had a shadow on his chin. "Is it true? Is he going to live?"

Dieter released a slow sigh and nodded. "Looks like."

Emotions warred on the other man's face. "Right. That's good."

"Is it?" Dieter rubbed his eyes. "Look, Mike, sorry if I seem pissy, but I'm fucking tired, and I just want to go and rest, okay?"

Llewelyn's eyes flicked up to the mark on Dieter's brow and to his eyes. "Of course," he said. "You take care."

But when Dieter nodded, turned, and walked away, Llewelyn called after him, "I'm sorry, mate."

"What?" Dieter glanced over his shoulder.

"I should have been more careful," Llewelyn said. "I shouldn't have let him get through."

Dieter blinked stupidly at him. "Fucking right you shouldn't."

Llewelyn flushed but didn't say anything more.

Dieter didn't turn back again, walking towards his room. He swiped the pass with a trembling hand. The door slid open in front of him. He stopped on the threshold.

Tom Sanders sat by the window, skimming through a projection.

"What the hell do you want?" Dieter demanded, stepping into the room.

"To see how you are," Sanders said.

Dieter snorted. He stalked over to the sink and filled a glass with icy water. "So you haven't come to tell me I'm about to be fired?"

Sanders shrugged. "I made the call. Bellevue had it right. If he'd been anywhere else in his time, we would be upsetting the timeline. He would have died there anyway, but he was in the middle of nowhere, and even if we'd put him back, no one would have known."

Dieter looked down into the glass. It shook in his hand, and he fumbled as it slipped, dropping into the sink with a clatter. "Fuck!"

Sanders was on his feet in a heartbeat. "Sit down, Dieter," he snapped, grabbing Dieter by the arm. "Sit down before you fall down."

Dieter recoiled. "I'm fine!" he snarled, jerking his arm free.

Sanders drew his hands back, holding them level with his chest, palms open. "You haven't slept in over forty hours. Maybe longer. Do I have to get Bellevue in here to knock you out, or are you going to stop being an arse and sit down?"

Dieter stared at him, then nodded and made his way to the chair Sanders had vacated. He tugged at the knuckles of his left hand with his right as he sank in the seat. His legs shook, unsteady. When had he last eaten? He couldn't recall.

Sanders refilled the glass, brought it over to him, and sat down in the second chair. Dieter couldn't remember if there'd been two chairs before he left. Probably not. He felt like a kid in front of the headmaster.

Mutely, he accepted the glass, praying to anyone who might listen to an atheist that his boss wouldn't say the words which would crack the fucking bottle of nerves open: Are you all right? It wouldn't help anyone if he went to pieces. So he'd almost been killed two nights before. So what? He hadn't died. He was fine. He was fine.

"We have one of the other German speakers on duty," Sanders said.

Dieter frowned at him in confusion. "What?"

"You need a break."

Dieter snorted. The pot calling the kettle black came to mind. Sanders was fifteen years his senior and known for working himself to unconsciousness when he stepped onto the temporal floor. He looked as haggard now as Dieter felt, with shadows under his bloodshot eyes. It might have been a trick of the light, but there was more grey in his hair too.

"You said the man speaks German along with Hungarian," Sanders said.

"Badly. Basic sentences, but not much more."

Sanders's thin lips seemed to vanish when he frowned. "I thought the Hungarians all spoke German in that period."

Dieter was impressed at least someone had been paying attention in his briefing.

"They were expected to learn some, for their Austrian overlords," he said quietly, turning the glass in his hands. He knew the history of the period too well. The briefings always meant intense study for the historians and linguists in the agency. "But it doesn't mean they did. If they didn't come from the cities, they might not have bothered." He raised his eyes to Sanders. "He needs someone around who speaks Hungarian."

"Dieter, you need a break."

Dieter glanced around the room. "That's what I came here to do. He's sleeping now."

"And you were going to sleep?"

Dieter shrugged, avoiding his gaze. "Eat, sleep, shower. Whatever I wanted."

Sleep was lower down the list if he was honest with himself. He'd slept briefly when the Hungarian was in surgery. Bellevue had given him some kind of painkillers and pills to calm his nerves. He had slept, until he'd woken from a nightmare and found he'd burst the healing seal on the wound in his arm. It wasn't pleasant to wake up sodden in blood.

"Dieter..."

"Don't. I'm tired and I'm hungry. If all you've come to tell me is that you're sidelining me, you should go. Unless you have someone else in the building who can speak Hungarian and knows the situation, it'd be throwing them to the wolves."

He didn't say it would be fucking cruel to send anyone else into a room with a man who had already threatened to kill more than once. The bastard man would probably be capable of it once he came down from the meds he was on. Better no one else had to deal with him.

Sanders was silent for a long while.

"He's not your responsibility," he said finally.

It might be the case, but until the man could understand where he was and what was going on, there was no one else. It was easier to stay silent than to say anything and make his boss give him a lecture like he was a bloody idiot.

Sanders ran a hand over his face and blew out a noisy breath. "If you need to watch over him, you can do what you like. But don't neglect yourself in the process, Dieter. You have a job to do and it isn't babysitting a veteran of the second World War."

Dieter nodded. Work was good. Work was familiar. Work wasn't the sensation of the terrifying free fall he'd had when a gun was pushed so hard against his brow the skin had cracked open and the blood had run into his eyes.

"Send me a recording of the debrief," he said. "I'll look over it and the data they collected."

"After you rest," Sanders said, rising. "I'll have a meal sent along to you."

"Yes, boss." Dieter snorted.

Sanders gazed down at him. "If I think you're being compromised by this scenario," he said in a conversational tone, "I'll refer you to Bellevue. And you know her opinions."

Dieter nodded with a shiver. The woman had little patience for those who would not take care of their mental health, which was why her role was limited to that of medic. Sanders knew Dieter was treading on thin ice, and Dieter knew it too.

"I'll talk to Patil," he said.

Very few agencies needed to keep their own mental health staff on the premises, but sometimes the TRI agents were shaken up by where they had been and what they had seen. Patil was the one who helped them find some kind of equilibrium in the modern world.

Sanders laid a bony hand on Dieter's shoulder and squeezed once. "I'll send up the debrief file in a few hours."

Dieter nodded, looking down into his glass as Sanders left the room. He drained the water, so cold his teeth ached, and then got up. The en-suite bathroom was basic, but it had a shower. He stripped out of the round-collared T-shirt and running trousers, stepped under the steaming hot blast of water, and closed his eyes.

That was a bad idea.

He'd never really understood what a flashback was like before, not until the nightmares. Now, whenever he closed his eyes, he was back in the room, a gun to his head, praying he'd get out alive.

His legs folded beneath him, and he landed on his knees, bracing his hands against the wall of the shower. Acid burned up in his throat, and he drew gasping, spluttering breaths. He stared blankly at the water spiralling towards the drain.

The shower cut out long before he managed to get to his feet, his knees apparently made of jelly now, and he shivered as he wrapped himself from head to toe in a towel. Fucking ridiculous, he reproached himself. He was alive. There was no fucking reason to be shivering on the floor like a pussy.

He made his way out of the bathroom, stumbling all the way, the warmth of the main room smothering him like a blanket after the cooling dampness of the bathroom. He sagged onto the chair and sat in the daylight, wrapped in his towel, until he could stand again.

Some clothes had been delivered. They weren't his own, and he hadn't had a chance to go home and collect anything since the Hungarian had arrived. Still, they were dry and they weren't bloody, which was something.

The last set of borrowed clothes he left on the bathroom floor. He hadn't checked, but he was sure there were stains on them. Nagy had pulled his drip out and gotten blood and saline everywhere. He'd looked so bewildered when Dieter tried to help that Dieter wondered how much the painkillers were still affecting him.

He didn't like to be touched. He'd been very specific. Or treated like he was weak. A sign of the origins, Dieter supposed. Nagy was from a time when men were meant to wave their cocks about and be men. Men like him didn't want to be passive or helpless, especially not in front of a man who was as far from the textbook definition of masculinity as he could be.

The poor bugger was in for a shock.

Dieter put the soldier from his mind as much as he could, and towelled his hair dry. He didn't want to check himself in the mirror, all naked without his makeup. Superficial bullshit? Oh, 100 percent, but he also didn't want to ask someone to go and fetch some for him. None of his colleagues had seen him without it before, and he hardly recognised himself.

There was a comb, at least, and he smoothed his hair before taking a breath and raising his face to the mirror. There were deep circles under his bloodshot eyes, and the scabbed bruise on his brow looked like the fucking Olympic rings.

Behind him, the door hissed open.

"Knock knock!"

Dieter set down the comb and turned with a crooked smile. Of course Sanders wouldn't wait for him to go to Patil. He probably had the woman on standby, waiting for him to come out of the shower.

Sally Patil beamed at him. "Morning, sunshine." She had a tray balanced against one hip. With her free hand, she tossed a bag to him. "Catch!"

He fumbled it but righted himself, looking down at the bundle, unsure why she had thrown her handbag at him.

"I don't know if there's anything there to suit your skin tones," she said as she carried the tray over to the bed and hauled out the table. "But

I thought you might like to have some colour in your face, if you're going to be wandering around."

Dieter opened the bag. She'd brought her own makeup for him, and he blinked hard, his eyes stinging. "Thank you," he breathed.

Sally shot a smile at him. "Oh stop fannying about. Go and make yourself pretty, and I'll set the dinner out."

Dieter turned back to the mirror and poked through the array of makeup she had given him. He could never understand how someone with a job like hers could be so upbeat all the time, but he was grateful for it.

She was always the same, always smiling, warm, and welcoming. When he'd started with the institute, she was the last thing he'd expected. She looked every bit the traditional Indian lady in gorgeous, colourful clothes, and beautiful ornate jewellery. Then she opened her mouth, and she was as English as Mary Poppins and crumpets.

He listened to her humming to herself as she arranged the plates from the tray onto the table, and he glanced at the reflection of the room. "Did Sanders tell you to come?"

Sally snorted. "Please. They borrowed some clothes off Terry down in PR for you to wear. Have you seen what he wears?" She met his eyes in the reflection. "It was like kicking a man when he was down." Her face split in a grin. "I came to help you deal with the fashion trauma..."

He added some colour above his eyes. It shouldn't have helped as much as it did. "He does have fucking tragic taste."

"Ahem!"

A blush crawled up the back of his neck. Sally accepted pretty much everyone with a smile, but if there was one thing she didn't like from anyone, it was swearing.

"Sorry," he said. "I'll try and keep it in line."

"That's better," she said.

The bed creaked, and he glanced back to see her sitting on it, cross-legged, arranging her skirts over her calves.

"You mind if I steal a carrot? I'm starving!" she said.

He waved a hand, then returned to his makeup.

She was right when she said the palette wouldn't suit his skin tones, but there was enough to shade his eyes and give his cheeks a little colour. He breathed in, then out, feeling more like himself.

He crossed the floor towards the bed, and she tugged the table closer to herself to give him some room on the opposite side. He pulled his legs up, matching her pose, and took the fork when she offered it to him.

There were two thermos cups on the table, one of which she picked up.

"Tea," she said.

"Ah," he said wryly. "Your magic remedy for all ills."

She shrugged with a smile. "Well, it's a start."

He looked down at the food. "They were being generous. This is from the bistro down the road, isn't it?"

Her dark brown eyes met his. "They thought you'd earned it."

Dieter flushed, ducking over the food. Someone who knew him well had filled them in. The pork cutlet was excellent with the crispest applesauce he had ever tasted. To his surprise, despite being sure he'd struggle with even a sandwich, he cleared the plate, even licking the fork clean.

Sally had leaned against the pillows, sipping her tea. "Better?" she asked.

He hesitated. "Not really."

"And won't be for some time, I expect."

He could never tell when she had her shrink hat on, but right now, he didn't care. She would listen, and she wouldn't give a damn if he was being pathetic about it.

"Is it normal," he said cautiously, "to have flashbacks?"

She nodded. "Given what happened, it wouldn't be surprising. Have you?"

Dieter nodded. "And nightmares. Which is fu..." Her eyebrow rose. He caught himself. "It's ridiculous. It's not as if he really did anything."

"Except put a gun to your head and threaten to kill you," she observed.

A chill ran the length of Dieter's spine. He clasped his hands together in his lap to keep them from shaking. "Apart from that," he whispered.

Sally sat up and set her cup down on the table.

"Dieter, listen to me," she said, her voice calm and gentle. "Just because it was words doesn't mean it was nothing."

"He's a soldier," Dieter said in a whisper. "He thought he was in a war zone."

"But you weren't," Sally said. "You still went down there, knowing where he was coming from, and you managed to keep him calm and get him out of the way so the team could come home."

He laughed unsteadily. "I did, didn't I?"

She folded her arms on the edge of the table. "I know it doesn't sound like it will help much, but think about that. Next time you feel nothing happened, remember you put your life on the line to save our team. That's not nothing. The mark on your head is not nothing. The scar on your arm is not nothing. You walked into a scared man's personal war zone, Dieter, and you saved every person you went in there to save, including the soldier and yourself."

Dieter was startled at the warmth of tears on his face and lifted a shaking hand, brushing his fingertips across his cheekbone.

"Shit," he whispered. "There goes the mascara."

"We'll call it a Neo-Emo look," Sally said, leaning over to grab the box of tissues from the bedside locker. She set it on the table.

He took one, dabbed under his eyes, and tried to regain control of his unsteady breathing.

"I didn't feel brave," he whispered. "In there." His voice trembled. "Christ, Sally, he looked me in the eyes and told me he would kill me."

She reached over the table and covered his hand with hers. "And yet, here you are. And I hear you've been sitting in with him as well."

Dieter nodded, swiping at his cheeks with the tissue. "No one else speaks Hungarian. It wasn't right to leave him on his own."

"Are you scared of him?"

Dieter nodded, pressing his trembling lips together. It was fucking stupid. The man was unarmed—literally—and half-stoned on pain medication, but when he'd threatened Dieter again, it had been too raw and real, as if they were back in the temporal chamber, and he was on his knees, pissing his pants in terror.

"Then why do you sit with him?"

"Because it wasn't right to leave him on his own," Dieter repeated in a shaking whisper. "It doesn't matter if I'm afraid. He doesn't know anyone else. No one else speaks his language. He's in a new world, and everyone knows where he came from and what he did. Who else would go into the room with him?"

"You could leave him alone. Instead of being there, with him, all the time. Why do you need to be there all the time?"

He shrugged. "I don't know."

Sally propped her elbows on the table and rested her chin on her folded hands. "I know you'll be going back in there. I want to give you something to take with you. It might help."

"Is it a bulletproof vest?" he asked, only half joking.

She shook her head. "Right now, you have all the power in this situation. It might not seem like it because of the way he talks and acts, but this is your world. You have all the knowledge, all the experience. Your Hungarian is sick, weak, isolated, in a place he doesn't know, surrounded by people who could be his enemies. He doesn't even have his weapons anymore. All he has left are his words."

Dieter played his fingers along the crease of his borrowed trousers. It was true their…charming guest had shown a little gratitude, but it was only after he'd cursed and threatened. Dieter blew out a shivering sigh.

"I don't know what to tell him," he said. "The whole world he knew is gone. I don't know if he understands he can't go back now."

Sally tapped the painted tips of her nails on the table. "Does he even understand where he is?"

Dieter shook his head. "Probably not. He must have been out of his mind with pain when he came through the door. Doc Bellevue said he was half-dead from malnutrition and dehydration on top of the septicaemia."

"It'll take a lot of adjusting," she murmured. "He would need someone who could guarantee to be there for everything, a stable factor."

Dieter twisted the makeup smudged tissue tighter between his hands. It was the thought he'd been trying to crush down. He wasn't fucking stable himself, so how the hell was he meant to support the man who had shot him in the arm?

Sally pushed the table to one side and covered his hands with her own, her bracelets clattering around her wrists. "Take some time. He's sleeping just now. You should try to do the same. Then think about it when you've rested."

"Ha!"

She looked at him with reproach. "That's why I said 'try.' I know it'll be difficult, Dieter, but you'll make yourself ill if you try and stay awake, and you know it."

He gazed down at their linked hands. "I might need help," he admitted, lifting his eyes to her.

"It's not a crime," she said with a small, crooked smile. "And things might be a little clearer with some rest."

Dieter nodded, trying not to think about the coming nightmares. The worst part was knowing the whole mess had dug up memories he thought he'd safely buried with his mother when her body was repatriated.

She had died being stupidly heroic, trying to save members of her regiment in a gunfight in some town he couldn't even pronounce. That was what they told him when they gave him a box with a medal on a red ribbon. He threw it in the river two days later, because if she wasn't coming home, he didn't want a fucking piece of army crap as a reminder her regiment was more important to her than her flesh and blood.

Funny how fourteen years and a near-death experience could change a perspective.

He tugged one hand free to swipe at his cheeks, blinking hard.

Sally plucked another tissue from the box and knelt up in front of him. "Here." She dabbed at his cheeks. "You're making yourself look like a zebra."

His throat tightened, and all he could do in response was stick out his tongue.

She wrinkled her nose in response and dried each cheek in turn.

"I'll let you get some rest." she said as she unfolded her legs and stepped down from the bed.

"Is that my doctor talking or my friend?" Dieter asked, uncurling his own legs and letting them dangle off the edge of the bed.

She put her head to one side. "Maybe a little of both. I'll speak to old Bell and see what she would recommend to help you sleep, especially with your knock on the head."

Dieter lifted his hand to his brow, touching the marks there. "I don't think it was hard enough to cause brain damage."

"Not physically, anyway." She patted his hand. "Your tea should still be hot. I'll send someone along with some magic pills for you soon."

He retrieved the thermos cup as she danced towards the door, her beaded slippers sparkling.

"Sally," he said when the door opened. She glanced back, dark brows arching. "Thanks."

She flashed a brilliant white smile at him. "Oh shut up, you silly queen. Just make sure you don't use all my eyeliner."

She vanished out the door in a swirl of turquoise, and Dieter crawled along the bed to lean against the pillows. His head ached, and he was tired as hell. She was right, of course. He needed to sleep.

He wrapped his hands around the thermos cup. Warmth spread through to his hands. As always, tea was a comfort when everything else went down the shitter.

His lips twitched wryly. Half his life spent in Germany, and a cup of tea made him come over all British.

Chapter Five

The world was very different.

After several days of consciousness, Janos was more and more dazed. He didn't need to be told he was in another world. One look out of the wall-wide window of his room told him that.

Shining buildings of glass and metal towered as far as the eye could see. Far below, cars moved around like ants on grids of roads. He lost count of the times he stumbled from the bed to the window just to peer out and convince himself it was real.

Everything was different.

His room had a bathing chamber with a toilet, a proper one, indoors. The water in the bathing room flowed both hot and cold, even in the shower device.

The first time in the shower was a revelation. After so many days and nights spent filthy and cold, he just stood under the searingly hot water until he got dizzy and was pink from head to toe.

The medics had to pull him out, cursing but too light-headed to push them aside. His bandages had to be replaced, but he didn't care, his skin thrumming with warmth. He couldn't remember the last time he had been so clean or so warm.

There was a moving picture-box, a flat-screened one, in his room. He had heard of them, of course, but never seen one. When people spoke of them, they did not speak of the colours or the hundreds of different pictures to choose from. He couldn't understand a word, but he stared at the images, the faces, the places it showed him.

The boy returned each morning, painted up once more. He was formal and cordial, but kept his distance. He gave little information about their whereabouts and when they were, but he would answer questions about the war and what followed.

There was so much to take in.

It did not help when the doctor provided more and more capsules for him to swallow. She said they were necessary, but all he noticed was that after he swallowed them, the pain seemed to dim. They were drugging him with opiates once more, keeping him passive. As soon as he realised, he started tucking the pills into his cheek and disposed of them down the toilet when the medics left him alone.

The unfortunate result was the return of the pain.

Nothing compared to a rotting limb, but it was there and constant. His wounds throbbed and ached. When the doctor checked his arm and his side, she would often leave frowning.

The pain did not ease, and the throbbing grew worse.

By night, stretching shadows haunted his dreams and he woke with his sheets sodden with sweat. He often found he had torn at his bandages, scratching at an unbearable itch, and his head swam.

The doctor was concerned, and the boy spoke of fever and infection. Janos didn't care.

All he wanted was the throbbing to stop. He slept more and more, and could scarcely eat or drink anything. He woke screaming one night, thrashing at grasping shadows that held him down, cutting his limbs from him.

The door of his room hissed aside. The rectangle of light from the corridor nearly blinded him, and he sobbed, his arms flung up over his face. Hands closed on his arms, and he screamed again, lashing out and scrambling away, off the bed, back, back, away.

His assailant spoke then. "Janos."

Janos cringed into the corner of the room. The boy. The boy was there. Using his name as if they knew one another. Another of the perils of the nightmares. The boy would make him forget himself, and he would make foolish, foolish mistakes, and they would hurt him for it.

The smaller lamp above the bed was switched on, directed away from him, and he put his arms over his head. Too bright. Too bright, and his head throbbed and swam, his legs giving way beneath him.

"Get out!" he whispered raggedly, pushing his bare feet against the cold floor, trying to shove himself farther back, but trapped by the walls. "Leave me be!"

It was cowardice and childishness and terror all tangled in one, yet he could not seem to fight it. His legs were weak, and he shivered as if chilled, but his blood boiled in his veins.

"Janos," the boy said again, his voice as steady and calm as it had been on the first night they had met, the night when the boy had quailed and knelt and lowered his head, passive and weak and afraid.

But how could he have been afraid when he spoke with such calm?

And now, he was just as calm, and Janos was terrified. Terrified of what the boy wanted, of what he might do, of how weak the boy might think him, curled up and sobbing like a child at the terrors of the night.

"Janos," he repeated. "Look at me."

Janos shuddered violently but forced his arm down.

The boy knelt on the floor, not close enough to touch, but close. He was half-clothed, in short underpants, his skin pale in the lamplight, as if he were carved from marble. He must have been sleeping, Janos thought hysterically. He was half-clothed, his hair in disarray, his face clean and bare.

God above, he was beautiful.

Janos stifled a curse, putting his hand to his eyes.

"Leave me alone," he pleaded.

"You were screaming," the boy murmured. "I could hear you from my room."

Janos's breath was coming too fast, the room too closed in, trapping him, stifling him.

"Go to hell!" he screamed out. "I don't want you to be here!" The stump of his arm beat uselessly against his chest, trying to push away the tightness there, and he wept, shaking, sobbing. "Please, leave me be. Please."

"You're in pain." It was said without pity, a statement of fact.

Janos shook his head, pressing his hand harder to his eyes. It had to be a trap. There was no other reason a handsome young Aryan German boy would approach him. Not out of compassion. It had to be a trap, something to test him.

He doubled over, retching, but there was nothing in his stomach to bring up.

The boy was beside him in an instant, his hands on Janos's shoulders. Janos flinched away so hard he struck the wall. He stared at the boy, like a wild animal caught in a snare, saliva and blood on his lips. The boy pulled back, as if he had been burned, holding his hands up, empty and bare.

"You need to get onto the bed," he said. "I won't touch you, but will you let the medics help you?"

Janos stared at him, trying to make sense of his words, and then nodded. The cold floor should have eased the heat in his veins, but it only made him shiver more, and he folded over again, his stomach clenching.

The men who were his wardens came into the room on the boy's request. They pulled him up, but his legs slipped and slithered beneath him as if they were nothing but limp sacks of water. The men spoke to him, words he couldn't understand, and lifted him onto the bed.

The boy didn't look at them when he spoke to them, his eyes on Janos, who avoided his gaze. Janos's hand shook so much he could barely tug the blankets around his body. He didn't dare protest when the boy leaned closer and drew the blankets closed. As he'd promised, he didn't touch, his hands only grasping the blankets, Janos noticed dizzily.

Janos's breath rasped, the only sound in the silent room

The boy sat on the edge of the bed, pulling one leg up under him.

He didn't speak.

Maybe if he had, Janos could have summoned up some fury from the panic and fear. But he didn't speak. He just sat there, breathing soft and shallow, and Janos's own frantic breathing gradually slowed to the same rhythm.

"Your face isn't painted," Janos whispered, his voice hoarse.

The boy's lips twitched. "It would make a mess on the pillow." He tapped his fingertips on his own knee. "I had to call for the doctor. You're ill. I think your wound may still be infected."

Under the blankets, Janos wrapped his hand around the stump of his arm. "I won't let you take more," he whispered. "You keep trying to drug me, and now you want to take more."

"Drug you?"

Janos nodded and regretted it at once, the world whirling around him. He leaned against the pillows. He swore he could feel the blood throbbing from his temples to his toes.

"Your doctor gives me pills to keep me quiet," he said, his voice low and dark. "I do not want them any more than I want your needles and tubes."

The boy stared at him, shock written on his face. "Jesus Christ. You haven't been taking them, have you?"

Janos stared defiantly at him, clenching his teeth.

The boy shoved a hand through his hair. "Fucking hell, you idiot! Those weren't to sedate you! Those were medicines to stop the infection spreading! They would have let your wounds heal and destroyed the infection!"

Janos ground his teeth together. "Liar," he whispered.

"Am not," the boy snapped. He reached up to his right arm and peeled a strip of linen away to show a healing wound where a chunk of flesh had been gouged out a hand's span below his shoulder. "I'm using the same things for this. Do you see the difference?"

Janos blinked at the wound in the boy's arm. A gunshot? He leaned closer, putting out his hand and touching the healing scar. The boy froze but didn't pull away.

It was strange, Janos thought. For some foolish reason, the sight of it made him angry, angrier than the loss of his own arm. It was stupid to pity the enemy, even if he was fair. "Who did that?"

The boy looked at Janos's hand, still lingering against the wound, and back at Janos's face. For the first time, true amusement reached his blue eyes. "You did, you stupid fucking Magyar."

Janos shook his head. "I did not."

"You might have been halfway to unconscious at the time, but it's no excuse," the boy said with a snort. "You fucking shot me, and I can show you pictures if you need proof."

Janos traced the edge of the wound with his fingertips, and he stared at it as if he'd never seen such a thing before. No wonder the boy had recoiled from him so often, if he had been wounded by Janos's hand. It was still reddened, as with his injuries, but not hot to the touch.

He frowned in confusion at the boy, startled to find the bright blue eyes watching him with the familiar guarded expression. Self-consciously, he tugged his hand from the boy's arm and pulled the blanket tight about him like a shield.

"Why?" he asked, lost.

"Why did you shoot?" The boy's slim shoulders lifted. "You were holding a gun. It went off in your hand."

"No." His voice sounded small and hollow. "Why did you stay here with a man who shot you?"

The boy's gaze dropped to his hand, which was resting on his bare knee. "Because you didn't have anyone else."

Such a simple statement.

Janos's throat tightened. It couldn't be as simple as kindness. The years of war had stripped away the need for kindness. Friend turned on friend. Neighbour on neighbour. You did not know who might be the enemy, so you did not lower your gun for anyone. A German boy had no reason to help a Hungarian who had shot him.

Janos looked gratefully towards the door as it slid open. The doctor was a safe distraction.

The boy rose from the bed and went to the doctor, speaking quietly to her. She glowered over at Janos and her features tightened as she stalked closer to the bed. She reminded him of his stern, fierce grandmother, and he could picture her coming after him with her wooden spoon.

Whatever she snarled at him, he didn't need a translation. He shrank against the pillows as she checked his vitals and let the boy's translation wash over him in a soothing tide. Pills. Taking. Injections. Antibiotics. Healing. Stupid, foolish, arrogant man. When she stormed out of the room, he closed his eyes, shivering with relief.

A cool hand pressed to his brow.

Janos jolted, his eyes flying open.

"Do you want a compress?" the boy asked. "You're burning up."

Maybe it was a trap. Maybe the boy was there to lure him into a false sense of security. Maybe he would end up in more pain before his time was done.

But now, he was tired, and he shook and ached down to his bones, his skin hot and too tight. Even if he was a fraud and a liar, the boy in front of him was offering to show Janos some little kindness.

Through dry lips and a parched mouth, Janos whispered, "Yes."

Chapter Six

"He's afraid of me."

A spoon clinked against the rim of a china cup. "Oh?" Sally said.

Dieter looked out the window onto the rooftop garden. He didn't know how Sally had managed to get the only room with a natural view for her office. She probably played on the fact that psychiatric patients would appreciate a calming environment.

The whole room was designed to be welcoming, with low shelves of books and photographs and a couple of flowering plants. Some landscape paintings adorned the wall, and the fourth wall was glass, overlooking the garden.

"Yeah," he replied.

The blind terror in the soldier's face as he cowered in the corner of the room had shocked Dieter. It was true Janos was delirious with fever after he abandoned his regime of antibiotics, but it didn't make his fear or his frightened pleas any less real.

Dieter frowned at his reflection in the polished window. He turned to her where she sat in her armchair. The large soft chair was big enough for her to tuck her feet up under her. She gazed up at him over the rim of her teacup.

"You knew," he said.

"He might be afraid of you?" She nodded. "I suspected."

He had his arms wrapped around his waist, his fingers biting into his sides. "How?"

She motioned for him to take a seat on the plush couch.

"You've been distracted by what's going on," she said as she poured tea for him. "Think."

He shook his head. "I don't know."

"If I'm dealing with people who have returned from the past, what's the first thing I could do?" she prompted.

"Review..." He looked up from the teacup to her face. "You saw the footage."

Sally nodded. She dropped a perfectly square sugar lump into his tea and slid the saucer across the polished glass of the circular table between them. "I needed a starting point so I could understand what was going on."

Dieter picked up the teacup and saucer, staring at the blue and gold pattern. "Bet they find it funny I pissed myself." He remembered it well, the spreading humiliating heat, the smell of it on his skin. Like a child, a frightened kid, he hadn't been able to stop himself.

"You don't think they haven't done the same in a frightening situation? They're human beings, not robots, Dieter. They get scared as much as you."

He said nothing, sipping the hot tea. It burned his tongue, but safer to hide in that than acknowledge she was probably right. He shifted his weight on the edge of the couch. He wanted to be up, moving, pacing, something, but she would read into it too.

He set the cup and saucer on the table and folded his hands together, squeezing them until the knuckles went white.

"He didn't seem scared of me," he finally said, remembering the gun, the violence, the anger.

"Because you didn't expect him to. You went in expecting a soldier, so that was what you saw. But the first thing he did when you walked in there was recoil away from you."

Dieter stared at her. "It doesn't mean he was afraid. He was giving himself room."

Sally raised her eyebrows. "Do you believe that?"

Dieter wanted to argue, but he thought about it: the way the soldier had retreated, the way he shied from him, the wariness and the hostility of his words when he snapped in his broken German, and he knew she had touched on something he'd overlooked.

"But I'm not frightening," he said, shaking his head.

"It depends on the context." She unfolded from the chair, went over to one of the shelves, and returned with two small plates and a tin of biscuits. "For example, what would you expect him to be afraid of?"

"Soldiers," he said at once. "Enemy soldiers. Big ones. With guns. Not skinny blonds with no weapons."

She set biscuits onto the two plates. "And why would they frighten him so much?"

He rolled his eyes. "You know why."

"Yes, but I want to know what you think."

He pushed himself up against the couch and crossed his arms over his middle. "Enemy soldiers are the ones who can kill you. What soldier wouldn't be afraid of them?"

"The soldiers who know the enemy is the same as them," she reminded him.

Dieter felt like she had struck him in the chest.

Of course his mother's files were on his record. Everyone in the agency had to undergo a thorough background check, and she was right. His mother had been a soldier, and she had never hated or feared the people she fought. They were doing their job, guided by their commanders, as she was.

He swallowed hard. "That doesn't answer the question. Why would a soldier be afraid of me? Rather than the enemy?"

She nudged the plate of biscuits towards him. "You're the historian. Tell me why a runaway Hungarian soldier might be wary of a well-dressed, blond-haired German in a military facility. Especially when that German looks and sounds calm and confident."

Dieter opened his mouth in astonishment.

"Fucking hell," he groaned. "He thinks I'm a fucking Nazi." He scooted forward, snatched up the teacup, and took another mouthful. "Jesus Christ. Of all the things for him to think of me..."

Sally's lips twitched. "Well, you do come across as a masterful Aryan, and you could have been a poster boy for their eugenics campaign."

"Yeah," Dieter said with a snort, "except my grandfather on Dad's side was Jewish." He pulled a face. "And I don't think they'd appreciate that I like to take it up the arse."

"Mm." Sally nibbled on the edge of a biscuit.

He turned the cup in his hands. "No wonder he was confused by the eye shadow. I don't remember any pictures of Goebbels or Goering sporting eyeliner."

"He was?" Sally inquired.

Dieter nodded. "When he had his night terrors." It had been one fucking bizarre night. The wardens at Janos's door had fetched him when the Hungarian started screaming, and it had all gone arse over tit from there. "He was out of it. Probably hallucinating, the old Bell said. But he said my face wasn't painted."

"Well, that's one way to put it," Sally said with a chuckle.

Dieter nodded, picking up one of the biscuits and turning it over between his fingers.

Janos Nagy, veteran Hungarian soldier, survivor of the Second World War, was afraid of a makeup-wearing queer, to the point he flinched when Dieter touched him. It was fucking ridiculous. His hand stopped halfway to his mouth, and he stared at the biscuit.

No.

The stupid fucking Hungarian was afraid of the blond German he saw, not the queer. He didn't see that part. He just lined up an image of a Nazi, and it was what he feared. Even though Germany and Hungary had been allies, something about them scared him. Something about physical contact made Janos beg him to go away, made him scream.

Fuck.

It couldn't be that simple, could it?

"Dieter?"

Dieter set down the biscuit. "I need to go. I need to get some other books."

Sally nodded. "You know where to find me."

It was several hours before he returned to the medical level, and he was carrying more books. They had shipped in some Hungarian history books about the end of the war for Janos to read up on, but Dieter had a feeling the man needed to know about more than the war and what followed.

There was only one warden now. They were hardly needed.

The soldier was weak as a kitten, made more helpless by the infection that had torn through his body. Doctor Bellevue insisted on kick-starting his immune system with injected courses of antibiotics, and he'd been too exhausted to protest.

The improvement was already noticeable. Janos's features were still flushed with fever, but he was spending more time awake. He had taken to reading with a book propped on the table unfolded over his bed, to learn about the changes to the world.

He was also quieter.

Dieter knew it all stemmed from the night when Janos had woken screaming.

That was when the soldier had broken, revealing the man beneath the anger and bluster. Dieter spent two hours sponging the stinking sweat from him, trying to cool the fever, while the doctor's remedies were poured into the man's bloodstream. Janos had shivered at his touch, turning his face away. Then, Dieter believed it was purely because he didn't want to be seen as weak.

Now, he knew better.

The door hissed open in front of him when he swiped his pass against it.

Janos was sitting up in the bed, the blankets still wrapped around him. He was poring over a book. When he raised his eyes, Dieter saw the way he drew himself up. He was a proud man, and even now, wanted to maintain the illusion of strength.

Dieter hesitated in the doorway.

If he was right, he knew he was about to help Janos understand the new world. If he was wrong, then he was about to insult him.

Still, better to find out sooner rather than later.

"Good book?" he asked, approaching the bed.

"Enlightening," Janos replied. His fingers curled into the blanket around his shoulders, drawing it a little closer, a shield to hide within.

Dieter gazed at the books in his hand, then at the man in the bed. "I'm not a Nazi."

Janos blinked owlishly at him. "What?"

"A friend of mine pointed out that you might think so."

The soldier paled, licked his lower lip, and looked down at the book. "I never said anything of the kind."

"No, you didn't." Dieter sat down on the end of the bed. "But I'm not one of those kind of people. They were beaten in the war. They lost. Their regime fell apart, and now, they are reviled."

Janos laid his fingertips against the edge of the pages of his book. "I never said," he repeated.

"You didn't have to." One side of Dieter's mouth turned up. "I know I'm all pretty and blond as fuck and everything, but it doesn't mean I walk to the beat of their drum. My mother was English, for fuck's sake. My grandfather's Jewish. I'm a fucking atheist. I cross-dress when I'm bored. Hell, I fuck men. They would have killed me for a hundred different reasons, no matter how Aryan I was."

Janos's head jerked up, his eyes wider.

Ah.

So it was an accurate guess, then.

Dieter set the stack of books on the table. "You might find these interesting."

Janos closed the book he was reading, marking the page with a strip of paper from his small notebook. He picked up one of the newer books, turning it over to read the blurb. Colour burned up in his features. He set the book down.

"Why would I want to read them?" he demanded.

Dieter shrugged and pushed himself off from the bed. "Like I said. Interesting." He glanced at his watch and then at Janos. "I'll leave you to it. I have some place I need to get to."

Janos nodded guardedly, watching him as he walked away.

Dieter left the room, oddly calm.

For the first time since the Hungarian had come through the temporal portal, Dieter didn't feel afraid. It was strange, as if a huge fucking weight had been lifted off him, and he drew and released a breath.

"You okay?"

He glanced at the warden, a tiny, red-haired lady called Shona. He knew for a fact she could break a man's arm with one hand. She was also one of the wardens who could speak German, which was why she had been chosen to stand guard on the room.

"I'm good," he said. "Just thinking it's about time for a night off."

"Aye," she said. "You've been hanging around like a bad smell for days."

"Charming." He snorted but couldn't help grinning. Relief, he realised. He'd been walking blind for days, but now he understood at least part of what was going on. It was a glimpse of light, and Christ, it felt amazing. "I'm going home. If anyone asks, I'll be back in the morning."

She looked him up and down, smirking. "So you might stop looking like a hobo?"

"Oh piss off, you ginger cow," he retorted with a laugh. "Keep an eye on him for me?"

Her expression sobered. "He's been resting easier. Hopefully, no more nightmares."

Dieter was relieved. "Do you have the whole night?"

She shook her head. "Some other poor sod'll see your face when you get back." She waved him away, settling more comfortably in her chair. "Off with you."

It felt strange to be leaving the building at all.

On a regular day, when his job was done and the teams were back, and all information reviewed, he would have been home with a chardonnay and a cigarette by seven o'clock. It had been more than three weeks since he'd left the agency. It was so long since he could. First, there was the jump to deal with, and then, the Hungarian.

He glanced down at the loose T-shirt and trousers he was wearing. They were too big for him, and under his black woollen coat, he suspected he looked like a prisoner in disguise, trying to make a break for freedom.

God, it would be good to be in his own clothes.

They'd offered, of course, to go and fetch him something else to wear, but his work life and his home life were always kept separate. No one from the agency had ever gotten anywhere near his home. The only reason they knew where he lived was because of his personnel file.

It was raining outside, the thick, heavy grey rain that swept in off the coast. He turned up the collar of his coat, peering around for a taxi pod.

"Hey! Dieter!" An old-fashioned car pulled up by the curb, the window open. Some pretentious dicks still preferred them to hands-free shuttles. Compensating, he always figured. The driver leaned over the passenger seat, waving him down.

Of all the people, Dieter thought with wry amusement, it had to be Paul. Seven years Dieter's senior, Paul occasionally met up with him for casual fucks. Neither of them had any interest in anything long-term. Paul thought Dieter was too academic, and he found Paul's repertoire of wit limited and his friends annoying. Still, Paul was good-looking in a broad-shouldered, beefy, Anglo-Saxon way, and Dieter appreciated the simplicity of having someone he could enjoy sex with, without the need to commit to tedious intimate suppers and banal conversation.

His cock twitched.

It was a happy coincidence, he thought, as he hurried down the steps towards the car. Right now, he wanted to tear off his clothes and run naked in the rain. He wanted to do all the crazy stuff he kept buttoned down under his tie and waistcoat. Christ, he wanted a fuck.

Paul flung the door open for him, and Dieter scrambled in.

"I thought you—" Paul didn't get a chance to finish speaking as Dieter kissed him.

The intensity of it startled Dieter himself. Maybe it was the near-death experience. Maybe it was the fact that he might never shag someone again. He didn't know. All he knew was he wanted to get the man in front of him naked and buggering him as fast as fucking possible.

Paul caught his shoulders, pushing him away, panting. "Dieter, what the hell…"

"Your place," Dieter growled, claiming another urgent kiss, sliding his hand along Paul's thigh and down between his legs—he was already getting hard. Dieter knew the feeling. "A hotel. Christ, here, if you don't get a fucking move on."

Paul swallowed hard and licked his lips. "At least shut the bloody door," he said hoarsely.

Dieter laughed, twisting in the seat to pull the door closed behind him as Paul floored the accelerator, tearing them off through the streets.

They didn't get as far as Paul's flat. There was a hotel less than a mile away, and Dieter grinned like a smug cat as Paul swung into the parking lot below it. Paul was trying his best to be placid and stoic, but Dieter saw he was hard as rock as they headed into the lobby, and colour rose up the back of his neck as he requested a room.

They barely got through the door of the room before Paul swung around and pinned Dieter hard against the door, kissing him as if his fucking life depended on it.

Dieter's coat, the T-shirt, and the trousers were dispatched as fast as possible, but the bed went neglected. There was a couch, a fancy number, and Dieter caught Paul by the tie and dragged him towards it. For all he was a big, imposing fucker, Paul was such a vanilla bastard anything outside of a bed was considered an adventure.

They were spent in no time at all, sagging against the couch, sweat-sodden and panting. Dieter pried his hands away from the back of the couch and shoved at Paul's shoulders.

"Shower," he said, by way of explanation. He stumbled like a newborn gazelle towards the bathroom, leaving his lover sprawled on the floor.

By the time he emerged, his skin pink from the heat, his hair slicked against his scalp, Paul had managed to drag himself up onto the bed. He lounged against the pillows, reading something on his tablet.

Dieter swiped water from his neck with a towel. "I don't know if I should be insulted or not. I left the bathroom door open and everything."

Paul grinned up with amusement. "You're not usually so keen."

Dieter shrugged. "Call it a fresh appreciation for life." He wandered over to the phone by the bed. "You want something to drink?"

He did, and room service arrived less than five minutes later with a bottle of scotch.

Dieter stretched out on the bed, propping himself against the end of it with a pillow.

Paul watched him curiously. "Is this because of what happened?"

Dieter shrugged, sipping his scotch. He didn't drink it often, but he liked the way it burned on his tongue. "It's given me a taste for life I didn't have before." He lazily curled his toes against the bedding.

Paul set aside his reader. "What's he like? The soldier?"

Dieter swirled the whisky in his glass. "I'm not sure. He's not a big talker." He took another mouthful of the drink, letting it rest on his tongue for a moment before swallowing. "He's got a lot to learn."

Privately, he was wondering if Janos would deign to look at the books he'd dug out for him. The man was a stubborn son of a bitch—that much he knew—and if he was as deep in the closet as he seemed to be, he might as well have been in fucking Narnia.

"Still, you're watching out for him?"

Dieter shrugged. "No one else speaks the language. What am I meant to do? Leave him on his own?"

Paul was silent for a moment. "How does he look?"

Dieter snorted. "You're asking me if I've checked out a half-starved invalid who barely got out of a war zone alive? The bastard's like a toast rack on legs. I've seen anorexics with more flesh on them."

Paul shook his head. "You meet someone from history, and you don't check them out?"

"Toast rack on legs," Dieter repeated. "You say *I'm* skinny. This fucker's half my weight right now. He doesn't look like they do in films, that's for sure."

"Well, that's less interesting," Paul said, setting aside his glass.

"Mm."

Dieter didn't feel inclined to disagree, but privately, he found himself thinking about the man who was back at the headquarters.

Janos had been fucking terrified, and now, if he was right, Dieter knew he had shown himself as an ally. He wondered if it would make any difference at all. He couldn't remember what it was like being queer without someone knowing about it. The idea of being forced to hide it, of being at risk of death if it wasn't hidden...

If Janos was so fucking scared, there was no guarantee he'd believe a word Dieter said, and if he didn't, then he'd hold onto his secret. He might consider Dieter an enemy, and it would be even more of a mess.

He drained the last of his whisky, shuddering as it burned down.

"All right, you big bastard," he said. "I need to get home in a couple of hours, but until then, distract me."

Chapter Seven

The books were an education.

Not the improper ones, of course, but the rest were.

As his arm and body healed, Janos had little else to do but read and rebuild his faded strength. He admitted to being educated, at least a little. His family's losses after the first great war put an end to any ambitions he might have had. Still, he could read.

Admitting it felt like he was displaying a weakness, that he might have been a spy or a tool of the enemy. Still, he told them, and it was enough to get them to provide him with books in his language. He devoured them without hesitation.

Some of them were old, leather bound, but when he opened them, they showed a publication date a decade after the beginning of the war. It was one thing to weave a tapestry of lies, but to make a fake book, in Hungarian, and age it sufficiently in such a short space of time was unbelievable.

So he read and learned of the fall of the Third Reich. He learned words he had never heard before, and wished he hadn't. He read about the camps, places he had heard muttered about in the army but they had been dismissed as the propaganda of the enemy forces. Germany was their ally after all.

He remembered the whispers. He remembered seeing people taken from their homes. He remembered a friend, a dear friend, who had always been unashamed of his sinful proclivities. A group of soldiers from their army had taken Ferenc away with others rounded up for the same immoralities. His village had stood by and let them be taken. He had stood by.

The soldiers returned. His friends didn't.

The same day, he had enlisted in the army.

Safer to hide in plain sight, to pretend he was one of them, than to be led into the forest and left to rot in the wormy dirt. Soldiers saw a uniform and saw someone who was like them, so that was what he became. He donned the uniform, raised his hand in the salutes, and every night, prayed his eyes would be blind to any distraction.

He knew he was not the only one.

They marched. They fought. They killed. They bled. They died. They were brothers at arms, and some secrets could not go unnoticed. In the cold and the darkness, hands fumbled, and lips met, but by the daylight, whispers spread. The last time he had kissed Szilveszter's lips, they were cold and tasted of dried blood and vomit.

No one knew it of him though. No one suspected. As ashamed as he was of hiding, he was not brave enough to declare Szilveszter's secret lover was standing among them. He was too afraid to die as cruelly as Szilveszter had.

At night, when he closed his eyes, all he could see was his lover's mutilated corpse. They castrated him before they killed him, and he had screamed, long and high and terrified, before they cut his throat. Janos was on patrol in the forest, and the distant screams had chilled his blood before he knew who it was. It was only luck that had him on the burial detail. It was the last chance he'd had to whisper an apology to the man his affection had killed.

They had believed their squad to be their friends and trusted allies.

That was the day Janos realised allies could not be trusted.

And now, this pretty German boy offered books which suggested he suspected the secret Janos had kept so carefully hidden. He spoke of having male lovers as if it were no crime or sin. He said it so freely. There had to be some kind of trap beneath it.

Sodomy was a sin as old as the commandments. Times could not change so much.

It had to be a trap.

The boy wasn't helping matters.

It was easier when he came in the first days, when his face was barely painted and he wore clothes too large for him. He'd been as uncertain as the green cadets. Then came the day when he brought the unwanted books and left for close to a day and a half.

When he returned, he walked tall, smiling and confident. The oversized clothing was gone, his tailored trousers and shirt fitting him neatly as a glove. He wore his fair hair slicked back, a streak of cobalt blue at his left temple, and he lined his eyes with cosmetic powder which made them seem larger and bluer than they had been before. He also wore a gleaming ring through his lower lip.

To Janos's shame, the damned boy crept into his dreams. The ring and the painted lips mixed with the image of the boy kneeling before him, and he woke, flushed and hard, and mortified. Wary of being watched, he rolled from the bed and stumbled to the bathroom, forcing himself into an icy shower.

It would do no good to think on the boy, no matter how he looked.

When they spoke, Janos was curt to the point of rudeness. He asked for facts, and the boy gave them without hesitation. He provided details of the improvements in Janos's health and did not hesitate to show him new technologies.

Despite it all, Janos found himself enjoying the foolish boy's company.

He was younger than Janos, at least by some years, and when he spoke, he did so with an eagerness bordering on childlike enthusiasm. He knew much history and admitted he enjoyed languages. Janos snorted and informed him his Hungarian could use a lot of work, which made him laugh and say that was what he was doing.

Each day he came, and they would talk, and each night, Janos would step into the shower and let it chill him until he was blue with cold. It rarely helped, each morning beginning the same way.

One morning, the throb in his groin was too persistent, and the icy shower was doing nothing to drive it away.

Janos braced his ruined arm against the wall of the shower and put his other hand down, wrapping his shivering fingers around his cock. It was hot against his palm, and his hand twitched around it, squeezing too hard for satisfaction as he thought about reddened lips and a ring that would drag against sensitive skin. He raked a nail up the underside of his cock and shuddered, spilling seed over his fingers.

He was a disgrace.

It was a wonder he had lived as long as he had, if he couldn't keep his cock under control. What a reason to die, for some pretty little German boy who painted himself like a whore and smiled like a fallen angel.

The boy arrived soon enough, but Janos had no stomach to face him. He demanded one of the German-speaking people, someone else, anyone else. The boy stared at him with pained astonishment.

"Did I do something wrong?" he asked.

Janos pushed aside the books on his table. "Do you want me to depend wholly on you?" he demanded more sharply than he intended. His words came out clipped and hostile. "Is that what you want? Am I to have no freedom from you?"

The boy's features became waxen and still. He rose from his chair at once.

"I only wanted to help," he said, turning away. "You're under our protection, but you're not a prisoner. If you want other company, I'll find some for you."

"Yes," Janos said curtly. "I do."

The boy's face was flushed, and Janos couldn't tell if he was embarrassed or angry. He walked from the room, the only sound the tap of his shoes on the polished floor, and closed the door behind him.

He was gone, and it should have been a relief, but it wasn't. It felt like cowardice, hiding from the reality. Janos knew he was burying his head in the sand, trying to ignore the attraction that had almost killed him in another time and place.

The only mercy was he had to work hard with German to be understood by his new companion. It took all his concentration, and he could put aside thoughts of how the boy had looked half-asleep, his hair a mussed mess, his face free of any paint.

His dreams still troubled him, but he hoped it would be easier to dismiss them as distant fantasies when he did not have to face the boy every morning. His cold showers did not stop. He tried to focus on the small German-speaking woman and, more often than not, any desire or fantasies flagged immediately.

She was harmless, and though her accent was difficult to comprehend from time to time, she was patient with him when he stumbled on his words. Sometimes, she offered to fetch the boy, as if she could tell how much he was struggling with German, but he shook his head and fought with the words until they made sense.

He had his books in his language. He could read them and then speak to the woman and clarify what had happened. He didn't need to speak to the boy, or listen to him or have him around. He could close his hand around his cock and think of other men from other times, other places.

And yet, each and every time, the boy's smile cut across his vision like a blade, and he would drag his nail slowly up his cock, and it was the thing to put him over the edge each and every time.

Even though the boy wasn't there, he haunted Janos.

The books the boy had provided were still in the small cabinet beside his bed, sitting like an unexploded bomb, waiting to go off. Part of him was curious about the content, but the rest of him was afraid of what he would learn.

Fear controlled Janos, and he hated it, but he had spent so many years hiding who he was. To bare himself felt like suicide, the death of the façade he had worked so hard to maintain, and which had saved his life. He remembered the abuse hurled at people of his kind, the cruelty, the violence, the death. The world could not change so much. There would always be people who hurt men like him. He didn't know whether the people in the agency would be a threat, but he didn't want to take the risk.

So he spoke in broken sentences to the woman called Shona. He let the doctor check his wounds and the state of his health. He listened impassively to the man in charge of the facility as he spoke through a translator, explaining while Janos was not a prisoner, he could not be freed into society for the security of the institution.

It was a prison. A fine prison with a comfortable bed and hot water, it was true, but a prison no less.

They allowed him some freedom, within the confines of the building.

If accompanied by a guard, he was permitted to go up to the rooftop where there was a garden. The windowed walls of the building surrounded it on three sides. The fourth side revealed the view out over the city, a sprawling mass of shining metal, dull concrete, and shimmering glass.

The city below seemed alien, as if he were in another world. They were in a city called Manchester, somewhere in the north of England, but it was nowhere he had heard of and nothing like anywhere he had ever seen.

They gave him a machine to learn. It was a database, they said, to let him search for any facts he might want to know. Smaller than a book, the device had a gleaming glass screen which showed images and records in dozens of languages. He could tap words into the screen to find anything he wanted—pictures, maps, books all stored in the small, thin machine.

The advances in technology were terrifying but incredible. He tried to learn more about them, but there was so much, too much, to understand at once. He took refuge in history instead, seeking out places he had known.

It shocked him how much the world had changed, in ways he could never have predicted. The small town his family once lived in was no more. It had been flattened, replaced with factories, and he read about communism, gulags, and more deaths and losses. His family were not important enough to have been taken there, but they were gone now nonetheless.

In the night, when he turned the machine off and the lights were dimmed, he lay with his back to the door and pressed his cheek to the pillow. If he wept for his family, his keepers would never know about it.

Day bled into night and into day once more.

His health returned little by little. His wounds healed. He no longer struggled so much with German, though it still took time to put sentences together. They allowed him use of the exercise facilities within the building to use machines and weights to regain some of his lost strength.

His dreams, though, remained much the same.

The boy didn't come back in to see him, but once, they crossed paths when Janos was on his way to the rooftop with one of the guards. Janos chose to look beyond him, hoping against hope the glimpse of a small, hesitant smile wasn't enough to reawaken his desires.

It was, of course, and he scarcely slept for fear he would waken to sticky sheets and shame.

He knew then that he needed distraction.

Reading and learning was fine, but being closed within the four walls of the building wasn't enough. If he was bound to the institution, then he would make himself useful. He could not stand to be useless and helpless. He had not survived battles and travel across time to spend his days festering away in a sterile box, lustful, shameful, and pitiful.

He spoke to his warden, who spoke in turn to the man responsible for the agency.

Less than three days later, Janos was called to his office.

Sanders was not what Janos expected in an official. A slight, thin man, he was perpetually haggard and tired, his tawny hair threaded with silver. His dark eyes gleamed, shrewd and watchful in his narrow, vulpine face. He spoke politely, but he never sat still, one hand always drumming on the desk or toying with a pen. A man with ideas, Janos thought, a man who wanted to do too much and forgot he was only a man.

"What can I do for you?" he asked through Shona.

Janos rubbed at the stump of his arm through the woollen pullover they had given him. It was still uncomfortable, but it was an anchoring point, a reminder this wasn't all some strange dream. He would never have dreamed his arm away.

"I have been told I must stay here," he said. "They say I cannot go back, and I cannot leave this building."

On the other side of the desk, Sanders leaned back in his seat. "Can you think of a reason we should let you? You attacked one of our men, broke into our facility, and took one of my linguists hostage, which resulted in him being shot." His expression was cold. "Why should we release you?"

Janos gazed at him. "Why should you save my life?" he challenged. "You did not save me just to keep me as an experiment in your cage."

"Can you be sure?" Sanders replied, his voice level. "You know what was happening in your time now. How can you be sure things have changed?"

The thought sent a shiver down Janos's spine, but all the boy had said, all the books he had provided—almost all—showed things were different. The boy said it was so, and as much as it discomfited Janos to think about him, he knew Dieter hadn't lied to him.

"Because I have to believe the world could become better," he said finally.

One side of Sanders's mouth turned up. "A good answer." He sat up a little straighter, and the directness of his gaze made Janos pull himself up, as if on inspection. "That doesn't change the fact that you threatened and wounded one of my staff."

Janos flushed. "He looked like an officer."

Sanders raised his eyebrows in amusement. "Dieter? An officer? The man couldn't be more civilian if he tried."

Janos blinked at him. "He's not trained in combat?"

Shona stifled a laugh, spitting out her translation, and Sanders's eyes widened in astonishment.

"I think you misunderstand when I said he's a linguist," he said, motioning for Shona to translate. "Dieter is a historian and linguist with no experience in the field or any kind of combat training."

Janos shook his head, frowning. "Why would you send such a person to deal with an armed intruder?"

"What makes you think I sent anyone?" Sanders said. "He thought you would react badly to armed men. He knew we needed to clear the temporal doorway to get the team home without anyone getting hurt. He came in to stop you killing anyone."

Janos tightened his hand on the stump of his arm, squeezing until it hurt.

He remembered when the boy entered the room. He seemed pathetic, a coward, kneeling and submissive, but he drew Janos from the room and closed the door behind him, doing what he had set out to do. He had not only kept Janos from doing something stupid, but had saved his colleagues, and earned a bullet for it.

"That stupid little idiot," he hissed.

Shona gaped at him in surprise. "What do you mean?"

"Putting himself on the line like that," Janos snapped. "I thought he was a soldier. I thought he was the enemy. I might have killed him! He should not have been in there!"

Sanders cleared his throat. Shona glanced at him and translated.

What Janos had said clearly met with the man's approval. Sanders drummed his fingertips on the edge of the desk, watching him.

"You want to make yourself useful?" he asked.

Janos nodded guardedly.

"Do you have any skills we could use?"

His words failed him. As much as Janos hoped he could be useful, he had not expected it to happen.

"I worked with machines," he offered finally, trying to recall the few skills he'd had a chance to develop in his youth. His heart sank. "But I don't know your machines now."

"No," Sanders agreed. A line creased up between his brows, making him look older, sterner. "But you know the machines from your time." His focus returned to Janos, and he inclined his head. "We may have a part you can play after all."

It shocked Janos how immediate and dizzying the relief was. "Thank you."

Sanders moved one hand in a dismissive gesture. "You will need to learn English. We have an international team, but everyone speaks English."

Janos nodded at once. "I will try," he promised.

Chapter Eight

Tea and bitching had become a thing.

Okay, technically, some people might call it therapy, but there was still a stigma with talking about feelings, and it was fucking ridiculous.

That was the problem. It needed to be done, but Dieter had been raised by his grandparents. His grandfather was a quiet, insular man, and his grandmother could talk the arse off a donkey, as long as it wasn't about anything serious.

In the year after his mother—their own fucking daughter—died, they hadn't mentioned her after the funeral.

Dieter wondered if it was the British stiff-upper-lip thing, or if his grandparents were really holding out on him. He suspected it was the former. They were opposites of one another, but they had to meet in the middle somewhere, and everything they did was to keep the worst of the world away from him.

Not exactly helpful when he was a teenage boy who hated his parents: his mother for getting herself killed, and his father for not coping and shipping him off to grandparents he didn't really know.

For the first time in a decade, he'd tried to be there for someone, and said someone told him to piss off. It shocked him how much of a blow it was. He'd thought he was being helpful, giving the man some information he might find comforting, but instead, all it had done was push the poor bugger deeper into the closet, scared shitless that he'd been found out.

So Dieter had gone for tea and bitching with Sally.

He hadn't mentioned his theory about Janos's issues, but he suspected he didn't have to. Sally could read people like a book. She'd read Dieter cover to cover.

She probably had notes about why he was fucked up. He'd stubbornly isolated himself for as long as possible because it was easier than getting attached to anyone. It was easier not to when you'd been shipped from place to place. People came and went; that was the way it was. It was why work and home were separate. The only people who ever came by his place were the one-night stands he sometimes had, or his grandmother.

That wasn't to say he didn't have friends. He did, but they were the ones who'd stuck around, the ones who hadn't drifted away because he was fucking useless at keeping them.

Sally was one of the few, and he knew he wouldn't be able to get rid of her, even with a crowbar and some lube.

They sat across the table from one another as usual, Dieter sprawled on the couch, his teacup balanced on his belly. He crossed his ankles and propped his heels on the arm of the sofa.

"He said he didn't want me there when he spoke to Sanders." He was trying to sound glib, but it wasn't working.

"You said he didn't want to depend on you," Sally reminded him.

Dieter frowned, staring at the ceiling. Why was it still bothering him so much? It wasn't like he was even friends with the fucking idiot. Could you be friends with someone who threatened to kill you and shot you?

But he wanted to help the stupid bastard.

He knew what it was like to end up in a place that wasn't his home, isolated and surrounded by strangers. He'd come to Britain speaking English—and two other languages—fluently, but his name and his accent betrayed him and told them he didn't belong. It didn't matter how diverse the country was, there were still bigoted fuckwits who liked to make a lonely kid feel even worse.

"Settling in a new place is bad," he finally said, "when you can speak the language. He can't. I thought I could help with the transition."

Sally nodded, leaning forward to claim a biscuit. "Brave of you."

Dieter flushed. "It's not brave. I wish I'd had someone there. I thought he might want the same—someone he could talk to about what was happening." He lifted the teacup over and set it on the saucer. "Shows what I know."

"He's still afraid," Sally murmured. "Of you most of all."

Dieter didn't look at her, fixing his eyes on a pattern of flowers picked out on the ceiling. He didn't need to be told. Of course the stupid poof was. Aside from Sally, Dieter was the only one to suspect the Hungarian's preferences. And he'd been bloody stupid enough to try to force the man to out himself.

He blew out a noisy breath. "It shouldn't bother me," he muttered.

"Why?"

Dieter shrugged. "We're not friends. The daft bugger shot me. Why should I care?"

"Why shouldn't you?" Sally said. "It's human nature to feel compassion for someone who is clearly afraid. It's not wrong to want to help them." She put her own saucer down. "He's from another time, though, and it means you have to approach him differently."

"How?" Dieter asked, shaking his head. "We crossed paths in the lobby, and he wouldn't even look at me."

Sally glanced towards the window. "Well, he's in the garden again, so you could go out and be casual at him." A crooked smile curled her lips. "You could discuss the weather. It's a nice, neutral topic."

Dieter sat up, frowning. "What's he doing up here?"

"He comes up most days," she said. "A change of scenery from his room, I suppose."

Dieter rose from the couch and approached the window, shielding his eyes from the morning sunlight. One of the wardens sat by the door leading to the elevator, reading from a console, and the Hungarian meandered around the gravelled pathway of the garden.

It had been nearly three weeks since Janos told him to leave, and several days since they had run into one another in the lobby. He seemed like he had finally started to gain some weight, but it was difficult to tell. He wore an oversized overcoat which hung to his knees and flapped loose in the breeze, and his hair whirled around his face.

He seemed distracted and walked in a slow circuit of the garden. He was probably still weak, Dieter thought, drawing back from the window. Strong enough to walk, but judging by the casual air of the warden, not strong enough to overpower anyone.

"You should say hello," Sally said with a smile. "What can it hurt?"

Dieter shifted uncomfortably. It was one thing to be pushed away by someone. It was something else entirely to push back. Janos had made it clear he was unwelcome, along with his knowledge. If Sally was right, it was out of fear. But if she was wrong...

Dieter's thought slammed to a halt as the Hungarian approached the wall which was low enough to take in the view over the city. Janos stopped there, resting his hand against the ledge, then glanced towards his warden. The man was engrossed in his reading. Dieter's heart faltered when Janos braced his forearm and hand on the edge of the wall and pushed himself up onto it.

"Shit!" Dieter was running before his thought could catch up with him.

The gravel crunched and gave beneath his feet, and he nearly tripped, leaping over a couple of the bushes in his headlong rush towards the far side of the garden. The warden glanced up, startled, but Dieter waved him back frantically.

He skidded to a halt on the edge of the terrace, half a dozen paces from the wall.

Janos sat with his back to the garden, peering down on the streets far below, his legs dangling over the sheer drop. All it would take was a strong gust of wind. Or a push from his remaining hand.

"Janos." Dieter's voice trembled. Strange, he thought. Gun to his head, his voice had been calm. Here, though, it shook so much it sounded like a stranger's.

Janos tilted his head to glance at him. "What do you want?" He sounded tired.

Dieter swallowed hard. "I'd like you to come down from the wall. I-I know things are difficult, but please. I can help." His heart thumped against his ribs, and it took him back to when he'd knelt, a gun at his head. He offered a shaking hand. "Please come down."

Janos was silent for a terrifyingly long moment. His eyes searched Dieter's face. "Why?"

Dieter's vision blurred. Tears. Fear or desperation, he didn't know which.

"I don't want you to fall," he said in all honesty. "Please."

To his shock and relief, Janos swung his legs back over the wall. He slid down off it, catching Dieter's hand with his own to steady himself. His skin was cool but his grip firm, and he didn't immediately let go.

Dieter swallowed hard and released a quivering breath. "Don't you scare me like that again, you stupid fuck."

To his surprise, Janos's hand tightened on his. He stared at Dieter with visible confusion, as if he couldn't believe he had intervened.

"I wasn't going to jump," he said. "Or fall. I wanted to see the city. I like high places."

Dieter stared at him, his hand shaking in Janos's. "Oh." It was barely a breath of a sound, and Dieter was shocked at the heat of tears on his cheeks.

Janos drew his hand free, which wasn't a surprise. Too much weak sissy emotional queer for him. He didn't step away though. Instead, he stepped closer, and Dieter stared at him, lost and confused, when Janos brushed the tears from Dieter's cheek. He stared at the tears as if he couldn't understand them.

Even if the arsehole didn't like being touched, Dieter couldn't have stopped himself.

He stepped forward and hugged him as hard as he could.

"Don't you ever fucking scare me like that again," he whispered this time. "I don't fucking like it."

Janos's faint laugh puffed against his ear. The soldier patted him awkwardly on the shoulder but didn't push him away.

"I'll try not to," he said, his words soft and close to Dieter's ear. "I don't want to upset my translator."

Dieter was the one who finally stepped away, and he rubbed at his cheeks. "Stupid fucker. What kind of idiot climbs on a wall over a twenty-storey drop?"

Janos studied him with a cautious, uncertain smile beneath his ragged beard. "That would be me."

Dieter snorted. "Arsehole." His heart had slowed to its more normal pace, and he shoved his hands into his pockets. They still shook more than he would have liked, so he balled them into fists and squeezed them hard. He nodded across the garden. "You want something to drink? Sally's got tea and biscuits."

Janos hesitated, then nodded. "It's cold out here. Tea would be welcome."

Dieter led the way back across the garden.

To his relief, Sally didn't smirk or say anything smug as they entered her office. She just smiled in welcome, holding out her hand to Janos. The Hungarian bowed at the waist, taking her hand as if to kiss it. He froze halfway into the bow, straightened up, and settled for shaking her hand awkwardly instead.

She inclined her head, and with her other hand, motioned for him to sit.

Janos sat uncertainly on the couch as she fetched another cup.

"She is a friend?" he asked Dieter, who had perched on the arm of the couch.

Dieter nodded. "And a doctor of the mind. She helps people to understand their troubles and how to deal with them."

Janos glanced across the room at her and then at Dieter, his brow furrowing. "And you were here."

Dieter studied his hands, clasped in his lap. "Everyone has problems," he murmured.

Janos looked away, flushing. "They do," he agreed.

Chapter Nine

Everything had changed.

Janos had a place within the agency, or he would once he learned to communicate with more than a tiny handful of people. He and Dieter had come to a fresh understanding when Dieter had intervened in what the silly boy seemed to think was a suicide attempt. Janos had been provided with a selection of false arms to choose from.

The world kept turning, he thought to himself.

The wardens were dismissed, and he was assigned a new room. Dieter was permitted to take him on a tour of the institution. The place was huge, with so many levels of the building. There were lecture rooms, massive chambers filled with clothing from dozens of eras, weapon stores, and archives.

Dieter explained most ventures into the past had so far been within the last two hundred years. It was safer, after their one foray into the Medieval period had gone terribly wrong. They had emerged in the middle of an undocumented siege, and one of their team had been badly wounded and had never recovered.

"Why go back at all?" Janos asked. "If you can't change things?"

Dieter considered for a moment.

"There are some places where the truth is still unknown," he said. "Where people died and no one knows why. Or where a battle went wrong and there's no record to explain it. We have to learn from the past. It's why we exist."

"But you can't save people."

Dieter shook his head.

"You saved me."

There was something in the way the younger man flushed.

"You were in our timeline," he said. "You had disrupted your own. That's a different set of rules."

They continued down the corridor, and after a few paces, Janos cleared his throat. "Thank you. I wasn't ready to die."

Dieter shrugged, avoiding his gaze. "I just did what any decent person would do. It's nothing special."

Janos walked beside him in silence.

He remembered what Shona and Sanders had told him: Dieter had walked into a room to confront an armed man. He had done so in the hopes of saving the rest of his team from being stranded in the past, putting his own life on the line to do so. Then he had broken all the rules to save the man who had threatened him. It took courage to do so, or recklessness. Janos wasn't sure which in Dieter's case.

Doctor Bellevue had confirmed he was fit enough to leave the medical wing earlier that day, though he was still under order to report to her for check-ups. Janos was privately relieved to be away from the sterile walls and clinical smell of antiseptic.

"It's not much." Dieter showed Janos how to swipe a card across a metal panel beside the door to gain access. "We don't have a lot of accommodation available here."

"I don't need much," Janos murmured, stepping into the room after him.

It was larger than his room in the medical wing, and the walls were neutral colours instead of plain white. Along the tall windows, half-opened floor-to-ceiling blinds allowed some of the afternoon light in, striping the polished floor.

A miniature kitchen took up a corner of the room, with cooking surfaces, a small table beside the window, and several cupboards. A wardrobe, bed, and desk filled the rest of the room, and a door led into the adjoining shower room.

"If you want to cook for yourself, we can get food ordered in," Dieter said, walking over to the kitchen. "It's basic, but some people prefer to make their own. If you don't want to, there's the staff canteen, or you can ask for something to be sent up."

"So people do live here? Not just prisoners?"

Dieter looked at him with something like surprise. "You're not a prisoner anymore."

"But I can't leave."

"It's for your own safety, as much as for the institution. The world outside…" He hesitated. "Until you're settled and more familiar with how much it's all changed, it could be dangerous for you."

Janos walked over to the window. They were on a much lower level, and from this height, he could make out people on the pristine streets. Their clothing wasn't so different, though the shiny metal pods shuttling along the roads in place of trucks and carts were strange.

It was frightening, but he had spent long enough hiding from a man who only wanted to help him. If he kept hiding, the world would pass him by.

"Maybe," he began carefully, "you could accompany me? If I was supervised, I probably wouldn't do something stupid."

Dieter was quiet for a moment.

"Stupid like sit on the ledge over a twenty-storey drop?"

Janos's lips twitched. Of course the boy would bring it up. It was, after all, the moment that had changed everything. He hadn't expected Dieter to be so alarmed at the prospect of him being hurt, and it was embarrassing how it warmed him.

He glanced over his shoulder. "Perhaps."

Dieter stood by the kitchenette, his fingers pressing against the counter, his eyes on his hands. "I can ask." He looked up. "I don't go out much myself. Maybe someone else would be better."

"I want you."

The words escaped before Janos could stop them.

He glanced at the window, the heat already rising in his face.

Dieter was silent again. Janos closed his eyes, his heart pounding. His words could have been innocent, but then, they could have been taken another way, and they had only just found a stable footing.

"I'll ask," Dieter finally said and tapped his fingertips on the edge of the counter. "Do you need me to get anything for you?"

Janos shook his head.

Dieter was halfway to the door before Janos remembered himself.

"Wait!" he said, turning. He wrapped his right arm cross his middle, his hand cradling the elbow and stump of his left. He swallowed nervously. "Those books you brought me. I-I left them in the cabinet in the other room. I..." He drew an unsteady breath. "I think I would like to read them now."

A brilliant smile lit Dieter's face and warmed Janos down to his toes.

"I'll bring them down," Dieter said as he stood at the door. "We could go to the canteen for dinner, if you like. Later, I mean."

Janos shifted. "I think I would prefer to eat here," he said, tightening his hand around his arm. It was one thing to make careful overtures towards an attractive man. It was another thing to be seen with him.

Dieter's eyes flicked to Janos's arm, and he flushed. "Oh. Of course. Sorry. I'll have them bring you something."

He should have said something, said it wasn't because of his arm, but he didn't. A last haven of safety, in case he was making a fool of himself. Let Dieter think he was worried about his clumsiness and disability. Janos nodded and turned to the window, gazing out into the city.

The door slid closed.

Dieter was as good as his word. He brought the books for Janos later that day and carried in the tray of food himself. Janos couldn't help noticing the food he'd chosen was cut into small pieces, which would be easier for him to eat. The boy didn't stay, though, and Janos wasn't sure if he was disappointed or relieved.

Left to his own devices, he ate and then settled on the bed with the books. The subject matter alone made his heart pound faster. Dieter seemed to think it would be beneficial to know, but some part of Janos was terrified he was about to learn worse things still happened to men of his tastes.

It was not the case.

It seemed across the world, tolerance and acceptance had become the norm.

Men were allowed to marry men, and women were allowed to marry women.

People could love whom they chose.

There were, of course, people and places that frowned upon it, but the more he read, the more Janos felt weak with relief and wonder. It had all changed so much. He would not be marched into the woods. He would not be shot and left to rot. He would not be cut and left to bleed. He would not die because of the way he was born.

In this world, Szilveszter and Ferenc would have lived.

He put the book down and covered his eyes with his trembling hand.

They would have lived. They and their friends and their lovers all would have lived.

It seemed foolish to weep for what had passed, but his friend and his lover had no one left who would weep for them. In silence, he sat and let the tears flow, remembering his secret trysts with Szilveszter, his merry discussions with Ferenc, the friends long gone because of who they happened to love.

They could not live, but Janos decided he *would.*

It did not matter if his desire for Dieter was not reciprocated. What mattered was he had the chance to show his interest without the risk of being harmed. It was as terrifying as it was liberating, and he rose from the bed on unsteady legs to go to the bathroom.

For days, he had avoided his reflection out of fear of what he might see.

A ragged beggar of a man stared back at him. Clean, yes, but his too-long hair tangled around his shoulders. He touched his chin and the straggled beard there. He looked like the kind of man who spent too many nights in a tavern and too little time tending himself.

No man with eyes would desire someone like that.

Janos pushed his fingers through his hair. He couldn't leave to have himself tidied up, but the institution had people responsible for dressing the agents who went to the past. If they could make someone fit for history, then surely they could groom him to appear as if he belonged in the present.

But it was difficult to find time.

He had been assigned a teacher from outside the institution to teach him English, a young woman called Stacey. He didn't know what details she had been told, but she believed he was some kind of war veteran in a rehabilitation facility. He could have told the truth, but it would sound like madness.

Physiotherapy occupied the rest of his time. They had provided him with a false arm, and he needed to learn to use it. It functioned almost as well as his other limb, the machinery delicate and intricate, covered in a fine layer of synthetic skin.

He was sceptical when they connected it to his arm with wires and pins. But his thoughts could direct the movement of the new limb, and he watched in astonishment as the mechanical hand picked up a ball and threw it in the direction he wanted. In awe, he turned the hand palm up and folded each finger in turn.

The doctors told him to try it for a few days to see how he handled it.

He wasn't sure if they meant it would cause pain or if there was something wrong with how it was connected.

"Some people are uncomfortable with them," Dieter explained when he brought Janos's food that evening. "Some ask to have them removed. They don't feel like the arm belongs to them, so they prefer to do without."

Janos turned over the hand again, examining it. It was true he didn't feel any sensation in it, but when he wanted to curl his fingers, they curled, and when he wanted to move his hand, it moved. He picked up both knife and fork for the first time since his arm had been wounded and ate in silence, wondering if he *could* dismiss such an incredible piece of technology.

Dieter sat on the opposite side of the small table. "I asked about a day out, by the way. Sanders said he'll give his approval, but you have to wear one of the tracker chips agents wear."

Janos frowned. "All agents?"

"Anyone who has ever been in the past. Just in case anything happens, past or present. We had a team who returned with a nasty strain of flu which didn't present symptoms for several days, and by the time anyone realised, two had gone on leave, and we were lucky to avoid an epidemic. You should be clear by now, but just in case..."

"So it isn't because he thinks I'll run?" Janos challenged.

Dieter winced. "Maybe a little. I hope you won't. I don't want to get in trouble."

Janos's lips twitched. "Well, I wouldn't want that."

Dieter smiled, and Janos had to stare down at his food, paying a little too much attention to cutting up the slices of potato with his fork. He was relieved when Dieter got up from the table.

"I should get to work," Dieter said. "Don't want to piss off Sanders and make him cancel our day out."

"When will it be?" Janos considered biting his tongue for being too direct, and laid down his cutlery self-consciously. "I mean, you have work, but it would be...good to see something aside from this building."

"If the weather's decent tomorrow afternoon, we could try?"

Janos nodded. "Sounds good," he said, hoping he sounded casual.

Dieter's grin flashed across his face like lightning. "Try not to sound too excited," he said, straightening his tie. "I'll come by and fetch you at about two."

"Two, tomorrow, if the weather's good," Janos echoed.

He waited until the door slid closed behind Dieter before hurrying over to dig the small radio out of his bedside cabinet.

He hadn't officially been given one, but Shona had slipped one to him, in case he had any problems with the technology, like getting himself locked in an elevator again. Dieter could help with communication, but Shona confided to Janos that the younger man didn't have the best knowledge of machinery.

Janos had spent an evening tinkering with the small, handheld device. He found he could patch himself into various frequencies in the building, but Shona was the one person he knew he could ask for help when it came to venturing outside. She was the one who had persuaded the wardens to let him out for air on the roof, and she would know who to talk to for something to wear.

She came half an hour later, and when he explained what he needed to do, her eyebrows disappeared up beneath her fringe.

"I always thought Dieter would have offered to take you," she admitted. "He's the kind of person to dress up."

Janos flushed. "I've bothered him so much already. I didn't want to ask for this on top of taking me out of the building."

To his relief, she didn't ask any more questions. Instead, she took him straight through to the wardrobe manager, a tall, bone-thin woman, who listened to her, then scrutinised Janos.

She ordered him to stand by a wall painted pure white, his feet apart and his arms extended to the side; then she held a small machine up. Bands of light cut across his body from it, stripes of red and blue.

"What is it?" he asked warily as he was ordered to turn and face the wall.

"She's taking your measurements," Shona replied, a flicker of mischief in her eyes. "You want to wear something that fits and looks good, don't you?"

His heart stopped. Did she suspect? Had he given himself away somehow?

It was only when she turned away to talk to the wardrobe mistress that he caught his breath and remembered it didn't matter. He was in a place where it was safe to be himself. He could be who he wanted and do what he wanted.

"Lea will take care of you just now," Shona said, turning to him. "We don't have a huge pool to choose from in modern clothing, but she'll be able to find you something. You understand yes and no in English, don't you?"

Janos nodded. "Stacey thought it was useful."

"That should be enough," Shona said and slapped him on the shoulder. "Good luck."

He didn't have a chance to ask what she meant, but within moments, he found out as he was pushed, prodded, pinned, unpinned, stripped, re-dressed, pinned again, and left shivering in his underpants.

Complaining would do no good. Even if Lea didn't understand Hungarian, she would guess what he was saying from his tone. He folded his arm across his middle and prayed she would at least put him in something suitable which wouldn't make him stand out too much.

Two hours later, mercifully, Shona came to collect him.

He knew it was two hours.

He had been staring at the clock, willing the time to move faster.

Still, he had been provided with a couple sets of clothes. The outdoor ones were similar to what he had worn in his youth—trousers, a shirt, and an overcoat—with finer tailoring, more expensive fabric, and a different cut.

Lea grunted in acknowledgment when he offered her thanks, a sour look on her thin face, and disappeared out of the room with a cigarette.

Shona helped him carry his acquisitions to his room. "I think she likes you," she said. "Most people don't make her miss her cigarette break."

"If she 'likes,'" he replied, "I wouldn't want to see dislike." He used his card-pass to open the door, then set the folded clothes on the bed. "She didn't like me enough to give me a kerchief for my neck."

Shona laughed. "Most people don't wear them now."

Janos touched his neck self-consciously. "I feel bare without it."

"I'll see what I can do." She set the shoes beside the bed and hung the coat on a peg. "We've got someone who can do your hair and beard tomorrow." She studied him. "Look up some modern haircuts on your computer. That way, you'll know what kind of styles are fashionable."

Janos nodded. "I don't want to stand out." He touched his tawny hair, resting against his shoulders and uncomfortably long.

"At least you have hair you can cut," she observed. "Better than a shaved head."

He tried to smile, but it felt unconvincing.

She left him then, and Janos sank onto the bed.

He examined at the folded shirt and trousers. They were smart, but not too smart, and the woollen coat to go over them was designed more for practical warmth than to catch the eye. Simply clothing. Nothing to draw Dieter's attention.

He took a shaking breath.

It felt like it was though.

As if he was preparing himself for something, anticipating a response that might never happen. He didn't know if Dieter had a lover or not. He hadn't dared to ask, for fear of what the answer might be. For all he knew, he might not be the kind of man Dieter found attractive.

He fell back against the pillow and stared up at the ceiling.

Better to get it over with. Perhaps the humiliation of rejection would be enough to drive the fantasies away. They had grown more intricate of late, sometimes taken straight from when he and Dieter had walked or talked together. Dieter had a habit of tugging on his lip ring with his front teeth when he was thinking, and it was distracting.

Janos pushed the thought of Dieter away hastily.

There were other things to be done. He couldn't just run and hide in the shower every time he thought of the way those white teeth plucked at the pink lip and the gold ring.

Janos rolled from the bed, picked up the clothing, and set it in the wardrobe. The other clothes given to him—loose trousers and soft, buttonless shirts called T-shirts—were more like undergarments than proper clothing, but Dieter had assured him they were worn casually.

Beside them, the shirt and trousers looked formal.

He ran his hand down the fabric.

Hopefully, he wouldn't look like too much of a fool. Hopefully, he wouldn't make too many mistakes in the world outside. And, secretly, privately, he wondered if it was too much to hope Dieter would like what he saw when they were away from watchful eyes.

Janos pressed his fingers to his eyelids, massaging them.

"Enough," he murmured. "Enough."

He would find out tomorrow.

Chapter Ten

"I'm not sure this is a good idea," Dieter said again.

Sally rolled her eyes. "You've already agreed to it."

They were walking from the canteen where they'd had lunch, towards the elevator. As it crept closer to two o'clock, Dieter became more worried. It was fucking ridiculous how terrified he was, with every possible way the situation could go wrong running through his head.

"There are so many ways it could go wrong," he said. "Sally, he's from a hundred years ago. What if he panics? What if he steps in front of one of the shuttles? What if he can't deal with it all?"

"That's a lot of what ifs." She caught his arm and drew him to one side.

He looked down at her hand and then at her face. "I don't think I'm the best person to be doing this. I'm a linguist. What do I know about keeping people safe?"

"He's a grown man, not a child. How about this— What if someone else takes him who doesn't have the vocabulary to explain things? What if he asks questions only you have the capacity to answer? What if it worries him more?"

"He might..."

"Or he might not," Sally said, pressing the button for the elevator. "If he's uncomfortable, you can just bring him back."

Dieter ran a hand over his mouth. She was right, of course. Fucking woman always was. "I'm worrying too much, aren't I?"

"Tiny bit." She slipped her arm through his. "You'll be fine. He doesn't seem like the kind of person to panic and bolt, even if he is alarmed. Just take him to quieter parts of the city and let him get out of here for a while."

"And if he does run off," Dieter said wryly, "he's got a tracker. Sanders made sure of that."

Sally knocked her shoulder against his arm. "Well, you're practically thinking positive," she said as they stepped into the elevator. "I'll walk you there so you don't get cold feet."

He wrinkled his nose at her. "Piss off," he said as the elevator rose. "I don't need a chaperone."

"Call it moral support," she suggested with a grin. "And I need to go to the same floor anyway, so I might as well tag along with you."

"And make sure I don't run?"

Sally widened her eyes in feigned shock. "I would never suspect that."

The elevator pinged as it slid to a stop, and the doors opened.

Dieter rolled his eyes. "Fine. This way."

Various rooms lined the halls, many of the external ones serving as temporary offices for people preparing for missions. Those rooms had internal walls of glass to allow daylight to filter through, though the accommodation block at the far end of the corridor did not.

"Is he the only one in just now?" Sally asked as they walked by the rows of doors. "Or is Telford in the doghouse again?"

"I thought Marta was staying, too, but I haven't seen her around, so maybe she decided to seek some home comforts," he said, after a second's thought. "Alex is definitely here again. Something about the wife and a wedding anniversary."

Alex Telford was notorious across the agency and seemed to spend more nights at the TRI than at home.

Dieter paused in front of Janos's door, his hand on the access pass at his belt. Normally, he would just let himself in because Janos wasn't great at answering the intercom. It would be a good excuse for him to leave it, if Janos didn't open the door.

Of course, if Dieter did, he'd be a fucking great coward. What did he have to be afraid of? Janos had coped with time travel. He was in a building with shiny pass cards to open doors and false arms hooked into his brain. If he could cope with that, why the hell would he panic at the sight of a modern version of a car?

So why did it frighten Dieter so much?

Maybe it was being responsible for the poor bugger's safety. Not because he was afraid of Janos anymore, but being responsible for him was something else. Or maybe because he tried to keep work and his life outside it as two separate things. Janos would see places Dieter knew, and no one else in work had done that. Work and life: two separate things. But they were overlapping now, and Dieter knew why.

He'd offered to find someone else when Janos asked if he could leave the building with a guardian. Dieter had offered, and he wouldn't forget the expression on Janos's face when he said, "I want you."

The stupid arsehole trusted him.

Of all the people in the whole bloody building, he trusted Dieter to guide him and watch his back.

And it fucking terrified Dieter.

People counted on him, yeah, but for information or words. This was something different. Janos was different. Not because Dieter was the one who could speak his language. Janos *trusted* Dieter enough to keep him safe.

Dieter stared down at the pass in his hand.

If he didn't swipe it and go in, he'd be letting Janos down. But how the fuck was he meant to keep someone safe, if he didn't believe he could?

Sally squeezed his arm, and he looked at her. How long had they been standing there? It didn't feel like very long, but it could have been hours.

"You can go forward or back," she said. "It's up to you."

"Your shrink-hat is showing," he said a little unsteadily.

"It happens sometimes." She slipped her hand down his arm to squeeze his fingers. "I'll be upstairs until seven tonight, so whatever you choose, you can come by if you want. I've just got appointments between three and five."

Before he could say anything, she rose on her toes and kissed his cheek, then hurried away down the corridor, her jewellery jingling.

He didn't know how much longer he stood there, squeezing the pass card so hard it cut into his palm. Minutes maybe.

All he knew was that his watch had beeped to remind him it was two o'clock, and he had an appointment.

He looked down again at the pass card.

Time to decide whether he had any balls at all.

"Fuck it all," he muttered and swiped the card over the key plate.

The door slid open, and Dieter took a breath before he stepped into the room. It was empty, but a coat lay on the bed. Water was running in the bathroom, and he breathed out, curling and uncurling his hands by his sides.

He could still turn and walk out the door, but he'd come this far, it would be fucking stupid to turn chicken and run.

He was still standing there like a twat when the bathroom door opened, and Janos stepped into the room. Dieter's mouth fell open in astonishment. No one had warned him Janos was going to get a fucking makeover!

Jesus Christ, a man could use a bit of warning.

The arsehole was all clean-shaken and high cheekbones and fucking sleek, short, golden hair brushed back from his face. And buggering hell, who had given him clothes that fit him like a fucking glove? And how in the name of fuck had Dieter not noticed the son of a bitch had put some meat on his bones?

He dragged his eyes up to Janos's.

Janos stood stock-still in the doorway, wary, a half-folded towel in his hands. "What?"

Dieter gestured at him. "You have a fucking face! What happened to the rat's nest?"

Now he could see the bugger's face, Dieter could also see the colour rising in his cheeks.

"I thought I should blend in," Janos said.

Blend in. Right. That was what they would call it.

Christ Almighty, he should have walked out the door.

Just what he needed: a day spent in the company of an attractive bugger who was still halfway in the closet and probably a fucking virgin on top of everything else. A bit of warning would definitely have helped.

Janos shifted self-consciously. "Are the clothes wrong?"

Dieter tried to gather his scattered wits. "No. No, they're great." He let his gaze flick down as if he gave a shit about the clothes. "They suit you."

Janos's face broke into a small, cautious smile. Without the beard obscuring his face, he seemed younger. Hell, maybe he *was* younger. War had made him ragged and old. He didn't look either now.

Dieter nodded towards the coat on the bed. "You were getting ready?"

Janos nodded, draping the towel over one of the chairs. He then crossed the floor to pick the coat up.

"I wanted to be ready when you were," he said, glancing over his shoulder. "Thank you for coming. I wasn't sure you would have time."

Dieter swallowed hard, unable to meet his eyes. "I wasn't sure either." He looked up. "I'm glad I did."

The cautious smile widened a little, and Janos turned away to pull on the coat.

Christ. Dieter groaned, closing his eyes. Just what he needed.

"Can I use your bathroom before we go?" he asked.

"If you need to." Janos gestured towards the room and sat to put his shoes on.

Dieter went straight in and closed the door behind him. He pressed his hands to its cool surface and rested his forehead between them.

"Shit shit shit," he whispered under his breath. "Jesus fucking Christ." He reached down, groped for his phone, and flicked through his contacts to Sally's number. She didn't pick up right away, and he paced in a tight circle in the middle of the floor.

"Dieter?"

"Christ, Sally," he whispered. "I'm fucked. I'm so fucked."

"What happened?" Worry tinged her voice.

He crouched down by the sink, pressing his hand to his forehead. "He went and got fucking hot," he whispered, his voice shaking. "I mean really. Christ. No one warned me!"

There was silence on the other end. "Dieter, don't tell me you want to…"

"In a heartbeat," he said, knocking his head against the wall. "Jesus Christ, Sally. Bad enough they cut his hair and got rid of the mess on his face, but someone put him in fitted clothes. Have you seen his shoulders?"

"I didn't look," she admitted. "It's not such a bad thing."

"Bad thing?" Dieter forced his voice down. "Bad? Sally, the poor sod comes from a place where buggery was illegal! Even if he is queer, which I'm not sure he is, I'd scare him shitless if I came on to him."

Sally sighed. "I didn't say hit on him, you silly queen," she said. "You have some self-restraint, don't you? So what if he's good-looking. Just enjoy having a crush. It's been a while, hasn't it?"

"God, yes." As much as Paul scratched the itch, Dieter couldn't remember the last time he'd seen someone and felt the crackle. "Sally, if I fancy someone, I flirt. What if I scare the poor sod? All he wants is a day out of here, not some stupid fucking queer giving him the eye."

"You're taking him into the modern world," she said. "I think he'll be distracted enough."

Dieter's breath shivered across his lips. "Christ, I hope so. If I scare him, he's coming to you for his therapy."

"Don't blame me for this one," Sally retorted. "You're the one whose brain isn't doing the thinking."

"Oh, piss off," he muttered and then severed the connection. He unfolded from the floor, flushed the toilet, and ran the tap so it at least sounded like an authentic toilet break. He looked at himself in the mirror.

"You'd better fucking behave."

He straightened his jacket, smoothed his hair, and opened the bathroom door.

Janos stood by the window, but he turned with the same quick, careful smile.

"All ready?" Dieter asked, slipping a hand into his pocket to find the old key ring in there, a round metal disk with an intricate labyrinth picked out on the surface. He traced his thumbnail along the edge of the pattern, a habit picked up whenever he needed to concentrate. He once jokingly called it his worry beads. Now, it didn't seem so funny.

Janos adjusted the collar of his coat and nodded. "I think so."

The first thing to do was get out of the fucking building.

Release papers had to be signed at the front desk, and Dieter ignored the stares as they made their way down.

Only a few people had seen Janos around the building, but everyone had heard of the man from the past. Dieter shot a few cursory glares around at the nosy fucks, and they hurried off to do whatever it was they were meant to be doing. Janos didn't notice as he put his mark on the form.

"Is that everything?" he asked, looking at Dieter.

"One more thing," Dieter said, holding out his hand to the desk warden. A metal band was placed in his hand. "This needs to go on your wrist."

"The tracker?" Janos guessed.

Dieter nodded, shaking his sleeve to show the ring around his wrist. It would be easier, he'd told Sanders, if they both wore them. "A security thing. Do you mind if I...?"

Janos held out his hand, drawing up the sleeve with his prosthetic fingers. He had adjusted to the false arm with surprising ease, but Dieter could see any movement with his left hand was made with concentration and care.

Dieter opened the band, setting it around the Janos's wrist. It closed with a click and a hiss, contracting to fit against his skin. Dieter wrapped his hand around it, moving it to check there was still some give. "It's not too tight?"

Janos stared at the band and Dieter's hand. Dieter remembered how he had recoiled from contact and self-consciously pulled his hand back.

"No," Janos said at once. "It's good."

Dieter led the way out of the building and onto the steps of the plaza. He waited for Janos to catch up, unsurprised by the dazed awe on the other man's face as he stared up and around at the gleaming buildings.

"It didn't look so tall from above," Janos said, shaking his head. "Is it all like this?"

"A lot of it is." Dieter raised a hand to flag down one of the taxi shuttles with his mobile beacon. Things had become lazier when applications were created to do every fucking little thing. The pod that stopped was one of the larger, sleeker passenger vehicles. Most of them didn't have drivers anymore. They weren't needed, just as it wasn't necessary to raise a hand to stop a cab.

"That's an automobile?" Janos said sceptically. "Where's the room for the engine?"

"They've managed to downsize them," Dieter said as they walked down the steps towards it. The door panel slid aside, and he stepped back to let Janos get in first. Janos hesitated, but ducked in, clearly surprised by the broad, comfortable chairs.

He sat, testing the texture with his fingertips.

"A bit different to your days?" Dieter asked, sliding into the opposite chair.

Janos nodded, sitting.

"State your destination," the automated voice said from the speakers above the window.

Dieter hesitated. He had no fucking clue where Janos might like to go, and the only thing going through his head was home, which was definitely not on the table.

"D'you have somewhere you'd want to go to?" he asked, slipping his hand into his pocket again.

Janos looked out the window, a frown creasing his brow. "Is there a river?" he asked. "I'd like to see a river."

"Salford Quays," Dieter answered for both Janos and the auto-recognition software, hesitated, then added, "Midspeed." It wouldn't do for the fucking thing to take off like a bullet and scare the living shit out of Janos.

The pod hummed to life, drawing away from the building.

Janos leaned sideways to look out the opposite window, watching the building vanish behind them. It was quiet, but Dieter heard the small, relieved sigh. No wonder. It had to be a relief to see his not-quite prison drop out of sight. He turned his attention to the city flicking by.

Dieter took the moment of Janos's distraction to study him. It was as if he were seeing a different person, and for all the shock he'd had, he wasn't about to tell Janos to get it all undone.

It wasn't that he was particularly handsome, all things considered. His nose was too long and aquiline, his eyes were deep-set under a prominent square brow. But he also had strong cheekbones and a jaw some people might call chiselled if they were pretentious dickwads. And Jesus Christ, his lips. There was a scar cutting across them both, just left of centre, and across his chin, as if he'd been caught by a blade.

It was a bad start to the outing if he couldn't stop staring at the way the scar plucked at Janos's full bottom lip.

Dieter forced himself to look out the window as well.

"Where are we going?" Janos asked as soon as Dieter turned his attention away.

Dieter darted his tongue along his lower lip. "Salford Quays. They've done some work there recently. There's a place to walk along by the water." He glanced at his watch. "At this time of day, it should be pretty quiet."

Janos's eyes were on the streets, the rushing pedestrians, and the vehicles speeding along the roads. "Quiet would be better," he said, his voice strangely flat.

Despite his intentions, Dieter leaned forward and touched Janos's knee lightly. "We can go back any time." He kept his voice as calm and steady as he could. As he had the first time they met. Christ, why did he have to think of that? There was no fucking gun. They were going out in a peaceful part of town, with no fucking weapons. He swallowed hard, pushing aside those thoughts. "If you want to, just let me know."

Janos turned from the window. "Is it all so big?" He sounded like a child, and there was no disguising the trepidation in his eyes.

"Most of the cities are now. They expanded upward as well as out."

Janos muttered something like a profanity, staring out the window. "I thought Szerencs was big." His voice was barely audible.

"Szerencs?" Dieter prompted as gently as he could. Better to make him talk than let him shut down in shock. Sally had warned Dieter it might happen. She'd be fucking proud of him for paying attention, and he knew he'd never hear the end of it.

"The city closest to my home," Janos said without turning to him. The fingernails of his right hand were pressing in a pattern on the back of his left, leaving half-moon indentations in the synthetic flesh.

"You weren't from a city yourself?"

Janos shook his head. "A village."

As far as things he should have asked about before they went, Dieter was starting to realise asking the poor sod if he'd ever been to a city before was pretty fucking high up the list. "I didn't realise," he said stupidly.

Janos looked at him, pale-faced and solemn. "Why would you? I didn't say."

"We can go back."

Janos shook his head. He glanced down at Dieter's hand, still resting on his knee. Before Dieter could think to draw it away, Janos moved his hand to cover it, as if to stop him turning the car around.

"I don't want to go back right away," he said. He took a breath. "It feels like weakness."

Dieter stared at him. If there was one thing he hadn't expected, it was that the soldier would be as scared of their outing as he was, but for completely different reasons. But he'd gone because he was a stubborn arsehole too.

"I almost didn't come," Dieter said, acutely conscious of the warmth of Janos's palm over his hand and the tremors in Janos's fingers. "I didn't think I would be any help to you outside of the building."

To his surprise, Janos laughed.

It was strained and tight, but it was a laugh.

"You're helping."

Dieter turned his hand enough to squeeze Janos's fingers. "Good."

Chapter Eleven

Salford Quays was a good choice.

Janos fought down his embarrassment about his behaviour in the automobile. He tried, but he wasn't able to crush down the panic at a world so much vaster than anything he had seen before. From above, it didn't feel so bad, but surrounded on all sides by towering buildings, he felt small, smothered, and inconsequential.

The place Dieter had chosen was as unlike that as possible.

The buildings along the riverside still looked modern to his eyes but were years older than the towering blocks in the newest and busiest part of the city. They were also much lower, and the spaces between them had been filled with green areas.

He walked to the nearest one as soon as he got out of the automobile, sinking onto an ornate wrought-iron bench. His legs shook beneath him. He closed his eyes, drawing unsteady breaths, taking in the scent of the grass and the nearby waterway.

Dieter's shoes tapped on the path as he approached a moment later.

To his relief, Dieter didn't speak. If asked if he was all right, Janos knew he would have lost what little self-control he had left. Instead, Dieter put his hand on Janos's shoulder, a silent offer of support. It was comforting, a solid point of contact for Janos. There was nothing threatening or intimate in the gesture, simply comfort, a man helping another man.

It took several minutes for Janos to gather himself.

"We have a few choices," Dieter said casually, as if discussing the weather. "There's a pathway by the side of the river we could walk along. Or we could just sit and enjoy the sun for a while. Or if you get hungry, there are quite a few restaurants along the quay."

Janos curled his fingers against his own palm, remembering how Dieter had clasped his hand as if to assure Janos he was there and would help. This man whom he had shot—no matter if it was accidentally—was willing to take time to reassure him, as he had each day since Janos had woken in the present.

If Dieter could walk into the room of a man who had shot him, day after day, how could Janos let a few buildings reduce him to knee-knocking panic?

"A walk would be good," he said, rising, hoping his legs would hold him.

Dieter's hand dropped away from his shoulder, and for a moment, Janos wished it hadn't. He opened his eyes and made himself gaze around. On the far side of the grassy area they occupied now, the shimmer of the crisp afternoon sun glimmered on the water.

There was something safe and familiar about it. His family's home had been on the banks of the Tisza, and some small part of him always found the sound and scent of water reminded him of a brief, peaceful time before the wars ruined everything. He glanced at Dieter and found the other man watching him with concern.

"Walk with me?" It was hardly an exciting proposition, but it was all Janos had. He wanted Dieter to know his presence was not unwelcome. Far from it.

Dieter's smile was quick and bright. He stepped alongside Janos as they started walking towards the river, the grass soft and springy underfoot. "If we're lucky, we won't get shat on by a seagull," Dieter said gravely.

Janos glanced at him, unsure if he was being earnest.

Dieter slanted a mischievous look at him.

"You are a very strange man," Janos observed.

Dieter nodded with a quiet laugh. "It has been said."

They emerged between the buildings onto the path along the riverbank. A cool breeze rose from the water, and Janos breathed it in. It wasn't the same, of course. They were not in the middle of the countryside. It was similar, though, fresh and crisp.

"This way," Dieter suggested, motioning with one hand. His other hand was in his pocket again, the shape of it visible through the woollen coat he wore. He was holding onto something, and Janos knew that sentiment, the press of his trimmed nails against his palm.

He took a deep breath, then set off along the path, the sun at his back.

The walkway had meandering patterns picked out in different colours of stone, images of ships and a representation of what the city must once have been like. A few painted barges were moored along the bank with signs suggesting they were permanently docked.

Dieter walked abreast of him, and Janos could tell by the way his shadow fell that the younger man was glancing at him from time to time. Or *was* he younger? Janos couldn't remember asking. It hadn't seemed important when he tried to distance himself from Dieter, but now, there didn't seem any reason not to ask.

"How many years have you?"

Dieter blinked in surprise, as if it was the last question he expected. "Twenty-eight."

Janos searched his face. "You don't look it."

Dieter snorted. "Thanks. I think." They walked a little farther in silence. "What about you? How many years?"

Janos uncurled his hand to rub his neck, frowning in thought. "Thirty-four, I think. I don't remember what month we were in. We marched so often, all the days seemed to go together."

"Of course," Dieter said, his voice quieter. "You were in the army."

Janos gazed ahead, trying not to think on their first encounter again, in that moment when he thought he had stumbled into a hidden German base. He often wondered who had been more afraid in the metal bunker. Dieter had seemed calm, but then Janos believed he was in control of the situation. It was becoming very clear he was as far from in control as it was possible to be.

Dieter, on the other hand, always seemed calm, except for the day on the roof.

Life or death, Janos thought. It all came down to life or death. Not his own. Other people.

"It was easier," Janos said finally. Dieter's shadow stretching on the path ahead of them told him he was being watched. When he spoke, it was carefully, precisely, offering what he prayed was enough of himself. "To be in the army was easier than not being in the army. If you were not in the army, people asked questions."

Dieter drew a breath as if to speak, but remained silent.

Janos clenched and unclenched his hands by his sides.

Words were not his strength.

They walked onward until they reached a bridge, and only then did Dieter speak again.

"What did you do before?" he asked.

"Before?"

"Before the army? Before the war?"

Strange to think of that time, now. Stranger still to talk of it with a man he had considered as nothing more than a coward and a pretty face. That man was not meant to care if he had a past, and yet here he was, giving Janos freedom and company.

Janos wrapped his hand around the false fingers of his prosthetic limb. "My family tended a farm for the man who owned the land. I wanted to study, but after the first war..." He remembered the hollow shell his father had become, sitting silently in his chair and staring out the window, rising only to get another drink. He shook his head. "We needed all hands there. I stayed until the soldiers came."

"Fucking brave of you," Dieter murmured. "Signing up in the middle of it all."

Janos bit down a bitter laugh at the irony.

Bravery had been the last thing on his mind.

Naked terror, the memory of the sound of gunshots from the woods, the moans and cries of the women whose men had been taken—those were the things that stood out on that day. He could still remember the scent of new-turned earth and the fresh smell of torn-up grass. It was a day full of life, the start of a new season.

But the soldiers were hungry and bitter and angry. They had marched for days from the Eastern front. Food had run short, and they wanted someone to punish, so they punished the ones who were foolish enough to be seen. Brave enough to be seen. Brave enough to face death, instead of running.

The knuckles of his false hand pressed painfully into his palm.

"You said there are places to eat here," he said. "Is there somewhere to get a drink?"

"Of course." Dieter nodded across the bridge. "There are a few places there." He hesitated and then pointed out one of them, a brick building which looked much older than the ones they had passed so far. "That one is probably the quietest."

Janos nodded, heading towards it. Dieter may only have been a hand-span shorter, but he had to hurry to keep up with Janos's long-legged pace. Janos pushed the door open, and it was as if he had stepped into a time closer to his own.

The bar might have been a more elegant version of any inn he had visited in his youth. There was something traditional about it, the bottles on broad wooden shelves behind the bar, the wooden counter with a hatch lifted up against the wall. Even the lamps on the wall were from another age.

Dieter brushed his hand against the base of Janos's spine. "What do you want to drink?"

Janos shook his head. All he had thought on was alcohol. Something to numb the rising panic. He remembered the distant gunshots and the birds bursting from the treetops in a wild flurry. Remembered another day, another time, and running like the coward he was. His chest ached.

"Some spirit," he said tersely. "Something strong."

Dieter nodded towards a table half-hidden from sight. "Go and sit. I'll bring them over."

Janos's legs shook beneath him. He walked with care to the table and folded into the corner, concealing himself from view. His breath came too fast, his head spinning. He brought his hand to his face, covered his eyes, and tried to remember how to breathe.

He must have only been there a heartbeat when a hand touched his shoulder, and he recoiled against the wall, eyes flying open.

"It's just me," Dieter said, drawing his hand away. He held out a glass of some kind of amber liquid in his other hand. "You look like you need this."

Janos dragged his tongue along his lower lip, his mouth dry as sand. He took the glass in his shaking hand and knocked back the contents. It burned down his throat, and his breath caught, his eyes stinging.

"Thank you," he said hoarsely.

Dieter glanced at the bar, raising a hand and making a gesture. "Another?" he said to Janos.

The liquid pooled in Janos's stomach. He should have eaten something, but he had foregone any food since breakfast. Too nervous. Too uneasy. He nodded, though it was probably a bad idea. Anything to make him feel like breathing wasn't a trial. He closed his eyes, drawing a slow breath.

The leather of the booth shifted as Dieter sat beside him, and when Dieter's hand covered his again, he didn't flinch. He just turned his hand enough to grip the other man's fingers, hold them fast.

Dieter was quiet for a moment, then said, "Your German is shit."

Janos flicked his eyes towards the younger man who met his gaze, not with pity as he feared, but with concern. "You can talk," he retorted, trying to keep his voice even. "Your tenses are wrong. You sound like a mentally deficient child."

Dieter arched his eyebrow. "Maybe I'm doing that for you since you act that way."

Dieter's thumb brushed soothingly along the back of his hand. Janos didn't dare glance down at their linked hands, in case the moment was broken, in case he took too much from something only meant in comfort.

"And now, you're trying English?" Dieter said. "God help my mother tongue."

"German isn't your first?"

Dieter's worried expression gave way to a winning smile, and for a moment, that and the alcohol drove some of the panic away. "Oh, I'm a language-whore." The gleam in his eyes was wicked. "I'll use my tongue on any of them."

Janos's mind slid off track in a heartbeat, his gaze flicking to Dieter's lips. As if the boy could read his mind, Dieter self-consciously tugged on his lip ring with his teeth.

Both of them turned away from one another in the same moment, and Dieter was the one to draw back his hand.

"I'll fetch the drinks," he said, rising.

Janos said nothing, keeping his face averted, and in the brief moment when Dieter was gone from the table, shifted in his seat, arranging his coat better. God above, it was the height of idiocy to have such ideas, especially here in a public place where anyone might see.

When Dieter returned, it felt like a wall had been placed between them, but Janos couldn't tell if it was all his own making or if Dieter had retreated too. They spoke of the bar, of the area they were in, of the new buildings, and vehicles used, of all manner of meaningless and harmless things.

So Janos took refuge in the glass Dieter had brought him.

There was food, also, but he had no appetite.

"We should walk," Janos finally said, pushing aside his glass. "I need air."

"As you like," Dieter replied, his tone sombre.

The breeze had quickened, and Janos shivered as they stepped out of the inn.

Instinct made him move his hands in his pockets, but the fabric on the left side gave way. The false hand, he recalled. Sometimes, he overextended, or moved it too quickly. It was attached to him, but it wasn't his yet.

He hoped Dieter hadn't noticed. As Janos walked on ahead, he glanced down at the pocket, wincing. The edge of the pocket was curled away from the coat, split stitches and torn fabric visible. He pressed his arm and sleeve closer to hide the damage as Dieter caught up with him.

"There's a mile of walkway," Dieter offered. "If you want some time on your own, I could wait here."

The trust implicit in those words made Janos come up short. If he chose to walk away, run away, Dieter would be held accountable. Though he had the tracker on, Janos knew he could find a way to free himself from it, and he would be free of the agency, his would-be prison, and all that came with it.

"Why?" he demanded, the words made bold by alcohol.

Dieter turned to him in confusion. "Why what?"

The wind picked up around them, and Janos held his coat tighter against him, both hands—real and false—clenched in the pockets. "Why are you here? Why are you showing me any kindness?" Anger seeped into in his voice, but he couldn't rein it in. "What do you want of me?"

Dieter stood, silent and still, as if carved from marble. His face betrayed no expression, and the only movement was the wind tossing his pale hair around his face.

"You needed someone who could help you," he said through barely parted lips. "Was I meant to stand back and let you suffer?"

"Yes!" Janos exclaimed. It would have been better. It would have been right. "I put a gun to your head! I threatened your life! You bled at my feet, you stupid child! You should have spat in my face! You should have left me to rot!"

Dieter swayed as if he wanted to retreat but stood his ground. "What would it have accomplished?" His voice was calm, always calm. Too calm. It could not be real. It was impossible that he had no bad reaction to their first encounter, about the gun, the humiliation, the piss and blood.

Janos shook his head. "I don't know. I don't know! But if someone hurts you, you have the right to fight back!" He pulled his hand from his pocket and pushed at Dieter's shoulder. "Do you fear nothing? Don't you care you might have been killed?"

A muscle twitched in Dieter's cheek. "I fear enough," he said.

Janos searched his face, so close now the warmth of Dieter's breath whispered on his skin. "I could have killed you," he whispered. "I could have, and you stand here, with me, as if I did nothing."

"You could have." Dieter's voice was just as low, his face ashen. He didn't seem afraid—he never did—but he was pale and drawn, and looked older. "But here we both are. We're both alive, and I'm going to fucking help you, okay? And being a dick about it isn't going to change that."

Janos's breath shrilled between his clenched teeth. "You're a fucking idiot."

"And you're a fucking Hungarian," Dieter snapped. "At least I can be less of an idiot."

It was like something broke. They stared at one another and then both laughed. Strange and uncertain and stuttering, but it was a shared laugh.

Janos took a step away, giving Dieter space, and rubbed at his eyes. "I shouldn't have drunk. It's gone to my head."

"I'm glad there's something in there," Dieter said, his toner gentler now. He was still for a moment, then reached out and touched Janos's shoulder. "Come on. If we walk, your head may clear itself."

Janos nodded cautiously, as though he was watching everything at a distance through the hazy warmth of the alcohol, and if he tried to think for himself, only foolishness could follow. He let Dieter take the lead and walked alongside him, keeping both hands closed away in his pockets and his mouth shut.

For a long while, they were both silent.

When Dieter spoke, it seemed more to himself. "You know, before all this happened, I used to want to be a time agent. It always sounded exciting—going to the places in the past I had only read about."

"Used to?" Janos murmured.

Dieter nodded as they turned the corner onto a fresh strip of flagstone path. "I saw the state you were in when you came through. Our people don't go back to times of peace. We need to resolve information about conflicts." He glanced sidelong at Janos. "I don't think I could walk away from people who were hurt."

"Break the rules," Janos murmured.

Dieter stared ahead. "I have a bad habit of doing what I shouldn't. I'd be smuggling people home with me. I'd fuck up the space-time-continuum or some kind of bullshit."

Janos screwed up his eyes, trying to make sense of what he was saying. "I didn't understand anything you said."

"It's time-travel science," Dieter said, waving one hand. "Apparently, we can't change things because it'll fuck up now, if we change then. If someone is dying there, they have to die there." He shook his head. "We couldn't stop it, even if it was right in front of us. We couldn't help them. We couldn't warn them." There was something angry and bitter in his voice. "We have to stand by and watch, knowing what's coming, because we can't let any fucking thing be changed."

Janos glanced at him, surprised by the colour in Dieter's face, the fire in his eyes. "You have to protect the past," he said slowly, as if putting the sentence together carefully, one word at a time.

"But not the people," Dieter said with quiet vehemence. "They live, they die, but the past is preserved as it was."

Janos studied at the flagstones beneath them as they walked. He felt detached from his feet, and dozens of stones had passed underfoot before the thought came to him. When it did, he said it aloud. "You helped me."

Dieter nodded. "Doctor Bellevue and I."

Janos shook his head. "You," he said with more clarity. "If they wanted to get their people back, I was expendable. You changed it. You spoke to me, instead of sending in men and guns." He stopped walking and looked at Dieter. "You saved me twice."

Blue eyes stared at him, then turned away. "I don't like to let people die," he said, resuming his brisk pace.

Janos fell into step beside him.

It seemed he had said too much because Dieter didn't speak again, his eyes on the path. Maybe saving Janos had landed him in trouble. Maybe he didn't want to think about that. It was understandable.

They reached the end of the walkway in silence, and as much as Janos was loath to go back to the agency, the cold had seeped to his bones. It would do little good to anyone if he caught a chill.

"Maybe," he suggested, "we can go back now?"

Dieter nodded, still drawn, as if thinking of the past had tired him. "I'll call a car."

They had to walk to the road for the vehicle, and the silence hung too heavily, suffocating. Dieter was unhappy. Janos could see it in his expression, the slump of his shoulders. They shouldn't have talked about the agency and the past. It upset him.

"I read the books." The words fell from Janos's lips. "Those books you brought for me."

Dieter blinked at him, and for a moment, his expression brightened. "You did?"

Janos nodded. He pressed the edge of his thumbnail into the side of his forefinger until it stung. The books said things he hadn't dared to believe possible, but admitting it out loud was a step too far, like putting his head in a noose. "Are they right?"

"They're not wrong," Dieter replied, his voice cautious.

Janos watched his feet as they walked. Dieter was being careful and quiet for him. He had provided books and knowledge and helped Janos as he said he would. He had shown the world was not so bad, and all for no good reason.

"Things are better, then," Janos said finally, his words as slow as his dragging feet. It was as close as he dared to come to a spoken confession, but he knew Dieter had guessed, and understood.

"They are," Dieter agreed as they approached the road and the shining car waiting for them.

Chapter Twelve

Steam from the shower had misted the surface of the mirror.

Dieter opened the bathroom door. The waft of cool air raised gooseflesh across his body from head to toe. He padded across the floor, leaving shining wet footprints on the tiles, and wiped his hand across the mirror.

Slick and pale and colourless, his ghostly reflection stared back at him in the dulled surface.

It had been a very strange day.

Less than two months ago, a half-starved gun-wielding Hungarian had put a gun to his head and threatened to kill him. Today, the same man had been indignant about the fact that Dieter hadn't tried to hurt him in turn. It was not what he'd expected when he agreed to take Janos out of the institute for the afternoon.

The whisky might have been to blame.

Or it might have helped.

Janos was not a talkative man from what Dieter could tell, but after two glasses of scotch, he'd broken the awkward silences more than once with a vehemence that had caught Dieter by surprise. He seemed angry and confused when Dieter wanted to help rather than punish him for what he'd done. He seemed to expect violence and retribution, even think he deserved them, and it unsettled Dieter more than he cared to admit.

What could he have done to believe he deserved punishment?

It was about more than what happened in temporal chamber.

It had to be.

The man was a fucking soldier. He'd been in the army. No soldier worth his salt would have given two shits about knocking down a suspected enemy. But Dieter remembered how shaken up Janos was when they were out of the agency.

From what he could tell, he was a walking panic attack waiting to happen.

It wasn't just the city either.

When they'd talked about the past, when he'd said Janos was brave for joining up, it was when things went strange and tense. Janos went as rigid as a statue, white as a fucking sheet, and he'd knocked back two glasses of whisky. It gave him some colour and drained some of the tension from his shoulders, but if he hadn't drunk, Dieter couldn't help wondering how much of a fucking mess he'd have been in.

Something meant as a compliment had left Janos shaking like a leaf. Dieter wished he knew how the hell he was meant to work out what to say when the bastard was as tight as a duck's arsehole with information.

The mirror was misting again.

Dieter abandoned it with a sigh, reached for the towel, and dried himself.

He was exhausted, and it wasn't as if he'd done anything. He'd gone into the offices, done some translation work for one of the next briefs, and taken Janos out for a walk, like an oversized, stupidly attractive Hungarian puppy with PTSD.

That was a complication he hadn't expected.

For weeks, Janos had resembled someone who lived under a bridge. Sure, he he'd been taken in, cleaned up and dressed in clothes too big for him, but he hadn't been anything special, and suddenly, he'd walked through a door all clean-shaven and solemn and fucking hot.

There had to be rules about eyeing up the poor sod who had almost killed him. He brushed his fingers across the scar Janos had left in his arm. The doctor had done what she could, but when a wedge of arm was gouged out, it stayed pretty fucking gouged.

Even if Janos did feel bad about it, it was fucked up to think about looking at him that way. Janos might have read the books, he might have suggested he supported the content, but it didn't mean he was ready to have some fucking great queen curling up beside him. Especially not when said fucking great queen was still having terrifying nightmares about him from time to time.

Dieter abandoned the towel and padded out into his flat.

A stack of laundry sat beside the washing machine, which was already whirling. He added his most recent socks and underpants to the pile awaiting attention on the black-and-white tiled floor.

The dishes from his breakfast and evening meal still sat on the counter. Half a dozen mugs had also migrated in from different rooms, still half-full of forgotten tea, cold and greying, skins of age tweaking the surface.

Dieter ran a hand over his face.

He had some energy to burn, and the sensible option would be to clean up. After all, if he left things lying much longer, they'd start to smell, and he didn't want anyone thinking he had a fucking corpse stuffed under his bed.

He hooked his fingers through the mugs, dragged them as far as the sink, and emptied them all, stacking the plates and bowls in with them. A blast of hot water filled the sink with bubbles and drowned the dishes. He surveyed his handiwork. It had been a long day, and it was about as far as he was willing to go.

What he really wanted was a fucking drink.

An exploration of the cupboards located half a bottle of vodka and some kind of cognac that had been someone's unwanted present last Christmas. Dieter was never one to see a bottle of booze homeless, so he'd shoved it under his coat as he left the office party.

The bottles in one hand, he snagged a glass with the other, and meandered through from the sharp contrasts of his kitchen to the warm browns and creams of his living room. None of the flat matched, but he didn't care. The kitchen was sharp and clean for cutting and cooking. The living room was warm and comfortable. And the bedroom...

Well, there were two things he did there, and it catered well enough to both.

He sat on the edge of the butterscotch couch and set the bottles and the glass on the coffee table in front of him. It was a gorgeous piece, a round cross-section of an old oak, varnished and polished, on four carved legs. It was the first piece of furniture he'd ever bought himself.

Dieter glanced at the television. He could have put it on. Hell, he could have retreated to his study and worked. He could have done any one of a thousand things, but his head was overcrowded with thoughts, and he poured himself a measure of vodka.

"Skol," he murmured to himself before knocking the stuff back.

It burned for a moment, and he poured another, then he sprawled against the couch, propping his bare feet on the edge of the coffee table.

It was all a mess.

A huge part of him screamed to back off now. The last thing he needed was get too involved with an emotionally fucked war veteran, especially one from a century ago. It was one thing to help the poor bugger find his footing, but he couldn't keep his mind on the job because he was distracted by the way Janos glanced up at him through his lashes.

"Christ," he muttered, draining a second glass. "Couldn't just stay simple, could it?"

Janos wasn't trying to be coy or flirtatious, and it made it worse. He was uncertain, cautious, and shy as if he'd never been hit on before, but there was an edge to him, sharp and full of anger and loss, and the mix was fascinating as hell. Most shy people weren't so hard, and most people who'd been so beaten up by life didn't have the tentative innocence Janos had.

Dieter abandoned the glass on the table and leaned forward to snag the bottle instead.

He needed to sleep. He needed to get Janos out of his head, and if it meant drinking himself unconscious, he would fucking do what was necessary, even if it meant working with a hangover in the morning.

Wasn't going to be easy.

He'd been mentally taking Janos home with him every night, trying to think of new ways to help make the transition from past to present easier. He'd spend hours poring over the Internet to search out books and information that might be useful. He'd researched Hungary in the period as much as he could, trying to find home comforts.

Guilt, he'd figured.

He was the one who'd helped keep Janos alive, so he had to make sure the poor bugger didn't lose it when faced with a world he didn't know. If Janos couldn't deal, if he broke, Dieter would blame himself for it, which was fucking stupid. It wasn't like he'd made the idiot come through the portal or anything.

All the same, he was Janos's main link to the world, and he didn't want to let him down.

Maybe, he mused, declaring he was an atheist had done the trick. Some almighty beardy old git in the sky had sneered down and decided to smite him by making the subject of his attention suddenly and unexpectedly hot as a punishment.

He snorted and took a swig from the bottle.

On the whole, there were worse punishments.

Although, having to look and keep his distance was a new one, and a pain in the arse.

Dieter knew he lacked restraint. It was a flashing great big personality flaw. He had a bad habit of crashing headlong into a situation. That was how he ended up in the bunker with Janos to begin with.

It was a hell of a thing to try to keep flirtation in check when there was a good-looking man right in front of him, choosing to spend time with him. Especially when the stupid son of a bitch got all emotional and passionate and intense.

True, it was scary as fuck, remembering the first night when that intensity had been pointed at him. But Janos's face had been so close to his, his eyes blazing, his cheeks flushed, and fucking hell, Dieter was so torn between the terror of the memories battering at him and getting turned on at the gleam in those green eyes.

He drained the last dregs from the bottle and gave it a sullen glare. Empty too fast, and he couldn't feel the effects. Shouldn't have had anything to eat before he started. That was the problem. He'd had food, and now, he was going to have to work for oblivion.

He leaned forward and retrieved the cognac, abandoning the empty bottle on the floor.

He'd always hated the stuff, but free booze was free booze.

It took three mouthfuls before his tongue was numb to any flavour, and he slid down on the couch, his heels propped on the table.

It was fucking typical, he grumbled to himself. He hadn't fancied anyone in fucking years, and the one person he shouldn't, the one person who should never have crossed his path, the one person who had scared him shitless in his whole life, was the one who gave him a fucking hard-on with one look.

Didn't help at all that he'd ended up on his knees the first time they met.

It shouldn't have taken his brain on the track it did, but his brain was a fucking wanker.

So what if he'd knelt for him? It wasn't out of an invitation to give him a blow job. It was because of the fucking gun pressed against his head. Dieter lifted his free hand to trace the crescent scar, half an inch above his left eyebrow. Another fucking souvenir of the fan-fucking-tastic night.

But for a moment, when he'd walked into Janos's room and Janos had just stood there, all grave and broad shoulders and fitted clothes, Dieter's cock had not given a fuck about the scars, the gun, or the fact that he'd pissed himself in terror because of Janos. Dieter's cock didn't jump to attention for just anyone, but Jesus Christ, something about their refugee from the past got to him.

He glared down at the rebellious piece of meat.

Thinking about Janos's expression was a mistake, especially the scar on his lips, the intensity in his eyes. It was a fucking mistake to remember the way the son of a bitch slid his tongue along his lower lip before speaking.

Dieter's cock didn't care.

"I hate you," he informed it and took another mouthful of cognac, making a face. It wasn't working. If anything, it made him think more about golden hair and broad shoulders and the scar-tugged lip, and he didn't want to be doing it, any more than he wanted a fucking boner at the thought of him.

Dieter pushed himself off the couch, swaying a little as he came to his feet. He kept a grip on the bottle and meandered through to his bedroom. The bed was as he'd left it, the burgundy covers shoved in a pile at the foot, the pillows scattered across it. He sat on the edge, setting the bottle on one of the matching bedside cabinets. They'd come in a set, and no one ever used the other one.

The room was cool, the air still stale from the night before.

Dieter scowled down at his cock.

The fucking thing was looking back at him. Reproachful.

He rubbed his eyes and pinched the bridge of his nose. Christ, he was drunk. Drunk and not in the way he'd wanted to be. He pushed himself onto the bed, waving a hand to the motion sensor to bring the lights down.

Some things were better to do in the dark.

When he wrapped his hand around his cock, when the heat of it throbbed against his palm, he closed his eyes and pressed his head against the mattress. It was high up the list of stupid fucking things to do, but he let himself think of Janos, of his broad hand, imagining it in place of Dieter's. He'd be rougher, probably, grip a little tighter, a strong grip.

Dieter's teeth caught on his lip ring and tugged. His hips twitched, and he dragged his hand down with a roughness to make him shudder. He imagined Janos being hesitant, then stronger as he got confident. He would leave fucking bruises, that man, whether he meant to or not.

Christ, when he realised he could do what he wanted, he'd probably turn Dieter on his fucking face and take him up the arse. The thought drew a strangled sound of want from Dieter's throat. He'd plaster himself against Dieter's back, silent, not a fucking word, never a fucking word, and he would fuck him hard and desperate.

Dieter's feet pressed against the mattress, and he pushed his hips up, as his hand moved harder and faster. His other hand, though, was over his eyes. Bad idea. Very bad. But he couldn't keep his hand from moving any more than he could stop himself from thinking about the stupid soldier.

His cock throbbed, and he squeezed just a little harder, and one, two, three more strokes and the hot spatter on his chest. His hand kept moving of its own fucking accord, and he sagged on the bedding. The cum slid down the hollow of his belly, warm and wet.

"You fucking idiot," he whispered into the darkness. "You stupid bloody wanker."

Chapter Thirteen

Janos wasn't surprised he'd slept badly. He was surprised he slept at all, if he was honest with himself. For once, his dreams weren't torrid and shameful but filled with towering buildings on all sides in a city where no one could understand him, and the one person who could help him as always just out of his reach.

He tossed and turned between nightmares and eventually gave up on the idea of sleep at all.

As much as he disliked being confined within the building, it wasn't a bad prison. It never closed. People came and went at all times from different departments. It meant he didn't have to self-consciously pad through the halls. He was just another face to most of them, another colleague.

The building was made up of training facilities, offices, and research rooms. But one level had been put aside for the well-being of the staff including a gymnasium, which he hadn't had the courage to face yet. He liked the bathing room best.

A vast, tile-walled pool took up most of the room, the waters a clear, chemical blue. The smell had taken him by surprise the first time he visited, but now, it spoke only of hygiene. When they provided his synthetic arm, they told him he would have to exercise with it, and he was surprised when they said swimming would be a good way to build his strength and grow accustomed to the new limb.

It was one skill from his past that wasn't outdated or irrelevant.

He wore a T-shirt and things called boxer shorts to sleep in, and he shed them before slipping into the water. There had been an unfortunate incident before involving chastisement and a screaming woman, but it was four in the morning, and he didn't imagine anyone would care if he was swimming naked or not.

The pool was warm enough to be bearable but cool enough to drive away the last vestiges of sleep. He watched the ripples spread outward, then braced one hand and his feet against the tiled wall and pushed off.

He swam length after length and lost count somewhere after twenty, back and forth, back and forth. It was easier than thinking on anything else. All that mattered was the next stroke, the next reach of his arms, the next kick of his legs.

He only stopped when his limbs ached. When he set his feet down on the smooth floor of the pool, his legs shook beneath him. Too much, he realised belatedly. He had pushed himself too hard. He stumbled to the ladder, pulled himself up, and sat heavily on the cold tiles, shivering.

Exercise was good. Strength was good. Being exhausted to the point of collapse was not.

The cold seeped into his bones through his aching flesh, and he forced himself onto quaking legs. He pulled the T-shirt and boxer shorts on and made his way in the direction of his room, leaning against the wall with every step.

At the elevator, he pressed the control button with relief. Only a little farther to go. The machine whirred, and the door slid open, revealing the shiny metal box which had made him recoil the first time he saw it.

There was something unpleasant about closing himself in a box, trusting in wires and cables to keep him from falling.

He stayed as close to the door as he could, bracing both hands on the handrail that circled the inside of the elevator, and closed his eyes, counting under his breath as the elevator rose. It stopped, less than halfway up, and he opened his eyes as another passenger stepped in.

The dark-skinned woman, Sally, smiled at him.

"Good morning," she said in English.

His lessons were going well enough to reply. "Good morning, madam."

It made her smile as she pressed the button for the top floor. She had a room on the roof level, and he remembered Dieter said she helped people with their problems. He closed his eyes, breathing in again.

"Are you well?" she asked as the elevator moved upward.

He forced his eyes open. She stood on the opposite side of the lift, leaning against the wall as he was, but she seemed at ease. He tried to remember his words to make an answer. "I am well, thank you. Are you well?"

She nodded. "Thank you. Yes, I am." She glanced down at him and back up at his face. "You swim?"

He didn't recognise the word, frowning, trying to remember. She seemed to realise and held up one hand to mime swimming.

He couldn't help a brief smile as she jingled her way through the pantomime.

"Yes," he said. "It is good for…" He frowned, blanking on the word, and patted his left arm with his right hand. "Makes strong."

The elevator pinged softly, and he glanced up at the display above the door in surprise. He hadn't noticed it had been moving so fast. Sally just smiled, inclining her head to the doorway as the doors opened.

"Be well," she said.

He nodded, bowing slightly, before stepping out of the elevator.

The muscles in his shoulders and legs were still twitching when he reached his room, so he stripped out of his damp clothes and stretched out on the bed to stare up at the ceiling.

He pressed false and real fingertips together, parting them and bringing them to meet again without looking. It was more challenging than it should have been. His left hand still moved a split second behind his right as the machinery tried to follow the impulses from his mind.

It didn't feel like his own hand.

It was true it did what he wanted, but sometimes, it was a moment too late, sometimes, too hard, and sometimes it barely responded at all. He was starting to understand why the doctors wanted to give him time to adjust to it before he made the decision about whether to keep it or not.

He wondered if it was normal to have a new arm granted and to reject it. He didn't know.

The more he saw, the more he realised how much he didn't know.

That was why the previous day had been so smothering: while he had seen out of the building before, nothing could have prepared him for just how different the world outside was, so many years in the future.

It made him feel small and helpless again, and he hated it. He hated being isolated, whether by the knowledge of what he was or the ignorance of his surroundings. He didn't know how anything worked. He didn't know why someone who looked like Dieter could be as brave as he was to stand up to someone who might hurt him.

He was so far out of his depth, and it scared him.

He sat up and held out his false hand, turning it over in the pale morning light.

One absolute certainty was the hand wasn't his.

No matter if they rewired it and changed it and made it work perfectly, it was not his arm. It would never be his arm. His arm was lost because he was involved in a war, and no amount of wires, cables, metal, and false skin could undo it.

He remembered the veterans of the first great war, when they came home, when they had lost limbs in combat. People tried to pretend it was not so, but they were whispered about with pity for what had happened to them. Here, he had far more to worry about than people pitying him for a missing arm.

It was too much, trying to grow accustomed to having a machine attached to him on top of everything else.

Perhaps when there was less knowledge vying for his attention, when he was less terrified by the world around him, he would be more secure in using such a machine, but now, it was just another piece of unfamiliar and discomfiting strangeness in a world that was starting to suffocate him.

He rose from the bed and went to the closet. There was no reason to dress up when he was staying within the building—and he wasn't ready to venture out yet—so he pulled on a T-shirt over some loose breeches, stepped into his shoes, and headed out into the halls.

The medical staff weren't in yet, but he had little else to do but wait for people.

He went into the waiting area, forcing himself to go to the window. He sank onto the chair and gazed out. The world was still as big, but from higher up, he didn't feel quite as small or stifled, the whole city dulled and unimposing in the bleak grey morning light.

He was still sitting there, brow resting against the glass, when Doctor Bellevue arrived and hung up her coat.

She cleared her throat to catch his attention.

It was only when he stood and turned to face her he realised he had no one to translate for him. His English was improving from constant classes and watching their films and moving pictures, but he didn't know if he could explain. Yet, he didn't want to have Dieter there. A doctor would understand why he wanted to change things, but it would mean explaining things through Dieter, and Dieter would be concerned.

Doctor Bellevue folded her bony hands in front of her. "Can I help you?"

He gathered his words. "I want arm to go," he said as carefully as he could. "It is not right."

The doctor searched his face and then nodded, motioning for him to come with her.

She opened the blinds, letting what little natural light there was pour into the spacious room. A desk, polished and grand, took up much of the floor and cabinets lined the walls. She walked behind the desk and indicated for him to sit opposite her.

Janos perched on the edge of the seat, cradling his left arm in his right.

She rested her forearms on the desk and spoke slowly and clearly. "If it causes you pain, it can go today if you want."

Janos shook his head. "It is not pain." He hesitated. "It is not mine. I need…" He frowned, hunting for the words. "All is new. I want things not new for me. I want something just me. Arm is too many new thing."

The doctor nodded gravely. "I understand. Later, if you want to have the arm again, you can."

Janos looked down at the false hand. The fingers were loosely spread, and to his surprise, they were trembling as much as his own hand. Maybe, once things were not so overwhelming, he might be ready to learn how to live with it, but now, he wasn't.

"Maybe for later," he agreed quietly, folding the shivering fingers against the false palm and covering it with his hand.

She rose from behind the desk, circled around, and sat in the chair on his left. She held out her hand. "May I see your arm?"

Janos held it out to her. She touched the joint where false became real, then slid down to touch the hand and turned it gently.

"Close your hand," she said, holding up her own and demonstrating.

Janos clenched it into a fist.

"Open slowly." She used her own hand to show one finger at a time, led him through several more exercises, and then released his arm. He gathered it to his chest, cradling it with his right. "You work well," she informed him. "If you want the arm later, it will work well."

It was a relief to know she understood his reasoning, and that he might be able to use it again in future.

"How long for not work?" he asked, wondering if there was a limit between the loss of the arm and the attachment of the false limb.

She smiled, and the lines of her face deepened. She was a hard woman, a strong woman, but a good one too. "It will work any time." He shook his head, not quite certain of her meaning, and she patted his shoulder. "All times, it will work."

He rubbed the synthetic flesh of the fingers. "Later. Later is good."

The doctor returned to her side of the desk. "I will speak to the team."

He could tell she was pausing to think through each sentence to simplify it for him, and he was grateful.

"I will make a time for arm to go," she said. "Good?"

He released a breath he hadn't realised he was holding. "Good." He rose from the chair and bowed to her. "Thank you very much, doctor."

She lifted her glasses farther up her nose and waved him away. "Go. It is time for breakfast. You should eat."

He clicked his heels together. Four years in the army had made it an unbreakable habit. She reached for her computer to switch it on, and he turned and walked from the room. A weight had been taken off his shoulders, one he hadn't noticed was there until it was lifted.

It was true he would have to work differently without his false arm, but better to adjust to the world without the additional pressure of the machine strapped to him.

He made his way through the halls to the canteen. The staff was used to him now, and fewer people nodded towards him and muttered when he entered, which was a blessing in itself. He knew they had all eyed him with suspicion for what he had done, but now, it seemed they tolerated him.

The breakfast was a buffet with hot and cold options, most of which had been sitting on heat plates just long enough they still looked appetizing. Janos snatched up a tray and piled a plate with the heavy, warm food the British seemed to favour. With the climate being as miserable as it was, he couldn't blame them.

He filled a large mug with coffee, set it on his tray, and glanced around the room. There were maybe twenty people already in, but one caught his eye: Dieter sat at the farthest table, arms propped on it, his hands wrapped around a steaming cup. He looked like hell.

Janos glanced down at his tray and back at Dieter.

If he was to face the world directly, he would prefer to start with someone who had helped him and taught him.

Steeling himself, he walked the length of the room and set his tray on the table opposite Dieter, who flinched, as if the rattle of the cutlery hurt him. He hadn't shaved, and he was paler than usual.

"Fuck off," he muttered without looking up.

Janos hesitated, then pulled the chair out and sat down. "No."

Dieter raised his head, squinting. His eyes were bloodshot, and he seemed surprised, even a little confused. "Janos?"

Janos transferred his plate from the tray to the table and set his mug down beside it. "You look like shit."

Dieter snorted and winced, touching his forehead gingerly. "Yeah. Cognac and vodka don't go well together." He glanced at Janos's plate and away quickly, green around the edges.

"You should eat something." Janos picked up one of the pieces of toast from the edge of his plate and held it out. "If you don't, it'll be worse."

Reluctantly, Dieter took the piece of dry toast and nibbled on the edge. He glanced at Janos's face, frowning. "What about you? You look like you went backwards through a fucking hedge."

Janos lifted his hand to his hair. It was standing in all directions. "Forgot to comb it after swimming." It was as good an excuse as any.

Dieter snorted again around a mouthful of toast. "At least you have an excuse. Mine is self-inflicted."

Janos nodded in brief agreement, skewering some bacon with his fork. He wondered why Dieter had been drinking, whether it was something to do with their discussion or if he had been out with other people in the evening.

"You had a social evening?" he asked.

"Mm?" Dieter had abandoned the toast to go back to nursing his coffee.

"Vodka and cognac?"

A little colour tinted Dieter's pallor. "Nah. Quiet night in. Not enough left in one bottle, so I mixed my drinks." He took a sip of his coffee and grimaced. "Forgot I had an early briefing this morning."

Janos winced sympathetically. "Eat the toast. It'll help."

Dieter picked up the toast again, wrinkling his nose. "Yes, mother," he grumbled. "Fuck off."

Janos laughed, surprising himself. "If I was your mother, I would thrash you for that."

Dieter chewed on the toast, making a face. "Only for that? Shame."

Janos's fork stopped halfway to his mouth, and he stared across the table.

Dieter's eyes were wider than they had been, as if he was alarmed at what he'd said. He swallowed the toast, lifted his cup to his mouth and gulped a mouthful of steaming coffee.

Janos glanced awkwardly down at his plate, then up. He'd heard of people with interesting tastes and games they might play from the books Dieter had provided, but he'd never considered them before, not with the last places he'd had lovers.

"Shame?" he echoed.

"Shit," Dieter muttered, setting down his mug and pressing the heels of his hands to his eyes. "Just fucking shoot me, okay? Get your gun and just finish me off. It'd be easier than this."

Janos's blood ran cold at Dieter's words. It wasn't just the hangover talking. It wasn't just the headache. No one would joke about the gun or being shot. He set down his fork. "This?" he said quietly. "What this?"

Dieter's elbows were propped on the table, his fingers curling into his hair. "Forget it."

Janos's mouth was dry. He could just walk away, but Dieter's words about the gun, about finishing him off, had shattered what was left of his calmness. There had been very little as it was, and the idea he would kill Dieter…

"No," he snapped. "You ask me to kill you then tell me to forget it? No!"

Dieter shook his head behind his hands. "It was a joke. Just a fucking joke."

Janos slammed his hand down on the table. "That is not a fucking joke!" He heard chairs getting pushed out, other people coming to their feet. In that moment, he knew they were still suspicious and afraid of him, of what he might be capable of. He leaned across the table and grabbed one of Dieter's wrists, jerked his hand away from his face. "Look me in the eyes."

One bloodshot eye stared at him, then Dieter lowered his other hand, his face pale and tight.

"What do you want me to say?" he asked in a low, unhappy voice. "I'm a fucking idiot? Fine. I am." He took an unsteady breath. "I shouldn't have said that."

Janos stared at the miserable, exhausted man in front of him.

All those things had forced the words from his lips, words he might never have said, but when hungover, it was the first thing to come to his mind: that Janos would be willing to harm him, or worse, kill him.

The anger drained away, leaving a gaping hollow in Janos's chest.

"Do you believe I would do that?" he said, shaken. "Do you believe I would hurt you?"

Dieter didn't say anything, but his eyes flicked to Janos's hand, which was still wrapped around Dieter's wrist.

Janos released him as if he'd been burned.

Dieter shoved the chair away from the table and rose.

"Dieter?"

People surrounded them, some of them armed.

Dieter squinted around, as if he couldn't quite make sense of what was going on. He rubbed his brow and then waved them away. "It's okay," he said in English. He looked up at Janos. "He won't hurt me."

Janos felt a muscle in his cheek twitching. "Get something to eat," he snapped in his own language. "You're an idiot when you're drunk."

He turned away, then, and pushed through the gawkers.

He didn't know where he was going. There was nowhere he could go, not when the building was coming to life. There were few places he wouldn't get in the way, and all he could think now was he wanted to break something, or scream, or be in a world where the prejudices were simpler.

He found a doorway to the staircases and started upward.

He ran, hitting every step with something between fury and hurt.

Yes, he'd taken Dieter hostage at gunpoint, but it was before he knew what was going on. Did he seem the kind of man who would shoot someone just for being confusing? What kind of man did Dieter take him for if he believed that? If he believed Janos would willingly hurt anyone?

By the time he got up six floors, his chest was aching, and he slowed his pace. For a brief, brilliant moment, he'd believed things were going to get easier. He'd believed he had someone who might be able to help him, despite everything that had happened.

To know that person expected to be harmed at any moment turned everything around.

Janos smacked the side of his fist against the wall. He slowed, then turned and sat down, halfway up a staircase. Just when things seemed to be getting better, they were suddenly getting worse all over again.

Trial by fire, he thought dully, leaning sideways against the wall. Even if you passed the test, you would still get burned.

Chapter Fourteen

Dieter was an idiot.

No.

Worse than that.

If idiots had a kingdom, and they voted in their ruler, Dieter would have won a fucking landslide victory.

Just because he was a neurotic asshole with issues coming out the wazoo and the inability to think when he had a drink in him, he'd gone and alienated the man he was trying to help. Of all the things to tell Janos, bringing up guns and shooting was the worst he could have done. Having graphic nightmares about it was no fucking excuse at all. Janos didn't know about them, so how the hell was he meant to know what the problem was?

Dieter couldn't go after him, either, not when he had a major briefing.

It was amazing how fast Janos's outrage and shock had sobered him up. Worked better than dousing him with a bucket of ice-cold water and a dozen mugs of black coffee. It didn't make the hangover go away, but he was mortified as he watched Janos storm out of the canteen.

People were staring too.

They didn't know what was said.

All they knew was Janos seemed angry, and had grabbed him.

"You okay?" One of the men touched his shoulder.

Dieter lifted his mug in shaking hands and drained the dregs. He didn't need it, not now he was stone-cold sober. Yeah, Janos had grabbed his arm, but it wasn't in threat. He wouldn't hurt him, not anymore. Dieter knew it. He fucking knew it, and he'd still told Janos to shoot him.

"I asked for it," he admitted.

He'd known the bugger for months, and after the first two days, Janos had been nothing but quiet, grave, and polite. He'd never shown any sign of hurting anyone, and Dieter knew it, but some part of his fucked-up little brain remembered the smell of blood and piss and metal walls on all sides.

He got up and made his way towards the breakfast bar, snagged a bowl of porridge, and headed for the door. He needed to eat. He needed to be away from staring eyes. He needed to be in the briefing room in ten minutes.

There were rest rooms near the canteen where people could read, review files, or relax before missions. Any one of those would be better than dozens of staring eyes watching him in the canteen as if he might go to pieces.

He stumbled into the first one he could find, fell into the seat, and groped for his phone in his pocket. Sally was probably in already, so he hit dial, but the phone went to voicemail. He hesitated, wondering if it was a good idea to leave a message to let her know what kind of fuckwit she considered a friend.

No. Better to do it directly.

He cut the connection and forced himself to eat the porridge.

Jesus Christ, he was King of the Arseholes.

Janos had come over to check on him because he looked like crap. He'd offered some of his own breakfast to help Dieter get over the hangover, and Dieter had let his tongue wag, and had managed to both insult and hurt Janos. He could tell from the expression in the man's eyes.

Sanders found him there, five minutes later.

He stepped into the room and shut the door. "What happened?"

"I fucked up," Dieter said, getting up.

"You did? Or did he do something?"

Dieter shook his head, though it made his brain rattle. "All on me. Said something I shouldn't have." He took a steadying breath. "I'll fix things after the briefing."

Sanders folded his arms. "You sure you're fit to do it?"

Dieter nodded. "I'm not an invalid. Just an arsehole."

Sanders opened the door for him. "You can't let this affect your work."

Dieter didn't meet his eyes. "I'm trying, okay?"

"You came into work drunk, Dieter," Sanders said quietly. "It's not like you at all."

Dieter ducked his head. "Am I in trouble?"

"It's the first time," Sanders said, closing the door of the rest room behind them. "Don't make a habit of it, okay?"

Dieter followed his boss meekly through the building, keeping his eyes down. The events in the canteen would have started spreading already. Everyone in the agency knew about Janos. Everybody knew Dieter was helping him out. And in the few moments since Janos had stormed out, there were probably a new flurry of rumours running through the gossip mill.

"Do me a favour," Dieter said as he and Sanders stepped into the elevator.

"You want a paracetamol?"

Dieter shook his head. "Can you let them know Janos didn't do anything? The rest of them who saw? I think Ojukwu was ready to take him down, but Janos didn't do anything." He glanced sidelong at Sanders. "They didn't believe me."

Sanders studied him. "Did you look as crap as you do now?"

"Probably worse."

Sanders rubbed his brow. "I'll do what I can. But you need to clean up before we go in. At least wash your face."

Dieter made a brief stop at the first bathroom they came to and then followed Sanders into the briefing room. His files were already there and waiting, and the team to be briefed filed into the room a few minutes later.

Panic, guilt, porridge, and a large cup of coffee had gone a long way to making him feel conscious. As he took his place at the head of the table, Dieter tried to push Janos's face from his mind. Sanders was right. He had a job to do, and he couldn't let his brain get in the way.

It was the first briefing of a new jump.

Those were always the easiest, and thank fucking Christ for that. He lit up the screen and switched to autopilot, pretending he didn't feel like he was about to throw up on his shoes.

It didn't hurt that the new jump was heading into a time before either of the World Wars, where the conflicts were building momentum. Dieter had always been fascinated with how quickly Europe had erupted into the wars, and he'd focussed on the periods surrounding the wars at university. A bit too intensely, some said. It would never come in useful, they said, like a degree in ancient languages.

Sometimes, Dieter considered sending them a cheerful "Fuck Yourself Sideways" card to let them know just how wrong they were.

He started off with an image of a man he'd read far too much about.

"Let's start with some of the big facts of the period we'll be in. Some of you may recognise this man," he said, motioning to the screen. "This is Franz Ferdinand, the man whose death allegedly caused a war."

There were murmurs of acknowledgement around the room.

The assassination of the heir to the throne of Austria, in Serbia, was seen as a trigger for the First World War. Europe was a simmering mess of political instability, from east to west, and it hadn't taken much to stir up something nasty. Austria struck back, then other countries were drawn in, and everything escalated from there.

And Dieter knew the ins and outs so well he could just let his mouth run while his brain took a much-needed nap.

"There's always been speculation about whether Franz Ferdinand was a liability within his own country. He was too liberal for many of the traditional politicians, and it has raised questions about whether his dispatch to Sarajevo was part of a plan to get him out of the way."

Dieter gazed around the room. "There were warnings to Vienna that he was an intended target, but they still let him go, despite the civil unrest."

"Aren't the Habsburgs the ones who are completely batshit anyway?" asked Nicky Downie, one of the older agents. "Because it sounds like something a crazy person would do."

Dieter couldn't help smiling crookedly. "I'll go with inbred and insular. They didn't get to run half of Europe for centuries without having some brains in there." He pulled up the projection of the archduke in question. "This man wasn't one to do what he was meant to, and it concerned people. He argued with the emperor a lot, and his views weren't in keeping with what his country was aiming for."

"Would they have killed one of their own?" Mike Llewelyn asked, frowning.

"We have no idea," Dieter said. "We do know the assassins were part of the Unification of Death or the Black Hand. They had ties with the Serbian government, although if you asked the Serbian government at the time, they'd probably put their fingers in their ears and sing 'lalala.'"

Images of the key players in the assassination with their names lit up on the screen.

"Gavrilo Princip," Dieter said, tapping the picture of a solemn, dark-haired young man. "This was the assassin who succeeded. He was one of six organised by Danilo Ilić."

Dieter pulled up a series of pictures from the day of the assassination. "We know they were working to kill someone, and they didn't care who. Franz Ferdinand was the poor bastard who drew the short straw."

"Why him?" Borowski asked. "Was he their biggest target?"

Dieter shook his head. "Sheer dumb luck. They'd tried going after other people, and things went wrong—not enough weapons, too many guards, all kinds of shit. Franz Ferdinand was the first available target when they were all ready."

"Bad luck on him," Downie amended.

"And his wife, Sophie." Dieter sifted through the pictures and brought up the image of the archduchess. "He'd married below his station, for love, and they weren't allowed to be seen in public, except when he went on military business. And can you guess what Sarajevo was?"

Downie winced. "So he got killed for trying to show off his wife?"

"For their wedding anniversary, no less," Dieter said. "Happy anniversary. She died first, he died after."

Another picture flicked onto the screen showing the car, the buildings, and crowds of people.

Llewelyn leaned forward, frowning. "Is that the archduke too?"

Dieter glanced up. "No. You're watching for Archduke Grand Fluffy Hat and Moustache." He scaled up the image. "This man is Governor Potiorek, the man in charge of Sarajevo. He was responsible for the archduke's visit and played ride-along with him for it. He was a target too, according to Princip, and high on their to-kill list, since he worked for Austria and controlled Sarajevo.

"He was probably the one who laid the route." Dieter pulled up an outline of the route of Franz Ferdinand's convoy. "It's pretty self-explanatory. They did the barracks first, at the west of the city, then went to do a 'Yay We're Pompous' display at city hall." He tapped a point on the map. "This is where a failed bombing happened."

"Wait, there was a bombing first?" Downie asked, frowning.

"A pretty close one too," Dieter replied with a nod. "The bomb bounced off Ferdinand's car and rolled under the one behind it. Needless to say, he wasn't a happy camper." He traced his finger along the map. "And this is where the biggest cock-up in security history happened. Someone forgot to tell the driver—on account of the great big bomb—

they were changing up the route, in case there were any other assassins just...y'know...lying around. So, the driver turns up this street when he's meant to go straight on, and gets a bollocking from Potiorek. He tries to reverse. Car stalls. Assassin, on his way home from the whole shambles, sees his chance, and Franz Ferdinand and his wife are fucked six ways from Saturday."

"Jesus," Downie murmured.

Dieter picked up a glass of water and downed as much as he could. "So"—he set the glass down—"we're examining at events leading to this."

"Like who hired the assassins?" Borowski asked.

"You know you don't get details until before the jump," Sanders said when Dieter opened his mouth. "Let's just stick to background just now."

Dieter ran a hand over his face. It felt like shit, having to think while his head throbbed. "We're going in earlier, before the assassination. So now, boys and girls, we're going to have a lesson in European politics, and it's going to be boring as hell, but sit up and pay attention, okay?"

The break at midday was a welcome respite, and Dieter swallowed a pile of sandwiches, then put his head down on the desk and slept for half an hour. It was broken by fragmented dreams, and Sanders had to shake him awake before the others returned from their lunch.

Members of the team only raised a few questions. He answered as best he could, but until the days before the jump, the details of the mission were always restricted.

Sanders leaned back in his seat as the team filed out of the room.

"God knows what'll happen if we ever try and visit uncharted territory," he said as he dragged his hands over his face.

"Probably get eaten by some kind of mythical beasties," Dieter replied after drinking his eighth tumbler of water. He glanced at his boss. "Has anything been done about the proximity sensor? We can't risk someone else coming through."

"Working on it," Sanders replied. "We can't afford to shut down the operation while we wait for it to be developed, but we're going to reduce the opening to the smallest possible size while the team is through. They'll have to provide a code before we open it wide enough for them to get through."

"Why wasn't it there before?" Dieter wondered if he should have been angry at them for their sloppy security, but he was too tired, and it didn't seem worth it. "It would have stopped Nagy coming through."

"We aim for unpopulated areas," Sanders said, "and a life-sign scan is done before the door is fully opened. Maybe the scanner was broken. Maybe Nagy was just out of range. We didn't know it would be necessary, since the door is hardly visible from the other side."

"Well, now you do." Dieter pushed his chair back. "You need me to sign off on the papers?"

"I can take care of it. You go home. Get some rest."

Dieter braced his hands on the edge of the table. "There's something I have to do first."

Sanders searched his face. "Don't get too caught up with Nagy, Dieter. I know you want to help him, but I need you on form. If this man is causing you any kind of problems, I can order you not to interact with him."

Dieter shook his head. "Civilian, remember. Anyway, I owe him."

"Owe him what? You already gave him his life."

Dieter rubbed his eyes with both hands. "I have to do this. I have to at least know he's going to be okay." He lowered his hands and met Sanders's gaze defiantly. "If I don't do something, I'll be worse, believe me."

"I do." Sanders drummed his fingers on the edge of the table. "But if I think this is affecting your well-being or your judgment, Dieter, I'm signing you out. You'll work externally, and any access to the building will be limited. Do you understand?"

Dieter nodded. "I'll be fine." He wondered if it was true.

Sanders sighed, waving him away. "Go on. Go be a hero."

Chapter Fifteen

Janos ended up on the roof again.

The garden was calming, even if the icy winds whistled around the building. He didn't have a coat with him, and it was cold, but he didn't care. He didn't want to go to his room in case Sanders's men were waiting for him. All he wanted was to be left alone, and if being cold was the price he had to pay, then that was fine.

His stomach growled in protest at his abandoned breakfast, and he pressed his fist against it, remembering times when he had been much more hungry than he was now. He could go without one meal. He'd gone without worse.

He followed the meandering path in a circuit around the garden.

Much of his anger had been run out on the stairs, charging up ten levels in a fury, and now he was tired. He walked on and on, retracing his steps in the gravel and scowling every time he passed the place on the wall where a man could climb up and sit to look out over the city.

The wind gusted, and he shivered, wrapping his arms across his middle.

Dieter had embraced him when he climbed down from the wall, as if he gave a damn. It stayed with him, as much as Janos hated to admit it, because for the first time in years, he'd felt another man's heartbeat against his chest.

He kicked his foot through the gravel impatiently.

Sentimentality would help no one.

It didn't matter how relieved the boy had been that day. It clearly meant nothing.

Janos turned, gazing at the wall, then walked towards it and hoisted himself up to sit on the broad stone ledge. The wind tore at him, tossing his hair around his face, bitterly cold, chilling him to the bone.

Would the boy care if he saw him now?

What had changed?

He didn't know.

He hadn't harmed anyone, least of all Dieter, since his first night in this new place, but they all still looked at him as if he might be dangerous. The first moment he had shown any anger, twenty of them surrounded him as if he were a criminal.

Janos cursed under his breath, then leaned out over the drop and spat as far as he could.

It didn't make him feel any better, but it didn't make things any worse either.

He sat there until the cold got too much, seeping from the stone through his clothing. Janos swung down from the ledge, wincing as his cold-stiffened legs throbbed. He crossed his arms over his chest, rubbing his hands up and down, and started circling again in steady loops of the garden.

It was like the reaping—following the same path at the same pace. Now, though, he didn't need to think about the swing of the scythe or check for obstacles. All he needed to do was walk. It warmed him, and the stiffness left from swimming and running the stairs dissipated.

Just when things had seemed to be settling, everything was turning on its head again.

His arm would be dealt with, and with it gone, he hoped things would be calmer for a little while, no more changes.

And that was the problem.

Nothing had changed.

They still looked at him as a dangerous enemy soldier.

All of them, including the one who had chosen to help him.

What energy Janos had left was spent, and he sagged onto the nearby bench and let his head rock back to rest against it. The rain had stopped, at least. He watched the grey clouds rolling and tumbling across the sky.

He didn't know how long he had been sitting there when he heard footsteps on the gravel, and sat up.

Sally trotted along the path towards him, bundled up in a thick coat.

He scrambled to his feet, offering her a curt nod.

She smiled at him and motioned to her office. "Please come in. It is cold here." She raised her face to the sky. "It will rain soon."

Reluctantly, Janos nodded. It was easier than going into the main levels of the building to be stared at again. To his surprise, she slipped her arm through his, her hand warm on his bare forearm as she led him inside.

The warmth made him shiver, and out of habit, he rubbed his hand against the prosthetic. The lack of warmth of friction made him start, and he stared down at the false hand. He lowered both hands, hoping Sally hadn't noticed.

She hung her coat up on a peg and seemed unaware of his discomfort.

"Tea?" she offered.

"Yes, please."

Sally shooed him towards the couch and bustled around the room, filling a silver kettle with water and switching it on. Janos sat down in the middle of the couch, glancing around self-consciously, his hands resting on his thighs.

The silence felt awkward, but he didn't trust himself to say anything when she returned to set a pot of tea, a cup, and a plate of biscuits in front of him. He frowned, puzzled. She had not made tea for herself.

"You do not drink?"

She shook her head. "I go now. I have meetings." Off his expression, she frowned and amended, "I talk to people. I go to them."

He started to rise. "I go."

Sally held up both hands. "You stay. It is warm here. Quiet." She came around to sit beside him on the couch. "No one will bother you here."

He stared at her. "Why?"

She smiled and patted his hand. "I help people. I help you now."

"You are friend of Dieter," he said quietly.

She nodded. "I am. And you are a friend of Dieter?"

He looked down at her small brown hand on his. "I do not know."

Sally gazed at him with eyes so dark they seemed black. "No."

She leaned forward and poured him a cup of tea, dropped two square lumps of sugar into it, and set the pot down. "Sometimes, friendship is not simple." She rose from the couch and reached for her bag. "Stay here. For quiet."

He picked up the cup of tea, cradling it in his hand. "Thank you very much," he said quietly. "You are...very good."

She shook her head with a smile as if denying it, and then hurried out of the door which did not open onto the garden. Janos didn't know where it went, but he assumed it connected with the main part of the building.

He sipped the tea, hot, black, and sweetened with sugar.

It felt like hours since he'd abandoned his breakfast, and after that, a pot of tea and a small plate of biscuits felt like a feast.

Outside, the wind was picking up, and raindrops pattered against the glass. If Sally hadn't taken pity on him, he would have still been sitting on the bench, getting soaked to the skin.

He set down the cup and went over to the window again, watching the raindrops tracking down the glass. He touched the cool surface with his fingertips, chasing the drops downward. If the clock on the wall was right, he was missing his English lessons, but he didn't care.

The quiet was better, especially somewhere no one would find him.

Sally seemed to know he needed to be alone, and he was grateful.

It felt strange to be doing nothing.

Life in the lower levels of the building was constant: he was seeing doctors, he was having lessons, he was being shown new things and places.

Here, he could sit in silence and just catch his breath.

He returned to the couch and finished off the tea and biscuits. He then carried the dishes to the sink and washed each one carefully, making sure not to chip the delicate china.

There was no hurry, no pressure, no rush to be elsewhere. Once he was done, he sat on the couch, leaned against the cushions, and closed his eyes. The modern world wasn't just big and bright. It was fast, and it was loud, and he hadn't noticed how fast or loud until those two things were taken away.

In the still and the quiet, he felt at ease.

By the time Sally returned, Janos had slipped his shoes off and was lying on the couch. He had fiddled with the radio controller until he found a channel playing orchestral music, and for several minutes, he did not notice Sally had returned.

She closed the door quietly, but the sound was enough to startle him, and he sat up. She smiled. "Good music?"

"Very good," he agreed, hastily putting his shoes back on. "Pardon me. I did not see you."

She shook her head. "It is all well. You are welcome."

He glanced up at the clock. "I stay too long." He got up. "This is your place."

"Very well," she said. "Please come again."

Janos nodded, bowing deeply at the waist. "Thank you very much."

Her eyes sparkled, and she curtseyed playfully. "I will see you again."

He made his way back out into the garden, shuddering at the chill of the drizzling rain, and hurried across to the doorway to the elevator. For the first time, he didn't feel smothered in the metal box as it descended.

He hummed the melody of the music he had been listening to as he made his way down the hall.

It was later than he'd expected, and the residential halls were deserted.

He swiped his key card at his door, stepped quickly into his room, and turned to shut the door behind him. A movement from the corner of his eye caught his attention, and he spun around, heart pounding.

Dieter was there.

Dieter was on his bed.

Janos's mouth went dry.

Of all the people he wanted to see, Dieter was the last, but Dieter was there, blinking sleepily. It seemed he had been woken by the sound of the door.

"Janos?" he murmured, sitting up. He squinted around, disorientated, rubbing at one eye and smearing his eye paint across his cheek. Janos could see the moment he realised where he was, and Dieter flushed. "Oh."

Janos remained standing where he was, folding his arms. The fingers of his right hand bit into his left elbow. "What do you want?"

Dieter didn't get up. It would have been better if he did. They would have been eye to eye, and it would have been simple. But he remained seated, twisting his hands together in his lap as if he was awaiting confession.

"I came to apologise," he said. "I was drunk, and I was stupid, and I fucked up."

"You were," Janos replied evenly, "and you did."

Dieter's thumb traced circles around the knuckles of his other hand. He watched it, his head bowed over his hand.

"I'm sorry." He looked up, still as pale and drawn as he had been that morning. "I owe you an explanation." He took an unsteady breath. "I've been having nightmares about the night we met."

Janos stared at him, unfolding his arms. "Nightmares?"

"You don't remember," Dieter said, lowering his eyes. "The only reason I'm here was because Doctor Bellevue knocked your hand aside." He touched his right arm. "This was a miss." He moved his hand to his throat. "This was where the gun was pointing."

Janos's stomach roiled. It would have been a killing shot, when he hadn't been conscious enough to remember. No wonder Dieter was having nightmares. If Janos could nearly kill him when half-dead, how much more of a threat was he when fully conscious?

Dieter watched his thumb circle his knuckles again. "Last night was...shit. I drank too much, and I slept too little, and I spoke without thinking." He raised his eyes back to Janos. "I know you wouldn't hurt me. Not intentionally."

Janos's nails bit into his palm. "Do you?"

Dieter nodded. "You scare the ever-loving fuck out of me, but I know it's because of what happened then."

"Oh."

Dieter pressed his hands to the bed on either side of him. "So, yeah," he said, gazing at the floor. "I'm sorry I'm such a fuckwit and I didn't think before I spoke, and I'm sorry I'm scared shitless of you sometimes."

Janos stared at him. "You're apologizing for being afraid of me?"

Dieter shrugged, barely lifting his shoulders. "I wanted you to understand why."

Janos shook his head. He walked across the floor and sat in one of the chairs beside the table. "I almost killed you," he said quietly. "You should have told me."

"I didn't think it would bother me so much."

Janos stared across at him. "You're an idiot."

Dieter raised his eyes from the floor. "We've had this discussion," he said, a suggestion of a small, tired smile on his lips.

Janos offered a brief smile in return. "It doesn't change the truth."

Dieter made a face, pushing himself up off the bed. "You're lucky you're good-looking, or I might be insulted." He approached Janos. "Do you want to go down for something to eat?"

"Together?"

Dieter shrugged again. "We gave them the wrong idea this morning. If I go with you, they'll know it was my fault." He offered Janos his hand. "This way, they know we're good." He hesitated. "Aren't we?"

Janos gazed at Dieter's slender hand and then up at his face, his nervousness visible, but there was hope there too.

Janos laid his hand in Dieter's. "We're good," he agreed as Dieter pulled him to his feet.

Chapter Sixteen

The air was thick with the smell of sex and sweat.

Dieter twisted his hands into the sheets, his brow pressed against the pillow, his breath ragged. He didn't open his eyes as a kiss was pressed to the back of his neck, but he shivered as broad hands dragged down over his sides.

It ruined the illusion when there were two, since Janos had had his prosthetic removed.

"Is this going to be a habit?" Paul asked, breathless. He drew away and sprawled on the bed next to Dieter, watching him.

Dieter turned his face away, rolling onto his side, his back to his lover. He'd practically begged, and, to let his imagination run wild, he'd made sure he couldn't see who it was doing the fucking. It had been the best fuck he'd had in months, and all because he'd been picturing someone else's face. It was getting ridiculous.

"Must have been missing the contact," he lied, using the corner of the sheet to dab at his skin, wiping up the worst of the mess. "It's been a while."

Paul ran a hand along his hip. "You've been busy. That soldier-boy's been taking up all your time."

Like he needed a fucking reminder.

After the brief fallout and the reconciliation, he'd been spending much more time than was healthy with Janos. They went for weekly trips to the Quays to help the poor sod get his fear of the vast world under control. They practiced Janos's English. They took meals together more often than not, when Janos didn't have more lessons, and Dieter wasn't working.

It was like being in a relationship, only one half of the relationship had no idea it was happening.

It was worse than being turned down.

At least it would have been final.

But no. Instead, Dieter spent his time with a man he was drawn to more and more every fucking day, and sometimes the man smiled at him, and for a brief moment, he could believe he had a hope in hell of something happening.

It never did.

It never would.

Janos saw him as a friend, nothing more.

And so, once more, he was in Paul's bed, trying to get some relief where he could.

Dieter rolled away from Paul's hand and sat up at the edge of the bed. "Mind if I have a shower?"

Paul waved towards the hall. "You know the way," he said, leaning across the bed to grope through the drawers for his cigarettes. He pulled one from the packet with his teeth and offered the pack to Dieter. "Want one?"

Dieter shook his head as he rose. His legs ached, and his arse was protesting such enthusiastic abuse, but he didn't care. "It's been a long day. Should've cleaned up before we started."

Paul snorted and took a drag from his cigarette. "Like I'd notice. You're the cleanest bugger I know." He shoved himself up the bed and propped himself against the pillows, one hand behind his head. "You want to eat?"

Dieter shrugged noncommittally. "If you want. Get something delivered?"

Paul blew a plume of smoke towards the ceiling. "Sounds good. Go and get cleaned up."

The light was on in the living room, illuminating the hallway of Paul's flat, and Dieter put out his hand to stabilise himself against the wall. The flat was just like Paul: too big, rigidly organised, and just a little bit messy around the edges.

Dieter groped blindly along the wall for the bathroom light switch. It hurt his eyes when it came on, the white room too bright after the street-lamp-illuminated gloom of Paul's bedroom and the half light from the living room.

He closed the door behind him and didn't hesitate before locking it.

He wasn't in the mood for interruption.

Paul's bathroom, wall-to-wall white tiles, felt like it should be in a hospital, but the shower was one of the few saving graces. The showerhead was practically as big as Dieter's torso, and the water could be turned up to such a force, like being pelted with warm hail.

Dieter turned up the pressure as high as it would go and stepped under the steaming water. He hissed through his teeth at the heat and braced both palms against the tiles, letting his head fall forward.

He was being a selfish prick. He hadn't come over to see Paul. He'd come around just to take advantage of the fact that Paul liked to shag him, and he needed someone to fuck him hard enough to take his mind off a certain idiot he couldn't stop thinking about.

It hadn't worked.

He'd imagined every which way Janos might've touched him: hard, soft, gentle, rough, silently, loudly. He didn't have a fucking clue, and he knew he probably never would, so he'd closed his eyes and pretended Paul was someone else and pressed his forehead against his knuckles and come harder than he had any right to.

The water beat down on him, the pounding of it echoing through his head, and he hit the wall as hard as he could. Red blazed behind his eyes, the pain driving the breath from his body.

He turned over his shaking hand in the stream of water, a small sharp sound escaping his throat as the hot water streamed, scalding, over the cracked and bloodied knuckles.

"Shit!" he hissed, reaching out with his other hand to turn the water off.

The blood dripped into the pool of water at his feet in blooming tendrils of red against the white.

Dieter grabbed one of the towels and bundled it around his hand.

He stepped out of the shower, leaving faint, bloody footprints on the tiles.

"Shit," he muttered again, sinking onto the toilet, cradling his wrapped hand. "Shit, shit, shit."

All the steam was clearing, and it was fucking cold, and he had blood on his hands and feet.

Paul would know. How could he not? It was his bathroom and his towels. Of course he would know.

Dieter gingerly unwrapped the towel, wincing as fresh blood welled up in the folds of stained fabric.

Better to face it head on than fanny around and pretend everything was all right.

He wrapped his hand up again and unlocked the door. His fingers shook, and Dieter swore under his breath. He'd already made a fucking mess. The last thing he needed was to go all hysterical and emotional.

The hall was much brighter now, and Paul had put some music on.

"Paul?" Dieter stood in the middle of the hall, not sure which way to turn.

Paul poked his head around the living room doorway, and his eyes widened. "Jesus Christ!" he exclaimed, striding down the hall. He'd put on his T-shirt and boxers, and Dieter was starting to feel very underdressed with nothing but a towel on one of his hands. "What the hell happened?"

Dieter stared at a knot in the floor as Paul unwrapped his hand. "I fell."

Paul's brown eyes lifted from the wounded hand. "Fell," he said, but Dieter avoided his gaze. "Right." He put his hand under Dieter's arm and guided him through to the living room. "Sit down. I'll get bandages."

Dieter sat in silence as Paul knelt as his feet and cleaned the cuts. The bleeding was slowing, at least, and Paul laid a strip of gauze over the broken skin before wrapping Dieter's hand in the bandage.

He sat back on his heels, gazing up at Dieter. "If I ask, are you going to tell me what's wrong?"

Dieter closed the fingers of his left hand gently over the bandage. "I fell."

Paul curled a finger under Dieter's chin, lifting his head and staring at him searchingly. "It's because of that bloody soldier, isn't it? That's what bothering you."

Dieter felt tired suddenly and shook his head. "Just leave it," he said quietly. He got up. "I shouldn't have come."

"Dieter..."

Dieter held up both hands, stepping around the other man. "No," he said, his voice sharper than he intended. "I said leave it. This is my problem, and I'm going to deal with it. You don't have any part in this."

"No," Paul said quietly. "I don't, do I?"

Dieter stopped in the doorway. "You knew this wasn't going to be anything serious." He touched his fingertips lightly to the doorframe. "You knew it when we started. Nothing's changed."

"You have."

Dieter turned back. "The hell I have," he said, his voice hoarse.

Paul met his eyes evenly. "You have. When was the last time you gave a damn about someone else?"

Dieter stared at him, his heart pounding. "What the fuck are you talking about?"

"This Hungarian guy. It isn't just work, is it? You're there all the time, even when you don't need to be." Paul fell silent, his eyes widening with realization, and Dieter wanted to turn and run before Paul could think it or say it out loud. "Jesus, Dieter." His voice was soft, not angry, not shocked, but quiet. "Don't tell me you want him."

Dieter shivered. He should have denied it. Lied. Said something. Anything. Anything that wasn't just standing there, staring wildly like an animal caught in the headlights of an oncoming car.

"Dieter…" Paul took a step towards him.

Dieter flinched back. "Don't," he whispered. "Don't tell me how fucked up it is. Don't tell me what I already know."

"I wasn't going to." Paul held out a hand. "Come on. Sit down, you silly wanker."

"Why?" Dieter asked, his voice cracking.

Paul sighed. "Because I already ordered takeout for two, and I'd feel bad letting you wander out into the night in the buff." He beckoned Dieter towards him, and Dieter stumbled and was caught in a broad-armed hug. Paul sighed against his wet, tangled hair. "You are a bloody idiot, you know."

Dieter nodded. "Literally," he whispered.

Paul cuffed the back of his head gently. "Now, you're staying for food, okay?"

"Yes, dad," Dieter said, his voice still unsteady.

Paul grimaced. "Don't go down that road. Go and get the bathrobe, would you? You're dripping on the floor."

Dieter obeyed, unresisting, and returned to sit on the couch cross-legged. It felt strange, having someone know, especially someone who knew him so intimately, yet not at all. He tugged at the frayed end of the bandage as Paul got out dishes for food.

"Does he know?" Paul asked when he returned with the dishes.

Dieter shook his head. "Don't know if he's queer or not." He took a shivering breath. "I'd rather not talk about it, if it's okay."

Paul frowned with concern. "I know it's none of my business, and I know I'm just a bit of fun for you, but I worry about you, y'know."

"No need," Dieter said quietly.

"Maybe not, but it doesn't stop it from happening."

Dieter looked up at him. "You deserve a decent boyfriend. Not a mentally fucked arse like me."

Paul chuckled. "Do I really seem like the commitment and boyfriend type? Nah. I'll take a mentally fucked arse from time to time." He poured two glasses of wine and brought one over to Dieter. "It keeps things interesting."

"Masochist." Dieter took the glass carefully.

Paul's smile was softer than usual, more genuine. It wasn't his usual sharp grin. "Takes one to know one." He held out his glass to Dieter. "I think we should drink to being played in the game."

"Oh, fuck yes," Dieter agreed, clinking the glasses together.

Chapter Seventeen

"It's heavy."

Janos hid a smile at the man's surprise. "This is very old gun," he said, as Mike Llewelyn turned over the handgun in his hand. "Metal is in forge. It is very heavy. This make pistol heavy. Your gun now? It is small. Not heavy. Made by machines."

Llewelyn nodded, shifting the weight in his grip. Twenty people had gathered in the training room—male and female, tall and short, every ethnicity Janos had ever seen—all there to listen to him, and that dazed him.

Janos had been called upon to demonstrate how to blend in when in the field. Many of the agents who went to war zones in the past carried prop weapons, and Janos had critically informed Sanders they only handled their weapons as they imagined a soldier would.

Llewelyn was one of the first to agree it was necessary. After all, he had been the one identified by a Hungarian soldier who had promptly disarmed him, stolen his clothing, and breached security.

"How do I hold it?"

Janos took the gun from him. It was like being back with his brigade before things had gone wrong. He could speak English well enough now to make himself understood, and they no longer stared at him as if he might attack them.

"Many wear gun in belt," he said, demonstrating by slipping it through the belt at his left side. "No holster, but comes out very quickly." He pulled it and held it straight out at arm's length, held it without sighting, and pulled the trigger.

A murmur ran around the room.

"How do you aim, if you shoot so fast?" asked Johnson, a tall, dark-skinned woman who—according to the reports Dieter was allowed to show Janos—was also the best shot in the agency.

"In war, is difficult to aim," Janos said, setting it down. "Much noise. Smoke. Is best to shoot quickly. Steyr Mannerlich is not so good." He pointed it again. "You shoot. Gun might fire. Bullet might stay."

"A bad make?" Johnson asked.

Janos nodded. "It is better shoot fast in case it does not work." He put the gun down and picked up one of the more reliable pistols. "This gun is better. More heavy, but bullet does not stay in it when gun is fired."

Dozens of weapons lay spread along the table, covering nearly a century's worth of weaponry, and Janos had laid hands on many of them while in the field.

The Hungarian army was grand in name, but that was about all. There hadn't been enough weapons to arm all their troops, especially not after the financial disaster following the first great war. Many soldiers had carried weapons belonging to their families to make up for the shortage, some of them old, some of them more dangerous to the one wielding them than their target.

"What gave me away?" Llewelyn asked. When Janos glanced at him enquiringly, Llewelyn hesitated and rephrased his question. "How did you know I did not come from the army?"

Janos selected the gun most like the replica Llewelyn had been carrying that night, months earlier. Despite the heavier weight, he hefted it up in his right hand and propped it in the crook of his left elbow. He noticed a few people glanced elsewhere, as if ashamed to stare at the concealed stump of his arm. He almost snorted aloud.

"This," he said, to Llewelyn. "You carry like it is not weapon." He nodded down at the gun in his arms. "Is gun. Is not baby."

Someone sniggered, and Llewelyn flushed with a sheepish grin.

"What about this one?" he asked, picking up the smallest of the handguns. "This looks like the ones the Nazis use in films."

Janos grimaced in distaste. "Is very good. There is much power." He searched the table, picked up the holster, and put it against his ribs where it would lie. "Is small. Good for keeping inside uniform."

"Did you ever use one of these?" another of the female agents asked. She had a Turkish look about her, but Janos couldn't recall her name. She pointed to one of the old muskets which was more than a little familiar.

A rueful smile turned Janos's lips. "It is my grandfather's gun." He wouldn't be able to pick it up one-handed, so he didn't try. "It is first gun I use when very small. Very strong. Strong enough to fall me down."

Several people chuckled.

"How old were you?" Another voice, another name he had yet to learn.

"I had seven summers. My father was in war. My grandfather show me how to shoot." He shook his head. "We did not have rabbit for long time." He forced a brighter smile. "I have bruise on backside for many days. Is embarrassing."

Strange how little some things had changed.

A man could divert people from how they truly felt by joking and smiling. Sometimes, he made his English sound worse, so they wouldn't realise how much he understood. Though they were growing accustomed to him, he still sometimes heard mutters. No one could come from the past and stay so levelheaded, they said. They expected him to fall apart soon, and he had no intention of doing anything of the kind, at least not anywhere they would see it.

At least now they spoke in tones of concern rather than fear.

It was better.

He smiled again and called their attention back to the weaponry before them. He could not pick up half of them anymore, so he hauled Llewelyn to the front. The man didn't mind. In fact, of all of the team, he'd proven the most eager to learn, and Janos used him to demonstrate how each weapon would have been carried formally and informally.

Some of it was not quite true, but it was still better than what they had been doing. Janos could see they had been briefly trained by military people, but they had been very modern lessons, out of place in the past.

The agents took photographs of one another holding the weapons correctly with small, palm-sized cameras. They scrutinised each other, pointing out when one of their colleagues was holding one of the guns wrong before Janos needed to say a word. They teased one another, and more than once, Janos heard the comparison to holding a baby.

It was as if they had accepted him.

As much as he wanted to believe it was genuine, it dredged up painful memories of Szilveszter. So long ago, they had trusted their comrades at arms too, and those were the people who held Szilveszter down and tortured him before they killed him, simply because he did something they disapproved of.

Times had changed, and Janos wanted to believe it was for the better, but doubts still crept in.

Llewelyn approached him. "Thanks for doing this."

Janos shrugged. "I want to have use. Your people, they go to my history many times. Is better they are not..." He clicked his fingers, trying to remember the word. "To be noticed. It is better to be not noticed."

Llewelyn grimaced. "Yeah. We wouldn't have room for more people in the accommodation level."

It was said in jest, and Llewelyn slapped him firmly on the shoulder, but sometimes, Janos wondered just what Llewelyn thought of all that had happened that night in the forests of southeast Austria. He admitted he had made mistakes in his actions in the past, but Janos knew none of them had been trained to deal with a half-starved, terrified, wounded Hungarian soldier.

Janos placed his hand firmly on Llewelyn's shoulder. "Do not worry, my friend. I will help you. You will not be seen again."

Llewelyn grinned. "That's what I'm here for."

The rest of the training went well. Janos liked to know he was being useful, and Sanders had made it very clear he intended to use him as much as possible as their agents specialised in the period surrounding the two great wars.

It was also safer, Dieter told Janos one evening. They had good records of major incidents in more recent history, but the further into the past they went, the more the chance of emerging into an unpredictable and unprecedented situation.

Sanders and his people had plans to develop technology to secure all doorways and prevent any damage to the historical period they were about to enter. The well-being of the agents was of the highest importance, after the preservation of the past. The last thing they wanted was to get anyone else injured or killed in the line of duty by walking into a battlefield.

So Janos became their living archive.

While he freely admitted he was no expert, it surprised him how much he had learned from his time in the army. His brigade had crossed the breadth of Hungary and infringed on many of the bordering countries during sieges and battles.

When an army rested, waiting for the next call to arms, there was little to do but watch people, noticing all the little differences. Janos hadn't thought it useful until he'd sat with Dieter, to work out how to teach the agents, and now, they liked him checking clothing, shoes, weapons, haircuts before agents went into the past.

Once they were dismissed and the archivist had come to collect all the weapons in their trunks, Janos fell into one of the chairs by the table, his head flopping back.

It was not the same as working the fields or marching for days, but it was no less tiring.

He barely registered the hiss of the door sliding aside.

"Mr. Nagy?"

Janos lifted his head, squinting at the new arrival. It wasn't someone he recognised: a tall, solidly built, tawny-haired man with the beginnings of a thick beard on his chin.

Out of habit, Janos got to his feet and straightened up. "The training is finished," he said.

The door slid closed behind the man. "I know," he said, remaining where he stood in front of the door. He was bigger than Janos, and though Janos knew there were cameras all around the room, he felt the familiar knot of panic in his gut. He was closed in, and this man—who did not appear friendly—blocked the way out. "I wanted to speak to you privately."

Janos rested his fingertips lightly on the surface of the table between them. He raised his chin in a feigned show of confidence. "How can I be helping you?"

The man folded his arms over his chest. His suit suggested he worked in an office, but the breadth of his arms showed it wasn't his only pursuit. "I wanted to speak to you about a friend of mine."

Janos raised his eyebrows in silent question.

"Dieter."

Janos inclined his head. "He is my friend also."

The stranger's lips pressed together in a grim line. "I know you believe it. But you're driving him to distraction, and it's not good for him."

Janos pressed his fingertips harder to the table until they ached. "I do not understand," he said carefully. "You say I must not be friend for Dieter?"

"A person should know when their friend is unhappy."

Janos stared at him. Dieter? Unhappy? It was true Dieter had come in recently with a bandaged hand and a solemn expression on his face, but he'd insisted it was only tiredness. If he was not happy, surely he would have said something.

"He is very busy man," Janos said.

"Because of you. He spends too much time here, because of you. You encourage him."

Janos was confused. "I do not make him stay. I do not ask him."

The man released an explosive, frustrated breath. "That's just the problem. You don't have to!" Janos gaped at him, and the stranger's brow furrowed in a frown. "And you don't know it, do you? You don't know why he stays?"

"He stays because he help me," Janos murmured.

"And you don't mind, of course." It sounded like he was sneering, but he appeared confused, even concerned.

Janos stared down at his fingertips. "It is not your business," he said, his voice low. "He is my good friend. I am his good friend." He was surprised at the bitterness in his voice. "We are good friends together."

"And that's all?"

Janos's cheeks burned with heat, and he raised his eyes. Was that the real problem? Did the person think he should not be looking at Dieter in such ways? He drew himself up as tall as he could, raising his chin defiantly. "It is not your business."

The man stared at him, then swore under his breath. He unfolded his arms and ran his hand over his face. "Jesus Christ, how stupid can two people be?" he muttered to himself. "I don't know you or like you, but Dieter is my friend, and he likes you a hell of a lot. Even if you just fuck him once and get him over it, just do it already. I'm sick of him moping around like an idiot."

Janos's mouth went dry as his brain tried to make sense of what was being said. "What?"

"You like him; he likes you. Do I have to draw a diagram?"

Janos took a step back, and the chair pressed against the back of his knees. He folded onto the seat, still staring. "He is my friend."

"He'd like to be a lot more." He shook his head. "Why the hell do you think he is spending so much time with you? It isn't just because he wants to help you. No one's that noble."

Janos put his hand to his mouth, his fingers trembling. "Why do you tell me this? You think I will..."

He didn't know what to say. Was it a trap? Was it to make him do something stupid, so he would drive Dieter away? "Why do you do this?"

The stranger sighed. "Because Dieter is my friend, and right now, I would ask the Pope to fuck him if it was what he needed to cheer him up." He put his hands in his trouser pockets, pushing his jacket back from his hips. "But he doesn't want the Pope. For some reason, the stupid bastard wants you. So either you tell him you're not interested, or you do something."

The world contracted around him, and Janos drew a deep, gulping breath.

Dieter wanted him.

Dieter *wanted* him.

In this new world, it was impossible to know the difference between simple tactile behavior and interest. Dieter was so free with his emotions and expressions that Janos hadn't dared to guess.

He rose from the chair and walked towards the stranger. "If you lie," he said quite calmly, "I will find you and hurt you."

The man looked down from three inches above him. "Good luck with that," he said then stepped aside and opened the door.

Janos stepped through, buoyed up on sheer panic and hope, and headed into the hallway.

Chapter Eighteen

"Several of you are fluent in German already. We need you to get even better."

The team looked shit-scared, and that was good.

Sometimes, people got complacent when things were easy, but when there were challenges ahead, and they had to be at the top of their game, fear was a good motivator for anyone.

"What if they call us?"

Dieter smiled crookedly. "You've all been to exit-strategy training, am I right?" There were nods around the table. "Anyway, as long as you keep to your character and don't do anything stupid like steal their cars or knock them out, they'll probably not even care enough to notice you."

Borowski raised a hand. "I can use Polish?"

Dieter nodded. "It's near enough for a migrant worker," he said. "Even if no one speaks Polish in the area, they may recognise it." He paused, scratching his chin. "Actually, I'll get back to you on whether or not they'd have a problem with it. Don't want you to get a kicking for being a dirty foreigner stealing their jobs."

Borowski snorted. "Do you enjoy stating the obvious?"

Dieter grinned. "Sometimes." He flicked through the last few screens. "Downie, you and Llewelyn are our best speakers, so you're going to have the face-to-face if it becomes necessary."

"Chances of that?" Llewelyn asked.

Dieter hesitated. "I'm not going to lie; you'll have to interact with people, just in passing. We need to make it so you wouldn't be noticed, someone local, someone boring, someone not worth any attention."

"Well, he knows how to make a girl feel good," Downie said, shaking her head. A couple of the team members chuckled, a little of the tension easing. "You going to check on our linguistic prowess?"

Dieter nodded. "I'll send you a timetable for refresher classes." He glanced around. "Any more questions?"

There were none.

Dieter dismissed them, and the team filed out, talking to one another.

"Good job."

Dieter looked up from the projection table at Sanders. "It's what you pay me for," he said, shutting down the images of maps and data.

Sanders grunted. "Yes, and I know how difficult this time frame was."

Dieter straightened up from the chair he'd occupied for much of the meeting and winced as his lower back protested. He knew it was pointless arguing with Sanders, because he was right about it.

They were focusing on a period between 1910 and 1915, tidying up loose ends of points in the pre-war history which were still unclear. Finding pre-war records in particular regions had been a challenge, especially with the wars and all that followed. So many buildings had been destroyed, and later, changes in politics meant more records vanished.

"I hate fucking communists," he declared as he got up.

"Many do," Sanders replied. "At least you'll be able to sign off on this one soon."

"Three weeks," Dieter reminded him, grimacing. He was marking the days until the scheduled time jump off on the calendar.

Ensuring every agent knew as much as possible about their destination and dangers meant intensive training for weeks. They didn't know where they were going yet, but at least the basic groundwork had been laid. The next few weeks, though, would mean working solidly, without days off.

A new jump always meant things went mental, right until the team returned.

Sanders gathered up his files. "I've approved the leave afterward. Go away somewhere that isn't here."

Dieter picked up his coat. "Is that an order?"

"Does it have to be? You've been doing twelve-hour days for far too long."

"I'm fine," Dieter said. "If that's everything?"

Sanders nodded in dismissal, and Dieter strode from the room.

Everyone was sticking their oar in. So what if he spent more time in the institute than anywhere else? He had bugger all to do outside of work, even if they didn't know. Why not make himself useful?

"Dieter?"

He stopped short, spinning around as Janos rose from one of the chairs lining the wall outside the meeting room. He seemed flustered, which made Dieter frown. Janos was implacable. To see him anxious meant something serious was bothering him.

"Are you all right?" Dieter asked, walking towards him.

Janos glanced down and then back up. "Is there somewhere we can talk? Privately?"

"Of course." He touched Janos's upper arm. "This way."

Dozens of smaller glass-walled offices lined the floor, and it didn't take long to find a vacant one. Dieter swiped his pass, opening it and letting Janos enter first. The door slid closed behind him, and he drew the blinds to shield them from prying eyes.

"So what is..." He turned, and Janos was right in front of him, his green eyes searching Dieter's face. He seemed scared shitless.

"Janos?" Dieter said, touching his arm. The heat of Janos's skin through the fine shirt fabric made Dieter spread his fingers, pressing his palm close. "What's wrong?"

Janos's face broke into a smile, uncertain and tentative, but brilliant.

"Nothing," he said, and then his lips met Dieter's.

Dieter's mind went blank.

He was pretty sure he hadn't drifted off into a daydream. Fairly certain. And how was he meant to help himself if his lips parted to Janos's, and how was he meant to stop his tongue from darting against the other man's?

Janos moaned.

It was barely audible, a ripple of sound against Dieter's lips, low and hungry, and enough to make Dieter's cock throb to life. Dieter pulled back, panting.

He'd never imagined Janos making sounds anything like that in his fantasies, and it made it real, and they were holding onto each other, too hard, too fast, as if the moment might slip away. Dieter stared at Janos, one hand at Janos's arm, but the other slipped around Janos's waist, his hand pressed to his back.

"Jesus, Janos," he whispered.

Janos's fingers tangled in his hair and curled, trembling, against the nape of Dieter's neck. He pressed another kiss, gentler, to Dieter's lips, and then another until they were kissing again, as if they would never stop, and Dieter pushed him back, step by step, until he was pressed up against the wall.

Janos tightened his hand, and Dieter hissed as his hair was tugged. In reproof, he nipped at Janos's lower lip, tugging, and slid his hand over Janos's hip, down, and squeezed his arse through his trousers.

Janos jerked back, eyes wide and darker than Dieter had ever seen them.

Dieter stared back at him. "What the fuck?" he demanded, his voice hoarse, thickened beyond recognition. "What are you doing?"

Janos drew his hand down, sticky with hair product, to touch Dieter's cheek. His thumb grazed along Dieter's lower lip, flicking against the lip ring, his eyes following the movement, and then he raised his eyes and the heat in them took Dieter's breath away. "Kissing you."

Dieter laughed unsteadily, in disbelief. "Spotted that, you dopey fuck," he whispered. "Why?"

Janos lowered his eyes, and a shy smile crossed his face. He looked younger, less fucked by life. "Because I can. Because I want to."

Well, fuck, Dieter thought. How could he not kiss him again after that?

He moved his other hand up Janos's arm and sank his fingers into Janos's shaggy blond hair. Janos's other arm circled his waist, and there wasn't an inch of space between them, letting Dieter know he wasn't the only one getting something out of the contact. Janos slid his hand down to Dieter's neck and around, cradling the back of his head. Dieter smothered a groan as Janos's teeth tugged at his lip ring.

He broke away from the kiss, breathless, leaning into Janos.

"You...oh *Christ*..." he whispered, pressing his hips against Janos's, rocking on the balls of his feet. That earned another of those low, throaty sounds from Janos, whose eyes were half-closed, his features flushed. "Where the fuck did this come from?"

Janos kneaded the back of his neck. "You want to stop?"

"The hell I do." Dieter pressed his lips to Janos's jaw, lower, down his bare throat, dragging his teeth and his lip ring against the stubbled skin.

Janos's breath hissed against his ear and his arm tighten around him.

He nipped at Janos's earlobe. "How long?" he asked, shivering as Janos matched the rock of his hips, their cocks grinding together through their trousers.

Janos arched his neck, his fingers in Dieter's hair again. "All the time," he breathed.

Dieter pulled away, staring at him, hard-on forgotten for a moment. "All?" he asked, dazed.

Janos met his gaze. "Yes."

Dieter shook his head in incomprehension.

Janos lifted his shoulders in a small shrug.

And in the silence, there was a quiet buzz of machinery.

Both of them peered up, and Dieter groaned. "Shit."

Janos turned to him. "A camera?"

"Security," Dieter admitted, flushing. He drew away reluctantly, smoothing hair which was standing in all directions. "We should get out of here."

Janos raised his eyebrows as he wiped his gel-sticky hand on his shirt. "We?"

Dieter glanced at the bulge in the front the man's trousers. "Well, if you want to handle that fucker on your own..."

He'd never seen a grown man blush as red as Janos did in that moment.

"I-I have not...for some time."

Dieter knew he was grinning like a fucking idiot. It wasn't every day his fantasies and daydreams started coming to life. He caught Janos by the hand, lifting his fingers to his lips. "We'll find somewhere without cameras, and we'll change that."

Janos tugged his hand, pulling him closer, and they were kissing again, Janos's tongue slick against his. He didn't kiss like a fucking virgin, or touch like a virgin. When he loosened his other arm from Dieter's waist, Dieter could tell he was about to walk the halls like fucking John Wayne.

"You absolute fucking bastard," he groaned, reaching down to adjust the front of his trousers.

Janos smiled like a hungry tiger. "You may want to hurry. I've waited for too many months already."

Dieter wasn't sure how the hell they got out of the building. They must have stopped for Janos's security band at some point, and he must have hailed one of the autocars, but he couldn't remember any of it.

All he could recall was Janos sliding into the car and giving him such a heated look that he forgot all about propriety. He had the naughty bugger pressed against the seat in a heartbeat, his legs straddling Janos's thighs, and his mouth crushed against Janos's so hard their teeth clattered together. They both laughed as Janos's broad hand spread on his back, as their mouths opened to one another, and every fucking rock of Janos's fucking hips was matched by a thrust of his tongue against Dieter's.

Janos's mouth moved down Dieter's throat, and Dieter threw his head back. He hissed through his teeth, burying his hands in Janos's hair as Janos bit at his throat. There would be marks. Christ. He would have Janos's mark on him. The thought made him press his hips harder, more demandingly against Janos's.

Janos's hand moved over his hip, to his belt, and he tilted his head, panting, to look at Janos. The other man drew back, watching Dieter's face as he loosened the belt, the tip of his tongue visible between his parted lips and teeth.

It felt like forever before he undid the button of Dieter's trousers, slid down the zip, and Dieter let out a sharp, shrill sound as his cock was freed. Jesus Christ, he was on the very edge, and if Janos even…

Broad fingers closed around the shaft, dragging up and down. Dieter's eyes pressed shut, and small, stuttering groans escaping him. "Christ," he whispered.

"Look at me," Janos whispered, his voice raw. "I want to see you."

It felt like the most challenging fucking thing in the world.

His hips jerked with every stroke of Janos's hand—and Christ, his fingers were just as rough as Dieter had imagined—and he could hardly fucking breathe, but he forced his eyes open and found Janos's green gaze fixed on him, drinking in his expression.

Janos's hand tightened, and Dieter grabbed at his shoulders to keep himself from pitching back, his knees braced on either side of Janos's hips, his own hips thrusting hard, hard, harder. Christ, Janos was squeezing, and God, his face…

Janos's tongue ran along his lower lip, his eyes dark. He shifted his hand, just enough to make Dieter groan as he bit his fingers hard into Janos's shoulders, as his cock throbbed and spurted in Janos's hand.

They stared at one another, both panting. The autocar had stopped at their destination, but Dieter couldn't give a fuck if someone could see in from the street. All he saw was Janos beneath him, cum on his shirt and hand, his cock tenting his trousers, and a shit-eating smirk on his face.

"You dirty bugger," Dieter breathed.

Janos just smiled the wider, lifting his hand to his lips and licking every drop of cum from his fingers.

So much for the worry he was a blushing virgin.

Janos dragged his hand down Dieter's thigh. He was still watching Dieter's face for something, but Dieter didn't have the capacity to figure out what. He tried to catch his breath, and he leaned forward, knocking his brow against Janos's.

"That was a surprise," he said, his voice hoarse.

"Perhaps." Janos glanced out the window into the street, which was fortunately not too busy. "Where is this place?"

Dieter glanced out, and his heart stuttered. He must have snapped a direction without thinking as soon as they got into the autocar. He couldn't remember, but it didn't change the fact that they were outside the main entrance of his apartment block.

He looked at Janos.

Of all the people to bring home with him…

"Wrong place?" Janos murmured, his hand falling away from Dieter's thigh.

Dieter stared at him.

Fuck it all.

He leaned closer and kissed him again.

"You're coming to my place," he whispered against Janos's lips. "Now, put my cock back in my pants, or I leave you in the car."

It took them several minutes to get from the car to the doors, and when they did, the lobby was deserted. Dieter caught Janos by the hand, leading him to the elevator, knowing if he stopped or thought, he would panic and leave.

So he was bringing a lover to his flat. So it was a lover from work. So what?

But it was Janos. The Hungarian time traveller who had been in his dreams—for good or ill—for the past three months. The man he couldn't keep out of his head, sleeping or awake.

The elevator doors slid shut around them, and Dieter felt Janos's hand tense.

"You okay?"

"New place," Janos murmured. "Enclosed." He looked at Dieter in helpless appeal. "Distract me?"

The elevator mirrors were misted by the time they reached Dieter's level on the nineteenth floor.

Flushed and out of breath—both of them—Dieter pushed back the fear. Janos was with him. Not the Hungarian. Not the soldier. Janos, who had kissed him senseless, and touched him, and who wanted him.

Wordlessly, he led Janos down the hallway, unlocked the door, and pushed it open.

Janos hesitated there, on the threshold, his fingers still tangled in Dieter's. "You're sure?"

Instead of replying, Dieter pulled Janos's head down and kissed him again. They stumbled into the apartment together, fumbling with clothing, knocking into the walls. The door was kicked shut behind them, and Dieter groped for the lights, his mouth too busy to go for voice command.

Janos broke the kiss. "Which way?"

Dieter stared at him in the half light cast by the evening sun. Way? Jesus Christ. It was like he'd been given a metaphysical conundrum that would decide the fate of the fucking world.

"What?" he asked, feeling like an absolute tit.

The smug little smirk was back. The bastard knew what he was doing. "Where is your bedroom?"

Dieter gaped at him. He'd imagined every which way: on the couch, bent over the kitchen counter, on his expensive coffee table. Bed wasn't high up there. "In the bed? Really?"

Janos's eyes were smoky in the faint light. "I have never fucked someone in a bed before," he said, his voice little above a murmur. He leaned a little closer, and his lips grazed Dieter's. "You would be my first."

Embarrassingly, Dieter *squeaked* but was quickly smothered as he claimed another kiss, spreading his hands on Janos's chest. He darted his tongue between Janos's lips as he tugged at the buttons, pushing the shirt off Janos's shoulders. Janos let go of him, just for a moment, to shake it off. It fell in a crumpled heap on the floor.

"Your room?" Janos purred between kisses.

They got there, somehow. Dieter couldn't remember if he'd made the bed that morning. He struck at the lights, getting them on midway, enough so they wouldn't trip over the shoes scattered all over the floor.

He risked a glance towards the bed, relieved he'd at least changed the bedding sometime in the last week.

"It's a mess," he apologised, turning to Janos.

Janos's fingers threaded through his hair, his mouth slanting over Dieter's and his tongue sliding demandingly against the roof of Dieter's mouth. The hot swell of Janos's cock pressed against him through his trousers. Dieter's hands skittered on warm, bare skin, sliding over Janos's ribs, up his back, down over his arse.

There were scars, and Christ, he wanted to lick every one of them, but Janos wasn't giving him a chance to think, let alone breathe. Janos nudged him back, one step then another, one of his legs insinuating between Dieter's, and rubbing, and Christ on a fucking carousel, Dieter's head spun.

"Is something wrong?" Janos's tone said he knew exactly what he was doing.

Maybe it was the way Dieter's fingers bit into his flesh that gave him the clue. Maybe it was the way Dieter's breathing was growing more and more ragged. Maybe it was the fact that he was getting hard again already.

"You...bastard," Dieter panted, shifting to press against Janos's groin. It earned him a low growl, and the hand in his hair twisted, and Christ, Dieter wasn't in love, but dominant and hair-pulling and sexy as sin? He was fucked.

But not quite literally yet.

"On the bed," Janos whispered against his lips. It wasn't an order, but it sent a shiver of pleasure down Dieter's back.

Dieter slid his hand between Janos's belt and trousers, then edged towards the bed, pulling Janos with him. He undid the buckle as he went, only pausing when the edge of the bed knocked against the back of his knees. Part of him was tempted to start working his way down Janos's body, tasting every one of those scars, but right now, he knew he had to see to believe this was all happening.

He drew away from Janos's kisses, meeting his eyes, as he pulled the belt free, then reached for the buttons of his trousers. Janos's fingers kneaded at the back of his neck. Janos's teeth gleamed between his parted lips, his tongue pressed to them, his lips trembling with each breath.

Once the buttons were undone, all it took was a shift of Janos's narrow hips to make the trousers slide down, and he pulled Dieter closer again, kissing him again, catching Dieter's lower lip between his, tugging on the lip ring with lips and teeth and brushing the tip of his nose against Dieter's.

"You have too many clothes on," Janos said, the ball of his thumb tracing along the curve of Dieter's jawline, then down his throat, down over his chest. Dieter swallowed hard as one button of his shirt, then another was flicked open with such slow deliberation he knew the kinky sod was doing it on purpose.

"I can do that," he said, lifting his hand.

"No." Janos's hand went still. "I want to." His lips grazed Dieter's again, a whisper of contact. "I've thought about it."

Dieter was suddenly very glad the bed was right behind him. His legs weren't going to hold him much longer if Janos kept it up. Still, he wouldn't be himself if he let Janos completely take the lead, so he ran one hand across Janos's belly, the muscles quivering beneath his palm.

"Thought about it?" he asked, only a little breathless as the last button of his shirt was undone. "About me?"

"Mm." Janos spread his palm on Dieter's belly, warm and callused and enough to make a shudder of want run through him. Janos's lips curved up, and he pushed the shirt first from Dieter's left shoulder, then his right, letting it slip down his arms. "Too much." He tugged on Dieter's lip ring with his teeth. "Let it fall."

Dieter couldn't help agreeing with the marvellous idea, and withdrew his arms to loosen the cufflinks to shake himself free. Before the shirt even hit the bed, Janos wrapped his fingers around his upper arm and pulled him into another brutal kiss.

Flesh against cloth was one thing, but nothing compared to Janos's skin hot against his.

The smell of sweat and sex made Dieter's mouth go dry. He reclined back, tipping them both onto the bed, and Janos half sprawled over him, their mouths open to one another, tongues twining as Janos rocked against him.

"W-wait," Dieter panted, groping for the waistband of his trousers.

Janos cursed in amused protest, making mischief by tracing his fingers across Dieter's chest, tweaking at his nipples and drawing ticklish circles on Dieter's skin as Dieter tugged at his trousers.

"Stop that, you fucking cock!" Dieter exclaimed, unable to keep from squirming.

"Not a fucking cock," Janos complained, sprawling onto his side, as naked as the day he was born, his cock right there.

His voice dropped a level as he added in a murmur, "Not yet."

Dieter stared at him, then rolled onto his side and kissed him once, hard, his fingers briefly dragging through Janos's hair.

"One minute," Dieter said, then managed to sit up and get rid of the trousers. He stood up to kick them off, heard the bed creak, and yelped when an arm wrapped around his waist from behind and a broad chest pressed to his back.

Janos pressed his mouth to the nape of Dieter's neck, sucking gently, and then less gently. He added the pressure of teeth, and Dieter's legs trembled as Janos slid his hand down Dieter's belly and closed it around his cock again.

"I want to fuck you, Dieter," he whispered. "Here. In your bed. Do you want me to?"

"Christ, yes," Dieter groaned as Janos's mouth moved to the side of his throat, his hips twitching towards Janos's hand.

Janos drew him down onto the bed, and Dieter groped at the dresser. He always kept supplies, just in case of fucking emergencies. He twisted in Janos's arms to face him and touched one shaking hand to Janos's cheek.

"Wait," he said, quiet, breathless. "There's something I need you to..." He opened his other hand.

Janos offered a small, crooked smile. "I think I have read of these things. In case I bring sickness?"

"Or in case I do. You're not my first."

Janos lifted his chin with a fingertip and kissed him. "Nor you mine." He gestured at himself, and the wicked, impish smile returned. "Dress me to your liking."

Of all the times to feel as nervous as a virgin...

Dieter had put dozens of condoms on dozens of men, but his hands had never shaken quite so much before. Anticipation was one rush, and despite more than a month of fantasising, he'd never thought to focus on this detail.

One hand pressed to Janos's thigh, the other unrolled the condom, and when he closed his hand around Janos's sheathed cock and squeezed, the sound Janos made was enough to curl his toes.

"Good enough?" Janos's voice seemed deeper.

Dieter replied by leaning up to kiss him, carding one hand through Janos's hair. With the other hand, he pressed the tube of lube into Janos's hand, the cap flipped up. "Fuck me," he whispered against Janos's lips. "Fuck me hard."

Green eyes stared at him, pupils wide and black. "I want to see your face," Janos growled.

Dieter nodded, pushing away enough to drag pillows down. He sprawled back, his feet pressing to the bed, legs spread in wordless invitation. Janos just gazed at him for a moment, eyes scorching their way all over his body, then leaned forward, propping the stump of his left arm on the pillow by Dieter's head as he bent and kissed him again.

It was gentle this time, teasing little kisses, flirtations of lips and tongue, and Dieter tangled his hand into his hair again, his breath catching at the brush of Janos's fingers, slick with lube, tracing the length of his cock and teasing across his balls.

"Lift yourself for me," Janos murmured against his lips. Dieter pressed with his feet, tilting his hips, pinned by the intensity in Janos's eyes as broad, strong fingers stroked down the crease of his arse.

Green eyes held his.

"You're sure?"

Dieter nodded. "Fuck, yes," he groaned, shuddering as two warm, slick fingers pressed into him. He pushed his hips against Janos's hand, pressing his head against the pillows as Janos's fingers slowly spread. "Fuck!"

Janos's brow rested against Dieter's, his breath unsteady as his lips parted. His eyes half-closed, and his hips twitched as he stroked his fingers in, then curled them and slowly withdrew them, the sensation making Dieter hiss through his teeth.

Janos's lips brushed Dieter's. "Catch your legs," he whispered. "Draw them up."

Reluctantly, Dieter withdrew his hand from Janos's thick, soft hair, letting Janos sit back on his heels and watch, rapt, as Dieter caught his hands behind his knees and drew his legs up to his chest.

Janos gazed down at him, so exposed, so vulnerable, so bloody horny, and he smiled.

"What?" Dieter asked, his breath catching as Janos's fingers thrust deep, spreading and opening him mercilessly.

"You have no idea how beautiful you are, do you?" Janos murmured.

Dieter's lips trembled, and the sounds he was making verged on pathetic. "Christ, Janos," he groaned, rocking his hips against the thrusting fingers. "Just fuck me already! Please!"

Janos's fingers were gone in an instant, and Dieter's eyes ran down his body, over the broad shoulders, the scarred ribs, the flat, muscled belly. And he watched as Janos's tongue darted along his lips, as Janos wrapped his hand around his cock, stroking until it glistened with lube. The scent of the stuff finally reached Dieter, and Janos noticed too.

"Strawberries?" Janos asked with a quirk of his eyebrows.

Dieter smiled helplessly. "What? I like strawberry."

Janos slid closer on his knees and stroked his hand up the back of Dieter's left thigh. "I prefer cherry," he murmured, holding Dieter's eyes as the tip of his cock pressed against Dieter's arse.

Dieter's fingers dug into his thighs. "Fine," he whispered. "Next time, cherry." His breathing quickened, and he shivered as Janos slowly pushed into him. Finally. Finally. He pressed closer, a little at a time, and Janos's hand covered his on his thigh, tangling their fingers, just for a moment. "Jesus..."

"Exactly," Janos panted. He released Dieter's hand, braced his arms on either side of Dieter's head, and started moving his hips. Slowly at first, barely withdrawing at all, and then sinking in, the coarse trail of hair low on his belly rubbing against Dieter's cock, Janos's eyes fixed on Dieter's face, and his stroke quickened.

Dieter pulled his legs harder, keening as Janos thrust deeper with each stroke, his stuttering breaths caught against Janos's lips, their kisses clumsy and careless as Janos pounded harder and harder against him.

Janos threw his head back, his fair hair clinging to his face, his expression both pain and pleasure, his hand tangling into Dieter's hair. "Look at me," he whispered. No. Pleaded. Desperate. And Dieter's eyes— half-closed from surging pleasure—flew open. Janos's face was so close to his, his breath hot on Dieter's face, his hand in Dieter's hair as he thrust and thrust again, his whole body tensing like a coiled spring.

Dieter released one of his twitching thighs to touch Janos's face, knowing just what he meant. Too many days of waiting. Too long. "I'm here," he panted. "I'm here, Janos."

Janos whimpered low in his throat, turning his face into Dieter's touch, his eyes pressing closed as a couple more ragged strokes finished him, leaving him shivering, panting, and slick with sweat.

Dieter curved his fingers along Janos's cheek. "Worth the wait?"

Janos's breaths were hot and rapid against his palm, and he turned to Dieter, his eyes dark and unreadable. But when he leaned down and kissed Dieter again, he didn't have to say a thing.

Chapter Nineteen

Sudden movement woke Janos.

He had been a soldier too long to sleep heavily.

The sudden chill of the air on his bare skin told him the sheets had been pulled aside, and he propped himself up on his arm, squinting in the darkness. Dieter's silhouette was outlined against the floor-to-ceiling windows as he groped around on the floor.

After they'd fucked, after he'd gathered his scattered wits, he'd finished Dieter with his hand again, and they had sprawled together in the bed, sated, too tired to consider moving. There was enough space for them to lie apart, so they did, on opposite sides of the bed. It didn't seem right to curl up and coo together like lovers, not so soon.

So they slept, though it must have been for only a couple of hours.

"Dieter?" he murmured.

"I shouldn't be here." Dieter's voice trembled. He spoke in English, which he never did around Janos. "I-I-I'm sorry. I'll go."

It was as if he'd been doused with ice water. Janos sat up and reached for the bedside table and the lamp. Illuminated in the soft, golden light, Dieter shrank away, blinking, turning his face away.

He trembled as if terrified, ashen. He was afraid, and Janos's stomach twisted. Only days, weeks earlier, Dieter had admitted nightmares troubled him, nightmares of their first meeting. To wake in a bed with the man who was the cause of those nightmares...

It didn't matter they had returned to the apartment together, or that they had fucked, and that it had been much more intimate than Janos had expected. None of it mattered, because Dieter was afraid.

"Dieter," Janos said again. "You don't need to go anywhere. This is your home."

Dieter turned a shirt over in his hands, twisting it tighter and tighter. "I shouldn't be here," he said again in a whisper, his eyes wide and dark. His ribs rose and fell with unsteady, shaking breaths. "Please, let me go."

No, he definitely was far from fully awake.

Janos remembered the night Dieter had come to him after his own nightmares. He had stayed at a distance, calm and quiet. It might not work, but it was better than doing nothing. Janos drew away to the other side of the bed, sat against the wrought iron headboard, and laid his hand in his lap.

"You can go, if you want to," he said. "I won't stop you."

Dieter remained where he was, glancing anxiously towards the door. "You won't hurt me?"

Janos folded his arm over his stomach and wrapped his hand around the stump of his left arm. "I swear I will never hurt you again," he said as steadily as he could. Dieter continued to stare at him, blinking hard. "I can go, if you want me to."

Dieter stared down at the shirt in his hands. "I want to sit down," he said plaintively, like a tired child.

Janos drew his legs up the bed, sitting cross-legged in the tangle of sheets. "As you like," he murmured, digging his fingers into the flesh just above his elbow.

Dieter took three awkward steps and sat on the far corner of the bed. He laid the crumpled shirt across his knees and smoothed the material out with still-trembling hands. He stroked it over and over, and gradually, the roughness of his breathing eased, and he closed his eyes. His makeup was smudged all down his cheeks.

"Do you want something to drink?" Janos suggested quietly. It worked to calm him. Perhaps it would help Dieter the same way.

Dieter shook his head. "Not again," he said, his voice hoarse. He lifted his head and gazed at Janos with so much guilt and shame Janos wanted nothing more than to ruffle his hair and reassure him all was well. "I'm more foolish when I drink."

"Warm milk, then," Janos said. "My grandmother would swear by it." He swung his legs off the bed, the polished floor cool under his one bare and one sock-covered foot. "Do you have cinnamon?"

Dieter stared at him. "Um. Yes. There's a rack with spices on the counter."

Janos nodded and strode out into the dark apartment. He had to bat at the walls to find the lights and stubbed his toes more than once, but it wasn't a large place, and the kitchen was easy enough to find. He rattled through the cupboards and dug out a pan, filled it halfway with milk, and set it on the stove.

Fortunate, he mused, that Dieter used simple technology for cookery. Just a dial to be turned to switch the heat on. So much easier than some of the machinery they used within the agency.

While there was cinnamon, the cupboards were half-empty, not even a jar of honey to be found. He clicked his tongue impatiently and returned to stirring the milk, adding a pinch of cloves as the milk warmed.

He didn't immediately notice when Dieter appeared in the doorway.

Unlike Janos, he'd pulled on a pair of shorts. He'd cleaned the makeup from his face as well, as bare and young as he had seemed the night of Janos's own nightmare.

"What are you doing?" he asked, his voice quiet.

Janos continued to stir the milk. "Making us both a warm, comforting drink. It seems like you need one."

Dieter looked down self-consciously. "I'm sorry."

Janos waved the spoon. "You have seen me in worse states. You don't need to apologise."

Dieter approached, folding his arms over his chest, and leaned his hip against the counter. He stayed at arm's length, watching as Janos stirred the milk with a plastic spoon. "What's floating in it?" he asked.

Janos scooped one of the cloves up with the spoon to let Dieter see. "For flavour." He resumed stirring. "Do you have a sieve? So we can take them out when the milk is done?"

Dieter slipped around him, touching Janos's back with his fingertips as he reached for a rack on the wall. That brief moment of contact brought more relief than Janos had anticipated, a frisson of warmth running through him. Dieter was afraid, but not so afraid he would let it come between them.

Dieter set the sieve down on the counter and glanced at Janos in concern. "You're cold."

"I am?" Janos frowned down at his body in surprise. After the Russian winters, being at room temperature didn't seem like a hardship.

Dieter touched his upper arm, drawing his hand down lightly. "As ice." He met Janos's eyes. "Don't go anywhere."

He disappeared from the kitchen, and Janos turned his attention to the pan. It took careful balance to prop the strainer on the mug and pour the milk without knocking the strainer off or spilling the milk all over the counter.

It was a small victory, but a victory nonetheless when he lifted the strainer off the second mug with not a drop spilled. He set the empty pan in the sink and filled it with water, turning with a brief smile as Dieter came back into the room. He eyed the bundle in Dieter's hands, raising his eyebrows.

"What is that?" he inquired.

Dieter shook out a flare of soft blue fabric. "Something for you to wear. I don't want you to catch pneumonia."

Janos peered at the robe in amusement. "You own it?"

Dieter wrinkled his nose and pulled a face. "Yeah. And you're going to wear it. I'm not having your bare arse leaving imprints on my sofa."

Janos couldn't hide a smile. The worst of Dieter's panic seemed to be abating, and if letting him play dress up helped, Janos was content to oblige. He still sighed impatiently and held out his arms.

Dieter opened the robe and helped him into it, then slipped around in front of him, drawing it closed. He didn't raise his eyes to Janos as he tied the cord in a knot tight enough to preserve modesty, but loose enough so it would come undone with a single tug.

Janos gazed at him and brushed an errant strand of Dieter's hair from his face. "I suspect," he murmured, "I have never looked so homosexual in my life."

Blue eyes met his, wariness replaced with the more familiar mirth. "I don't know," Dieter said, his hands on Janos's hips. "You looked pretty gay when you had your dick up my arse."

Janos snorted. "You are an idiot."

Dieter leaned up and kissed him. "And you're the idiot who fucked me." He withdrew, his hands lingering for a moment. "Come on. The sofa's the place for warm milk."

"Not bed?"

Dieter picked up the mugs. "Warm milk isn't a sexy drink, you silly sod. I want to keep the bedroom sexy, not turn it into a geriatric's den."

Janos followed him through the apartment. "Well, I am over one hundred years."

Dieter shot a grin over his shoulder. "Pervy old bastard."

Janos shrugged with a modest smile. "Sometimes."

He glanced around the living room as they entered, surprised at the decor. Dieter's bedroom was all hot, sexual colours and dark metals, the bedframe a playground for hands to grip. This room, by comparison, was all soft edges, cream and golden colours, speaking of warmth and comfort.

Dieter set one of the mugs on a table and dropped onto the broad sofa, propping himself against the far arm.

Not wishing to press his attentions, Janos sat at the opposite end of the couch, one foot braced on the floor, the other leg folded up in front of him. He took up the mug in his hand and sipped the contents, a safe distraction from leaning forward and touching his distressed lover again.

Dieter watched him. He had his hands wrapped around his own mug, and between sips, he propped the cup on his upraised knee.

"It helps," he murmured.

Janos made a small sound of inquiry.

Dieter held the mug up. "This. Helps." He gazed down into the mug. "Thank you."

Janos offered a slight smile. "I was the cause. It's only manners to provide the cure."

Dieter didn't argue, sipping some more of the milk. "I feel like a fucking arse," he confessed. "Jesus Christ, Janos. I know you. I know you wouldn't hurt me, but one nightmare, and I'm ready to cry for my mother!"

Janos unfolded his leg, his calf brushing against Dieter's foot. "I spoke with Sally about nightmares. She says they are the way the brain tries to make sense of trauma."

"Yeah, she would say that." Dieter set the mug down with a sigh. "It's all fucked up."

"I shot you," Janos murmured.

"By accident."

"I put a gun to your head."

Dieter looked away. "Do we have to talk about it?"

"If it's still giving you nightmares…"

"It is, okay?" Dieter snapped. "And now, with the added feature of you forcing me to my knees and making me give you a fucking blow job." He pushed his hand through his hair with a shaking laugh. "My fantasies are mixing up with my nightmares, and I don't know where one starts and one ends."

Janos knew the feeling well, but his own nightmares were of isolation, of violence, and he didn't know how to say, more than once, the body he laid in the grave in his dreams no longer wore Szilveszter's face. Dieter didn't know about Szilveszter. He didn't know what fed Janos's nightmares. He didn't need to.

So Janos said, "Is that your fantasy? Doing that?"

Dieter laughed unsteadily. "Fuck no! It's fun, and I'm good at it, and men like you like it, so that's why I thought it." He hesitated, then added, "I like it the other way around."

Men like you.

So, for all that he liked to have a dominant lover, he didn't want it to be all.

Janos set the cup to one side. "May I touch you?"

Dieter's lips twitched. "Now you ask?"

"Now, I do."

Dieter's tongue darted out to wet his lips, and he nodded.

Janos braced his hand against the arm of the couch behind Dieter and leaned closer to kiss him. He tasted of milk and cinnamon, and his mouth opened as Janos's tongue stroked along his lips. Between their bodies, his legs unfolded, splaying gracelessly, and Janos smiled against Dieter's lips as nimble fingers tugged the cord of the robe, letting it fall open.

"No," he whispered against Dieter's lips. "No touching me now."

Dieter nipped on his lower lip. "Why?" he asked, one hand skimming closer to Janos's cock.

"Because," Janos replied and kissed him again, stealing what breath he had. Dieter's hands slid around him, skittering along his sides, over his back, and he was gasping as Janos's lips moved from Dieter's lips and lower.

Janos took his time, leaving sharp, stinging bites down the length of Dieter's throat. He returned from time to time to claim another kiss, but from there descended again. Dieter hissed and cursed and squirmed when Janos nipped and licked at his nipples, dragging teeth and tongue over them, and then lower still. Dieter pulled his hands from the robe and tangled them into Janos's hair instead, combing through, guiding.

Janos felt the impatience rising in his lover. He tasted the sharpness of Dieter's ribs, the rapidly rising and falling curve of his belly beneath his ribcage. He dragged his stubbled cheek against the sensitive skin and slid from the couch to kneel on the floor.

"Turn?" he asked.

Dieter, panting, breathless, flushed, nodded. One leg splayed off the couch, and through the thin fabric of his shorts, little hid his eagerness.

Janos met his eyes, curled his fingers around the waistband of those shorts, and dragged them down. Dieter lifted his hips just enough, and his cock slipped free, the head already gleaming and wet.

Dieter stared at him, one hand beating against the arm of the couch. "You don't have to," he ground out, his hips twitching.

"No," Janos agreed, leaning closer. "I don't."

The flavour of spiced milk was still warm on his lips as he closed them around the head of Dieter's cock. The tang of salt and maleness was familiar, but not the same, and he drew his tongue in a circle, earning a stuttering groan from Dieter.

Fingers twisted into his hair, stroking. Dieter's hips were trembling. He wanted to thrust, and he was holding back. Janos smiled. So "men like him" didn't like to do things like this?

Something else his innocent little lover didn't know about him.

He brought his hand up to tease Dieter a little more, his mouth skirting the head of the throbbing cock with licks and nibbles and long strokes of his tongue as he stroked Dieter's balls and occasionally wrapped his fingers around the shaft, dragging down then releasing.

"Christ!" Dieter gasped aloud, his foot skittering on the floor. "Jesus fucking Christ!"

The sounds he was making were a delight, and Janos moved hands and lips to earn more, and only when Dieter was all but whimpering did he stop. He went still, completely still, and raised his eyes to Dieter's face.

Dieter—flushed and shivering with want—stared back at him wildly. Janos smiled, dipped his head, and took damn near every inch of his lover's cock in his mouth, swallowing around him—a little trick learned after too many nights of stained uniforms.

Dieter yowled like a cat, his fingers tightening in Janos's hair as his hips bucked, and he came, hot and urgent, and Janos swallowed, hard. He sucked again, drawing every drop, until Dieter fell against the couch, gasping, his hand still clenched in Janos's hair.

"Jesus," he whispered. "Where the fuck did that come from?"

Janos drew his head away, dragging his tongue lazily over the head of Dieter's cock, then with the back of two fingertips supporting the limp shaft, laid it down with mocking solicitousness against Dieter's thigh. "'Men like me' have to pass the time somehow."

Blue eyes stared at him, wide and unblinking. "Where'd you learn?"

he demanded breathlessly. "I can't even do it!"

Janos knelt up. "That is a story for another night." He retrieved his mug and braced his other arm on the table to get back to his feet. "Now, I think we both should sleep. We have a busy day tomorrow."

Dieter rose too. "Aren't you…" he began, nodding at Janos's groin. "I mean, don't you want to…?"

"Fuck?" Janos suggested with a half smile. "Your favourite word and you forget it?"

Dieter laughed, his smile lighting his eyes. "Oh, piss off, you cheeky sod. The offer's there if you want it."

Janos drained the last of his milk and put the cup on the table. "I may take you up on it," he said, smoothing Dieter's hair. "But it's late, and we both have much to do tomorrow. Fucking can wait."

Dieter caught his hand and kissed his palm. His eyes searched Janos's face, and when he spoke, he was uncharacteristically serious. "You're all right, you know."

Janos grazed his cheekbone with his thumb. "You also. Now, bed."

When the lights were finally turned down and the sheets drawn up, Dieter squirmed around in the darkness until he nestled against Janos's back, his arm around Janos's waist, their legs tangled comfortably together, and in the peace, Janos smiled.

Chapter Twenty

"This is the target."

Dieter tapped the pointer against the map projected onto the wall. It was an old-fashioned technique, but once, he'd caught operatives talking between themselves and brought the stick down so hard on the table they'd jumped. It had been a lesson that stuck.

"According to the records we've been able to gather," he continued, studying the operatives' faces, "there are a few settlements in the area where the gateway will open, but enough that we'll have to leave someone to stand watch as a precaution."

Mutters and looks were exchanged.

It was rare for the temporal techs to open a doorway near populated areas, but days and weeks of research hadn't been able to change the facts: the information they sought was in a town, and the town was fringed on all sides by farms and people.

Sanders rose from his chair. "We know this is unorthodox, but necessity demands it, which means you're all going to have to be a lot more careful than you otherwise would be."

"What are we going for?"

Sanders and Dieter exchanged glances.

The final big briefing before the jump meant it was the time for the reveal.

For every jump, there were preliminary briefings, so the team knew the place and time, along with general details of the kind of situation they might be entering so they could start preparing, but the last briefing was always the most important one.

In the week before a jump, the agents had to cut all communication with the modern world and were isolated within the building, even from other teams. Restricted to the dormitories and training rooms, they were only allowed to speak to people with clearance.

If someone found out about the destination and plans too soon, they could be leaked.

Once, an agent had made the mistake of making off with documents retrieved from a jump, in order to make a profit. She'd set up a buyer beforehand, with knowledge of what she'd be collecting, and it had caused all kinds of problems for the institution. They couldn't sue her for breach of contract or have her arrested for theft since the institution technically didn't exist, nor could they let it happen again.

Precautions had been put in place.

The teams would be housed together until the jump, and once they returned, they had a two-day decontamination and debrief period. Anything they'd collected would be taken from them on their return. Nothing modern went through the gateway and nothing historical left the building with any of the agents.

That wasn't to say they didn't bring anything back with them.

Dieter picked up the controller and flicked through a few screens. "You'll remember our old friend, Franz Ferdinand."

Borowski groaned, and Downie buried her head in her folded arms.

"I think that's a yes," Sanders observed dryly.

"It's kind of hard to forget Archduke Who-Started-a-War," Llewelyn said, leaning back in his seat.

"Technically," Dieter agreed. "Technically, his death was a big part of it, but don't forget problems were building there already." He rubbed his hands together. "What you're going for is something that could rewrite the history books."

"You mean all the history you just taught us?" Downie said grumpily, raising her head. "That history?"

"Wait," Llewelyn added. "Rewrite history books? You mean change something?"

"No." Sanders's voice snapped like a whip. "You know the rules."

"Then how?" Llewelyn demanded.

Dieter smiled. "By confirming how events actually happened."

"Don't we...know already?" Borowski asked. "I mean, you told us many details."

"We know the assassins had a lot of information about Franz Ferdinand's movements," Dieter agreed. "What we don't know for certain is how they managed to have so much information about the archduke's plans, like specifics of numbers of men, times, places, how they would be traveling."

He brought a map up on the screen.

"There were theories that someone within the palace was leaking information, and we all know how valuable that can be. There have always been spies, and sometimes, those spies eventually got old and made a profit by writing their stories down." He highlighted one of the houses, a glowing line of red tracing the outline. "And conveniently, one of those spies left enough clues for us to follow him."

A flick of the controller drew the house out of the map, presenting it as a three-dimensional projection.

"Based on what our modest spy wrote, this place was the key," he said. "The information would change hands here. According to all records, from 1884 to 1917, it was an inn, and a stopover point for people crossing the borders in both directions. If he is to be believed, this is where the leak would disseminate his information on the day we're set to arrive. June 3rd, 1914."

"This guy seems to know an awful lot about the leak," Llewelyn said. "Is it possible it was him?"

Dieter shook his head. "That's not what we're there to find out. Our priority and target is still the information. If we can see it being passed on, great. If we can see who it was passed to, even better. But our priority is the person carrying it and what it says. Spy or leak, we want to clear up any doubts whether someone in the Viennese court was responsible for revealing Ferdinand's movements to the Black Hand."

"What kind of extraction do we have?" Borowski asked. "It will be just lying around? Or we will have to find it?"

Dieter stepped back with a nod to Sanders.

The older man moved to the fore and summarised the operation. The team of six would approach the town. Each of them would have a post to keep watch, while two—Llewelyn and Downie—would get into the inn. The spy's diary said the information would be handed over there, in the upper room. They would both have a button camera to scan the information if they found it.

"Will there be anyone around?" Llewelyn asked, surveying the image of the inn. "I mean, is it a market day or anything to bring in a lot of people?"

"Not that we're aware of," Dieter replied.

Sanders added, "But we have to allow for flexibility. If there are too many people around or the room is occupied, we can't put anyone at risk. You can interact if you must, but limited contact. We don't want anyone noticed or remembered. You know the drill."

They did, of course.

It was the first rule of the TRI: the past must be protected.

Dieter took a seat as Sanders went through the rest of the briefing. He was there to answer questions on the past, but the time-jumping aspect was all on Sanders, the man who had helped pioneer the system, and who continued to develop it with every successful jump.

Only one or two more questions came up about the historical aspects, though concerns were voiced about moving among the population in daylight. They'd had extra language coaching, but it was another thing entirely to fool someone from a different time.

"Janos Nagy has offered his assistance," Sanders said, rousing Dieter from his wandering thoughts. "The timeline may be a little before his own, but he'll be assessing each of you on the way you move and carry yourselves and your props."

"Like baby," Borowski muttered under his breath.

Llewelyn snorted in amusement. "Piss off, Borowski. Let's see what the old-timer has to say about the way you walk."

"You sure he's going to help us, boss?" Downie asked.

Sanders nodded. "The feedback I've been getting from his training sessions has all been positive. He's a decent man. He just wants to play his part and make himself useful. No reason to doubt him."

Downie glanced at Dieter. "He stopped being a jackass?"

Dieter smiled crookedly. "I think it's his default state."

Sanders laid out files on the desk. "These are your identities and aliases. You need to read over them tonight, get to know all the details. You'll be quizzed on them every day until departure. Your one-on-one sessions with Nagy will be scheduled, and you will receive the timetable in your inbox this evening." He glanced at Dieter. "Anything else?"

Dieter shook his head. "Unless there are any more questions?"

No one spoke, and Sanders nodded in approval. "Dismissed, then."

The team departed together, taking their files with them under the supervision of one of the security teams. They would be escorted to the accommodation suites and locked down for the evening.

Dieter rose from his chair and snatched up his jacket. "So Janos is checking them for accuracy? Those poor sods."

Sanders chuckled. "He wanted to be useful, and this time, we need to know they're not going to stand out. We've never done something quite as risky as this before."

Dieter nodded. "He knows what to watch out for." He slipped his jacket on, leaving it unbuttoned. "I guess it means he and I have to stay inside the building now we're both involved in this jump? Security bullshit and all that?"

Sanders raised his eyebrows and then glanced at his watch. "Ah. It's date night, isn't it?"

Dieter braced his hands against the edge of the table, hoping he didn't seem as rattled as he felt. He and Janos were keeping their tentative relationship quiet, not least because Janos was technically part of his job. "What do you mean?"

Sanders snorted. "You insist on getting him out of the building once a week."

Dieter rolled his eyes, more relieved than he expected to be. "Well, he's not a prisoner, and I don't know anyone else in the agency who would want to go anywhere with the grumpy arsehole."

"And you had something scheduled?"

"Just dinner somewhere that isn't here," Dieter lied cheerfully. "Maybe the cinema. He's been curious about it for a while now."

Sanders tapped his fingers on the side of his file. "Fine. He doesn't know the details of the mission, only that he'll be helping out. It's nothing new. If you want to get him out for one last night before he starts the spot-checking, fine. But once he's been working with the agents, he'll be locked down too."

"I think he can cope with being indoors for ten days." Dieter agreed, trying to keep the grin off his face. He threw a salute Sanders's way. "Don't wait up."

Sanders sighed, shaking his head as Dieter headed out of the room.

Janos was waiting in his room, as always.

They still met for breakfast and dinner in the canteen, but in the two weeks since their first night together, they'd tried to keep things as they were before: they only went out of the building together once a week, and it wasn't going to change. Suspicions didn't need to be aroused.

It did, however, mean the anticipation of those nights out had skyrocketed.

Dieter swiped his card and didn't bother going into the room. "You ready?" he asked, leaning against the doorway.

Janos's face lit up in his rare, brilliant smile. "Ready."

They had planned to go the river, but it was pouring with rain when they emerged from the building. Dieter was quite happy he had a contingency plan in place, especially when it meant he and Janos could have a little more time alone together.

"So you control the weather now?" Janos said dryly as he shed his long coat in the hall of Dieter's apartment.

"Eh?"

Janos nodded towards the windows and the rain lashing against them. "Very convenient that it starts raining and you have to bring me back to your house."

Dieter took his coat to hang it up on the hook behind the door. "Oh, piss off," he said, smiling. "If you want to go and wander along the quay in the rain and get a nice dose of pneumonia, you can do it on your own."

Janos tilted his head, gazing at Dieter. "No," he decided. "I think I will stay here."

Dieter pulled his head down and kissed him firmly on the lips. "Good. Now stop pissing and moaning like an old lady and come through to the kitchen. I'm going to make us some dinner."

While the kitchen wasn't big, there was a breakfast bar by the window with two stools. Janos pulled one of them out and perched on it, watching with interest as Dieter carried a stack of food from the fridge to the counter.

"Why are you cooking?" Janos asked finally as Dieter chopped onions and garlic.

Dieter glanced over at him. "What? Did you think I was just bringing you back for a quick fuck?" he said, widening his eyes in feigned shock. "Do you think I'm so shallow?"

Janos scratched at his chin thoughtfully. "Yes, but I think you're hungry too, so you want to eat first."

Dieter couldn't help the stupid shit-eating grin that crossed his face. "You're working out my cunning plan," he said sternly. "Stop it." Janos smirked at him. Dieter made a face. "Did anyone ever tell you you're an arse?"

"Sometimes," Janos said, leaning against the breakfast bar.

Dieter tossed the onions into the pan where they sizzled in the heated oil. "Oh," he said as he set to work on the meat. "Sanders said you're going to be helping the team to get ready for the next jump."

Janos shrugged. "He said it would be helpful for them to have someone look at them with old eyes. I told him I wanted to be useful." His smile was brief and small, but warm. "I think I'm being useful."

"You are," Dieter said at once. "Everyone has said so. You're teaching them a lot."

Janos made a short noncommittal sound, but he seemed pleased by Dieter's words. "Not so bad for a one-armed man from the wrong time."

"Oh, piss off," Dieter said with a laugh, tipping the meat into the pan. "You're not just a one-armed…" He paused, narrowing his eyes at Janos, who stared back at him with an air of wounded innocence. "Oh, I see what you're doing. You want me to keep complimenting you."

Janos stared up at the ceiling. "I don't know what you mean."

Dieter shook his head. "Arsehole." He added some spices to the pan and then put some water on to boil. He didn't notice Janos had moved until an arm slid around his waist from behind, and Janos pressed a kiss to his ear. A pleasant shiver ran the length of his spine.

"Do you mind?" Janos murmured.

"Fuck no," Dieter replied just as quietly, leaning into him. "It's been a hell of a week."

What surprised him was that it didn't turn sexual. It could have done, so easily, but instead, Janos was just there with him, his arm around Dieter's middle, and they talked about the coming week and Janos's role with the agents.

It was almost like they were a couple, which was as disconcerting as it was warming.

Dieter waited for the moment when it would become uncomfortable as they took the plates of food through to the living room. When he poured the wine, when he sat and gazed across the table, he couldn't help worrying it didn't feel as strange as it should.

No one ever came to his apartment more than once.

No one ever got invited.

And yet, here was Janos Nagy, back in the apartment for the third time, trying to work out how to manage noodles on a fork with one hand.

"Here." Dieter dragged his chair alongside Janos. "This is the easiest way." He showed him how to twist the noodles up and then looked at him solemnly. "If you get sauce all over the table and your face, I'll forgive you. I'll be pissed, but I'll forgive you."

"You are a noble and gracious host," Janos replied just as gravely.

They both lasted less than five seconds before sniggering.

Dieter scooted his chair along to his own food and propped his left arm on the table while forking the noodles. He waited until they'd both just about finished the food, then spoke again. "I was wondering why you don't just get the arm again? The false one, I mean. Wouldn't it be easier?"

Janos was silent for a moment, and Dieter winced, wondering if he'd managed to upset him again.

"No," Janos said. "I'm not...ready to have it there." He frowned, shaking his head. "I don't know if I can explain it. Everything is so new. I need to feel I'm part of it. Not me and a false part. Just me." He glanced at Dieter, uncertain. "Does that make sense?"

Dieter nodded. "You need to be yourself for a while."

Janos smiled fleetingly. "Yes." He stared down at the fork, frowning again as he tried to catch the last stray noodles. "I don't think I have ever been me before."

"Really?" Dieter stopped twisting his fork. "Didn't anyone know you for the arsehole you are?"

Janos chewed on the noodles, then set down his fork on the empty plate and picked up the wine. "Not really. It was a...bad time to be someone like me." He stared into the wine glass. "People died. Many of them. It was better to be quiet and unnoticed."

Dieter gazed at him. He then tugged his chair to sit closer to Janos, dragging his place mat and what remained of his food with him. "You don't have to be afraid anymore," he said, touching Janos's wrist with his fingertips. "You can be whoever you want to be here, and do whatever you want to do."

"You make it sound so easy," Janos said, his voice barely above a whisper. "In this place, it's safe, but outside? I've done so many things to keep people from seeing me." He put the wineglass down, and when he spoke, his voice was flat. "I've killed to hide who I am."

Dieter's hand remained where it was, resting against Janos's wrist, but his heartbeat had quickened. "Killed? When you were a soldier?"

Janos lowered his eyes, turning his face away. "He was in my regiment. He...made accusations. They were true, but if they were accepted as truth..." Janos trembled, and Dieter couldn't help tightening his grip on his wrist in mute support. "I had seen people killed for less, Dieter. I saw them bleed. I heard them screaming. Holy Mary, I was afraid. I was so afraid." He swallowed hard. "So I challenged him to fight for his lies." Janos's voice shook, and he took an unsteady breath. "He got a knife. We fought. I won. He died."

"Shit," Dieter whispered. "Holy shit."

"He had the knife," Janos whispered, staring at his plate. "I didn't want to kill him, but my arm...my chest...if I didn't kill him, he would have killed me."

"Your arm? He's the one who did that?"

Janos tugged his wrist free and crossed his arm over his middle to touch his stump. "Small price for a life," he said quietly, his expression bleak. "It was when I found my way to this time. I broke martial law by killing one of my comrades. I was to die, so I ran. I was still running, and then, there was a doorway, and then..." He laughed brokenly. "And then, there you were."

Dieter's mouth went dry. "Jesus Christ, Jan..."

Janos took an unsteady breath. "So now you know," he whispered. "I am a coward and a traitor and a killer." His eyes were bright with unshed tears. "That is who I am. Is that the man you want to see?"

Dieter leaned closer and caught Janos's face between his hands. "You are the bravest son of a bitch I have ever met," he whispered and kissed him.

Chapter Twenty-One

Janos walked in a slow circle around the man.

Mike Llewelyn spread his arms, showing off the details of his costume. He was the third person to stand in front of Janos. Lea from the wardrobe department waited nearby, her arms folded over her chest, her eyes narrowed.

"Who are you?" Janos asked in German.

Llewelyn didn't hesitate. "I'm a labourer. I've come south because the crops failed in my village, and I need work."

"Where did you get money for to buy drinks?" Janos said, stopping in front of him. His German wasn't as good as Dieter's, but the people the team would encounter would be the same.

"I helped a trader on the road," Llewelyn said. "His cart was broken. He gave me coin when I helped him to fix it."

Janos nodded. It was a good answer. He didn't *have* to ask questions, but it caught Llewelyn off guard, and the agents needed to be tested. As he checked the clothing, he asked about the weather, the village Llewelyn was meant to have come from, whether he knew this family or that family.

Llewelyn only stumbled once or twice, but it was enough to refer him to Dieter for another grilling. They each had their roles to play in preparing the team. He had to make sure they looked right, and Dieter had to make sure they sounded right.

"I will see your hands," he said, lapsing into English.

Llewelyn held both out, palms down.

Janos took one hand in his and turned it over, examining the fingers, and shook his head. "Too clean. Too soft. It is not obvious thing, but people see small things that are not right." He rubbed his chin pensively. "Put hands into salt. It will dry skin." He met the man's eyes. "It may be hurtful."

"We could get the makeup team in," Lea said from the side of the room.

Llewelyn shook his head. "We need it to be realistic. Salt'll dry them out. Makeup can make them dirtier."

"You will need much dirt," Janos added. "Men in farm, they do not wash. You will need skin to be brown from sun also. In summer, skin is red, then is brown." He tapped at the stubble on Llewelyn's chin. "This is good. Is messy."

"And the hair?"

Janos inspected Llewelyn's thatch of thick, dark hair. "It must be cut. Not so neat. Not so clean."

"And the clothing?" Lea asked curtly.

Janos stepped away, studying it critically. "It does not look old enough. It must look more used. Old stains washed, but still there. It is dirty, but it is new dirt, not old enough for a poor man. Poor man has two clothes—work clothes and church clothes. Work clothes must be tired like man. Make places where it is fixed. Where holes were. Loose thread."

"Easy enough," Lea said with a nod. "What kind of holes? Cuts from a blade? Or worn through?"

Janos frowned in thought. "What work do you do?" he asked Llewelyn.

"Field," Llewelyn replied at once. "Cutting, ploughing, reaping, carrying."

It brought back memories in a rush. Janos stepped closer and traced a curved line across Llewelyn's right thigh. "Make wearing here," he said to Lea. "Like a sickle. Some men dry sickle between cuts to keep sharp."

Lea leaned forward and traced a faint line with chalk on the trousers. "Anywhere else?"

"Which shoulder you carry things on?" Janos said to Llewelyn. "Left or right?"

Llewelyn stared at him. "What?"

Janos gestured impatiently. "You have big bundle of sticks. You have to carry. Which shoulder?"

"Right, I guess?"

Janos sighed, shaking his head. "You must learn more. These are things all farm men do." He turned to Lea. "Maybe put patch on shoulder?"

"Where the cloth is wearing through from carrying things? And maybe on the elbows too? The fabric would get worn there."

Janos nodded in agreement, then took her chalk and marked out patches on the clothing to be aged, frayed, stitched, and torn as necessary. Only when he was satisfied did he stand back and watch the way Llewelyn walked and carried himself.

It was a long day.

People in this modern world walked too tall, too confident, too fast. To slow them down, to make them understand how people of their stations would be bent and worn, he weighed them down with sacks and tools.

Not one of them walked correctly when they arrived in the room to be trained. By the end of the lesson, not one of them walked out as tall as they had walked in.

Only once they were moving to his satisfaction did he let them go. He then took himself down to the level where the gymnasium and the pool were.

It was a fine way to end an afternoon of training: swimming as many lengths as he could until his body ached with pleasant exertion. He must have been in the water at least an hour, maybe more. Long enough for the building to clear of day workers.

Since he was now involved with the time jump, he was under orders not to interact with anyone outside the jump team. His meals were delivered to his room, and it was easier to go there than to risk crossing paths with others outside the jump team.

After a day of using nothing but his broken English and German, of being surrounded by people and chatter, of concentrating and training, closing himself in the quiet for a while seemed like a good idea. Except for an emergency, no one would intrude on him there.

He stepped into his room, let the door slide closed behind him, and shed his clothes as he crossed the room.

The one downside of the pool was that it reeked of chemicals, and the first thing he did after every swim was retreat to his shower and scrub himself until he didn't smell like a walking laboratory. The heat of the shower would ease the ache in his muscles too.

He turned the water on, letting it heat as he stripped out of the remainder of the clothing. It was strange how easy it was to do things one-handed now. Practice, he supposed. Still, he left them in a crumpled heap on the floor. Folding could wait.

He hissed through his teeth as the searingly hot water streamed down over his body. Raking his fingers through his hair, he tilted his face up into the stream, letting it pour over him. It was the height of luxury, the one thing he knew he could not go without, if he ever had to return to the place from whence he had come.

Soap was an afterthought, and even after he had scrubbed himself as much as he could, he braced his forearm against the polished tiles and rested his forehead against his fist.

The door opened behind him, the curl of cooler air against his skin raising gooseflesh.

A small smile twitched his lips.

Only four people had access to his rooms, and only one of them would feel so bold as to walk into the bathroom when he was showering.

Dieter's footsteps didn't make a sound, shoes—and probably clothes—already off, and Janos drew a breath as long-fingered hands came to rest on his hips. Lips pressed to his shoulder, then parted, and teeth nipped at water-warmed flesh. Playful, gentle, an offer.

Mutely, Janos leaned into him in invitation and inclined his head to one side, baring his throat.

Dieter's smile was palpable against his skin, and he dragged his tongue from Janos's shoulder up his throat to the corner of his jaw. His hands moved too, sliding around Janos's waist, one of them splaying on his belly, the other slipping lower to fondle his cock.

Janos closed his eyes as Dieter sucked on his earlobe, then tugged it with his teeth.

"I missed you."

Janos laughed breathlessly. "We had breakfast together." He spread his legs just a little, for better balance, as Dieter's hand wrapped around his cock, teasing it to hardness.

"I didn't mean that," Dieter murmured, pressing to his back, caught beneath the spray of the shower with him.

Janos knew what he meant. To allay suspicions within the offices and have some little privacy, they still only went out of the building once a week. More often than not, they would go to eat or to shows, but without fail, the end of the night would find them in bed together. Once a week wasn't enough, not when they still took breakfast together, and could see one another, but do nothing.

"We both wanted discretion," he murmured.

Dieter rocked his hips against Janos's backside. "Fuck discretion," he whispered, and bit the nape of Janos's neck. Janos swore, letting his head fall forward, and Dieter chuckled in wicked delight.

His mouth moved down, then, his tongue tracing every jut of Janos's spine, his free hand outlining every scar on Janos's torso. It slipped to Janos's hip as Dieter's mouth moved lower and lower, and Janos cursed raggedly, pressing his forehead to his fist, as Dieter's hand shaped the curve of his rear.

Dieter released his cock, and Janos opened his mouth to protest until warm, wet lips pressed to the base of his spine. His hips jerked of their own accord, and he felt Dieter smile again, the smug little bastard, as he squeezed both of Janos's cheeks, then traced his tongue up the crease of Janos's backside.

Janos lifted his head enough to bite at his knuckles, shivering, as Dieter's mouth pressed against him, his tongue teasing as his hands kneaded at Janos's ass. He dragged his tongue in long strokes, and the flicker of the lip ring on skin made Janos shudder down to his toes.

Janos shifted his weight from one foot to the other, unfolding his arm to reach for his cock. One of Dieter's hands slid between his legs, cupping his balls, squeezing them, and Janos released a rasping breath through his teeth as their fingers brushed against each other.

"Dieter..." he panted out and then swore in surprise when Dieter bit him on the ass. He twisted around to see Dieter rising from his knees, grinning like an imp. His hair was soaked, plastered on his head, and his eyes were shining.

"What?" he said. "It looked as ripe as a fucking peach."

Janos abandoned his cock to catch the back of Dieter's head and pulled him the rest of the way up to kiss him. Dieter pressed him against the tiles, one hand combing through Janos's hair, the other reaching down between them, closing around both their cocks.

Dieter drew away from the kiss, his lips parted and swollen. He looked debauched, and his smile was wicked as he moved his hand. Janos inhaled sharply as Dieter's hot, hard cock rubbed against his.

"Better?" Dieter said with mocking innocence. His fingers tightened, and Janos couldn't say what was better: the pressure of Dieter's water-slicked hand or the throbbing warmth of Dieter's cock against his.

It didn't matter, he decided, pulling Dieter's lips to his, wrapping his other arm around his lover. Dieter leaned up into him, rocking his hips and moving his hand, and his tongue slid against Janos's with the same steady strokes.

Janos pulled away to tug at Dieter's lip ring with his teeth, his fingers tangled in Dieter's hair, and he swallowed hard, unable to tear his eyes from Dieter's face. The water still streamed over them both, and Dieter shook his head, laughing as spray flew, his throat bare and inviting kisses and bites, and Janos lowered his head obligingly.

Dieter's hand and hips kept moving, and Janos licked the water from his skin, catching the flavour of him as he left ruddy marks on Dieter's pale skin. It made his cock throb to draw away and gaze at his mark on Dieter, knowing he'd wear high collars to keep their secret.

He hissed as Dieter bit his earlobe again, his arm tightening against Dieter's back.

"Come for me," Dieter murmured, shifting his grip and dragging his hand up. He had a ring on, and it teased up Janos's cock with the same sensation that the lip ring would have. "I want you to come in my hand."

Janos made a small, explosive sound as his cock tensed. He didn't know if it was the words or the sensation or both, but his hips jerked, and Dieter stroked rapidly. Janos's head knocked against the tiles as, panting, he came, spatters of cum spilling over Dieter's erect cock and washing away in the misty spray from the shower.

Dieter grinned like the cat who had both the cream and the canary.

"Satisfied?" Janos said mildly, fighting a smile, as Dieter released their cocks.

To his surprise, Dieter shifted his weight, straddling Janos's thigh with both of his.

"Not quite," he said and buried his face against Janos's neck, his mouth leaving delightful, stinging marks along Janos's throat as he started to rock his hips against Janos's, his cock stroking up Janos's thigh relentlessly.

Janos curled his fingers in Dieter's hair, kneading the back of his neck until Dieter shuddered, and his cock twitched, leaving a trail of cum on Janos's thigh.

"Mm." Dieter's lips were close to his ear. "Now, satisfied."

"Little pervert," Janos snorted, though he made no move to push him away. He traced his fingers in a circle at the nape of Dieter's neck. "There aren't security cameras in here?"

Dieter nuzzled his throat. "Who gives a fuck?" he murmured, one of his hands lingering on the scar curved across Janos's right side.

That made Janos withdraw. "You were the one who asked that we keep this arrangement outside of work," he reminded him. "Against regulations, you said."

Dieter pulled a face, stepping from under the full force of the shower. "Don't start," he said with a sigh, rubbing both hands over his face. "Can't we just enjoy a minute of post-coital whatever?"

"I only want to understand what is permitted," Janos said. "This is all new for me."

Dieter lowered his hands. "I know. I'm sorry. I'm a selfish prick just now." He caught Janos's hand and pulled him under the spray, then gathered the soap and started lathering them both. "The next jump's in two days, and everyone's on edge." He looked up at Janos. "I just want to say fuck the regulations, just for a few minutes."

Janos laughed, rubbing a smear of bubbles across Dieter's chest. "Instead you said 'fuck the Hungarian,' I guess?"

Dieter's grin returned. "Maybe a little. He lifted a hand and left a blob of bubbles on the tip of Janos's nose. "I can't wait until this one's over. First time in five months, I'll have a week off."

Janos had been trying not to think about it. As much as he was settling in at the agency, and as much as he was trying to forge new friendships, the thought of Dieter being absent, even for a week, was jarring. He let the water rush across his face.

"Do you have plans?" he asked when he withdrew, shaking water from his hair.

Dieter scooped water onto Janos's chest, rinsing away the last of the soap. "I was going out of the city. Somewhere with no buildings and lots of fresh air." He turned the shower knob until the water slowed and then stopped. "Maybe up the coast if the weather isn't bad."

"That sounds pleasant," Janos admitted, stepping out of the shower and reaching for the towel.

Arms wrapped around his waist from behind. "I hoped you'd say so." Dieter propped his chin on Janos's shoulder. "I've got us a nice hotel room where we can fuck as often as we like without having to worry about getting a slap on the wrist."

Janos turned his head, startled. "I'm coming with you?"

Dieter gave his cock a playful squeeze. "Well, it's more fun that way." He pecked Janos on the lips and stole the towel from his hand. "You sound surprised."

"It's your break from this place," Janos said, bewildered. "Why would you take me with you?"

"Two reasons," Dieter replied cheerfully. "One, you're not work. And two, you like fucking me as much as I like fucking you." He snatched the other towel and tossed it at Janos. "If you want to stay here, you can, but I'd like to see you in the great outdoors, on your back in the long grass." He shrugged, a wicked smile on his face. "If you don't want to…"

Janos closed the gap between them and kissed Dieter hard. "I want to."

"Let me guess." Dieter sighed, poking at his chest. "You just want to see grass and nature. Nothing at all to do with my fine piece of man meat."

Janos made a noncommittal sound, swaying his hand from side to side, though he had to bite his lip to keep from grinning.

Dieter flipped up his middle finger, laughing. "Dickhead," he said happily. "Now get dressed so we can go and eat. I'm fucking starving."

Chapter Twenty-Two

The team was lined up, ready to go into the temporal chamber.

Janos did his last checks, making sure nothing could be considered too modern. Dieter watched him as he paused at Downie, instructing her how to tuck her hair away beneath the cloth cap she wore. She rolled her eyes at him, still smiling.

"He's doing well." Sanders stood with Dieter at the foot of the stairs leading into the hallway and temporal chamber. "Seems to have gained some confidence in the last few weeks."

Dieter kept his eyes on the team. He didn't want to think how much trouble he could get in for fucking one of the historical artifacts. Or how much it would scare the hell out of Janos. The poor sod was still adjusting to the concept of coming out, and the idea of anyone seeing them interacting like lovers terrified him.

"He just wanted to be useful," he said. "I think it helps that they've listened to him."

"Well, he was talking sense." Sanders was silent for a moment. "How about you?"

Dieter blinked at him in confusion. "What about me?"

"Your first involvement in a new jump since our Hungarian came through. You all right?"

Dieter glanced at the open doorway, remembering that night, months ago, when he walked into the confines of the temporal chamber to face a madman with a gun.

He remembered the terror well, the smell, and the taste of vomit on his tongue, but with everything he'd learned about Janos since then, the fear had gradually started to give way to other and unexpected emotions. The nightmares had become less frequent, though they weren't completely gone, but less was better than more.

"You've got someone guarding the gate this time," he said lightly. "At least I won't end up on soldier-sitting duty again."

Sanders was studying him with the stern expression he usually reserved for his kid. The expression that said, "I could call you on your bullshit, but I won't because I'm trusting you to come to me if you need help".

Still, Dieter felt like he had to say something. "It's all gone smoothly this far. I don't see why I should be worrying about anything. I've got no reason to go into the temporal chamber. I won't have someone point a gun at me." As an afterthought, he added, "It's fine."

Sanders exhaled. "I want you to take this one easy. You and Nagy. This must be strange for him as well. You can watch the departure, then I want both of you to go to the mess and relax, okay? We'll find you there if anything comes up, but it's not going to."

Dieter knocked his hand on the railing of the staircase. "Easier said than done," he said quietly. He turned to Sanders. "Just make sure we don't get any surprise visitors, and I'll be fine."

Sanders nodded. "I can guarantee it."

"All are prepared," Janos said, calling their attention. He returned to the staircase. "This is good as able." He glanced at Dieter, a worried frown creasing his brow as Sanders walked over to talk to the team. Janos stepped a little closer, switching to Hungarian, his voice lowered. "Is something wrong?"

"Just remembering the last time I was here," Dieter murmured.

Janos glanced over his shoulder. "It was in there?"

Dieter nodded. He laughed a little unsteadily. "At least I don't have to go in. And Sanders has given us the afternoon to relax as soon as the team go. Can't leave the building, but we can watch a movie or something."

To his surprise, Janos reached up and touched his hand on the railing, clasping his fingers lightly. It was only a split-second of contact but enough to make Dieter's breath catch.

"It won't happen again," Janos said. "You know this."

Dieter nodded. "Come on. We should go upstairs. We can watch the departure from the console room."

Sanders joined them several minutes later.

"Team is in the layover chamber," one of the techs said. "Awaiting connection."

Janos approached the desk to watch the screen as the connection to the temporal field hooked up. The lights flickered, and the coding on the screen rolled by in screeds of text and code. Dieter couldn't understand the science behind it all, but he could tell it looked fucking impressive.

"This is like telegraph, yes?" Janos said to the tech. "Instead of message, you are sending connection to another time?"

"Something like that," the tech said, astonishment clear on his face. "You mind stepping back a little, sir? I need to concentrate on this?"

Janos nodded at once, taking a step back but keeping his eyes on the screen, fascinated.

Dieter came alongside him. "You understand it?"

"Some of it," Janos said. "It uses a lot of power."

"You have no idea," Sanders said. "We have to stockpile power for months before we can attempt a temporal link, otherwise the energy companies may start wondering why we're using so much in one go. It's why we can only open the portals once every few months."

Janos nodded solemnly, then swore in surprise as the temporal chamber was flooded with light. "This is the connection?"

Sanders held up his hand to silence Janos. "Connection is formed," he said briskly, once the light had dimmed. "Team to the temporal chamber." They watched as the agents filed into the chamber. "Downie, dispatch the scanner."

"Scanner?" Janos murmured.

"To make sure there's no one around to see someone step out of thin air," Dieter replied just as quietly in Hungarian. "Like you."

Janos glanced at him. "They should have known I was there?"

Dieter nodded. "We don't know why it didn't register your presence."

"I know," Janos said, studying the screen as the scanner readings scrolled across it. "People are warm. That's what a scanner will identify. I was cold, half-frozen, and hiding in the dirt." There was a tightness in his voice. "A scanner wouldn't find something near-dead."

Dieter glanced at him. Janos said so little about what he'd been through, but when he did, it was hard to hear it. Dieter had seen the state of the man when he arrived, but he made the same assumption as everyone else: a soldier would only have been wounded by enemies during wartime. He felt like a fucking idiot in hindsight.

Without saying a word, he brushed his hand against the base of Janos's back.

"All clear, boss," one of the other techs said. She typed rapidly on her keyboard. "We have a wet day as well, and we're emerging late-afternoon."

"Good time," Dieter said, stroking his hand in a soothing circle on Janos's back. "It'll be when the day is winding down, and if it's raining, a lot of people will have retreated indoors, so there's less chance of witnesses."

"You hear that, Downie?"

"Loud and clear," Downie replied. "Ready to depart."

Sanders glanced at the clock. "In five."

Next to Dieter, Janos tensed as the doorway opened. One by one, the agents stepped through, vanishing from sight. It looked strange, seeing them go.

"What does it feel like?" he asked Janos quietly. "Coming through the door?"

Janos shook his head. "Like walking through a sheet of ice. Like that, but not like that." He turned away from the screens. "We can go now?"

Dieter nodded. "Sanders, we'll either be in the mess hall or in Janos's room."

Sanders waved them away, his eyes on the screen in front of him.

Dieter led Janos into the hall.

"Remembering?" he asked.

Janos nodded. "I had prayed for someone to save me," he said distantly, "and then I saw a doorway. Light." He shook his head, his laugh brittle. "I thought I was dying, and I..." He ran his hand over face. "I wanted it then. I wanted to be free. At peace."

Uncaring of propriety, Dieter drew Janos around to face him and wrapped his arms around the man. "I'm glad you didn't," he confided, his lips close to Janos's ear.

"I too," Janos whispered.

Dieter stepped away. "Want to go to your room? It'll be quieter there. No one'll bother us."

Janos nodded.

His whole body was rigid with tension until they reached the room and the door closed behind them. He crossed the floor stiffly, sank onto the edge of the bed, and braced his forearm on his knees, his eyes on the floor.

"I didn't think it would trouble me," he admitted. "Seeing it from this side."

Dieter remained where he was, undoing the buttons of his coat. "It's strange, the things that bother us," he said, slipping the coat off and hanging it up on the handle of the wardrobe. He approached the bed, sat beside Janos, and squeezed his lover's knee. "If you could go back—"

Janos shook his head before Dieter finished speaking. "I couldn't. I was a coward in their eyes, a traitor. What would I have to return to but death?" He smiled tentatively at Dieter. "I think I might be happy here."

Dieter suspected he had a ridiculous soft look on his face. He put his other arm around Janos's shoulders and leaned against him, resting his brow against Janos's. "You're trying to make me cry, aren't you, you fucker?"

A wry smile twitched Janos's lips. "Is it working?"

"Is it hell," Dieter said with a snort, belied by the way his voice cracked. He gave Janos a warm squeeze. "Now, we've got some time to kill, so what do you want to do? Because if we're going to spend the next few hours being maudlin, I'd want to get the drinks in."

Janos covered Dieter's hand with his own where it rested on his knee. He watched as he drew his thumb along Dieter's knuckles. "We could see a movie. Something ridiculous."

"Here? Or down in the mess?"

Janos's hand went still, and he was silent for a moment. "Here," he said finally. "I don't think I want to be around other people now." He glanced at Dieter hopefully, cautiously. "Just us is okay?"

Dieter nodded, leaning in to kiss him gently. "Of course." He turned his hand and squeezed Janos's fingers. "How about I go and get us something to eat from the canteen, and you pick out a movie?"

Janos's smile returned. "That would be good."

Dieter was only gone ten minutes, but by the time he got back, Janos had found a dozen pillows and arranged them all along the bed and wall into a makeshift sofa. He'd propped the screen on a chair in front of it, and gave Dieter a grin which suggested he was half-embarrassed, half-pleased with his work.

"Well," Dieter said, biting down on a grin, "once you get out of designing peasant fashion for the 20th century, you could always go into interior decorating."

"Fuck you," Janos said, his smile flashing across his face.

Dieter laughed. "Maybe later." He set a tray down on the table. "Food and movie, or food first?"

In the end, they settled for both, lounging against the cushioned wall as they ate, but once the food was done and a second movie put on, Dieter found himself leaning less against the wall and more against Janos. Janos didn't seem to mind, and when Dieter drew his feet up and curled down on his side, resting his head in Janos's lap, Janos released a small, soft sigh.

His hand carefully came to rest on Dieter's shoulder, as if he expected to be brushed away. He was always so convinced he would be rejected or any sign of affection would be pushed away.

If someone had made that mistake, Dieter was going to do his damnedest to prove otherwise. He rubbed his cheek against Janos's thigh, nestling closer. He couldn't help smiling as the hand drifted down, and Janos curled his fingers into his hair, combing through it with such a calming, light touch, and Dieter's eyes drifted closed.

He was woken by Janos shaking his shoulder urgently.

Dieter lifted his head, squinting. The lights were on, blinding, and it took a moment to recognise Sanders standing several paces away. It took him another second to realise he was still sprawled across Janos's lap, and he scrambled up, flushing.

"Boss?"

"We have a problem," Sanders said tersely, jerking his head towards the door.

Dieter stepped into his shoes. Acid rose in his throat. The jump was meant to go smoothly. There weren't meant to be any problems. Sanders never needed to call on him. The last time he called on him, they'd ended up with Janos.

"I should wait here?" Janos asked in English. He sounded tense, and no wonder. They'd just been caught cuddled up like a pair of lovebirds when the man hadn't even felt ready to come out to anyone but Dieter.

Dieter glanced at Sanders, who nodded.

"Good idea." Dieter tried to smile reassuringly, but he had a feeling the expression fell flat. "You stay put. I'll come back once we're done."

Janos nodded curtly, his face pale.

Sanders stalked out the door and waited for Dieter to follow. He didn't speak as they set off down the corridor, and Dieter glanced back as the door of Janos's room slid shut. Christ, he was in trouble.

"Boss," he began. "What you saw..."

"Right now, I couldn't give a shit." Sanders swiped his card at the lift panel, and the doors slid open. He stepped inside and didn't look at Dieter as he said, "We have more to be worrying about than where you put your dick."

Dieter closed his eyes. "Another breach?"

"Worse," Sanders said, his voice clipped.

Dieter felt sick. "How bad?"

"Possibly terminal." Sanders walked forward as the lift doors opened. Doors along the corridor, which normally stood open, were closed, the locks illuminated. The hall felt longer, darker, more oppressive than usual.

The door of the console room opened at a swipe of Sanders's ID card, and a wall of sound poured out. Dieter didn't need to be told twice that everything had gone to hell, and what was meant to be a simple extraction had been fucked up beyond recognition.

"Any word?" Sanders snapped.

"Working on picking up the feed from his buttoncam," one of the techs said.

Another spoke up. "Borowski is kitting up to go through with the tracker."

Sanders strode across the room to the screens, Dieter hurrying after him. "Get the images on the screen as soon as possible," he said. "If we can get the last footage from the cam, we need Borowski to know what he's heading into."

"What the fuck's going on?" Dieter demanded.

"The extraction didn't go well," Sanders said. "Llewelyn and Downie had to break cover and split up. Llewelyn didn't make it to the gate. His cam is down, but we're trying to retrieve the last data."

"Shit," Dieter hissed. Agents were told to only destroy their cams if there was a chance of being uncovered.

"Sir!"

The screens filled with crackling, blurred images. Llewelyn had been running. Dieter's heart pounded hard against his ribs, and he leaned both hands on the back of the chair. The room was deadly silent, all eyes fixed on the screens.

Llewelyn had been running towards the forest, scrambling up shallow hills, grasping at roots and branches. The trees weren't close together, but the thick undergrowth was slowing him. He was shaking, and he jerked suddenly, as if something had pulled him to a halt. His hand flew up, grabbing at the button concealing the camera, and the signal cut out, dissolving into black.

Dieter straightened up, one hand to his mouth, smothering the "fuck" that was trying to escape. The technicians were all talking at once over one another.

"Was he just—?"

"Oh my God…"

"Sanders, what do we do?"

Sanders was staring at the black screens.

"Borowski!" he snapped.

"Sir?" Borowski's voice boomed from the speakers.

"He was close to the edge of the forest ten minutes ago. He may still be there. If possible, extract without intervention."

"If not?"

Sanders ran a hand over his face. "Follow protocol."

Dieter stared at him.

Everyone knew about the protocol. If an agent was compromised and could not be liberated, they could be left behind with the intention of an extraction at a later date. A place and a time was always allocated before a team went through the portal, but it had never happened before. It had never been necessary.

Every eye was on Sanders.

"Protocol?" Borowski echoed.

Sanders closed his eyes and drew a breath. "Yes. Now."

Borowski appeared on the screen showing the temporal chamber. He raised a hand in salute to the camera and stepped through the doorway, vanishing from sight.

Dieter stumbled a step, sitting heavily on the edge of one of the desks. "Jesus," he whispered.

Sanders pushed his glasses up and rubbed his eyes. "Downie, report. Is everyone else back in one piece?"

"Minor abrasions and bruises." Downie's voice echoed around the room. She was silent for a moment and then asked, "Where do you want us?"

Dieter glanced at Sanders. He had one hand braced on the desk, the other over his eyes, as if he was holding himself together by willpower alone. To give him a moment, Dieter stepped closer to the microphone.

"Get into the layover room and start decontamination," he said. "We'll need to debrief straight away." What he didn't say was they were going to need to work out what had gone so fucking wrong.

Sanders had straightened up. "Dieter. You're with me. The rest of you, keep tabs on Borowski. We don't want to risk losing anyone else."

Dieter fell into step behind him. "Boss..."

"Don't say a word, Dieter," Sanders said, his voice tight and terse. "We need to know what happened before we get the luxury of basking in our failure." He strode towards the elevator. "We're going into the layover room. You going to be okay?"

Fucking hell.

What could he say? He couldn't piss and moan about going into that room, not when they might have lost someone.

"I'll cope," he said.

Sanders glanced at him as they waited for the elevator. "You're a shit liar."

"Yeah, well I'm not going to piss myself this time," Dieter said, clasping his hands together behind his back to stop them from shaking. "Immediate debrief, right?"

Sanders nodded as they stepped into the elevator. "Something went wrong. We need to know what it was. And I don't need the rest of the home team panicking if they tell us it's worse than we expected."

Dieter's fingers were closed so tightly around his other hand the skin had grown colder. It was probably just his imagination, but it felt like the temperature was falling as they descended to the lower levels.

Christ, he didn't want to go in there.

The nightmares had eased off, at last. He could try to pretend he didn't still think about his lover accidentally shooting him right there, his blood and piss and vomit all over the shiny metal floor.

He flinched when Sanders grasped his shoulder. "Dieter?"

"I'm going to fucking do this," Dieter choked out. "I have to. It's a fucking room. That's all."

Sanders's hand tightened on his shoulder. "And you're not alone this time."

The elevator pinged, leaving them at the top of the staircase leading into the temporal chamber. Sanders took the steps three at a time, swiped his pass card, and went straight into the passage to the layover room.

Dieter took a shaking breath and followed.

The four members of the team turned in surprise when the door opened. No one usually entered the room during decon, and a lot of that was for privacy. The cameras were off in the room to let them change out of the historical clothing and into the jumpsuits they would wear until it had been confirmed they weren't contagious.

"Boss!" Downie stood up. She was already in her jumpsuit, but blood had seeped through at the elbow on one side and across her thigh. It reminded Dieter all too clearly of Janos and the blood and the stink. He braced one hand against the wall, forcing himself to breathe deeply and not run out of the room like a coward.

"Report," Sanders said tersely.

It became easier when Dieter closed his eyes and just listened. Just like any other debrief. Not inside that room. With his eyes closed, he could imagine they were in the conference room upstairs.

Downie spoke quickly, clearly. They'd gone to the inn and taken advantage of the cover of darkness. She'd entered to distract the guests, while Llewelyn scrambled up the wall outside and through the window. Something went wrong. The room was meant to be empty, but it wasn't. She heard the sounds of a struggle. Llewelyn rushed out, out of breath, bloodied, and told her to run.

"I don't know if we ran because we were being chased or we were being chased because we were running," she admitted. "People came after us. We split up to divert them and head back to the gate. Llewelyn told me to take the shorter route because he could run faster." She nodded towards the door leading to the temporal chamber. "I thought he'd gotten through before us."

Dieter risked a glance at their boss. Sanders had one arm crossed over his middle, the hand of the other rubbing at his beard. His whole face was a mass of lines, and he seemed wound as tightly as Dieter.

"How many were after you?" he asked.

She shook her head. "I didn't stop to count. Llewelyn yelled something in the inn. I think he was trying to distract them, but a lot of them ran out after us."

"You're hurt," Dieter said quietly.

Downie grimaced. "I had to jump a wall. Caught my arm and leg on the way down. Just superficial." She glanced at Sanders. "You sure you should be in here, boss? Decon isn't over."

"I'll risk it," he said. "I didn't want people panicking without cause."

Some chance of that, Dieter thought bitterly. There was fucking cause. The whole console room had seen the footage. They knew how bad it was.

"You saw the footage, boss," Melville said. She was a wiry, dark woman, very quiet. "Was he hurt?"

Dieter turned away. Of course all they knew was the footage showed where Llewelyn was. They didn't know he'd made himself the bait so his team could get home.

Sanders's face gave everything away.

Downie's lips tightened into a line. "You weren't exaggerating when you said to follow protocol."

Sanders shook his head. "Worst case scenario." He nodded to the door. "We wait until Borowski comes back, and then we'll see where we need to go from here."

Dieter swallowed down bitter acid in his throat. The idea of waiting there in the room, closed in on all sides with the smell of blood and dirt, was too much.

"Boss," he said quietly.

Sanders nodded. "Wait at the stairs."

Dieter gratefully fled from the room to the welcoming rush of warm air in the staircase. He crumpled onto the bottom step, gulping in ragged breaths, propping his elbows on his knees and burying his face in his hands.

Jesus Christ, he had to pull himself together.

Sanders would need him to keep his head together if he was going to help them deal with this mess. The shit had hit the fan, and everyone was getting splattered. He couldn't just plead fucking panic attack and go and hide.

Part of him wanted to run up and find Janos and reassure himself that everything in that room was in the past. But the other part of him didn't want to set foot near his lover again until he could do it without thinking about that night.

Sanders wanted him there for a reason. He knew the history and what was meant to be going on in that place and time. He would be able to put his finger on whatever wasn't right. He should have known. There had to be something there. If something had gone wrong, it was on him. He was the one providing the intel.

Dieter lifted his head from his hands, curling his fingers into fists, and knocked his forehead against his knuckles. Something was wrong. There had to be something he'd missed, and he couldn't see it.

It should have been straightforward. All Mike had to do was get in, scan the stuff with his cam, and get the fuck out. There wasn't meant to be any problem. No chases. No drama. No stupid heroics.

His knuckles pressing to his brow as he went over everything he'd collated, all the data he could think of. He knew the details inside out and backwards. He had checked, double-checked, triple-checked all the facts, and he couldn't see what he was missing.

"Shit," he whispered under his breath. "Buggering fucking cunting bastarding shit."

He didn't know how long he'd been sitting there when the door opened, but his head ached, and his chest hurt. He glanced up and scrambled to his feet.

"Boss? Is he...?" Dieter's words caught in his throat.

Sanders looked a dozen years older. He stared blankly at Dieter and opened his hand.

A broken circle of metal—smeared with dirt—lay in his palm.

"Is that..."

"Llewelyn's tracking cuff," Sanders said quietly, his voice flat and emotionless. "Broken off. Buried."

Dieter stared at it in incomprehension. "But why would someone take it off him?" he asked, frowning at Sanders. "Or bury it?"

Sanders stared dully at him. "They wouldn't."

Chapter Twenty-Three

Dieter had been gone for hours.

Janos tried not to worry, but they had been caught in a compromising position by the head of the agency. Sanders had gazed at him with a strange, flat expression as he waited for Dieter, and Janos felt the disapproval.

They were both in trouble, but it went further than that.

Sanders had come personally to get Dieter.

Something must have gone very wrong.

Janos tried to distract himself by tidying up the room, putting the pillows in order, stacking the plates. Tried was the right word. No matter how much he did, every time he looked at the clock, the time barely seemed to have moved on at all.

He didn't know what was more worrying: whether there was something seriously wrong on the mission or whether Sanders viewed him as others had viewed Szilveszter in the past. The man's expression had given nothing away, but it did little to comfort Janos. He and Dieter were breaking the rules, and they both knew it. And now, so did Sanders.

He paced the floor. He tried to sleep. He tossed and turned, and when the sky started to lighten, daylight cutting into his room, he knew it was useless.

Janos got up from the bed and went to the door.

Even if he was no use in the chamber, he had to at least know what was going on.

He swiped his pass over the security panel.

The light stayed red.

Janos frowned, swiping his pass again.

It remained red.

His first thought was a technical fault, but when he took up the radio to contact anyone who might assist him, it was also dead.

He was locked in, cut off.

Janos stared down at the dead radio, his heart pounding and his blood rushing in his ears.

It was like being in another time and another place. There were no bars, this time, and there was no blood on his skin, but the doors were closed on him and the walls thick, and there was no way out. The instinct to claw at the door overwhelmed him, but Dieter had said he was safe, and he had to believe it.

There was an explanation, he knew. A simple one.

Even the thought did little to ease the tension in his chest.

He resumed pacing, following the walls, his eyes fixed on the lines of the floor tiles, until he was dizzy with it. He didn't know how many circuits he did. He didn't care. It helped as the swimming had: a rhythm, a steady, repetitive pattern like the reaping.

The sun was high above the horizon when the door finally opened.

Janos spun to face it and was greeted by two wardens in uniform, unsmiling and grim.

He stared at them in incomprehension.

"Can I help you?"

"Mr. Nagy," one of them said. "You have to come with us."

He must have retreated, because the window was suddenly at his back. He remembered the morning of the tribunal. He remembered soldiers then, opening his door, taking him before the martial court.

"Why?" he asked, wishing he had a weapon, a knife, a gun, anything.

"Mr. Sanders needs to see you," the warden said.

His nails bit into his palm. "I am locked in. Why?"

"Everyone is. Please come with us."

Everyone.

It should have been a comfort.

Janos silently nodded, clipping his pass to his belt, and let them escort him out into the halls.

Normally, there were one or two people in the halls at all times. It was a busy building, but now, there was no one to be seen anywhere.

The wardens took him to the elevator and faced the doors as the elevator descended. Standing between them, Janos closed his eyes and took slow, steadying breaths, counting each one until the doors opened again.

Even in the main business level of the building, the halls were deserted. The whole building seemed empty, and for one so large, it was terrifying.

Janos clenched his hand by his side, following them past room after room until they reached a door and one of them swiped his pass across the key panel.

The door opened, and the wardens stepped aside.

"Only me?" Janos asked warily.

"Yes, sir."

Janos tightened his fist, pressing it against his thigh to stop it shaking, and stepped into the room.

The sight that greeted him made him stop dead.

The room was larger and brighter but otherwise the same. A figure of authority behind a broad table, papers spread out before him, his face stern. Sanders did not seem as he had only the day before, much grimmer, much more difficult to please.

Janos glanced to the window.

Dieter stood there, his back to the door, his arms folded over his chest. He hadn't even turned to acknowledge Janos.

Janos's heart plummeted.

Behind him, the door slid silently closed.

"Sir," he began awkwardly. "You saw..."

Sanders raised a hand. "I don't want to hear about it." He motioned to the seat on the opposite side of the desk. "Sit."

Janos approached and sat down. He folded his arm over his middle and wrapped his hand around his left elbow. At least this time, he didn't have to stand. At least this time, he didn't have the throb in his wounded arm and the gash across his ribs. His chest hurt, but for other reasons.

"You trained with members of our team," Sanders said, examining a file. "All of the team we sent through in the current jump."

"Yes." Janos remembered well how to speak to superior officers. "On your orders, sir."

Sanders raised his eyes from the page in front of him. "Agent Michael James Llewelyn. He spent a lot of time with you. Additional training?"

"Yes."

Sanders set the page down. "Elaborate."

Janos stared blankly at him. "What you mean?"

"Why did he want extra training? What did you teach him?"

Janos tightened his fingers around his arm. "He wanted to make ready for jump. He asked to check all things. He wanted no one notice." His arm ached from the pressure. "He wanted no catching again."

By the window, Dieter released a hissed breath between his teeth.

Sanders glanced at him and turned to Janos. "Did you teach him everything you could?"

Janos nodded, glancing warily towards Dieter, then to Sanders. Was that wrong? Was he meant to keep some things from the team? "It is asked of me. You ask for me to teach. Mike Llewelyn is good student. He learn many thing."

Sanders removed his glasses and rubbed his eyes. "Shit."

Janos darted another glance at Dieter. It had been a long time since he had seen Dieter so rigid and tense.

"What I have done?" he asked, his voice more unsteady than he wanted it to be. "I have done wrong thing?" He turned to Dieter pleadingly, lapsing into Hungarian. "Why am I brought here like a prisoner? What have I done? Was my information wrong? Did someone get hurt?"

Dieter finally turned, his face drawn and his eyes circled by shadow, fixed anywhere but Janos. "We need to explain, boss," he said quietly in English. "He did what we asked. He wasn't to know he was being used."

"Used?" Janos echoed.

Sanders leaned back in his seat, rubbing his face, and then nodded. "Fine." He waved a hand. "Give him the summary."

Dieter sat against the window ledge, his arms still folded tightly over his chest. His fingers bit hard into his upper arms, and he still didn't meet Janos's eyes. When he spoke, his voice was dull.

"We think Llewelyn has gone rogue," he said in Hungarian. "He created a diversion, separated from his teammate, removed his tracker, and abandoned the team and the mission."

Janos stared at him in confusion. "But why would he do that?"

Dieter finally raised his eyes to Janos's, and something bleak in his expression made Janos avert his gaze. "Because he's going to change something. We've searched his rooms and his home. He didn't leave much behind, but there's enough to give us an idea."

"What?" Janos asked.

Dieter shook his head. "Better you don't know." His gaze was on the floor again, and he rocked against the window ledge. He took a breath and turned to Sanders. "He knows," he said in English, his words clipped. "Except the target. You want to ask, you do it now or not at all."

Sanders rubbed his forehead. "There are other options," he said, looking at Dieter.

"You know he's the only one who could get anyone up to speed in every way in the time we have," Dieter snapped. "Let him make the decision."

Janos dug his fingers anxiously into his arm. Half the words they were saying held no meaning. Dieter turned away, bracing one hand against the window frame.

Sanders removed his glasses, folded them, and set them on the table.

"We need to get Llewelyn back before he can do anything," he said finally, his expression grave. "We can't use people from the same team, in case they were helping him. We need someone to be trained up as quickly as possible, to be ready for a jump in ten days."

Janos frowned. "You say this is bad. Why not go now?"

Sanders shook his head. "Not enough power. We had to keep the gate open too long to try and sort out this mess. Used what energy we had." He tapped at his computer, then turned it, showing Janos the screen. "We've calculated as best we can, and ten days is the soonest we can open the doorway long enough to send one operative through." He nudged the glasses with his fingertip, lining them up with the edge of the computer. "You made Llewelyn invisible. Now, we need you to do it again."

Janos squeezed his arm. One person had gone bad because of his assistance. "You think this good idea?"

Sanders gazed at him, expressionless. "It doesn't matter what I think. You have the knowledge we need for blending in. You can tell when someone is moving wrong, acting wrong, speaking wrong. We need to get someone there without drawing unnecessary attention. We won't make you do it, but we will ask you this one time."

"And this one, he will come back?"

Sanders nodded. "This operative would find and contain Llewelyn without damaging the timeline. And we would gather enough power to send a retrieval team just over a week later."

Janos chewed on his lower lip. "I can do this." Maybe by training someone as well as Llewelyn, he could make up for Llewelyn's treachery. "It is not problem."

He turned, frowning at the dull thump of Dieter's head knocking against the glass.

"God, I wish you hadn't said that," Dieter whispered.

Janos stared at him. "Why? Who is person?"

Dieter turned around. "The only person in the agency who knows the history of that time inside-fucking-out," he said quietly.

Janos felt like a fool as minutes ticked by before his mind understood what his ears were hearing. "No," he said abruptly in Hungarian. "No. You are not going there."

Dieter's face was pale, and he looked exhausted. "You think we have a choice?"

"Of course you have a choice!" Janos exclaimed. "You have many teams! You have many agents!" He rose with such violence the chair scraped across the floor. "You aren't an agent! You aren't trained to do this job, to go into such places!"

Dieter remained seated against the window ledge, calm and passive, but his eyes sparked fire. "And that's why we asked you," he said, his voice quiet and even, and too calm. "No one else in the agency knows the history as well as I do. I'd recognise people and places other agents wouldn't. You can't teach it in ten days. But you can teach me to move the right way and carry myself so I won't be noticed."

Janos's throat burned with acid, his insides churning. It was true he had hidden himself in plain sight for his whole life, but Dieter wasn't like him, too free-spirited, unaccustomed to hiding who he was from the rest of the world. It was true Dieter kept some secrets, but hiding himself? If he went, if he tried, he would be seen, he would be recognised for who and what he was, and it would end badly.

"You can't," Janos said.

Dieter straightened up. "You think I won't learn?"

"I think if you put a sheet over a piano, people will still know it is a piano. Some things about yourself, you can't hide!"

Dieter's expression went blank. "You think you know me so well. You know nothing about me."

Janos flinched. He put his hand on the back of the chair, squeezing it until his palm hurt. "I know you are afraid you will be like Llewelyn. You said it yourself—you don't think you could just stand by and watch people being hurt. And now, you want to go. Do you believe you can keep yourself from interfering?"

Dieter's lips compressed into a thin line, and he took a step forward, his eyes blazing. "I will do my fucking job," he said through clenched teeth. "I'm going, with or without your help. So do you want to be fucking useful or just fret and whimper like an old woman?"

Janos stared at him.

It was a simple choice.

Help Dieter to walk into a world that could turn on him and kill him in a heartbeat or let him do it without any help at all.

He released a shivering breath. "Very well. I will help. But you have to do everything I tell you to."

Dieter nodded. "Agreed."

Chapter Twenty-Four

"No!"

Dieter stopped midstep and set his foot down.

Two days until the jump, and he was exhausted. He hadn't gotten a solid night's sleep since he rested his eyes in Janos's room. It wasn't getting any easier.

"What the fuck did I do wrong this time?" he demanded, wheeling around to face Janos.

"You need to move like you normally walk this way," Janos said. "You're concentrating too hard. I can see it. Other people will see it. You're thinking about how you walk."

"Of course I am, you arse!" Dieter exclaimed. "I have to!"

Janos turned away, walking the length of the training room. His hand was clenching and unclenching by his side, and Dieter knew he was trying to keep his temper in check. Well, he could be pissed off all he liked. It wasn't helping anyone.

Dieter went to the table standing by the wall and filled a tumbler with water. The jug shook in his hand. He wasn't sure if it was anger, exhaustion, or the ever-growing knot of fear which had settled in the middle of his chest.

Janos turned around at the far end of the room. "You must get this right."

"You think I don't know that?" Dieter snapped. "Every time I do what you tell me, there's something else, and then something else. How the fuck do you expect me to remember everything when you keep on finding new fucking faults with every fucking thing I'm doing?"

Janos strode towards him. "You asked me to help you," he said, his voice a low growl, "so I'm helping you. You said you would do everything I told you to do, but when I tell you to do something, you don't."

"I'm doing every fucking thing you tell me! First I'm walking too straight, then too slow, then too fast. Will you make up your fucking mind and set a fucking pace for me to walk at?" He downed half the glass of water, then set the tumbler down. "Jesus Christ! Like anyone pays so much attention to one man!"

Janos drew a breath through his nose, his chest rising and falling, his face flushed. "You think people don't pay attention? How naïve are you? You think no one sees you? You think no one can tell there's something you are trying to hide?"

Dieter leaned against the edge of the table, bracing his palms against it. His hands shook. That tone, that anger, was too similar to their first encounter, and those memories made his breathing come harder.

"Tell me what I did wrong this time," he asked, his voice quieter, flat. Better to calm the Janos down. No more shouting. If he wasn't angry, Dieter could pretend he wasn't scared shitless and get on with the job.

Janos closed his eyes for a moment, then opened them. "You start walking, then you change your steps, and it shows on your face. As if you have remembered you're meant to be walking a different way. You have to start walking as if it's the same way you always walk. Think first, then walk. Don't walk then think."

Dieter nodded, pushing off from the table. "Is that all?"

"All?"

Dieter spread his hands. "Every time I start, there's something new. Tell me everything I'm fucking up at once. Tell me all the things that'll get me noticed. Are my hands still wrong? Or the speed? Or the way I lift my feet? How many more things am I going to get wrong before I'm ready?"

Janos gazed at him. "You will never be ready for this."

Dieter had to turn away, or he could have grabbed something and thrown it. It was the one thing he didn't need to be told. He knew he wasn't ready. Of course he knew. How the hell was he meant to be ready for anything like this?

"Just tell me," he said through clenched teeth. "I'm going through that fucking gate in two fucking days. Tell me how to do it."

Janos was silent for a moment. "Stop whining."

Dieter stared at the wall in front of him. "What?" he said, unable to believe his ears.

"You heard me," Janos said, his voice slow and deliberate. "Stop whining. You want to know what you're doing wrong? Everything. You are too afraid of being able to do this so you make mistakes."

Dieter turned around. "Afraid?"

Janos's jaw was set. "Yes. Afraid." He hooked his thumb through his belt, his knuckles white. "Like the boy who pissed himself at my feet."

Dieter stared at him, then took a step towards him. "You fucking bastard," he said, stalking across the floor, one step after another. "You're calling me a coward when you had a fucking gun in my face?"

They were close, nose to nose, and Janos leaned that little bit closer. "Yes," he said. "Because it's still true."

Dieter stared at him, the challenge in his expression, the accusation, and he was angry. Angry of being afraid. Angry Janos was right. Angry that it was all his fault that he had to think about it.

His arm swung before he could stop it, his fist crashing into Janos's face. It was a crap punch, but so close, it knocked Janos reeling.

"What the fuck are you trying to do?" Dieter whispered, clutching his throbbing hand. "How the fuck is this going to help anyone?"

Janos lifted his head, wiping a trickle of blood from his burst lip. "Because when you're angry, you don't think so hard," he replied quietly. "And when you don't think so hard, you'll stay alive." He gazed at the blood on his fingertips then up at Dieter, his eyes too bright. "I will not have someone else I care about die because they can't hide who they are."

Dieter stared at him.

"Care about?" he finally said. "What the fuck is that?"

Janos shrugged.

Dieter shook his head. "If this is some new mind game to get me angry, it's not funny." He pushed by Janos and headed for the door.

"Where are you going?"

Dieter spun around. "I'm having a break, okay? I don't need to hear about you caring about shit, okay? We have a fucking job to do, and if you're just going to wind me up, I'm having a fucking break."

Dieter's rapid walk turned into a run down the deserted, quiet corridors because he didn't trust himself not to turn around and go and give the arsehole a piece of his mind.

How could he do that? Using that...that night against him when Dieter was about to go into a time jump and needed to focus? What kind of sick fuck was he to use it as a tool to make Dieter angry?

He was ascending the stairs when another thought crept up on him.

What if he was serious?

Dieter stopped and leaned heavily on the banister. "Shit," he whispered, the sound echoing off the walls.

It wasn't meant to be complicated. It was meant to be sex, nothing more. He wasn't meant to get attached. He could think of it as fucking and nothing more, and that was good. But now? Now, Janos used words like "care," and, Jesus Christ, it couldn't have come at a worse time.

He peered up the stairwell, wondering if Sally would be in, and wondering how much she would care to listen to him and the details of his tragic love life. Shit! No. Not love life. It wasn't serious. It couldn't be serious.

No.

He couldn't go to her. He couldn't out Janos to her, just to make himself feel better.

There were only two people in the whole agency who knew, and Sally wasn't one of them.

He made his way up the stairs, trying to gather his thoughts, but it felt like trying to hold onto handfuls of sand. It was too much, on top of everything else, and he needed to talk to someone, which was why he headed straight for the HR offices.

Half of the agency was on lockdown, but he had access to everywhere, and the HR department was still working, though they didn't have much they could do.

All eyes turned to him when he stepped through the door, and it took him a moment to remember he was dressed like a 20th-century civilian who looked like he'd been dragged arse backwards through a hedge.

Paul rose from his desk, frowning. "Dieter?"

Dieter rubbed his forehead. "I need to talk to you," he said, too tired to pretend everything was all right.

Paul didn't even look askance at his team leader. He just got up from his desk. "There's an empty office down the hall."

Dieter didn't wonder why he'd get up and walk away from his desk. It was because of what was going on.

Paul ushered him into the room, one hand between Dieter's shoulders, and closed the door behind them.

"What's wrong?"

Dieter crossed the room to the window and gazed down at the city below. "What isn't?"

"So it's true you're doing the jump." Paul dragged the seats out from beside the desks and pushed one to Dieter.

"No, I'm dressed like this for fucking fun," Dieter whispered, staring at his reflection in the glass. He wouldn't have recognised himself. He didn't look like himself, so how would anyone in the past be able to see him for who he was?

Paul sat down, gazing at him. "Sit," he said.

Dieter did so and knocked his knuckles together in front of him. What was he meant to say? He didn't talk about lovers. He didn't have lovers. He had one-night stands and people he fucked from time to time, but he didn't have lovers.

He stared at his hands and said quietly, "I've been fucking Janos."

Paul sighed. "Yeah. I thought you might have been."

Dieter glanced up at him, startled. "What?"

"I might have mentioned to him that you fancied him."

Dieter's mouth opened in shock. "You did what?"

"I was sick of seeing you getting strung along," Paul replied with a shrug. "You were miserable, and he had no idea you fancied him. I dropped a hint."

Dieter leaned back in the seat. "Jesus Christ on a submarine. I wondered what made him..." He shook his head, gazing across at Paul. "He's training me for the jump, and the silly sod just came out and said he cares about me."

Paul's eyebrows rose. "You're surprised?"

"Of course I'm fucking surprised!" Dieter exclaimed. "It was only meant to be sex!"

"The hell it was," Paul said with a snort.

"What the fuck do you mean by that?" Dieter demanded.

"How many people do you get to know well before you sleep with them? You always said you're in it for the sex, not for the personality. How many times did you get to know someone before you fancied them?"

Dieter flushed. "Well, he wasn't meant to fucking care!"

Paul gave him a rueful smile. "Die, you're a nice guy, but you're thick as shit sometimes. I'm a serial shagger. I know it, and you know it. But even I can tell your Hungarian isn't. He wouldn't just shag anyone."

Dieter buried his face in his hands. "Shit," he whispered. "Shit, shit, shit."

Paul leaned over and squeezed his knee. "Is it a bad thing?"

"It is when I'm going into the fucking past and I'm expected to stop one of our agents from..." He caught himself before he let slip the target and shook his head. "Paul, I'm not ready for this. I'm not ready to be an agent or have someone declaring they like me."

Paul shook his head with a crooked smile. "No one ever is. On both counts. Think of it this way— Do you like the man?"

Dieter nodded. "More than I should."

"Problem solved, then. You like him. He likes you. Enjoy it."

Dieter rubbed his forehead with two fingertips. "It's not that easy."

"Because you're going into the past?"

"Because he's a relic of it. For fuck's sake, he might have latched onto me because I was friendly with him. Or because I'm the first piece of eye candy who didn't run a fucking mile because he's a queer."

Paul didn't say anything, just raised his eyebrows.

"What?" Dieter demanded.

"I didn't say anything," Paul replied, holding up both hands. "I'm only saying you've got someone who gives a damn. Why not see where it goes?"

Dieter covered his eyes. "I knew I should have gone to Sally."

"She wouldn't give you any better answer. You know Sally. She'd give you tea and wait until you answered your own questions, and you'd be more pissy than you are right now."

Dieter peered between his fingers. "You're right." He pushed his fingers through his hair. It was unkempt, lank, and heavy without any gel or product, and he withdrew his hand, wrinkling his nose. "I must look like a fucking hobo."

"It's not actually too bad," Paul said, putting his head to one side. "I didn't recognise you without the blond."

Dieter squinted up at the shaggy dark mass hanging over his forehead. "Welcome to Dieter's natural colouring," he said with a snort. "I look like a reject from Goths-R-Us."

"At least it's only temporary. When you come back..."

"If."

Paul frowned at him. "When you come back, you can go all the colours of the rainbow. You've been trained. You're smarter than you think. You'll be able to pull this off, and Sanders'll give you a bonus."

"Yes. The bonus of not firing me for getting involved with one of the historical artifacts."

"I heard one of the girls from the Spain mission got frisky with one of the toys she found. So you're not the first."

Despite himself, Dieter smiled crookedly. "You're trying to cheer me up now?"

Paul shrugged. "I'm guessing you need it. How long is it since you've had a break from this training?"

Dieter shook his head. "No fucking clue."

"Right." Paul got up. "You're coming with me, and we're going to order in something to eat, and you're going to think about something that isn't this time jump for half an hour." He straightened his tie. "I'm your HR boss. I get to tell you what to do."

Dieter got up. "Christ, Paul, why couldn't I just fancy you? It would be so much easier."

"But then," Paul replied, "it wouldn't be half as satisfying." He caught Dieter's shoulder. "Come on, you daft sod. Let's get some food into you, and you can tell me how good a fuck this Hungarian is to get you all hot and bothered."

Dieter felt like a fucking schoolboy with a crush. "It's not that big a deal."

Paul snorted. "You're still a crap liar. I want details." He flung his arm around Dieter's shoulder. "You owe me that much."

"Pervert."

"And proud of it."

Chapter Twenty-Five

It was late.

Janos was worried, but it wasn't as if he could do anything about it.

He had admitted far more than he intended in the training room, hours earlier, and Dieter had stormed out. It was too much. You didn't tell someone you cared for them, not so soon, but he couldn't help it. Every time Dieter hesitated or his step faltered or his mask slipped, all Janos saw was Szilveszter's corpse.

It was true Dieter would be going to a time before the war, before the first war, but people like them were still treated with suspicion in those days. If he let even a little of himself show forth, he could be laid in the dirt, blood on his skin, his throat opened like smiling lips.

Janos paced in the training room for a while, but when it became clear Dieter did not intend to return at once, he returned to his own room. There was little to divert him, but he didn't want to go down to the pool in case Dieter returned.

So he lay on his bed and stared at the ceiling, and tried to push away the thought that he might have ruined everything between himself and someone who had become so important to him. Stupidity and sentimentality had made him speak. Dieter didn't need to know.

Janos closed his eyes, pressing his hand over his chest. He slid his fingers down his side and traced the narrow scar that had so nearly ended his life. He couldn't remember how Sanyi had worked out his secret.

All he knew was the man had spoken over the fire, mocking, taunting, insulting.

It was a bad night, that night.

He tried to be the better man, and told Sanyi to talk again when he had less drink in him, but Sanyi would not be silenced. When Janos got up and walked away, Sanyi followed him, hurling abuse at him. Between the rows of tents, Janos had turned to face him and made the greatest mistake he could have in challenging the man to fight him.

Sanyi was much bigger and stronger, and if he had been sober, the wound to Janos's torso would have been deeper and fatal. What Janos expected to be a brief scuffle turned bloody all too fast. His arm and chest were both sliced open before he managed to twist the knife away, and Sanyi lunged at him.

Desperation made a man mighty.

Janos couldn't remember what he did, but Sanyi fell away from him, blood spurting in ruddy gouts from his throat. He dropped, clutching at the wound as if he could stop it, the blood pooling around him on the ground, gleaming wetly in the dancing firelight. Sanyi cursed as he died, wide-eyed, shocked.

A sane man would have run then, but Janos felt rooted to the spot. He had killed before in battle, but this wasn't battle, not really. He stared down at the spreading dark stain, and Sanyi's friends were suddenly there, surrounding him, and Janos still had the bloody knife in his hand. So heavy. He couldn't remember taking it.

He was arrested, of course, but not before Sanyi's friends beat him.

It was the only reason he lived long enough to escape: they had to let his wounds heal so he could stand on his own two feet to face judgment. There was no sport in killing a man who could not lift himself from the ground. They caged him, spat on him, and when he was strong enough, they tried and condemned him.

Janos sat up, his breath coming in shaking gusts, and buried his face in his hand.

No one had ever known his secret but those he shared it with, yet someone had found out, and his life was turned upside down. If he—with so many years of experience masking himself—could be uncovered...

But Dieter was clever. Dieter had fooled everyone. They all thought he was unafraid even after everything that had happened to him. They didn't know about the nightmares. They didn't know he hid behind the laughing, smiling scholar.

Did any of them really know Dieter? Did he?

Janos rose from the bed and went to the small stove to warm some food. He could have gone down to the canteen, but he didn't want to face more people. He didn't want to face Dieter, not yet anyway. So he warmed some kind of pasta in sauce. It wasn't much, but it was food, and while he ate, he tried to distract himself with history books of a time before his own.

It was dark outside when he finally gave up and shed his clothes to retreat to bed.

With the shutters open, the lights of the city tinted the room in dim shades of blue and gold. He gazed at the ceiling, watching the patterns of light change as traffic came and went, and buildings darkened one by one.

It must have been close to midnight when the door slid silently open. The rectangle of light silhouetted a familiar shape, and Janos raised himself on his arm, startled.

"Dieter?"

One hand was held up.

"Don't speak," Dieter said quietly. His pronunciation was much more careful than usual, as if he was having to concentrate. "I need to tell you things."

Janos nodded mutely as the other man stepped into the room. The door slid closed, and for a moment, as Janos's eyes readjusted, Dieter was just a patch of shadow in the darkness.

"I'm scared." It was said with the simplicity of a child.

"Of what?" Janos asked quietly.

Dieter took two steps towards the bed and stopped. "You. This thing we have." He wrapped his arms around his middle. "Going there. Fucking up. Dying like people do in war zones. Being afraid." He laughed, unsteadily, and swayed on his feet. "Everything."

He came close enough for Janos to see him in the faint light, pale and trembling. "Don't be angry with me because I'm fucking terrified."

"I'm not angry with you," Janos whispered. "I'm scared too."

Dieter laughed, a strange, brittle sound. "Why? You're not going."

"No," Janos said unhappily. "I'm not. I wish I was." He curled his fingers into the blanket. "I don't want to lose you."

"Am I so useless?" Dieter sounded miserable. "Do I fuck up that much?"

"No. But I didn't, and neither did the last man I loved, and he's dead, and I almost was too." He met Dieter's eyes. "I don't want you to end up like he did. I don't want to see you get hurt or killed."

"Because this isn't just fucking, is it?" Dieter rocked on the balls of his feet as if he was getting ready to run. He didn't have shoes on, just socks. "This hasn't ever just been fucking."

Janos watched his fingers as he plucked at the sheet. "Not for me."

"Why?"

He curled his fingers. "You were kind to me when you should have been cruel, patient when I was unpleasant. You spoke to me because you knew no one else could. You helped me, without any motives, though you were afraid of me. You are one of the bravest men I have met." He gazed up at Dieter. "How could I not love a man like that?"

"You forgot fucking gorgeous," Dieter whispered, though his voice broke.

"Are you?" Janos cautiously teased.

Dieter sniffed quietly. "Piss off," he whispered, his voice tiny. "Prick."

Janos's lips twitched. Wordlessly, he lifted the blanket in invitation. There was enough room in the bed for two to curl close together. Dieter stared at him for so long he wondered if he had maybe misinterpreted, but Dieter shrugged off the shirt and coarse trousers and left them in a heap on the floor.

Pale and sleek in the faint neon lights, he slipped into the bed, curling with his back to Janos's chest, shivering, cold.

Janos drew the sheets and blankets close around them and slipped his arm around Dieter's chest. Dieter groped for his hand.

"You're cold," Janos said quietly as Dieter pressed closer to him.

"I was on the roof," Dieter replied just as quietly. "Spoke to Paul. Went up there to think. Drink too." He blew out a noisy breath. "Only way to make the words come out."

Janos propped himself up a little on his left arm. "Are you very drunk?"

Dieter tilted his head up at him. "Enough." A tentative smile crossed his lips. "Said things. More than usual." He clumsily patted Janos's cheek, puzzled. "And you love me, you silly fuck."

Janos lowered his head and kissed him lightly on the lips. "Not one of the smartest things I have ever done."

"Yes I am!" Dieter said with alcohol-softened indignation.

Janos gazed down at him.

In two days, Dieter would be gone through the gate, and neither of them knew if he would be coming back. They could hope, but both of them knew there was no guarantee.

It wasn't the time to say it, or to think it.

Janos leaned down instead and kissed him.

Dieter murmured drowsily into the kiss, shifting slowly, his hips rocking in wordless encouragement against Janos's. It was a gentle way to be roused, as their lips parted and their tongues slid against one another.

It felt strange to kiss Dieter without the ring through his lip, and with the beginnings of a beard, but it was no less welcome. Sweet wine clung to Dieter's lips.

Slender fingers circled Janos's wrist, guiding his hand downward. He lifted his head to watch the way Dieter's eyes pressed closed and how his lips parted in a sigh as Janos's warm fingers stroked his cock.

Janos moved his hand, tightening his grip little by little as Dieter's cock swelled and hardened against his palm. While the rest of him was still cold, his cock was hot. Janos pressed his lips to Dieter's shoulder. Dieter tilted his head to nuzzle at Janos's cheek.

"Can I stay?" he asked in a whisper.

Janos chased his lips over Dieter's, teasing with not-quite-kisses. "I'd be offended if you didn't," he murmured, smiling as Dieter tangled his fingers in Janos's hair, holding him in place so he could steal a kiss.

It seemed drink made him more playful in his affection. He nipped at Janos's lower lip, and his tongue soothed the bite, as he rolled his hips against Janos's groin, making his cock stir against Dieter's bare ass.

"Good," Dieter murmured, finally breaking the kisses. The tip of his nose brushed Janos's. "Want to have a good fuck before I go."

Janos stroked up and down, sliding his cock against the crease of Dieter's backside. "Only one?"

To his amusement, Dieter giggled. "Don't get fucking ambitious," he said, though his words trailed off into a yawn.

Janos couldn't help laughing. "Oh, that's how it is? Maybe I should let you sleep."

Dieter exclaimed in indignation, craning up to claim another kiss, his mouth slanting clumsily over Janos's as he thrust his hips more demandingly against Janos's palm. He squirmed, his usual coordination gone, and his legs tangled between Janos's, his skin growing warmer by the moment.

Janos hissed softly as Dieter rubbed his tailbone against Janos's cock. When he tightened his grip in response, Dieter made a short, stifled sound, his hips jerking. Janos felt the warm spill of Dieter's seed on his palm and lifted his head from Dieter's fumbling kisses.

Blue eyes blinked heavily at him. "Fuck…"

"Not quite," Janos said wryly, his hand sticky with cum.

Dieter obligingly nudged his ass against Janos. "M'good. Your turn."

"And you'll stay awake?"

"'Course," Dieter murmured, his fingertips tracing Janos's forearm down to his sticky fingers. "Y'want a fuck."

Janos idly rolled his hips, his cock rubbing gently against Dieter's ass. "I find it hard to believe," he murmured before lowering his lips to kiss Dieter's throat and trailing them up to Dieter's ear. "You'd be asleep before I got halfway."

"Mm-mm."

Janos nipped at Dieter's earlobe. "You're nearly there already." He laughed softly as the lazy rocking of Dieter's hips slowed and then stopped altogether.

"Mm."

Janos raised his head. Dieter's eyes were closed, his lips turned up just a little. His arm wrapped around Janos's, holding Janos's hand close to his chest. For the first time in days, the furrow in his brow had vanished, and he seemed at peace. Whether it was the wine or the sexual release, Dieter needed sleep, and though his own cock throbbed demandingly, Janos wasn't about to wake him.

Janos sighed quietly, studying his lover's face.

Sometimes, Dieter looked so young, but he was almost the same age as Janos when he enlisted in the army. Perhaps he hadn't seen as much of the cruelty of life as Janos, but he was not innocent or ignorant of it.

He was to go into the past though.

Janos buried his face in Dieter's now-dark hair.

It didn't bear thinking about.

In less than twenty-four hours, Dieter would step through the doorway into a place and time Janos was forbidden from entering. Sanders had been very specific; Janos was already alive somewhere in that period, and they could not allow him to cross his own time stream, no matter how he insisted.

He understood why, but it didn't make it any easier.

The knowledge was enough to smother any carnal thoughts, and he drew the blanket closer around them. It would have to be changed, but it could wait until morning, until Dieter had rested, until a few more of their hours together slipped away.

"Come back to me," he whispered, knowing he would be too afraid to say it aloud by the light of day. "That's all I ask."

Dieter's only response was to nestle closer, and Janos tried to scatter every unpleasant thoughts about what was to come. He needed to rest, as well as Dieter, and lying awake through the night was going to be no use to anyone.

He curled his left arm up beneath his head, behind Dieter's on the pillow, and closed his eyes, willing himself to think of nothing but peace and quiet and rest. With Dieter's back pressed to his chest, it was difficult with every breath pressing them closer, and under his palm, the steady beat of Dieter's heart. He wanted to stay awake and indulge in what hours they had left before the jump.

But they had training in the morning—last moments, last details.

He brushed his lips across the crown of Dieter's head and forced himself to sleep.

It came with disjointed fragments of wakefulness, when nightmares were vivid, and he had to lift his head—his eyes unfocused—to see Dieter was safe and still lived. Too many dreams came quickly, showing blood on pale skin, screams tearing the air, and a grave open and empty and waiting.

Still, there was some sleep. Not much, but enough that when the sunlight gently illuminated the room, he was rested.

In the night, Dieter had turned about in his arms, tucking his head under Janos's chin. Janos could not remember moving, but he was somehow on his back, pinned between Dieter's warm body and the wall. Janos gradually came more awake to the sensation of lips and teeth moving on his throat, then down against his collarbone. He opened his eyes drowsily, spotting the patterns of light reflected from buildings and vehicles on the street below.

"Dieter?"

"Mm?" Dieter's lips were occupied, teasing across Janos's chest.

"What are you doing?"

He felt Dieter's smile as fingertips brushed along his hip. Teeth scraped over his nipple, earning a short, explosive gasp, and he tilted his head to Dieter. Blue eyes watched his face from beneath sleep-mussed dark hair, and again, Dieter's smile flashed across his lips, bright and brilliant.

"What do you think I'm fucking doing?" he murmured.

Janos stared at him in sleepy incomprehension, which was knocked aside when Dieter slid lower, shoving the sheets down around Janos's knees. Janos blinked, then blinked again when slender fingers closed around his cock.

A profanity escaped him, and Dieter laughed, his mouth tracing the outline of the muscles of Janos's belly.

Janos's breath came quicker with every kiss that descended across his belly. Dieter's tongue darted into his navel, and Holy God, he wanted to twist his hand into Dieter's hair and guide him lower still. He couldn't though. He wouldn't. He remembered a night, only weeks ago, when Dieter spoke of nightmares and fantasies combining, and he would not add fuel to the fire.

Instead, he grabbed the sheet, twisting his fingers into the fabric. Dieter's hand stroked down his left thigh, even as Dieter's teeth grazed his left hipbone. A playful tug on his cock made him catch his breath, teasing him to hardness, but watching Dieter's lips move closer was doing more to rouse him than the hand could.

The second Dieter kissed the head of his cock, Janos pressed his head against the pillow, stifling a moan and trying his utmost to keep from demanding or forcing his desire.

The grip on his cock loosened, and Dieter dragged his tongue up from balls to head, before closing his mouth around Janos entirely. Janos's chest heaved, and he jumped when fingers brushed across the back of his hand.

Dieter lifted his head, withdrawing his attentions. "Look at me, Jan," he whispered.

Janos tilted his head, gazing down his body.

He was afraid it would seem like their first meeting, but he couldn't have been more wrong. Dieter smiled like the wicked brat he was, his eyes shining, and he darted his tongue across the head of Janos's cock, earning a near-violent shudder.

"You're going to watch," he murmured, sliding his fingers against Janos's clenched fist.

Mutely, Janos relaxed, spreading his fingers and threading them between Dieter's as Dieter lowered his head again, his mouth hot and wet and eager. Dieter's hand squeezed his as Dieter's mouth moved on him.

Janos watched, breathing hard, as Dieter's cheeks hollowed, and groaned low in his throat as tongue and teeth played along his cock. Blue eyes caught his, and Dieter gave a muffled laugh, the vibrations making Janos shiver. There had never been a place for mirth on the battlefield, and the sensation made his hips twitch up of their own accord.

Dieter took it as encouragement, tilting his head as he kissed and sucked his way down the underside of Janos's cock, lipping at Janos's balls and sucking at them before working his way up again and taking Janos's cock as deep in his mouth as he could. Janos couldn't keep his hips from lifting, though he forced himself to stillness when Dieter pressed lightly down on his hip.

A small, strangled sound escaped Janos's throat when roaming fingers slid between his legs and gently squeezed his balls as Dieter's mouth moved. Dieter's tongue swirled around the head of his cock, and then he brought his head down again, drawing on him so firmly Janos gasped out his name.

Shivers racked his body, and he threw back his head with a whimper as Dieter slid up and wrapped his fingers around Janos's shaft, even as his tongue curled on the head.

Dieter laughed around him, ticklishly, and he squeezed Dieter's hand hard as his hips jerked up, his cock throbbing with his release. He forced his eyes open in time to see Dieter gazing at him, eyes widened in mock virtue, cum spattered on his face.

Janos tugged his fingers against Dieter's. "Come here," he murmured.

Dieter crawled up the bed, draped himself over Janos, and leaned down to kiss him. His erect cock pressed against Janos's belly, and his lips tasted of salt and sex. "Morning."

"Well observed." Janos brushed Dieter's hair back from his brow. "You made a mess of my bed."

Dieter grinned. "I'm not the only one," he said, folding his arms on Janos's chest and propping his chin on his crossed wrists. "Thought I better make up for last night."

Janos shook his head with a rueful smile. "It's not a matter of taking turns. It doesn't matter if one receives more than the other."

Dieter's eyebrows rose. "That so?" He scrambled onto his knees and lifted one leg then the other to straddle Janos's thighs. Hands on his hips, he glanced down at his cock and then at Janos.

Janos's lips twitched, and he put his hand behind his head. "Do you want something?"

"You're going to make me ask?"

Janos gazed at him fondly. "I want to look at you first. I didn't get to see you last night."

Some men would have blushed, but Dieter struck an absurd pose, gazing off into middle-distance, an expression of deep contemplation furrowing his brow. It would have been quite striking if he hadn't started wiggling his hips, making his cock sway enticingly from side to side.

Janos forced his eyes up to Dieter's face. "Are you still drunk?"

Dieter frowned in thought. "Maybe a little." He gave his cock a pointed poke. "I just know I would like you to suck my cock again."

Janos pushed himself upright, now level with the cock in question. "We do this, then I have to shower, and we get breakfast. It's the last day we have to get you ready for the…"

Dieter pressed his finger to Janos's lips. "No talking. Just here, just now, okay?"

Reluctantly, Janos nodded. It felt foolish avoiding the topic, especially since it was looming so close, but the last thing he wanted was to drive Dieter away on their remaining full day together. He stroked his hand over Dieter's hip to squeeze his ass, then leaned closer and flicked his tongue around the head of Dieter's cock.

Dieter released a shaking breath. He wove his fingers into Janos's hair, curling and didn't say anything as Janos took his cock in his mouth. Janos lapped and sucked as Dieter's fingers tightened, but it was like being back in a forest where words couldn't be spoken, and he knew he should have kept quiet.

Dieter's other hand joined his first in Janos's hair as his hips started moving, his cock sliding in deep strokes into Janos's mouth. He rolled his tongue to tease it, and Dieter drew a breath between his teeth as Janos swallowed several times in rapid succession. Dieter's hips jerked against his mouth with his release, the cum hot on Janos's tongue. Janos lapped slowly, gathering every drop he could before drawing his head back.

He raised his eyes to Dieter gazing down at him, emotions warring in his eyes as he released Janos's hair and ran his thumb along Janos's cheekbone.

"Don't wait for me," Dieter said. "If I don't come back, don't you dare mope about like a fucking queen."

Janos's heart clenched. "You're coming back."

Dieter briefly touched his lips to Janos's and, before Janos could stop him, swung off the bed and snatched up his clothes. He had his trousers on and was halfway to the door by the time Janos untangled his legs from the blankets.

"Dieter!"

Dieter stopped by the door, pulling the shirt on over his head. "I'll see you in the training room," he said without turning as he swiped his pass at the door. "We've got work to finish."

Janos ran to the door, leaning out. "Dieter, for God's sake!"

Dieter didn't turn around or look back.

Chapter Twenty-Six

It was a mistake.

The whole night had been a fucking mistake.

Getting drunk had been just stupid, especially when Dieter tended to run off at the mouth with a drink in him. He'd been too open, and now, he had to try to gather the scattered pieces of his dignity up again.

He took breakfast up to the training room, away from anyone, and reread the background created for the identity he was to adopt. He ate without thinking as he read, his coffee going undrunk and cooling in the mug.

Trouble was he wasn't a fucking actor.

The teams had it easy. They went in under guidelines of noninterference, and interaction was kept to an absolute minimum. They didn't have to go into the middle of a city when the heir to the fucking throne was on display. There was an advantage of anonymity in large numbers, but there was the disadvantage of a lot more eyes to notice if he cocked up.

He gazed at the words on the data sheet.

They'd gone for a Hungarian identity because Janos said Dieter's rural Hungarian sounded more convincing than his rural German. They'd considered placing him as an officer, but Dieter knew enough about the upper circles of the army to know they would recognise an outsider. A common man, a trader down on his luck and seeking employment, was as good a role as any. Someone who had every excuse for looking like hell and staying out of trouble.

He threw down the data sheet and pinched the bridge of his nose.

He knew the character inside out and backwards, but remembering how to move like him? How to walk like someone who had been fucked over by life, who skirted the edge of the abyss? He'd never been around people so desperate before.

The door slid open.

Janos didn't hesitate before walking into the room, but he looked at Dieter like he wanted to say something, something he bit down on. Instead, he headed straight for the table by the wall as if there wasn't a fucking thing wrong and filled a glass with water.

He was good at playing casual.

Dieter stared at him.

Maybe that was the solution: be like Janos, the bravest son of a bitch he'd ever met. He'd lived through the wars, he'd lost everything, and no one would have guessed he was ever scared by anything around him. Dieter wanted to be like that, and he'd watched him enough to know how he carried himself, how he moved. It wasn't like remembering a whole new persona. It was remembering Janos, and Dieter could do it with his eyes closed.

He rose silently from the table, glancing up to the far end of the room at the mirrored wall.

It took no effort at all to angle his shoulders down just a little, like Janos did when he thought no one was looking. Dieter slowed his steps and shoved his hands deep in the pockets of his coat, staring at a point about two feet off the floor as he walked. It was only when he neared the mirror that he lifted his eyes and saw Janos's reflection watching him.

Dieter drew himself upright, like the soldier Janos was, pulling his pride about him, unwilling to let anyone see him weak. Only then did he turn around.

"Where did you find that?" Janos held the glass of water, his fingertips pressing white against it. Dieter didn't know if he recognised himself or not, but his face said Dieter had finally gotten it fucking right.

"I watched people," he replied quietly.

Janos put his glass down. "Can you keep it up?"

Dieter nodded, letting his shoulders slump forward again, and did a circuit of the room. His hand fumbled in his pocket. He needed something to fiddle with, something to keep the rising tension at bay. Without it, his nails—cut blunt and square as they now were—pressed into his palm, stinging.

Janos didn't move. He just leaned against the table and watched him.

Finally, Dieter dropped into a chair, splayed his legs in front of him, and raised his eyes to Janos, whose face was a blank mask.

"Better?" Dieter asked, praying it was enough. He didn't need another fight, another fucking declaration of affection, something else to shatter his already cracking nerves.

Janos nodded wordlessly. He turned away, reaching for his glass, his hand trembling. "There's nothing more I can do to help you," he said, his voice too steady, flat. "You're ready."

He was just begging for a fucking hug, but Dieter knew he couldn't let himself give a shit now, not when it was so close. If he let himself care, he wouldn't stop thinking about the bugger when he was gone, and it was the last thing he needed. He needed to be able to think on his feet, not moon around like a fucking idiot.

"We have a brief with Sanders in twenty minutes," he said, glancing at the files on the tabletop. Anywhere but Janos. "Then I'm into wardrobe to get fixed so I look right." He touched the thick stubble at his chin. "More dirt. Less clean."

Five fucking days without a shower. His skin was already itching like hell.

"I'll make sure they have the shower ready when you come back," Janos said quietly.

For the first time since Dieter had met him, he actually sounded sad.

Janos still faced the wall, his fingertips resting on the tabletop beside the glass.

"Don't get sentimental on me now," Dieter said quietly. "I don't fucking need that on top of everything else."

"Do you expect me to pretend I'm happy I have to watch you go through the gate?" Janos said. He didn't raise his voice, and somehow, that made it even worse. "To know what you might see? To know I can't do anything but watch? And if anything happens, I'm helpless to stop it?"

"You don't need to protect me," Dieter said. "I can get by on my own." Story of my life, he thought unhappily.

"You shouldn't have to," Janos said, turning to him.

"It's easier, Not to give a shit. Not to have to worry."

"Bullshit."

Dieter got up from the chair and started gathering the files together. "It's a complication. I don't want it or need it now, okay?" He shuffled the papers, even as Janos approached him. "Don't worry about me."

Janos's hand caught his shoulder, and he was jerked around. "The last person I gave a damn about," he said slowly, "died when I wasn't there." His voice was flat as he trembled. "They tortured him. They cut his throat. Because they knew he loved a man. Because he loved me. And you think I shouldn't worry?"

Dieter stared up at him.

A mish-mash of pieces fitted into place, and care had suddenly become a lot more emphatic. Christ, he wanted to hold him, but he couldn't, not when they were about to go their separate ways, maybe permanently.

"Then it's a good thing I don't love you," he said quietly.

It wasn't until he gave the words voice that he realised how much of a fucking colossal lie it was.

Janos went still as a statue, his face blank and waxen, and he loosened his fingers from Dieter's shoulder. "Yes. A good thing." He stepped away. "You should go to your briefing."

Dieter had to turn away from him. He gathered the pages up into a folder. "You're not coming?"

"There's nothing I would be able to add. You're ready. I can't tell you more."

Dieter ran his fingertips along the edge of the files. "You can come if you want. I won't stop you."

Janos shook his head. "It's TRI business. I have no place there. I'll go down to the pool. You speak to Sanders."

He turned and walked away, and Dieter let him go. Better now than later. Better than drawing it out.

Still, when the door shut behind Janos, Dieter folded into the chair and whispered, "Shit."

He was still sitting there when the alarm on his watch beeped. Reluctantly, he dragged himself upright, gathered the files, and headed for Sanders's office on the next level.

Sanders was already there, his desk illuminated with a map, and he glanced up when Dieter entered.

"No Janos?"

Dieter shook his head as he shut the door behind him. For all that the agency was the most modern building imaginable, Sanders liked his old-fashioned office with a door swinging on actual hinges.

"He says I'm ready," Dieter said without meeting Sanders' eyes. "Says there's nothing more he can add."

The chair creaked as Sanders leaned back. "God save me from personal entanglements." He sighed and waved Dieter to the chair on the other side of the desk. "Do you have everything prepared?"

Christ, he wanted to lie, say he needed more time. They were a time-travel agency for fuck's sake. They could shove him back to the same time, any time they wanted. But he knew if they waited, if they overthought things, if the news got out that someone could and had gone rogue without anyone being sent after him, then others might think they could do the same.

"As ready as I can be," he replied. "All the props are ready, and currency has been arranged."

Sanders nodded grimly. "We've got the gate set to open as close as we can risk to civilization." He scaled up the map and tapped a fingertip to it. "We're aiming for the edge of the forest here."

Dieter glanced across the map. "Decent distance from the city," he agreed, trying to keep his voice steady, as if it was any other brief. "And it'll be better if I look like I've been walking a while."

"You'll have a week to locate Llewelyn," Sanders reminded him.

Dieter nodded. A week to find a needle in a haystack. They could only guarantee one point in the timeline where he would be, but it would be too late by far. So, a week to find him. Llewelyn had already been running around for over a month, but he'd know how to avoid causing a lot of damage to the timeline. The less time Dieter was there, the better.

They'd gotten hold of some money of the period, which meant he'd at least be able to eat, and there were enough inns and taverns to provide accommodation. He was shitting bricks about not just speaking to people from the past, but dealing with them, buying and interacting.

One fuck-up and he could have a worse ripple effect than Llewelyn.

"And the exit point?" he asked, pushing the thought of failure aside for a moment.

Sanders scaled the map down with a touch of his fingers and drew it across, showing the western outskirts of the city. "This farmstead is the wait point. You'll have your tracker, but we don't want to have to infiltrate the city." He met Dieter's eyes. "You have to get to this place. We can't guarantee the exact time, but as long as you and Llewelyn are there for two days after the event, the team will come and get you."

The event.

Subtle name for the biggest fucking mess Llewelyn could possibly try to interfere in.

They went over the plans, such as they were, for the hundredth time. Sanders was on edge and no wonder. If they failed, if Llewelyn succeeded, they were fucked. There had only ever been accidental and small things changed in the timeline. If they did something big, they didn't know what the repercussions might be. That was why nothing was meant to be changed.

When Dieter's watch beeped again, he was forced to remember this wasn't a normal brief. He had props to get and last details to be added to his appearance, as well as the tracker chip to be implanted in his skin—a new precaution against loss or removal. He hit the button to switch off the alarm and took an unsteady breath.

"You want me to come down with you?" Sanders asked.

Through all of the shit of the last few months, Dieter recognised the gesture for what it was. Sanders was a miserable git most of the time, but he gave a damn about everyone in his charge.

Dieter got up, leaving the files on the desk, and put his hands into the coarse pockets of his overcoat. "If this goes to hell," he finally managed to say, his voice unsteady, "I want you to watch out for that stupid arse."

Sanders nodded. "He's one of ours now." He stood up too. "Lea'll be waiting."

Dieter nodded stiffly. "Yeah. Don't want my head bitten off." As he made his way to the door, Sanders called his name. Dieter paused, turning.

Sanders sat, resting both hands on the desk, and the light from the projections turned his features ghostly and ancient. "I'll meet you at the gate. Just keep breathing, okay?"

Dieter nodded, pressing his lips together, and hurried out into the hall. Christ, it would be just perfect if he had a nervous breakdown in front of the boss right before the most important fucking mission of his life.

He headed to wardrobe as if on autopilot.

One of the techs was waiting to implant the new tracker chip into the flesh of his shoulder. It had to be somewhere he couldn't reach it, in case he decided to follow Llewelyn's lead. Just a precaution, as they said.

Then, it was time for the costume.

He'd been wearing most of his costume for days, and it reeked, but Lea still smeared more dirt into it and into his skin. Dirt rimmed his nails, oils dragged through his unkempt hair.

When Lea was done, he stared at his reflection. He couldn't see himself anywhere in it.

His watch beeped, and he glanced down at it.

It was time.

He undid the strap and held it out to her.

"You're ready," she said, taking the watch and laying it on the work counter beside her. She picked up a small pouch of money and pressed it into his hand. "Good luck."

Her assistants were watching him, but he couldn't even force a smile. He closed his fingers round the purse, put it in his pocket, and made his way to the door. The only thing he had that wouldn't be going with him was his pass. Sanders would be waiting for him, to take it from him.

He gripped the pass, squeezing so hard it cut into his fingers as he walked in silence towards the elevator. There weren't many people about, and he was grateful. They would have stared. Wished him luck. Been fucking useless.

When he emerged at the top of the staircase leading into the temporal chamber, he had to stop for a moment. His legs shook, and the world wavered alarmingly around him. Going into the room was bad enough, but fucking hell, this was something else.

He started down the stairs on leaden legs.

"Dieter."

He stopped halfway down the stairs, didn't even have to turn. "What do you want?"

Janos's footsteps were loud in the silence as he descended the stairs. "I was waiting. I wanted to give you something."

Dieter turned. "I can't take shit through."

"Not modern shit." Janos held out a pocketknife. It was one of the few things he'd been carrying when he breached security, hidden inside his boot. "This was my grandfather's. It's old. You might need it."

Dieter stared at the carved handle and the small, sharp blade. "No."

"I want you to take it."

Dieter shook his head. It was all Janos had left of his family, and he couldn't be responsible for taking it from him too. "No."

"I know you'll bring it home."

It was the fucking straw that broke the camel's back.

Dieter dropped his head, shaking it, unable to speak. His eyes burned, and Jesus fucking Christ, he was crying. His throat hurt, and his chest hurt, and he squeezed his eyes tightly shut to keep the tears from falling.

Janos thudded down the two steps separating them, and Dieter couldn't even find the strength to push the soft bugger away when he embraced him. He just stood there like a fucking scarecrow, limp and ragged and fucking pathetic.

"I'll see you soon," Janos murmured, close to his ear. "Ten days. I'll see you then."

Then his arm fell away, and he retreated up the stairs. Dieter didn't dare open his eyes until he knew he was alone. He wiped at his cheeks with a grubby hand. It would only move the dirt around.

The rest of the stairs were even more of a trial, but Sanders was waiting, as he promised, at the bottom. He caught Dieter's shoulder, squeezing it hard.

"You ready, you overqualified little prick?" he said. At the look on Dieter's face, Sanders's lips twitched in a wry, tired smile. "You didn't expect some kind of motivational speech, did you? What kind of arsehole are you?"

Dieter couldn't help laughing weakly. "Thanks, boss." He turned to the door leading to the temporal chamber. "Get me in there before I change my mind."

Sanders opened his hand. "Your pass?"

Dieter gave it to him and took a breath. "Let's go."

For the first time, he could ignore the walls of the layover chamber as he walked through it, Sanders at his side. The temporal chamber, though, made his heart stutter. Christ, he'd forgotten how high the ceiling was, how large and oppressive it felt.

"How long?" he asked.

"One minute," Sanders said. "Dieter..."

Dieter held up a hand. "No. No sentimental bullshit, boss, please."

"I was going to say don't fuck up."

Dieter wasn't sure if he was laughing or crying as Sanders headed out of the room, closing the door behind him. Of all things Sanders could've said, it was the most fucking comforting thing Dieter could have asked for.

He backed up against the closed door, taking steadying breaths, and closed his eyes, trying to force away memories of this place, and guns, and Janos. Jesus, Janos. He was the one who had started everything. One life saved when it shouldn't have been, and that was what had driven Llewelyn to act, to rebel, to throw everything down the shitter in the hopes of making a difference in the world gone by.

A countdown started, and Dieter breathed in and out, trying to keep calm. He tapped his fingertips against the door with every descending number, turning his face away from the outline of the doorway as the count got lower.

When the light blazed, he could see the veins in his eyelids, and he took a last, shivering breath of modern air as he stepped forward.

"Sensors confirm the area is clear," a voice said over the speakers. "Depart at will."

"See you soon, you dick," Sanders added, his voice echoing.

On shaking legs, Dieter walked through the doorway.

Chapter Twenty-Seven

"The gate is closed."

Janos sat on his bed, his back to the wall when the confirmation was relayed across the speakers. Janos's insides tangled in knots, knowing it meant Dieter was gone, and he couldn't come back until the job was done.

It wasn't their normal practice either.

From his own experience, he knew the gates weren't normally closed during a mission. They were open until the team returned, rather than risk opening the gate at a different location that the team couldn't find. That was why he'd been able to find his way through.

This time, though, they didn't have enough power to wait for Dieter to do what he had to.

Dieter was kicked through without any direct connection to return, and they shut it behind him. All they could do was wait and hope he would be at the meeting place when the time came.

Janos rose from his bed and walked over to the small kitchen area. He scooped some water up in his hand and splashed it onto his face to keep his eyes from burning. Turning into a weeping mess would help no one, least of all Dieter.

He took refuge in the mundane, filling his kettle and setting it on to boil. He watched as steam gradually built and curled out of the spout, his hand braced against the edge of the counter.

He was still standing there when he heard the chime of his door.

Someone wanted to come in.

Dieter never even waited for permission.

Janos drew a breath, straightening up, and went to the panel to swipe the pass to open the door.

Sanders stood on the other side.

Janos wrapped his arm over his chest to squeeze his left elbow. "What do you want?"

Sanders held up a bottle of amber liquid. "I thought we could both use this."

Of all the things Janos had expected, this was not among them. "What?"

Sanders didn't wait for an invitation, brushing past him as he walked into the room. "You just waved your lover off on a life-or-death mission. I just sent a bloody linguist to play at being a hero. You think you're the only one who isn't scared shitless this is all going to go horribly wrong?"

Janos closed the door, then turned to watch Sanders pull out a couple of mugs and pour a measure of the spirit into each of them. Sanders set the bottle down and picked up the mugs, offering one to Janos.

"You think this help?" Janos said, watching him guardedly. "You have job to do."

"I can't do anything for the next twenty-four hours, so I plan to have a break while I can."

"With me?"

Sanders shrugged. "Figured you're the only person in this building more worried than I am."

Janos couldn't argue with his assessment. He took the mug from Sanders and sat down at the table, sprawling in the chair. He knocked back the contents of the mug in one mouthful, grimacing as it burned down his throat.

The other man approached and sat on the opposite side of the table, setting the bottle on the tabletop. He didn't say anything when Janos reached for it and poured another measure into his own mug.

They sat in silence for a while.

Janos wasn't a big talker anyway, and it seemed Sanders was the same kind of person.

They poured drinks, drank them, and gazed out over the city until the alcohol did its work, loosening Janos's tongue.

"You worry?" he said finally.

Sanders gazed at a point on the horizon. "I always worry when any of my teams are out there." He turned to Janos. "We have a tracker on him now. He's coming back."

"He does not think this," Janos said, reaching for the bottle.

Sanders got there first and poured another measure for each of them. "That's because he's an idiot."

Surprised, Janos snorted in amusement. The mirth didn't last long, though, with the thought of Dieter and the world he, himself, had come from. "You believe he comes back?"

For several moments, Sanders was silent, as if thinking how to reply.

"I have to believe it," he said. "Until the minute someone doesn't, I have to believe they will."

"Like commander of army," Janos observed quietly. "You send soldier out. Not all soldier come back."

Sanders's expression drew taut and grim, lines deepening briefly around his eyes and mouth. Here sat a commander who had lost soldiers, and who regretted it.

"That little shitbag is coming back," Sanders said, "if I have to jump in there myself and drag him by his ears."

Janos gazed at him in surprise. He hadn't expected such vehemence from Sanders, who always seemed to keep himself in check. Maybe the drink was affecting them both. "He is good here? You like him?"

Sanders set down his mug and nodded. "He's a stubborn fool, but he's also one of the smartest kids I know. I just hope he remembers both of those things while he's out there."

Janos examined the contents of his cup. "I am sorry," he said quietly. "For problem I am making."

Sanders waved his words away dismissively. "We always knew the doorway needed to be secure. I'm just shocked it didn't happen before." He leaned back in the chair, pushing his fingers through his silvering hair. "We're working on it. Always working on making things better." A distant look crossed his face. "At least the connection is stable now. We can pinpoint where and when it connects."

It spoke of a time when things must have gone wrong.

Janos glanced at the bottle. They had drunk a lot of it already, and he might say foolish things if he drank more. "I have coffee." He got up and hooked his finger through the handle of his mug. "Do you want?"

Sanders picked up the bottle and examined it, then set it down. "Probably a better idea."

Janos returned to the counter and added more water to the kettle to boil. "You say you have nothing for twenty-four hour?"

Sanders nodded. "Since we're not keeping the gate open for the duration of the mission, we can open it nightly—his and ours—for ten seconds, to check Dieter's health through his tracking chip."

The jar of coffee slipped in Janos's hand, and the glass clattered on the counter as he fumbled with it, his heart pounding like a drum. They weren't going to be entirely out of contact for the next ten days? They would be able to check on his well-being? The relief made his legs shake beneath him, and he steadied himself against the counter.

"Is good," he said unsteadily. "To know this thing, is good."

"If you want to be there when we make the connection, you are entitled as his significant other."

It was said so simply, so directly, that for a moment, Janos didn't understand.

He turned, uncertain. "Significant other?" he said, unsure he had heard correctly.

"Partner," Sanders said. "Lover. Whichever term you prefer."

The heat rose up his face, and he pressed his hand harder against the edge of the counter. "I-I do not understand," he said, his mouth dry. "We are not...he said he did not...that we are not..."

It's a good thing I don't love you. He heard the words over and over.

"Do you believe anything that came out of his mouth in the last ten days?" Sanders said bluntly.

Janos turned away. "It is private matter."

"It is. And one of the last things he said to me was to take care of you."

Janos pressed his lips together and stared at a patch of reflected light on the ceiling, blinking hard.

He remembered Dieter's tears as he stood on the staircase. It wasn't just fear. Janos knew that. He remembered Dieter's hands in his hair, Dieter telling Janos to forget about him when he was gone. Those weren't the words of someone who didn't care. And now, to know Dieter wanted him to be taken care of in his absence?

"He is idiot," he said, his voice unsteady.

Sanders chuckled quietly. "He is." The legs of his chair scraped across the floor. "Never mind the coffee for me. I think I could do with some fresh air."

Janos didn't turn to him, struggling to get his breathing under control. "You will call me for connection?" he asked tentatively, unsure if Sanders was serious.

"I'll send one of the techs for you." Sanders stopped an arm's length from Janos and laid something down on the counter. "I'm not good with the talking crap, but Sally's in if you need someone to talk to."

Janos nodded mutely, tapping his fingers against the counter. He held his breath until the door slid open and closed again, and he was alone. He released a gasp, scarcely able to believe the exchange had happened at all. Pushing off from the counter, he searched along the counter to see what Sanders had left behind.

A small, rectangular card, not unlike his own pass lay there.

Janos picked it up and turned it over.

Dieter's face gazed up at him from the pass card. He looked as he had the first time they met, only with purple in his hair. His eyebrow was raised, one corner of his mouth turned up in a half smirk.

Janos traced the outline of Dieter's face with the tip of his thumb. Something to hold onto until Dieter came home.

Chapter Twenty-Eight

Thunder rolled from the darkening sky. The rain was beating down as Dieter pushed the door of the inn open. Water ran down his neck, soaking his sleeves, and not a fucking thing he could do about it.

It was just luck he'd reached the outskirts of the city before the heavens opened, and he'd staggered towards the first inn he saw within the city walls.

His legs ached. Walking several miles hadn't been a problem. The terrain had been a fucking bastard, along with the crap shoes they'd given him. He'd grabbed a broken branch to serve as a walking stick to lean on, his feet blistered to all buggery by his shoes.

A dozen curious eyes peered up from their drinks, and he froze, rooted to the spot, but only encountered bored glances. They didn't give a crap who he was, and he forced himself to walk in as if he had every right to be there. Christ, it was like being part of a living exhibit in a museum. With his heart in his mouth and legs turning to jelly, he really, *really* wanted to hide.

The thought of being dry drove off some of the sheer panic of speaking to people from a different era as he approached the innkeeper. He kept it short to the point of rudeness, asking for a room.

He was offered a choice and took the cheapest—a small cubbyhole in the eaves of the building. The place was a shithole, but it was dry and out of the way, and it was all he needed. Better to be seen as poor and cheap than to draw attention because of his purse.

He retreated up to the room, stick in one hand and a stub of a candle in the other. No, not a room. "Room" implied space. He was renting a cupboard to sleep in. A fucking cupboard with a sack of straw on the floor.

Dieter propped the stick by the low doorframe and gingerly sank onto the sack, every joint creaking in protest. It was a hard day's work just to get his wet coat off. It slipped from his grasping hands, and something clattered across the floor.

Dieter stared blankly down.

He'd left the outer pockets empty. He'd been warned by Janos about the danger of pickpockets, so everything of value was within the inside pockets, buttoned away.

The object lying on the floor looked like nothing, but his hand shook as he reached down and picked it up. The wooden handle was cool against his palm, and he unfolded the blade, the metal shining and sharp by candlelight.

Janos's knife.

The last thing the idiot had of his family.

"You didn't..." Dieter whispered under his breath, his eyes pricking with uncalled for tears. "Oh, you stupid fucking arse."

He closed the blade and squeezed the grip hard. It was tangible proof of Janos's faith in him. The soft sod believed Dieter could do it, that he could find Llewelyn and come back and bring the knife with him.

It was ridiculous.

How could he trust him so much? What the fuck had he done to deserve that?

The most he could do was try his best and hope he wouldn't cock up too badly. He knew the history, he knew the area, he knew what to look for. He would try his best and get home to give the arsehole his knife back.

Hiding in a room wasn't going to get it done. He was going to have to go out there, interact, be an insignificant part in the lives of the people he had only read about in books and reports. Terrifying as fuck, but he had to do it.

No time like the present, he thought, then snorted. Or the past, for that matter.

He forced himself to his feet and pushed the knife into a trouser pocket, deep enough it slid to rest against his inner thigh.

A helpless laugh bubbled up in his throat. Jan's fucking phallic symbol was practically pressing against his cock. It was ridiculous how comforting it felt having it there: a reminder of the man waiting for him.

Okay, maybe he'd broken the poor fucker's heart before he left, but he'd had to. He couldn't have left them with the possibility of something when there was every chance he wouldn't be coming back.

He shook his head.

No use thinking about it now.

He had a job to do, and he was going to fucking do it.

His coat was still wet, so he tucked most of the money inside his boots, carrying only what he needed for a meal in the inn below.

The place stank of mould and dampness and the dank, stale smell of old sweat and ale. A haze of smoke from pipes hung in the air. Most of the tables and benches were occupied. Dozens of voices chattered at once in at least three different languages he recognised.

Dieter felt like a school kid on an excursion when he went up to the bar to ask for food and a drink—like the moment when Janos showed up. Every word he knew abandoned him. Even the simple ones. *Please may I have a drink?* Simple as fuck, but could he remember? Like hell he could.

Terror spurred him on, and he asked more abruptly than he intended. It fitted with how he looked, he supposed: someone shabby, exhausted and miserable, with a face like a slapped hairy backside wouldn't be polite.

The innkeeper pushed a cup of ale to him and an empty bowl and spoon, nodding across the room. Dieter turned and spotted the fire burning in the hearth and a large iron pot over the flames filled with some kind of stew or soup.

"One bowl only," the innkeeper warned. "Or more coin."

Dieter nodded, his mouth dry, and padded across the floor. He should have taken off his shoes, dried his feet, or something. Christ, he was in the wrong place.

He set the cup on the mantle and filled the bowl before searching out a seat somewhere in the room. It would have been easier to hide out in the attic, but he had to interact... His mother once told him the best way to learn to swim was to jump in the deep end. He'd tried it. He'd almost fucking drowned, but he did it, and he learned.

This was just like that.

Hiding in an attic wouldn't help anyone.

He had to jump in with both feet and hope like hell he wouldn't sink.

There was a vacant space at one of the busy tables, and he nodded to the occupants.

One of the men removed his pipe from his mouth, conferred with his companions, and waved Dieter over. Dieter swallowed the ball of terror choking him, made his way across the room, and sat on the end of the bench.

He stirred the bowl of steaming stew. Whatever it was, it smelled okay.

One of the men asked something in what had to be Serbian.

"Hungarian," Dieter said apologetically.

"Ah." One of the other men leaned over the table and said carefully in strongly accented Hungarian, "New come to town?"

"New today." Dieter and Janos had worked on his story, but now he was here, seeking some kind of employment didn't sound like a good excuse. The place was choked with merchants and farmers alike. They didn't need another one taking up space. "Passing through."

There were grunts of acknowledgment, but no one said anything more to him. Hungarian was a good language to hide behind. Few in the area could speak it, which meant fewer questions asked. He ducked gratefully over his food.

Some of the spices and vegetables seemed familiar. Not the meat, but he didn't really give a fuck. It was warm and it was filling, and he had made a start by interacting and not cocking up so far.

He remained at the table, drinking slowly, and listening, picking out the different nuances in the languages he recognised. It was one thing to learn Hungarian from a 20th century man and German in the 21st century. It was something else entirely thirty years earlier. Language always was fluid, and even sitting there, he could hear different phrasing and tones in the words.

He was sitting right in the middle of a living history lesson.

Seeing it that way somehow made it easier.

He wrapped both hands around his cup and sat there, listening and watching, and taking it all in. It was a linguist's wet dream, and he was right in the middle of it, picking out the ways some languages had adapted within thirty years.

Christ, he'd have a thesis to write if he got home.

He finished the ale and made his way up the stairs to the attic. He wasn't surprised to find someone had gone through his room for valuables. Janos had warned him to be careful, and he planned to be. His wet coat lay in a heap on the floor. He propped it up over the heavy stick he'd used for walking and sat down on the straw mattress. He eased off his boots, his feet throbbing, and glanced at the flickering flame on the stub of his tiny candle.

In the morning, he could start his work in earnest, but right now, he was fucking exhausted, and all he wanted was sleep. He blew out the candle, and in the darkness, slipped one hand into his pocket and wrapped it around Janos's knife.

Chapter Twenty-Nine

It should not have been one of the most terrifying moments of his life, but there it was.

Ignorance was as frightening as a blade to the throat.

Dieter was...too much to him. To fear for his life so much was far more than Janos had anticipated when he first kissed the man.

Janos stood behind Sanders's chair as they opened the gateway, glowing brightly on the monitors. Commands were snapped, people typed in codes and numbers, and screens blurred with information.

He didn't know if they had locked onto the tracking chip in Dieter's shoulder, or if the information flooding the screens was something else. He didn't know anything that was going on, and no one was saying anything he could understand.

He braced his hand on Sanders's chair to keep it from trembling.

The doorway winked closed after only ten seconds, and he blinked away the afterglow.

Sanders pushed the chair out and moved from one screen to another. It was all Janos could do not to beg for some kind of answer. The last time he had gone into the unknown, he had come back to find the ground mired with blood and a body waiting for burial.

It felt like hours, but it could only have been minutes at most, then Sanders turned, smiling.

He was alive and well. Alive, well, and resting based on the readings.

All the sound in the room faded to nothing, and Janos swayed as the world seemed to shift, and suddenly, he was sitting in Sanders's chair, Sanders's hand on his shoulder. The techs had fled, leaving them, and Janos squinted around in confusion.

"Where did they go?" he asked.

"Thought you might want a moment. You need a medic?"

Janos took a breath. "No. I am well." He covered his face with his hand to allow himself a chance to gather his dignity. Sanders said nothing, just squeezed his shoulder as Janos swallowed gulps of air.

"His blood pressure is normal," Sanders said when Janos finally lowered his hand. Sanders was studying one of the screens, but Janos had no idea if he was reading what was there. "No signs of distress in any of the readings. It looks like he might even be getting more sleep than we are."

Janos nodded, startled to realise he was shaking. "Good," he whispered. "Is good." He rose unsteadily from the chair. "I can go?"

Sanders glanced up at him. "You're sure you're okay?"

Janos avoided his eyes. "Is all good." He still felt light-headed, but it was a giddiness of relief. He needed some quiet, somewhere he could let the emotions get the better of him without anyone seeing.

Sanders slapped him firmly on the shoulder. "He'll be fine, your boy."

Your boy.

Janos forced a brittle smile, nodded, and headed for the door.

Your boy.

There was no guarantee it would be the case when Dieter returned. He could hope for it, but whatever Dieter was living through might change him. Dieter had already withdrawn from him, but there was still a chance he could go further.

Janos headed for the stairs. He could have used the elevator, but people were in the halls, and he knew some of them wondered why he was even allowed to be there when they opened the gate. They didn't know, and he wasn't ready to tell them.

The rooftop was the only place he could be guaranteed some peace, but it was raining, a steady, constant drizzle turning the world grey. He sat just outside the doorway, in the shelter of the alcove, and propped his elbows on his upraised knees, watching the raindrops on the flagstones edging the garden.

Dieter had survived more than twenty-four hours.

From some of the faces in the control room, it was more than they had expected. No wonder he believed he would fail if his colleagues didn't trust him to complete the job he had been sent to do. People spoke of him as if he was gone permanently. They eyed Janos as if wondering what he would do now his companion was gone.

They were right to wonder.

He didn't know.

What he needed to do was prove himself, that he wasn't simply some historical relic to be used when needed. He was seen as such—as something out of time and out of place—and it alienated him more than anything.

A slow smile turned up his lips.

So, they thought he was just some rustic man from times gone by? Well, he would have to prove to them he did not intend to stay a museum artifact for their amusement and education.

He got to his feet and extended his hand into the bitterly cold rain.

If Dieter was brave enough to go into the old world, how could Janos do anything less than take hold of the new one and shake it until it rattled?

He turned and strode into the building and bounded down the stairs. Fitting into this world was a challenge, but Janos's secrets no longer needed to be a concern. Here, he could do all he wanted and much more. Why try to remain hidden when there was nothing to fear? Why not use the skills he had?

People turned in astonishment as he stalked by them in the halls, making his way to the console room, and the techs who were there glanced up in bewilderment as he walked in. Some of the machines had been powered down, but half of them were still active.

"Sanders isn't here," one of them—a spiky-haired boy called Barry or Brian or something—said, speaking loudly and slowly as if Janos were a complete imbecile.

"This I can see." Janos grabbed one of the chairs and dragged it over to the console which had been flashing codes when they searched for Dieter's life signs. "You will show me this machine. You will show me how I use it."

The techs exchanged looks.

"You don't use computers, do you?" asked Tamara, a reed-thin girl, covered from head to foot in tattoos.

Janos glanced at her. "I use computer in my room. Is small and simple, but it is start." He darted his fingers across the control panel and studied the boxes on the screen. Some of the codes he recognised, others he didn't, but he had watched the techs working and had paid attention.

He typed a series of letters in, and Dieter's tracker file opened up.

"How did he do that?" B-boy demanded, startled, hurrying over.

"*He* is speaking English now," Janos said dryly. "I see code when Sanders bring me here. I put code. Code bring file." He glanced up at the young man. "I am talking too fast? You want for me to speak slow?"

The boy swore and stormed off. Tamara covered her mouth to hide her grin.

He turned to her instead. "You will help me? I want to learn."

She looked over at the other techs, who were either working or trying to pretend they were working. "I don't have much time just now," she said, dragging over a chair. "But we can do some basics." She gave him a crooked smile. "Learning during a jump isn't a good time."

He shook his head. "No. Is best time. This is when all things happen."

"All things," she echoed with a rueful chuckle. "Yeah. That might be an understatement."

He raised his eyebrows. "Understatement?"

"When you say something is a little busy, when it's really, really busy," she explained. "You understate it. You make it sound like it is not so bad."

He glanced at her in surprise. "Thank you."

"For what?"

"For explaining for me." He touched the screen, dragging through the images on the file. "Some people do not."

Tamara pulled her chair closer. "Some people are idiots." She nudged him. "Move over a bit. I'll show you the basics of this system. It won't be much, but if we speak to Sanders, he might let you sit in and watch us working during the day."

Janos glanced sidelong at her. "This is not problem?"

She grinned at him. She had large, very white teeth with a gap between the two front ones. "You want to learn. I'll be doing routine checks on the system. If you're going to be around for a while, you might as well see what brought you here. I can't guarantee you'll understand it all."

Janos gazed at the glowing screen in front of him with a slow smile. "Is not so difficult. I can build engine from all parts. Words on screens are not problem."

"And I thought you were a quiet, shy kind of guy."

He shrugged with a half smile. "Cocky asshole is better," he said, remembering the teasing epithets Dieter had directed at him.

She shook her head, laughing. "You're not what I expected for a historical guy." Her hands darted across the keys, taking them to the most basic screen.

"I am not historical guy. I am just guy."

Brown eyes glanced at him. "Yeah. I'm starting to get that." She pushed away from the screen. "Okay. Lesson one."

Janos leaned closer attentively.

Chapter Thirty

The town wasn't large, but it was large enough to make searching difficult.

Dieter slept badly. If it wasn't the mice skittering around nearby, the straw mattress was the most uncomfortable thing he had ever slept on, and the sting of fleas biting at him didn't help. He was filthy, disgusting, and absolutely exhausted.

Let the temporal agents say their job was difficult, going unnoticed and not living among the population. There was no fucking comparison.

It was only ten days.

Dieter told himself the same thing every morning when he crawled off the damp sack of straw. The mantra ran around his brain as he scratched the fleabites and bound up his cracked and blistered feet.

The past was a fascinating place, but Christ, he wanted to go home.

Five days and no sign of Llewelyn so far. And every day that went by was another day closer to the event.

From what Janos said about his additional training, Llewelyn wanted to know how to blend in and had specifically been trained in his last role—as a farmhand and labourer. If he attempted any other, there was the possibility he would slip.

The bastard might not even care anymore, in the final days before the event.

The thought of it made Dieter sick.

The event.

The assassination.

Franz Ferdinand was due to arrive in Sarajevo with his wife, completely oblivious to the fact that they had a great target flashing over their heads.

Everywhere Dieter looked, he saw their faces. From news sheets sold on street corners, black-and-white images of the couple stared reproachfully out at him. He tried to ignore them, but it was impossible.

People talked about it everywhere. The flags were going up. And their faces haunted him.

He knew them too well already. Years of research had seen to that. But now, the archduke and his wife were all over the newspapers, like any other celebrity royal. The archduke was aloof and stern, and she always appeared peaceful, but a little sad. There would be more pictures, too, of the children, and Dieter couldn't face it.

Seeing Franz Ferdinand and Sophie was bad enough.

They weren't just images on a page anymore. They were real people coming to the city to die.

Llewelyn wanted to stop it. He wanted to change everything.

It was a fucking incredible idea, the secret fantasy of every time agent—saving a man to stop a war that would tear apart a continent.

The trouble was it was a fucking delusion.

Stopping one assassination of one man in one place wouldn't make a difference to the world at large. Llewelyn had ignored it in his mad rush to play the hero. The continent was a powder keg. If Franz Ferdinand didn't die, then some other spark would send the world to hell.

Still, there was something messed up about letting an assassination happened.

No.

He couldn't think of it that way.

The past had happened. It had to stay the way it was. It couldn't be undone. They didn't have the right to make the decision over what was changed. If they took that right, why then couldn't people with more fucked-up ideas do the same? What if a sociopath decided he had the right to play God and turned the world on its head?

Rules had to be upheld.

They had to be, even if felt sick and wrong to stand by and do nothing.

So Dieter had to find Llewelyn before he changed the world.

Dieter's routine made the day go by quicker, working through the city block by block. It took longer than he would have liked, leaning on his walking stick like an old man as he hobbled through the streets. His feet were blistered to ribbons from the combination of rain, walking on bad roads, and old-fashioned boots wearing ragged.

Ten days.

It was only ten fucking days.

He had the tattered photograph of Llewelyn tucked in his inner coat pocket, ready to be shown to anyone who might be able to help the ragged Hungarian peasant who was seeking his lost brother. It was as good a story as any: a dead father, a brother needed at home, an inheritance promised.

Some people nodded approvingly for his filial duty, others snorted as if he was an idiot for being so honest with his brother's inheritance. None of them were able to help him. Either Llewelyn was hiding himself too well, or he wasn't even in the city yet.

Either way, Dieter was running out of time.

Still, he couldn't stop searching, so he walked, and he asked, and he walked and showed the picture, and he tried not to feel more and more ground down when people brushed him aside, ignored him, or spat in contempt at him, a ragged Hungarian vagrant.

Speaking to them in broken German seemed a farce. Reining in his language was harder than speaking Hungarian, and if Janos ever heard his forced pidgin German, he would piss himself laughing.

Dieter was known at the inn now, which worried him.

An agent wasn't meant to be noticed.

True, he was playing a part and had no choice in the matter, but it was enough people would remember him. He had hoped to avoid it, but a couple of the older men always nodded to him from their smoke-filled nook when he returned to the inn at the end of the day.

One evening, after another waste of a day, one of the stockier labourers had approached him and started speaking in strongly accented German. Dieter was so tired he nearly replied without thinking. He'd caught himself, but it was becoming too risky. He couldn't skulk off to his room. People would be suspicious of him.

Being on his guard all the time was as exhausting as the hunt.

A summer storm swept in while he trudged through the east side of the city. Dieter could be back at his inn within the hour, but he hadn't been sent there to shelter from the weather. He had a job to do, and if he caught pneumonia because of it, then the medics could deal with it when he got back.

He slipped his cold, wet hand into his trouser pocket under his coat.

Janos's knife was warm against his palm. Each day, it rested against his leg, a solid reminder he had to go home. The reason why he kept walking, because someone was waiting for the knife. Maybe for him too.

He tried the inns he had not tried before.

Inns were the best places to check because people of all ranks and stations crossed paths there. Some were loud, some quiet, some packed with travellers, others only with locals. He took out the increasingly fragile scrap of a picture, straightened his back, and became the desperate brother once more.

It was useless.

If Llewelyn had been seen, no one was admitting to it.

Dieter made his way across the city as night fell, his coat clinging to him, damp with sweat and rain. The mission felt more and more useless with every passing hour, the frustration burning his throat like acid.

He was later than usual, and when he pushed the door open, several conversations stopped, eyes turning towards him warily. He wasn't surprised. Franz Ferdinand and his retinue were due to arrive soon, which meant increased numbers of Austrian soldiers in the city.

Sarajevo might be a part of the Habsburgs' sprawling empire, but even those who weren't openly rebelling against the Austrian rule weren't necessarily happy about the heavy-handed overlords from the west any more than they had been about the oppressors in the east.

He nodded mutely to the old men in their nook.

If anyone was to grant approval, they were the ones to do it.

One of them was lost in the shadows, only the glow of his pipe visible, but one of the others leaned forward, a gnarled hand on the table, and nodded in response. The conversations began anew, and Dieter released the breath he'd been holding.

He limped over to the bar and laid a coin on the wood. The innkeeper pushed a bowl towards him without a word. Something was wrong, and he was fucked if he knew what it was. Maybe just the impending arrival of their future overlord. Maybe the soldiers. Maybe the weather.

Silently, he picked up the clay bowl and headed to the pot over the fire.

The mess that filled the pot was no more appealing than it had been on the first night, but it was food, and it was hot. Dieter scooped a ladle of the slop into his bowl and retreated to the first empty seat he could find.

The mood in the inn seemed different, a tension which hadn't dispersed even when he'd settled out of the way. People were on edge, voices lowered, furtive looks darting around. The hair on the back of his neck stood on end, and his stomach curled into a t knot.

It was one thing to read about "tensions" in the history textbooks, but terrifying to sit there with the whole world about to be blown to fuck.

There were a few days left.

It was Friday night.

By Sunday, it would be over, for good or bad.

No one spoke to him as he ate. Muttered conversations hummed around the bar, too quiet to be easily heard. He caught words, fragments, and though he tried not to, he could make out some of what was being said.

He lowered his eyes, fixing them on his food, and pretended he wasn't listening. The people around him didn't need to be any more fucked than they already were. Some of the whispers could easily be called treason.

Maybe they thought he'd want to join in their conversations. Maybe it was why the whispers were within his range of hearing. Maybe they were trying to gauge his stance on the disaster that was their region.

When he pushed his stool out and rose, his bowl scraped clean, he felt eyes on him, but he was too tired to give a damn.

They could think what they fucking liked.

He set his empty bowl on the counter, nodded silently to the old men in their nook, and dragged himself up the stairs. The mice were already rustling in the thatch, but he lacked the energy to even beat at the roof and drive them away.

Dieter sank onto the mattress, wincing.

He'd turned his ankle earlier in the day, and it was swollen, aching. He gingerly pressed his fingers against it, cursing through clenched teeth. All he wanted was take his boots off and sleep for a week, but if the boots came off, they wouldn't go on the next morning.

He pulled the neckerchief off and smoothed it out. Not much of a bandage, it was too thin to provide any support. He glanced at his walking stick. It would have worked, but if he tried walking without the thing, he'd get nowhere.

Reluctantly, he withdrew Janos's knife from his pocket.

The staff wouldn't be much support, but it was all he had without walking anywhere to find more sticks.

Dieter clenched his teeth as he wedged the handle into the side of his boot to hold it in place. It hurt like hell. His heart pounding, he pushed up his trousers to wrap his scarf just above the neck of his boot to stop his foot from moving, his hands shaking so much he could hardly tie the knot to pull it tight.

His head fell forward to rest on his upraised knee.

It was all fucked. Everything about the situation was fucked.

He pressed his eyes shut, wrapping his arms around his legs, and squeezed his calves until they ached.

Christ, he wanted to go home.

Sitting about like a fanny, crying, wasn't going to help anyone, but he couldn't stop it. Every inch of him felt bruised, and all he wanted was to open his eyes and be back in the shithole of a temporal chamber.

He was shaking so hard he bit down on his bottom lip and tasted blood. But he wouldn't make a fucking sound. He wasn't that useless. He would be quiet, and no one would have any clue he was falling apart.

He sat with his eyes closed tight and let the acid burn in his throat and the bruises swell under his fingertips, and cried in the darkness until everything was quiet.

He didn't remember lying down or going to sleep or anything.

He must have done because he was on the floor when someone kicked him in the ribs.

Dieter's eyes snapped open, and he scrambled to sit up. It was still dark, and someone outside the room held a flickering lantern. Shadows, figures, stood around him, and his mouth went bone dry, his heart racing.

"What do you want?" he whispered hoarsely.

None of them answered, but one reached down and pinned him against the wall, while another went through his pockets.

A robbery. Of all the fucking things.

The photograph of Llewelyn was pulled out of his pocket and held up in the light of the lantern.

"You're sure?" One of the men spoke in High German. No one in the inn spoke High fucking German, especially not any of the locals.

Dieter shrank against the wall, his heart pounding.

The only people in the area who would speak that were much higher up the social ladder.

Or worse.

Fucking Austrians.

"He listened in the inn."

Dieter recognised the voice—the son of a bitch who had almost fooled him into giving himself away.

"He replied in German when I spoke to him one time. He said he did not speak German before."

Shit shit shit.

He'd replied?

When had he fucking replied?

Jesus Christ, he was fucked. He was fucked so fucking hard.

He stared around wildly, but he was blocked on all sides, and even if he managed to get past them, he had a busted ankle. They'd run him down before he even got half a block. But if he let them take him, everything was fucked beyond the telling.

His breathing came in ragged gasps, and when they dragged him to his feet, he kept his eyes down. If they thought he was cowed, they might not expect him to try to escape, and he had no intention of staying locked up.

History was the main thing. It had to be protected.

They dragged him out of his room, down the stairs, and he bit down a scream as his ankle cracked against the doorframe. The pain was blinding, and he gulped in gasping breaths of the thick humid night air.

His eyes swam, but he peered around urgently.

A wagon took up half the street, but only a couple of men by it.

His combat training was limited, but after his first encounter with Janos, he could at least break free of people holding him.

He managed to knock one of them on his arse, and fled, limping and keening in pain. He barely got a dozen steps before something struck him hard in the back of the head.

Dieter swayed and folded at the knees.

The world whirled, darkening at the edges.

He stared, blank, dazed, down at the mud, thick and wet, and fell forward. Voices shouted orders, angry. He blinked slowly, mud in his eyes, his ears, his mouth. He tasted blood.

Boots appeared in front of his eyes and then faded into darkness.

Chapter Thirty-One

"Damn!"

In the monitoring room, Janos sat at one of the computers as Tamara led him through another computer programme. Many of the programmes were simple to follow, but this one had code in it he had never seen before. It scrolled across the screen as Tamara typed it in, her hands moving in a blur on the sensor keys.

Tamara glanced at him. "Problem?"

He clenched his fist, flexing his fingers. "I am doing what you do, but it is too fast."

She lifted her hands from the keyboard. "Okay. Which part is too fast?"

Janos took a breath, his teeth gritted together for a moment, before he faced her. She was one of the few people who seemed to overlook his infirmity. "Your hands. They are too fast. I have only one."

She flushed. "Oh, God. I'm so sorry. I didn't even think."

"No, no," he said quickly. "It is good. You do not see it is gone. This is good."

"But it doesn't help you when you can't keep up," she said, pulling her chair closer to his. "Let me see where you are, and I can talk you through."

He pointed to the screen. "This."

"Okay. This is what you need to do."

Painstakingly, he followed her instructions, but what had taken her less than a minute took him closer to ten, and he slapped his hand on the desk in frustration.

"This is useless," he snapped. "I waste your time."

"For a guy from the 20th century, you're doing much better than you should be."

"But not fast enough." He glanced down at the stump of his arm.

"It just takes practice. We can get new software to help you."

Janos was silent for a long while, rubbing his thumb against his fingertips. It seemed technology was everywhere to help someone maimed as he was: a false limb, something for a computer.

"You mean machine to help me?" he asked. "Because of one arm, I must use machine?"

"Not must. You *can*, but you don't need to."

He touched the concealed stump of his arm.

He remembered speaking to Doctor Bellevue about his arm, about not wanting or needing a synthetic limb. Dieter too. He'd wanted the thing removed because it felt too different, from another world he wasn't part of. But now...

By the light of the computer screens, with lines of code filling his mind, he knew he belonged in a world of science and technology now, where an arm could be attached and could function like his own limb.

"You will excuse me?" He pushed his chair out from the desk. "I must think."

Tamara nodded, gazing at him in concern. "You okay?"

He nodded. "Too many thoughts. I will come again. Maybe later."

She didn't ask anything more, and he was grateful. He left the computer room and retreated through the building up to the roof garden, away from everyone and everything. It was easier to think up there, without the constant buzz of electricity in his ears and people coming and going at all times of the day and night.

The sky was grey, overcast, but the rain had stopped for the first time in days.

Janos meandered onto the gravel path. It wove in a constant pattern, and it was easy to lose track of how many times he'd circled around it.

It should have been a simple conundrum. He was missing an arm, and he could get a new one put in its place. He could have two hands again, even if one of them was not quite his own. It would make things easier to learn in a world where speed was appreciated.

He glared down at the smooth stump where his forearm once was.

It would be useful, but it also felt like giving up.

He shook his head with a sigh of frustration and stopped walking.

Maybe it was unconscious direction or maybe chance he ended up there, but he stood at the door of Sally's office. He rubbed his thumb against his fingertip, staring at the door, then nodded, reaching up and knocking cautiously.

She opened the door and smiled in surprise. "Janos. How are you?"

He folded and unfolded his fingers. "Dieter tell me you help with...with thoughts? Is true?"

Sally opened the door wider, motioning him in. "It is. I can't guarantee I can give you advice you want, but I will listen and make suggestions."

Janos walked into the room and hesitated behind the sofa. There were sandwiches on a plate on the table. "You are eating," he said apologetically, "I will come again."

"Nonsense," Sally said firmly, closing the door. "Sit down. We can talk. Food can wait."

He sat uncertainly, self-consciously drawing his sleeve down his arm. "I do not know what to say."

Sally went over to the teapot on the counter and poured him a cup. "You don't need to tell me everything. Just what you're comfortable with."

He was silent, even when the cup was set in front of him, but finally, he said, "I have one arm now. Doctor Bellevue will give me two arms." He picked up the teacup, curling his fingers around it. "Is this weak? To take another arm? To be whole man again?"

She shook her head with a smile. "It's not weak. It's about what makes you comfortable and happy. If you are happy with one arm, then have one arm. If you think you will be happier with two, then have two. It is not strong or weak to choose."

Janos stared down at his tea. "It feels weak." He held up the stump of his arm. "I am broken."

Sally gazed at him. "I don't think other people see you like this. Your arm is gone, but people see that you are strong and clever. People do not see you as broken. Dieter didn't. Nor does Sanders. Or the people who learn from you."

"Some of them look." Janos remembered them staring.

"Some people look because they are not used to seeing a man with one arm." She picked up one of her sandwiches, nibbled on it, and set it down. "You should think about what it will mean for you. Pretend other people are not there. If you take this arm, it is for you. It is not for anyone else. It does not matter what they think." She nodded towards him. "It is only for you."

He took a mouthful of tea, drinking so quickly he burned his tongue, and set the cup on the table. "I do not know. I think..." He frowned, turning his arm. "I do many bad thing. To lose arm was to be punished for bad thing."

"So you don't want a new arm, because you are being punished?"

He raised his eyes to hers. "I am not good man," he said quietly. "People die because of me. Maybe, this make me remember."

She gazed at him. "Because of you?" she asked, and Janos flinched.

"All people I know," he said, his voice low. "People I..." He shook his head. "I care for people, and they die."

Sally came around the table to sit beside him on his left side, and when she reached out, she gently laid her hand over what remained of his forearm. Janos shivered, closing his eyes.

"It does not make you a bad person," she said quietly. "You don't need to punish yourself for something that wasn't your doing."

He met her dark eyes. "Dieter," he whispered, his voice breaking. "I came, and now, he is there. He did not want to..." He shook his head and rose unsteadily. "I talk foolishness. I will go."

Sally stood, stepping back. "If you want to, but you don't have to. I am always here, you know."

He closed his hand over the stump of his arm. "Thank you. You enjoy sandwich."

The garden didn't seem so comforting anymore, the sky too big and open. He retreated into the building and made his way down to the pool to lose himself in the steady repetition of lengths, pushing away all thoughts of loss and limbs and the man trapped in the past because of him.

By the time he climbed out of the pool, his body ached from exertion, muscles twitching in his arms and legs. He sat on the edge of the pool, feet trailing in the water until a familiar call came across the intercom.

"Gate connection in fifteen minutes. Report to control chamber in fifteen minutes."

On shivering legs, Janos got up, dressed as quickly as he could, and made his way to the elevator.

Sanders stood just inside the doorway of the control room. He glanced at Janos as he entered. "You okay?"

Janos nodded mutely, taking his seat at the desk beside Tamara. She offered him a quick nod, but her hands darted across the controls, her eyes fixed on the screen.

It was the routine part of the day.

Nothing happened.

The gate opened.

Dieter's vital statistics were fine.

The gate was closed, and they all went back to worrying for the next twenty-four hours.

"Connection made."

Janos watched Tamara's monitor.

He was the first one to see it: slow pulse, low blood pressure. Dieter's life signs were weak.

"Shit." Sanders was the second.

"Keep gate open," Janos snapped, getting up.

"Shut it down," Sanders snarled over the top. "Now."

Janos whirled around. "No."

"You're not going through," Sanders said, his voice hard. "Don't even think about it."

Janos stared at him. For a moment, he was standing on sentry duty, distant screams ringing out in the cold night air. He never forgot the sound, just as he never forgot the cold, stiff corpse.

He swung his arm; his fist crashed into Sanders's face, sending him reeling. In two steps, Janos crossed the floor and slammed him against the wall, his fist twisted in Sanders's shirt, his forearm pinning him by the throat.

"You son of bitch! You leave him there to die!"

Sanders held up his hands. Maybe to stop people attacking Janos. Maybe to calm people. Janos didn't care. Sanders's face darkened, his breath wheezed in his crushed throat, but he didn't fight. He just met Janos's eyes, calm and steady.

Behind Janos, the hum of the gate cut out, and there was silence.

Janos jerked his arm back, recoiling with a curse.

Sanders slumped against the wall, gasping. "You think you can help him." he said, his voice hoarse. "You can't."

"How you know this? You do not even try! You send him alone, and now, he is harmed! You leave him to die! You do not even try!" The words trembled in his mouth. "We will go too late. He will be dead!"

He groped out blindly with his missing arm, stumbled, and sat heavily against a desk. Burying his face in his shaking hand, his breath came too fast, his vision swimming. Tears or rage, he didn't know.

Sanders pushed himself upright against the wall. "Clear the room," he whispered, his voice so quiet it was hardly more than a rasp. Everyone obeyed, scuffling through the door.

"Boss..."

"Out!" Sanders barked.

When the door closed, Janos lowered his hand and stared at Sanders. At the bruising across the man's throat, dark and ugly, but he didn't care. "You leave him there," he said dully. "You leave him to die."

Sanders still leaned against the wall. "And what if I let you go through? How would you find him? Do you know anything about that time? That place? Where would you even start?"

"So you leave him."

Sanders took unsteady steps towards one of the chairs and sat down. "I trust him to do his damned job. He knew we wouldn't be able to come in after him. He knows the rendezvous point."

"And if he dies?"

Sanders met his eyes. "I don't think that way. Until the mission is completed or confirmed as failed, we have to presume the best, even if we expect the worst."

Janos stared at his hand. His knuckles were reddened from the impact with Sanders's face. He curled his fingers, wincing, then turned to the man. "How you can do this?" he asked quietly. "How you can sit and do nothing?"

"Because I've already risked one man." Sanders looked old, and he sounded tired. "I can't risk more. If I let another go, then another, and another, where would I stop?"

Janos nodded. "You are commander." He glanced over at the monitor which still showed Dieter's life signs, frozen in time. "I am sorry." He shifted self-consciously. "It is...difficult to not know."

Sanders nodded, rising. "Trust me," he said quietly, "I've been where you are now." Janos stared up at him, startled. Sanders smiled briefly, sadly, and laid a bony hand on Janos's shoulder. "At least you know he's still alive."

Janos glanced at the monitors, but by the time he turned to ask Sanders who he had lost, the man was gone.

Chapter Thirty-Two

Dieter tasted blood in his mouth.

He wasn't sure if he'd been asleep or unconscious or both. It was receding, whichever it was, and Christ, he wished it would come back. His head throbbed like a bastard, and every fucking inch of him felt like it had been beaten black and blue.

He forced his eyes open, the lashes gummed with dry blood.

Gloom surrounded him, except for a faint shaft of light cutting across the room from somewhere higher up the wall.

He gingerly turned his head to find his face pressed close to a damp stone wall. Straw pricked at his skin, and he smelled a piss bucket somewhere nearby. With shaking arms, he pulled himself up into a sitting position. The world swam, and he tipped sideways to lean against the wall, drawing shuddering breaths.

The pain that had started in his head was intensifying, and he squinted down at his legs. His aching ankle was worse—a great big fucking shackle was wrapped around it and his other leg.

He tried to pull his legs closer to check, and the metal bit into the swollen flesh. Pain blazed up his leg, white flashing behind his eyes. He clamped a hand over his mouth to stop from screaming like a fucking child.

"Looks like he's awake."

Dieter turned towards the voice, swallowing down bitter burning acid at the sight of bars separating him from the speaker. He was in a jail, not just a simple cell either. Thick walls. Shackles. Bars. The man on the far side wore a terrifyingly familiar uniform.

The Austrian Imperial household guard.

Another man stood by the door.

Dieter glanced from one to the other. He was in so much fucking trouble he couldn't even think. Locked up, and the heir to the throne's assassination due in God knew how long. Did he call their bluff? Did he keep playing the role? Fuck, he didn't know.

The two guards spoke quietly to one another, and then the one by the door strode out.

The other one approached the bars, and Dieter shrank against the wall.

Even that hurt, and he didn't want to work out why it felt like his ribs were broken. It wouldn't have been the first time soldiers took a chance to put the boot in when they caught a suspected enemy.

"We know you speak German, friend," the soldier said, smiling. A pleasant-looking man, but his expression was anything but friendly. "You should stop pretending. It will only end badly for you."

Dieter's tongue sat like a rock in his mouth, every thought was moving at a snail's pace, and even blinking stupidly at the man took so much fucking effort. Christ, his head hurt. Would it be better to keep his mouth shut or speak? Somewhere in the middle, he sat there, mouth open, staring like an idiot.

His head.

It had to be bad.

His words were all over the place.

Something tickled down his chin, and he touched his mouth. His fingers came away bloody, his bottom lip swollen, split.

"Water?" he asked in Hungarian, his voice frail. "Please?"

The soldier's eyebrows rose. He folded his arms over his chest and didn't move.

Dieter leaned against the wall, his head too heavy to hold up, and he closed his eyes, breathing deeply to keep himself from being sick. Christ, he was going to fall, even though there was nowhere to go.

It seemed like hours crawled by in silence, but it might have only been minutes. Everything was hazy.

Dieter caught a breath of fresh air as the door out of the cell block opened, and footsteps came closer. It was like listening to them through a tunnel, echoing through his head. He forced his eyes open and peered up, half expecting the captain of the guard to have come for his head.

Mike Llewelyn stood on the other side of the room, dressed in household uniform.

Dieter stared at him in incomprehension.

"So, Muller," the other guard said. "What have you to say for yourself? Do you know this man?"

Llewelyn approached the bars, doing an amazing job of not acting surprised. The bastard recognised him; it was clear in Llewelyn's dark eyes, though Dieter could only guess how, given the mess he was in.

"Dieter? Are you all right?" he said quietly in formal German.

Dieter shrank against the stone once more, shaking his head. It wouldn't do Llewelyn any good to be linked to a suspected spy. At least one of them could get out of the train wreck alive if he kept his mouth shut.

"Muller?" the guard snapped.

Llewelyn straightened up. "Yes, sir. I know this man. He is my brother." He looked over his shoulder and approached the guard, speaking quietly. "He is a simple-minded man. He was born so."

"He speaks Hungarian," the guard observed.

"Our grandmother was from Hungary. She taught us," Llewelyn said. "He does not leave our home often. He fears the enemies of our people will harm him." He gazed at Dieter with pity. "He must have used Hungarian so no one would suspect he was from our land, the little fool."

The guard eyed Dieter doubtfully. Llewelyn had handed him a role, and he had to play it, but gathering thoughts was about as easy as catching a fucking cloud in a colander.

"I'm sorry, Micke," Dieter whispered in German, his voice breaking. "Papa is gone, and I had to find you. Mama said you would be here, but you must come home at once." He covered his eyes, his head aching. "I did not mean to get you in trouble." He struggled onto his knees, crawling towards the bars, every inch of him screaming in pain. "Please, you must come home, Micke."

Llewelyn ignored the two guards to kneel by the bars, reaching through, and, Christ, Dieter couldn't help bursting into tears when Llewelyn hugged him like he really was his brother. He clung onto the other man, someone familiar, someone who knew he wasn't pretending to be absolutely fucking terrified.

"I'll get you out of here," Llewelyn muttered close to his ear. "Just play the village idiot, okay?"

He pulled away from the bars, and Dieter grabbed at him. He wasn't sure if he was playing the part or if it was terror at being left alone again. "Don't leave me, Micke," he whispered. "We have to go home."

Llewelyn reached through the bars and gently touched his head. He looked at the two guards. "Sir, may we speak elsewhere?"

The guard nodded abruptly.

Dieter didn't have the strength to crawl away from the bars. He crumpled there like a wet towel, the cold of the floor seeping through to his throbbing bones. More blood pooled in his mouth, his face hot and wet, and salt mingled with the metal.

He hadn't moved, still curled, shivering, when Llewelyn returned.

All at once, the shackles were removed from his ankles, and he was gently lifted onto a makeshift stretcher. The jolting of the stretcher jarred his head, and he gasped in pain a second before blackness descended.

When the light returned, he flinched as a cool cloth was drawn over his face, his eyelids flickering feebly.

"Easy," Llewelyn muttered. "Rest quiet, little brother."

Dieter didn't know what he expected. Did Llewelyn think he would leap up and run around, screaming they were time travellers? He opened his eyes, wincing at the late afternoon light cutting through a nearby window. It seemed the rain had finally cleared.

He was lying on a rough pallet bed, and Llewelyn sat on the edge of it, sponging the blood from his face. There were three other beds in the room. Not military dormitories, then. Staff quarters.

Another man stood nearby. Not in a guard uniform, but the look on his face suggested Dieter was still not as free as his self-professed brother might believe.

Llewelyn tilted a cup to Dieter's lips, and Dieter choked as he tried to gulp down the watered wine. It seared across cuts inside his mouth and burned his lip, but it was the sweetest thing he had tasted in what felt like weeks.

"Easy," Llewelyn murmured again, withdrawing the cup. "You'll be sick."

Dieter nodded as much as he dared, hissing through his teeth when Llewelyn unlaced his shirt. He tried to squint down at himself and had to turn away, his chest a mess of bootprints and bruises.

"You didn't make friends, did you?"

Dieter twitched his head tightly. "I want to go home." It sounded fucking pathetic and childlike, but it was only the truth.

Llewelyn sighed. "I know you were sent to find me, but you shouldn't have come."

Dieter groped for Llewelyn's arm, clutching at his wrist. "I had to," he whispered, trying to work out how to tell him just how much trouble he was in. "You know papa didn't like it when you went away without his permission. He was very angry."

Llewelyn helped him sit up and set to work binding Dieter's ribs. "Father was always too strict," he said quietly. "One rule for one child, another rule for another." He met Dieter's eyes. "It's too late now."

Dieter shook his head as much as he dared. "Come home," he whispered. "Don't do something stupid."

Llewelyn lifted his hand to Dieter's cheek. "I'm doing the right thing, little brother. I'll come home with you, if that's what I have to do, but not yet." He searched Dieter's face. "You understand?"

"Micke…"

Llewelyn's fingers dug into his ribs, hidden by the bandages. Dieter keened in pain, clutching at Llewelyn's arms as fireworks went off behind his eyes. He tried to push him away, but Llewelyn's thumb stabbed up beneath his sternum, and Dieter retched. He folded over and vomited over the side of the bed, spattering the floor.

"Water!" Llewelyn barked to the other man, hauling Dieter up as if he hadn't done anything. "Get some water for him, damn you!"

The man dashed out the room, leaving them alone.

Llewelyn pushed Dieter against the bed with a gentle but ruthless force that made his breath come short in pain. "You're going to stay here," he said quietly. "I've not got this far for you to get in the way now."

Dieter grabbed Llewelyn's shoulder, his fingers biting hard. "You don't know what you're doing," he hissed, his mouth bitter with blood, bile, and vomit. "You won't be stopping anything, Mike. This won't stop anything. This whole fucking place is a fucking powder keg."

"And Ferdinand is the spark," Llewelyn said coolly, pushing Dieter's hand from his arm.

Dieter hit Llewelyn's chest. "No, no, no, no," he groaned, his ribs screaming. "He's not the only thing. This isn't just about him, you stupid fuck! You can't change things! You can't! You can't know it won't make things worse!"

"You can't know it won't make things better," Llewelyn said, his voice low. "One man, Dieter. I'm saving one man. You've done the same already. You have no fucking right to get in my way."

"Because he was already dead in his own fucking timeline!" The whispered words were getting harder to say, and even breathing hurt. "For fuck's sake, Mike. I hate the rules as much as you, but they're there for a reason. You can't change the past!"

Mike clamped his hand over Dieter's face, pressing his head against the pillow, stifling him as boots clattered in the hall outside. Dieter gasped explosively when Llewelyn lifted his hand away, the pain in his head overriding the pain in his chest.

"We can go home on Monday, little brother," Llewelyn said, wiping his brow with a cloth as the guard strode in with a pitcher of water. He poured some into a cup and held it out to Llewelyn. "Only one more day, then we can go home."

Dieter clutched at him as Llewelyn slid a hand under his head. "Don't," he whispered. "Please don't make us stay."

Llewelyn smiled, but it didn't reach his eyes. "The archduke arrives tomorrow." He put the cup to Dieter's lips. The water tasted bitter, and Dieter choked on it, coughing. "I can't leave until after his visit."

"Micke..."

The muscle in Llewelyn's cheek twitched, and he moved his hand against the swelling wound across the back of Dieter's head. His fingers pressed hard, and Dieter retched again, his world spotting with black.

Llewelyn cradled him like a kid as the edges of the world went dark and blurred.

"I'm sorry, Dieter," he murmured, "I truly am."

Chapter Thirty-Three

The chain rattled as the punching bag spun.

Janos waited a moment and hit it again, this time with the remains of his left forearm before crossing with a punch. He'd always been good at sparring. Now, he tried to find his balance again while taking out his frustrations on the bag.

He had barely slept. All he wanted was to exhaust himself to the point he couldn't remember dreaming. Swimming wasn't enough, so he'd turned to the punch bag.

People came and went, but he ignored them, and as far he cared, they ignored him too.

His shoulders ached, and sweat had soaked into the back of his vest by the time someone stepped up and stabilised the bag. Janos swiped the sweat from his eyes and glanced sideways, expecting Sanders.

Instead, it was the man who had told him of Dieter's interest in him. Like Janos, he wore sporting clothes, and from the shine on his skin, he must have been using another part of the gym as well. He nodded to the bag.

"Want me to block it for you?"

Janos stared at him blankly for a moment and then nodded. It was harder to keep it from spinning when he didn't have two hands to hit with.

The man stepped behind the bag, bracing it with both hands, and Janos resumed striking.

Less than ten minutes later, he had to step back, rolling his shoulders.

"Thank you," he said. "That is very helpful."

"No problem. You okay?"

Janos shrugged, returning to the bench where he'd left his towel. He dragged it over his face and behind his neck.

The man was still watching him.

Janos didn't know what he was expecting, if he wanted anything, and he was too damned tired to ask. He folded the towel and gathered his key card and identification, looking at it, unsure what to say.

"I worry about him too."

That caught Janos by surprise.

The man offered a brief, half smile, mostly hidden in his beard. "He's still my friend, even if he's not very good at it. For someone who thinks he's a loner, Dieter has a lot of people who care about him."

Janos nodded abruptly, turning away. "That is good."

He didn't want to talk about Dieter.

He didn't want to think about Dieter.

That was the whole point of the exercise.

The man sighed behind him. "Do you want company? Or a drink? Or something?"

Janos stopped halfway to the door. "I do not want anything," he said as steadily as he could. "Thank you."

"You don't need to cut yourself off."

Janos's hand tightened on the towel, and he turned. "You do not know me. I do not know you. It is not your business what I do. You understand?"

"I understand you attacked Sanders yesterday." Brown eyes gazed at him placidly. "And I know people don't understand why. They're talking."

The edge of Janos's pass cut into his hand. "And you understand this? You are special?"

"I know about you and Dieter."

It was like a punch to the chest. He strode the four steps to close the distance between them. "You do not speak of this. You do not tell anyone of this. It is private for me and for him. It is not your business."

He held up his hands. "Fine. Just don't forget who told you Dieter wanted you in the first place."

Janos stepped away, blowing out a hissed breath. "Yes. I remember this," he agreed quietly, his hand still clenched around his pass. "But it is not your business. Not now. Not until he is coming home." He met the man's eyes. "You are understanding me?"

He nodded slowly. "Just speaking as a friend."

Janos shook his head curtly. "We are not friends." He turned on his heel and stalked from the room.

Most people avoided his eyes as he made his way through the halls. He didn't care why, only that he wanted to return to his room and away from anyone who would talk at him when all he wanted was quiet. All they would talk to him of was Dieter, with meaningless reassurances. He couldn't listen to them try to lie when they had no idea what was going to happen.

He tossed his pass and the towel onto his bed and headed for the shower. He stood under the steaming water until it ran cold, his shoulders twitching from exertion, his legs still aching from hours of swimming.

Finally, he emerged from the bathroom, his towel around his waist, and stopped short.

Sanders sat at the table.

"You were late," he said abruptly without turning. "You missed the gate-check."

Janos's heart sank. Sanders sat too rigid, too formal. "Dieter?"

"Better than he was yesterday. For god's sake, put some clothes on. I can't talk to you when you're half-naked."

Janos nodded mutely, towelled himself, and pulled on his sleeping clothes. He padded to the table and sat down. "You did not call on me."

Sanders gazed placidly at him, his face swollen where Janos had hit him. "I did. You weren't listening."

Gym or shower or pool. Janos didn't know.

"He lives?"

Sanders nodded, sliding a flat computer across the table to him. It showed the details from the tracker. The heart rate was stronger and steadier than the day before. Janos traced the lines with his fingertips. Dieter was still not showing his usual signal though.

It wasn't good news, but it wasn't bad news either.

"I hear you've been terrorizing the staff," Sanders said as he got up from the chair and walked over to fill the kettle.

"Terrorizing?"

"Mm." Sanders poked through Janos's cupboard. "Storming about like you want to smack someone." He paused, laughed wryly. "Well, someone else." He glanced over his shoulder. "I heard the punch bag got a good workout."

Janos gazed down at the screen. "What I can do?" he asked quietly. "I cannot help him."

Sanders turned and leaned against the counter. "You can find something to do. We have weapons and arms that need to be tested and catalogued. We have a wardrobe mistress who would be more than happy for you to work with her. Instead of beating the shite out of a bag, you could open your eyes and see we're not all sitting and waiting about. We're all worried about the little bugger, but we're keeping ourselves busy."

Janos flushed in embarrassment. "I work with computers."

"Not today. Not when you needed the distraction."

Janos glanced at the computer on the table. No. He couldn't have dealt with the computers today, seeing the information being sorted and put into neat little folders as if it wasn't about someone they knew.

Sanders made two cups of coffee, carried them over, and set one in front of Janos as he sat down. "Tomorrow, I've assigned you to the weapons and arms store. You know how those guns work. I want you to test them. There are machines to pull the triggers so you don't blow yourself to pieces, but since you need to do some violence, you can use the firing range."

Janos drew the cup towards him. "I did not mean to scare people."

Sanders sighed with a lopsided smile. "I know, and you know, but between you and me, you aren't the most approachable person on a good day. I don't blame people for avoiding you. Especially after..." He gestured to his face.

Janos looked down sheepishly. "It is looking bad today. I did not think I hit so hard."

"You weren't the only one who was surprised. People had gotten used to you being the strong, silent type. They didn't expect you to react like that."

"You did not tell them?"

Sanders shook his head. "Not my place. Your life. You tell who you like when you like. They just thought you were worried about him."

Janos tried to smile, but it faltered. "They are not wrong."

Chapter Thirty-Four

Dieter squinted into the darkness, unsure what time it was. Early or late. He didn't know.

The only sound was the breathing further down the room, one of them snoring.

With a wince, Dieter turned his head. His hair stuck to the pillow. Dried blood, he guessed, pulling free. It hurt like hell, fresh pain burning across the back of his skull, and he hissed between gritted teeth.

He had to get up. He had to. It was the day. The event. He had to stop Llewelyn from doing whatever he was planning.

Christ, he didn't know how.

He could barely think straight.

A hand touched his chest from the other side, and he flinched away, biting down on a curse.

"Easy," Llewelyn murmured.

He sat beside the bed on a low stool.

Dieter stared at him warily. "What time is it?" he asked, his mouth dry as a bone.

"A little before five," Llewelyn said quietly. "You should rest."

Dieter laid his head down gingerly. "What are you going to do?" he whispered.

"What I came to do."

Dieter closed his eyes. He was the last hope Sanders had of preserving the past. If he could knock Llewelyn out, it might be enough, but he could barely stand, let alone take down a man trained in combat.

Llewelyn poured some water into a cup and held it to Dieter's lips, helping him drink. It was even more bitter than before, and he turned his face away.

"Is there anything I can say to change your mind?" he asked.

"When I know you wish you could do it?"

"I wouldn't..."

Llewelyn nodded, his face featureless in the darkness. "I know. But you wish you could. Anyone who has gone back wishes they could." He brushed his hand across Dieter's brow. "You'll stay here."

Dieter stared at him blankly. He had Janos's knife. He could take it out. Hurt Llewelyn badly enough so he wouldn't be able to act. But if he did, they'd both be fucked. He couldn't get him to the rendezvous if they were both injured.

Dieter's head swam again, his tongue numb. The water. The bitterness. Oh, fucking hell.

"Mike, what did..."

"You need to rest," Llewelyn said gently. "Just a little drink to help."

Dieter groped for his arm, but it was like moving through quicksand. "Mike..."

Llewelyn caught his shoulders, pressed him down to the bed, his words muffled in Dieter's ears. Bastard, Dieter thought desperately. Fucking bastard.

He fought against the swirling dark clouding his vision—a losing battle. Like drowning in air, and the dreams it brought were vivid, sharp, and terrifying. He screamed in them, screamed until he tasted blood.

Something hit him.

Cold.

Wet.

Dieter jerked to wakefulness, gasping and gagging.

A man—the man who had been watching him and Llewelyn the day before—stood over him with an empty bucket.

Dieter stared at him, panting and shaking, soaked to the skin, his hair plastered to his face. "Wh-what..."

"You wouldn't shut up, and your brother wasn't here to wake you."

Brother?

Dieter put his hand to his head, wincing.

Llewelyn.

The bastard.

He'd drugged him.

Dieter tried to sit up but a tight pressure across his ribs restrained him. He winced, reaching for it, his hand encountering rope. His fingers trembled along it. If there were knots, he wouldn't have a fucking chance of undoing them.

"Can you untie me, please?" he asked, his voice hoarse.

"Sorry, boy," the man said. "You were to be left here. Muller didn't want you wandering off." He shrugged. "Enjoy the rest. Some of us have work to do." He headed for the door, picking up his coat on the way out.

"Wait!" Dieter called desperately. "Please. What time is it? When will my brother be back?"

The man glanced at him and then pulled out a pocket watch. "It's a half hour past nine." He paused in the doorway. "You have to be quiet, or someone will come in and gag you, you understand? We need quiet now."

Dieter nodded as much as he could, swallowing hard.

The man nodded in response and closed the door behind him. Dieter held his breath, waiting for the sound of a key in a lock, but none came. One fucking small mercy.

He took deep breaths, trying to clear his head. The water had helped, but not much.

Sitting up was impossible. The ropes across his ribs were meant to keep him there, and it hurt to even try to move against them. His arms were free, though, and his legs.

Dieter shifted his feet carefully. Both boots were still on. Maybe Janos's knife was still there. He drew his left leg up, his foot flat to the bed, and stretched his arm as much as he could. Yoga had to be useful for something.

His fingertips skimmed along the top of the boot and the edge of the scarf holding the knife in place. He couldn't feel the knife anymore, the pain in his ankle throbbing like a heartbeat.

He tugged at the scarf, his hands shaking so much he struggled to get a grip on the thing. His foot was too far out of reach, and he flopped, exhausted, against the pillow, panting, ribs and legs aching. Christ, if he didn't get a move on, the world he'd come from would go to fuck.

He took a slow, deep breath, reached down and grabbed his left knee, and pulled his leg up hard against his chest. The scream rose in his throat, and he bit down hard on his lip to keep it in. His mouth filled with blood. His hands shook, but he wrapped his right arm around his leg, held it fast, and blindly tugged at his left boot.

Shaking and sweating, he finally tugged the knot in the scarf loose. The loss of pressure around his ankle made it throb even more, his breathing coming hard as he fumbled for the knife.

There was something comforting about it in his cold, shaking hand, warm and solid and—most importantly—fucking sharp.

Dieter let his leg fall down and sawed at the ropes across his chest. They parted like thread under the blade, and he pushed himself upright, pressing his eyes shut for a moment as the world spun around him.

Okay.

Upright.

He dragged his legs off the edge of the bed and peered around. His coat lay on the stool beside the bed. His stick too. It looked like Llewelyn had been serious when he said they'd go home afterward, assuming there was a home to go back to.

Dieter struggled to his feet, grabbed the stick, and limped towards the window. The pain in his leg was so constant now he could ignore it. He took in the view, leaning against the window ledge. He had no clue where he was. Only mountains and forest, and, Jesus, if they were anywhere far from town, he was fucked.

He limped to the bed and sat down to retie the scarf around his ankle, then pulled on his rough cloth cap to cover his bloody head.

There wasn't any time to waste cleaning up.

All the assassins would already be in place around the city. Of course, only two of them were actually going to do anything: Cabrinovic with an unsuccessful attack with the bomb on the way to the town hall, and Princip with the fatal gunshots on the return journey.

Dieter's options were limited. He had no idea where Llewelyn was. Or hell, where he was himself. First, he had to find out, then work out what Llewelyn planned to do. If he was lucky, he'd be able to get in the way before Llewelyn managed to fuck everything up.

Or, there were two choices he didn't want to think about. Either one of them would get blood on his hands He was too exhausted to take on Llewelyn in hand-to-hand, and the second...

Princip had to be the assassin.

He had to be the one to kill the archduke and his wife.

He was the one in the history books, the man who pulled the trigger and rotted in jail for it.

Dieter got up gingerly, leaning heavily on the stick.

He'd work out the details on the way. What mattered was that he was free, on his feet, and had an hour to do something about it. He'd been given a mission he wasn't going to forget about, even if his head still felt like it was stuck in a fucking cloud.

He made his way cautiously out into the hall. The building was grand but basic, and voices echoed through the halls. If he was seen, he could be locked up again, so he kept close to the walls, recoiling into doorways at any sound of footsteps.

At a junction of two corridors ahead of him, two men in Austrian military uniform walked briskly across the hall. He shrank back to a door behind him, and he pushed it open a crack. It appeared to be empty, so he pushed the door wider and hastily stepped inside, only to trip over a prone body.

Dieter yelped in pain as his knees cracked against the floor. The click of the door swinging shut covered the sound, and he scrambled away, staring at the body—a man in a uniform he didn't recognise, tied up at wrists and ankles. Whoever he was, he was unconscious but starting to stir.

Dieter glanced towards the door. With all the men outside, one tied-up man in here was easier to deal with. Also, maybe he was a prisoner. But it didn't make much sense since he was locked in...

A glance showed weapons and metal and swords.

An armoury.

Who would lock someone in an armoury where no one would look for him?

"Shit," Dieter whispered to himself. He pulled out his knife, sawed at the ropes pinioning the man's arms, and rolled him onto his back. He had to be someone significant, but Dieter didn't recognise him.

The man blinked, his eyes unfocussed.

Dieter hesitated and then slapped him sharply. He flinched, eyes widening as he stared blankly at Dieter.

"Who are you?"

The words lined themselves up without Dieter even thinking. "No time to explain," he said in curt formal Austrian German. "We believe an assailant has infiltrated the party attending His Highness, the archduke. Did you recognise your attacker?"

The man shook his head, seeming to have trouble understanding. "He hit me from behind." He sat up, put his hand to his head, and blinked again as if trying to bring his eyes into focus. "What time is it?"

"Come close to ten," Dieter replied, hoping he was right.

The man tried to rise but swayed and fell back. "The governor! He asked for me to drive! I must be there!"

"Drive?" Dieter asked.

He nodded, grasping at Dieter's arm. "I am the governor's driver. He ordered me to bring the car for the Archduke."

Dieter stared at him. "Lojka? You are Lojka?"

He nodded, rubbing his bruised head again.

Dieter swore, scrambling up. Leopold Lojka was the man who had driven the wrong way and, while reversing, had put Franz Ferdinand straight into the line of fire. If he was here, then Llewelyn must have infiltrated the convoy, perhaps to drive the car himself.

If that was the case, Llewelyn would only have to drive the archduke and his wife the right way, avoiding the junction where the assassination took place altogether.

"I believe this man wanted to take your place," Dieter said, leaning on his stick. "You must get down to the cars immediately."

Lojka nodded again, got unsteadily to his feet, and stumbled towards the door.

Maybe it was a bad idea to put a concussed man behind the wheel of a car, but at least it would be more of a guarantee the archduke would end up dead. And if he didn't, someone else would have to step up to the plate and ensure history happened.

Dieter took a shaky breath.

Franz Ferdinand had always been little more than a name to him. An iconic figure. Not a person, but a symbol.

If Llewelyn already had the car, if Lojka was too late, if Dieter didn't make sure there was a contingency plan, the whole thing would have been for nothing. If Llewelyn managed to stop the assassination, Dieter would have to make sure it did happen, and he wanted to throw up at the thought.

It wasn't a symbol or a sign or an icon.

He would have to kill a man and his wife. He would have to find some way to make him dead. Them. Two happily married people who had children. He would have to take the parents of those children away. He would have to orphan them as war had orphaned him.

Christ, he wanted to be sick.

He stared around the room, staring at the racks of shining guns, then finally, reluctantly picked one up. He hated the fucking things, but Janos had shown him how they worked. Just in case, he'd said. Just in case.

He loaded it—hands shaking—and shoved it into the belt of his trousers. It was cold and heavy, and he wanted to throw the thing away, but if he didn't succeed in the first or second plan, he had to have something more than a flick knife.

In the distance, he could hear cheering, but he tried to put it from his mind and concentrated on getting the fuck out. It wasn't until he was halfway down a staircase that someone called out.

Dieter froze.

"What the hell are you doing in here?" The voice was unfamiliar, brisk, sharp German, and he turned to see a man in a military uniform bearing down on him from the top of the stairs. He was imposing, with bushy sideburns and eyebrows as big again. "You want to see the archduke, you wait outside! He will not see you here."

Dieter stared at him in incomprehension.

The soldier snarled an obscenity, grabbed Dieter by the collar of his coat and his arm, and frogmarched him down the staircase. Dieter stumbled on every step, yelping in pain, but the soldier ignored him, hauling him to a doorway—too small and plain to be a main entrance to such a big building—and tossed him out onto the step.

"Serb idiot," the man growled in German, slamming the door hard behind him.

Dieter was down the side of a building, and towards the front, he could see the crowds. They were cheering, and he'd barely started limping towards the opening of the alley when a car drove off. Another followed, and then another, this one with its hood down.

Dieter nearly stopped breathing.

He'd studied the wars enough to recognise the man's profile.

Franz Ferdinand.

Shit, shit, shit.

He was in a military building, and the archduke was leaving it.

The barracks. The first thing the archduke did in Sarajevo was inspect the barracks.

Dieter leaned against the wall. Of all the places to be held prisoner, in the place where the procession started was the most ironic. He drew shaking breaths, staring out at the crowd.

It was ten o'clock, then, and he was stuck in the west end of the city.

The procession would go east to the city hall, and on the way back was where the archduke was meant to die.

Out of habit, Dieter put a hand into his trouser pocket. The knife was where it belonged, and he held it tight.

Even if Llewelyn were driving, he could only diverge so far. If he tried to drive off with the archduke and duchess, he'd be shot as readily as any of the assassins. So, he'd be trapped in the main route.

Dieter nodded slowly. He needed to get to the junction where the assassination was meant to happen. He would stop Llewelyn and the car, somehow, if he had to jump out in front of it and get flattened in the process. He would complete the mission, if he had to die. Or worse, if he had to kill the archduke himself.

Swallowing hard, he started walking, keeping his head down. Wouldn't do any good to get noticed now. He leaned on his stick as much as he needed to, but terror and adrenaline were doing a good job of pushing the pain to the back of his mind. Not completely, because every bit of him screamed for attention, but he had a job to do and he was going to fucking do it.

People filled the streets, crowding in to see the archduke and his wife.

Some were happy enough, but a week in the city told Dieter a hell of a lot of them were pissed off. Franz Ferdinand was a symbol of the stupid empire which had bulldozed in and annexed the country, and that wasn't something people were usually thrilled about.

Dieter nodded in greeting when anyone glanced at him. He didn't have a clue how much of a mess his face was. His swollen, sore lip paled in comparison to the great dent in his head. No one stared, at least, so he had to assume he didn't look like the walking dead.

It was easy to get lost in the crowds, but he tried to keep his eyes open. The last thing he wanted was to run into any of the men from the inn, or any of the fucking bastards who had beaten the shit out of him.

He hadn't quite reached the main street when an explosion ripped through the air, echoed by screams.

Llewelyn knew about both assassination attempts. He would know to avoid the bomb. But maybe he'd mistimed. Maybe he wouldn't have been ready.

"Please be dead," Dieter prayed under his breath, hating himself for thinking it. Please. Please. Please.

If they were all dead already, if they were all gone, it would be better. Better for everyone.

Not even a kilometre to go, but it was the hardest walk of his life.

The babble of rumours was already spreading. He tried to understand, to tease through what little he knew of the languages around him, but there were too many. Too many people, too many voices and faces, too many flags everywhere.

If the archduke was dead, Dieter was sure he'd know about it. He was fucking positive. Everyone would be going ballistic, not talking in urgent hushed whispers.

By the time he reached the point on Appel Quay, the route of the convoy, the signs of the bombing were being cleared away. The crowd had quieted, but tension was thick in the air. People were eyeing those next to them, wondering if any of them might be the next to reveal a bomb or a gun.

Blood had spattered the road ahead, blackened stone, and shards of twisted, mangled metal.

A few of the Austrian forces prowled along the edge of the road, daring anyone to make a move, and then, shouts on the far side of the road. The crowd parted, and two uniformed men appeared, dragging the limp and battered body of a man between them. His clothing was thick with blood and mud, and he was unmoving.

"Is this the bastard?"

"Yes, sir."

The guard scowled down on the half-dead man with contempt and spat in his face. The man didn't even flinch. He was dragged away, his feet leaving twin trails of blood and dirt on the road.

Cabrinovic. The bomber. Caught when he tried to throw himself in the river, beaten, but saved from the mob to spend years in prison. That was right. So far, everything was going as it should.

Dieter wanted to cry with exhausted relief.

The crowds milled around uncertainly.

The archduke and his procession were meant to return this way, but being attacked with a bomb had changed the mood. They didn't know what was happening, and a lot of them were drifting away, making themselves scarce. Getting the fuck out of the way. Probably the Serbians in the crowd. If one of their people did it, they knew there would be reprisals, because people were more than happy to blame a whole culture when one person was a dickwad.

They were going to be in for it if Princip succeeded as he was meant to.

Dieter stopped to catch his breath. A clock on one of the towers showed it was coming up on half past ten. In less than ten minutes, the procession should start back. He knew where he was. He'd walked the streets so many times in the last week, he remembered every building, every corner, every fucking junction.

One block on was the corner where Lojka would make his fatal mistake.

Dieter stared at the pieces of wrecked car on the road, the bloodstains.

Lojka wasn't where he should be. Things could still change. The gun tucked in Dieter's belt weighed heavily, and he felt sick and cold at the thought of using it. If he had to, he would, but the idea of taking a life made him shiver. The thought of killing was bad enough, but knowing what would happen after? To the world? To him?

He leaned against the wall, swallowing down bitter bile.

Fucking hell, he was so out of his depth it wasn't even funny.

If he had to raise the gun, pull the trigger, he would be doing what he swore he'd never do. He'd have blood on his hands. He would be one of the trigger points in a conflict that would swallow Europe whole and spit out the bones of a generation of young men.

So what if he knew it had already happened?

That didn't make a bit of difference if he was the one who pulled the trigger.

He took a gulping breath and pushed himself away from the wall.

He could just say he was too late.

He knew he could.

But it could make things worse.

He didn't know how, but it was always a possibility.

That was why it had to happen the way it always had.

He brought his foot down hard, the jolt of pain from his ankle surging through him like fire. He needed to focus. The sooner it was over, the sooner he could be done.

He limped onward, leaning on his stick, his hand pressed to the gun at his hip, keeping it hidden, keeping it close. If he got to the corner and waited there, he could push through the crowd and stop the car if he had to. If he needed to use the gun, it was ready.

Somewhere nearby, a clock chimed the half hour.

The crowd was thinner now, and he could see the junction ahead. The very thought of what was meant to happen there made his heart pound in his ears and his palms cold with sweat.

There was a café there, and a shop. He'd passed it often enough in the last few days, but the street had never seemed so long before. He heard people talking urgently, excitedly. Everyone seemed to be gathered in groups, clusters of family and friends. Everyone except him.

He didn't know what caught his eye.

Maybe it was because everyone was milling around together that he noticed. Maybe because the man was on his own, sitting casually on the window ledge of the café. Or maybe it was because, out of the corner of his eye, Dieter had spotted a familiar face, and one that made his stomach drop like a fucking stone.

Gavrilo Princip.

Dieter pressed his hand to the gun at his side.

He could do what Llewelyn had failed to do so far, he thought, light-headed.

All he had to do was walk up to the man and put a bullet between his eyes. All he had to do. He was willing to do it to save history, but here was the man who pulled the fatal trigger. All Dieter had to do was pull a trigger first, and everything could change.

Everything would change.

His finger slipped to the trigger, his hand shaking.

The gun was loaded. He'd made sure of it. All it would take was three steps, one little tug of a trigger, and Princip would be nothing more than a spray of blood and bone against the window of the café.

One dead man for another.

One life for another.

One war...

Dieter stumbled and had to lean against the wall, his stomach clenching.

No.

No.

He'd signed up with the TRI, and even if it could change everything, history had happened. They couldn't change it. If he changed one thing, if he—one of the good guys—changed something, how the fuck could he justifiably stop some nutter like Hitler or Pol Pot going back and changing something else? Who had the right to decide the fate of the world? Not him. And not Llewelyn either.

He let go of the gun and pressed his hand—shaking—to his mouth, trembling.

No intervention. No changing.

He wanted to fucking cry, but he couldn't. Not now. Not yet.

He forced himself to focus on Princip who was lazing in the sun like a fucking cat.

Dieter had read everything about the assassination and Princip. Not one document indicated the man would be spending his last fifteen minutes of freedom sprawled on a window ledge of a coffee shop as if he wasn't planning to murder two people. He seemed calm, relaxed, not the panicking bundle of nerves Dieter was expecting.

The group of assassins were famously sloppy according to every record.

After the bombing went wrong, most of them scattered, and everyone presumed Princip had either backed out or was considering fleeing before the archduke's car took a wrong turn and presented him with his target, a very large fish in a motionless barrel.

The man in front of him wasn't fleeing anywhere.

He was completely at ease, and a chill ran down Dieter's spine.

The assassination was a failure. Princip's ally had been beaten and taken captive. He had no fucking reason to look like everything was fine.

Unless it was.

Unless the corruption with the Habsburg household extended out to those who held the reins of their lands for them.

Dieter limped over to the window ledge, sinking down to sit, trying to act as casual as the fucking assassin. He desperately riffled through the facts he could remember, but it was as if his brain had been replaced with cotton wool.

One person had the authority to change the route. One person shouted down any refusal to go another route. One person dismissed the police chief's concerns and his offer of extra men to ensure the safety of the archduke. One person riding in the car survived the shooting, despite allegedly being a target. The man who had given the order to stop the car right in front of Princip.

Potiorek.

The governor of the city.

Dieter cursed under his breath.

Someone spoke to him in Serbian, and he glanced sideways. Princip had opened his eyes and was staring at him curiously. Dieter recognised the words—a query if he was well—but he didn't have words enough to reply.

He made a show of wincing, rubbing his leg. He didn't even need to fake it, because it fucking hurt, but it was enough to make Princip nod agreeably and turn to gaze at the road through half-closed eyes.

Oh Christ, they were neck-deep in the shit.

He didn't know if Llewelyn was part of the cavalcade, but if he was, and Potiorek was still with them as he had been, Llewelyn would have no idea he was already part of a trap that had been baited and set.

In the distance, there were cheers.

The convoy was on the move again.

Princip straightened up from the window ledge. He took off his cap, smoothed his hair, and checked his reflection in the polished glass. Of course, if you were going to be arrested for assassinating the fucking Archduke of Austria, you'd want to look your best.

Dieter got up unsteadily, leaning on his stick, and flinched when a hand tucked under his arm.

Princip, again, smiling like a wolf.

"Let me help you," he said, like he was a fucking Samaritan.

Yes.

Use the cripple to get to the roadside.

People would move out of pity.

Dieter jerked his arm free. "No, thank you." The words came out clipped and sharp and German, and Princip's expression changed.

Dieter saw his hand move and knew the gun was there. It could just as easily be him who stopped it all, by being a fucking idiot and saying the wrong thing at the wrong time and taking the bullet with the archduke's fucking name on it.

He flinched, staring at Princip.

He could stay silent. He could fall to his knees. He could do anything to make Princip forget about him.

"He is coming."

The words escaped his lips in his voice, and Princip searched his face and then nodded.

It was like watching through a pane of thick glass, the images out of focus, as Princip walked forward towards the front of the crowd. The cheers were louder, but they sounded muffled in Dieter's ears, and he tried to move, tried to walk forward, stumbling like an old man.

The cars came, one by one. And Dieter saw the open-topped car.

Idiots. How could you say you weren't preparing a target by leaving the fucking roof down?

He blundered forward, and the crowd parted for the mad, lame man and his stick, and he saw the driver in the archduke's car. He saw Llewelyn, and Llewelyn had spotted him. The defiance all over Llewelyn's face was like a fucking blow, and the car was going too fucking fast. It wouldn't slow, and it wouldn't stop, and Princip would miss.

They were about to pass the turn. He was meant to turn right, but Llewelyn's eyes were fixed ahead, and he wasn't going to turn, and he wasn't going to stop, and Christ, if Dieter didn't get in the way, everything would go to fuck.

He stepped down off the slabs lining the road.

It was an old car. They could go fast, but not like modern ones. If it hit him, he might be lucky and not get hurt too badly. It'd have to stop. He swallowed hard and was about to run forward when the brakes screamed. He glanced up, startled, and saw Potiorek leaning over the partition behind the driver's seat, his hands gripping Llewelyn's shoulders.

Llewelyn jerked around, staring up at Potiorek in shock and disbelief. Dieter was frozen in place as Princip walked calmly out from the body of the crowd, smiled, lifted his gun, and fired twice.

Chapter Thirty-Five

Minute by minute, the days ticked by.

Janos worked. He took guns apart with assistance from the technicians. He put them together. He loaded them. He fired them if he could or recorded if he couldn't. He had lessons on new machines. He practiced his English with Sally. He ate in the dining hall. He nodded in salutation to people. He went to the gym. He swam. He hit the punch bag. He slept when he could.

And he waited and listened for the call on the speakers.

He didn't miss another connection.

He was there, by Tamara, each day, but the last connection had been the most important.

They knew Dieter was alive, and he had survived whatever he was meant to be surviving, even if he was far from his best. The event was over and from that moment, there were two days until there would be enough power to connect the gate, send a team, and get them back.

No one would tell him what the event was.

No one seemed to know, except Sanders, and he was calmer than he had been since Dieter stepped through the gate.

It had to be going right.

Janos was in the archive restoration room when Sanders came for him.

He didn't notice at first, lost in working on the intricacies of a neglected musket laid out on a sheet of cloth in front of him. Dirt and oil gummed the machinery, and he patiently cleaned each part with swabs of cotton.

"Nagy."

Janos stilled his hand, and he carefully finished cleaning the small coil before sitting up. His back ached in protest. "It is time?"

Sanders stood by the door behind him. "We're keeping it quiet. So people don't try and crowd in to see what's happening."

Janos set down his tools and wiped his hand on the cloth draped over his thigh. "This is good idea," he agreed, getting up from the workbench. He carefully folded the cloth over the musket to keep all the parts in one place and put away the basins of solvents.

His hand was shaking, he noticed.

Sanders didn't say anything to hurry him. He just stood by the door, waiting.

"All is good," Janos said finally, closing the store cupboard.

Sanders nodded, jerking his head towards the door.

No one paid them any attention as they made their way along the quiet hall to the elevator.

"You have to stay in the console room," Sanders said, breaking the silence as the lift rose. "I don't want to have any more people than necessary anywhere near the temporal chamber."

"I want to be there."

"And I'm giving you an order. You're emotionally compromised, Janos, and I'm not having more blood shed on my watch." Janos opened his mouth to protest, but Sanders held up his hand. "You already hit me. I don't want to imagine what you might do to Llewelyn for putting Dieter in this situation in the first place."

Janos's mouth snapped shut. He didn't need to imagine. He had already thought about it in graphic detail. It wouldn't help anyone to confirm Sanders's suspicions. It was true he had played his part, but Llewelyn had taken things further and deliberately. Too far.

"I am to wait?"

Sanders nodded. "I'll call you down when things are clear." He was silent for a moment. "I'll make sure Dieter's in the best hands, okay?"

Janos nodded unhappily.

They were silent until they reached the console room.

Tamara nodded in greeting, and Janos approached and sat beside her. "We're almost done," she said. "You want to log on?"

Janos nodded, typing in the code and watching the screen flare to life.

"I'll be in the temporal holding bay," Sanders said. "Janos will stay here."

Janos scowled at his screen. All eyes were on him, and the tension in the room was as bad as any courtroom. They all remembered what he had done to Sanders. None of them wanted to be the one to restrain him if he was told bad news.

Around him, screens glowed, and he watched in silence as the codes for unlocking a temporal gate were keyed in. The screens projecting the temporal chamber blazed white as the doorway opened, and Janos pressed his hand hard against the edge of the desk.

"Preparing to depart in three, two, one…"

The room was silent.

It seemed like everyone was holding their breath.

The echoing hum of the gate hung in the air. Janos stared blindly at the screens, his nails splintering against the desk.

"How far is meeting place?" he asked, his voice low. "How long?"

"Five minutes," Tamara murmured, "maybe ten."

He took a shaking breath, nodded, and glanced up at the clock, staring at the glowing numbers until the afterglow flashed across his eyelids.

"We have visual of the rendezvous. Will proceed with radio silence until contact is made."

Tamara's hand covered Janos's, and he stared down at it, startled.

She met his eyes, a strange smile on her face. "Not long now."

He stared at her and pulled his hand free. "We must wait," he said, turning to the screens. He curled his fingers into a fist. His nails were cracked. They scratched against his palm.

"Sanders." Downie's voice rang through the room. "Get a medical team on standby. Now."

Janos was on his feet in a heartbeat.

"Janos!"

Someone shouted—he didn't know who.

He didn't care.

He ran for the door and swiped at the security panel with his pass. The light flashed red. Locked in. They had locked him in. He cursed, slamming his fist against the door, then whirled around.

"Let me out from here!"

One of the techs stood. "No. Boss said you were to stay here."

Janos advanced on him, panting. "You think I care what he says? You think I will wait here when I know it is all bad? When Dieter is hurt?"

The tech recoiled. "I can't!"

Janos grabbed him by the front of the shirt. "You open door now!" he roared, shaking the man. "You have pass! Open door now!"

"I can't!"

Janos shook him furiously. "You lie!" He dragged the man towards the door and slammed him—and his pass—against the sensor. It flashed red again. "You undo this!"

"He can't," Tamara said quietly. She was at his side and wrapped her hand around his forearm. "Sanders told us you had to stay in here. That means we all have to stay in here too. He's put us in security lockdown."

Janos stared at her. "All of us?"

She nodded. "Let Brian go, okay?"

Janos uncurled his fingers and shoved the man away from him. He stalked across the floor, pausing to kick the door. "He should not do this," he whispered. "He should not make us prisoner."

"It's better for them if it's calm down there," Tamara said, holding up her hands. "He'll let us out once it's safe for everyone."

Janos turned his back on her, staring at the door. "Only he has power to do this?"

"He's the one who controls access," she said. "Janos, I'm sorry. If we had a pass that wasn't blocked, I swear we'd let you out."

Janos glared at the door and then down at his pass. It was blocked. So were the passes of the techs. He slipped his hand into the pocket of his trousers and touched the smooth plastic of another pass card. Dieter's.

Before anyone could stop him, he swiped it across the sensor, which flashed green, and lunged through the door as soon as it opened. Hands grabbed at his arm, and Tamara swore, but he didn't look back.

People chased. He knocked them away, hurled them aside, and ran.

The elevators would be locked down, or if they weren't, they would try to seal them, but they wouldn't expect him to use the stairs. He knew the stairs well, and he ran headlong. The pass still worked on the doors, and he burst into the stairway leading down into the basement, running as fast as he could. He took staircases in three long leaps and staggered to a halt at the doors leading to the temporal chamber.

Sanders had left agents guarding the door.

Ojukwu and Henderson. Big men. Gentle, but big.

"Janos?"

Panting, Janos nodded to the door. "I must go in."

Ojukwu shook his head. "You know Sanders doesn't want you in there."

Janos looked from one to the other. "Please," he whispered. "Please. I have to be there. I do not want to hurt you, but I have to be there."

Henderson took a step forward. He was broader than Janos, and if he wanted to stop him going in, Janos knew he could. "You swear you won't touch Llewelyn?"

"I don't care about Llewelyn."

Even as he said it, Janos was shocked to realise how true it was.

He didn't.

Llewelyn could live or die or whatever he wanted. He didn't matter.

Henderson glanced at Ojukwu, who murmured something into his comm. He was silent for a moment and then swiped his pass.

Janos nodded in wordless gratitude and stumbled into the passageway. He remembered it, and hated it, probably as much as Dieter. The layover room was already empty, the door at the other side open. He could see the glow of the temporal gate at the far end of the corridor.

He stumbled like a newborn calf, bracing his hand against the wall.

He remembered the room, but only in fragments, and he didn't want leave Dieter there, in the place of his nightmares, if he could help it.

There were agents, the team who had gone through. Sanders was there.

Janos heard them speaking, maybe to him, but pushed by them.

Dieter.

Dieter was there.

He was kneeling on the floor, head down, hands limp in his lap. He looked like he was resting where he had fallen, boneless and exhausted. He was kneeling, again, in this room, in this place.

"Dieter?" Janos's voice sounded like a stranger's in his ears.

When Dieter lifted his face, Janos barely recognised him. His hair was matted with blood. His face was bruised, his lips cracked and swollen, his eyes bloodshot. He stared blankly at Janos, and then his lips parted in a faint, unsteady smile.

One shaking hand rose from his lap, and he held it out, uncurling his dirt-stained fingers.

Janos's knife nestled on his palm.

"I brought it back," he whispered, his voice rasping and coarse. "I brought it back for you."

Janos crumpled to his knees and pulled the stupid idiotic man into his embrace as gently as he could, burying his face in Dieter's bloody hair.

"You came back too," he whispered, his voice breaking. He didn't care if he was weeping. Dieter was in his arms, and Dieter was clinging to him, and he was back, and he was alive, and Janos didn't give a damn about anything else.

Chapter Thirty-Six

It was too quiet.

No mice rustled in the straw. No sounds from the inn below. No wind whistling through the eaves. He was lying on something more solid than a sack of straw. Someone breathed nearby, low and slow.

Dieter's eyes flew open, his heart racing.

The ceiling above him was white tiles, and a soft light to his right illuminated the night-darkened room. Clean and bright, and he smelled antiseptic. Bandages were strapped around his ribs and ankle, a needle in his left hand, hooked up to a drip. The pain, a thousand miles away.

Home.

He was home.

He covered his face with shaking hands, trying to catch his breath. His fingers met bare, shaven skin. Clean skin. No dirt or blood or itching. He stifled a small, tight sob of relief.

Home.

"Dieter?"

He shook his head. It didn't hurt so much now, not so much at all. He didn't want anyone to see him—not shaking and breaking, not in all the pieces he was in.

A hand covered one of his, gently, and drew it from over his eyes.

"You are safe," Janos murmured in English.

That made Dieter's breath catch.

Janos sat beside the bed and smiled tiredly when Dieter looked at him. He threaded his fingers between Dieter's, squeezing his hand. "And we kill all fleas."

Dieter shook his head wearily. "Don't have fucking fleas."

"Not now." Janos pressed his cheek to the back of Dieter's hand and closed his eyes. He looked exhausted. "They were in hair and beard." He kissed Dieter's knuckles gently. "We spray you with hose." He slanted a glance between his lashes. "Very sexy."

Dieter choked on a helpless laugh, his ribs aching. "You dick."

Janos smiled against Dieter's hand, tracing his thumb along the side of Dieter's palm. "Only small part."

Dieter gazed at him, uncurling a finger to brush Janos's cheek. "Not that small."

Mischief glinted in Janos's eyes. "Tamara teach me," he said solemnly. "This is understatement."

Dieter's eyes stung. "God, I love you," he whispered.

Janos drew up in surprise. "You do?"

Dieter gazed at their linked hands, blinking hard. "Yes." The word came out in a cracked whisper. It was pathetic, but he couldn't make his voice any louder or clearer. He rocked their hands back and forth. "I lied. Before I left."

Janos was silent.

He drew his hand free, and Dieter let his own fall against the bedding. He closed his eyes, turning his face away. No fucking surprise. He'd fucked about with the man's emotions. He would deserve it if the poor bugger walked away.

Janos got up.

He didn't leave though. The edge of the mattress sank under his weight as he sat down close to Dieter's side, and he cupped Dieter's cheek, drawing his face around.

"Look at me," Janos murmured.

Dieter reluctantly opened his eyes.

Janos leaned over him, as drawn as Dieter felt, but fucking Christ, his eyes were stunning, gleaming green by the pale light.

"Tell me truth," he said quietly.

It could have been a demand, but there was a quiet plea in Janos's voice, as if he couldn't believe what Dieter had said.

Dieter touched Janos's wrist, his fingers trembling. "I love you."

"You idiot," he whispered into a kiss, running his thumb along Dieter's cheekbone.

In all the months they'd known each other, Dieter had never noticed how gentle Janos could be, not until that moment. Janos's hand slipped under Dieter's bandaged head, supporting it, and his kisses were careful against Dieter's bruised and cracked lips. He braced himself on his left arm against the headboard, keeping any pressure off Dieter's bound ribs.

Dieter put his arm around him, hand splaying on his back, and Janos murmured against his lips in approval. It was slow, lazy, comforting, and finally, Dieter sank down with a small sigh.

"You quite finished?"

Under Dieter's hand, Janos tensed. He turned his head, glaring over at Sanders, who stood at the door.

"You do not knock?"

"Not when I need to speak to him."

Janos pressed his hand against Dieter's pillow. "You will not disturb him now. He needs to rest."

Dieter kneaded at his back reassuringly. "S'all right," he murmured, still exhausted, but better than only minutes earlier. Janos searched his face. "I can talk to him."

Reluctantly, Janos nodded, rising from the bed, but Dieter caught his wrist. "Stay? Stay with me?"

Janos leaned down and kissed him again as if Sanders wasn't there. "Always," he promised, resting his brow gently against Dieter's, making Dieter shiver down to his toes. He turned and dragged the chair closer to the bed, and sat down, staring sternly at Sanders. "You can talk, but not for long time. Dieter must rest."

Sanders nodded, approaching the end of the bed. One side of his face was an ugly mess of yellowing bruises. "Not going to argue. But we need to do the debrief before we can decide what to do with Llewelyn. He's not speaking, and we need to know what happened to him."

Janos's hand covered Dieter's on the covers, tangling their fingers together. "Who gives a damn?" he muttered in Hungarian.

Dieter personally agreed. He remembered Llewelyn pressing on his wounds until he screamed, until he threw up, until he passed out. It was true the son a bitch had saved his life, but he'd also hurt him as much as the fuckers who took him prisoner.

"Lock him up," he said quietly. "The bastard did what he meant to. He changed things. He fucking broke history."

"Changed things?" Sanders's expression was unreadable. "What things?"

"He knocked out the real driver," Dieter said, closing his eyes and trying to concentrate, to remember. "He was trying to drive straight down Appel Quay instead of turning off towards Franz Josef Street so the archduke wouldn't end up in the line of fire." He couldn't help laughing bitterly, painfully. "He didn't know the conspiracy went all the way to the top. Potiorek went fucking mental and made him stop and turn."

"No," Sanders said, the frown audible in his voice. "The driver was meant to turn up Franz Josef Street, but he didn't. He stopped when the governor told him he was going the wrong way. That's when Princip got him."

Dieter opened his eyes. "What?"

"The car," Sanders said, talking slowly as if Dieter was an imbecile. "It was meant to turn up Franz Josef Street."

Dieter stared at him. "What?" he said again.

"The route," Sanders said patiently. "The route they were meant take went to Franz Josef Street, but the driver, this Muller person, tried to go straight down Appel Quay."

Dieter shook his head in disbelief. "Holy shit..." he murmured. "Boss, no one can do this again. He's changed things. He's changed things then, and those are the things you remember now. It wasn't this way before."

Sanders stared at him for a long moment, then circled the bed and sat at the opposite side from Janos. "Explain."

In fits and starts, Dieter put together the details of the assassination as he had known them before.

It was a simpler time, before they knew Princip was definitely planted at the street corner and waiting for his moment, before they knew some bastard who was meant to be loyal to Austria made sure the car slowed down and stopped right in front of the assassin with the gun.

Dieter remembered Llewelyn's face when Potiorek reached over the driver's seat and told him to stop, to turn. Dieter and Llewelyn had each been as shocked as the other. No one had guessed how keen the governor was to bring war on the Serbians.

By the time Dieter stopped talking, his throat was dry, and he was exhausted. Janos watched him with concern, holding Dieter's hand against his cheek.

"Potiorek? The governor?" Sanders said finally. "He was in on it?"

Dieter nodded. "Looks that way," he said quietly. "We don't know if it was orders, but he's the bastard who started the pogroms against the Serbians, and led the first attacks of the Austrian army after." He took a slow breath, his head and chest aching. "He could have been acting on orders. Or been paid off."

Dieter closed his eyes wearily, curling his fingers against Janos's. "Franz Ferdinand's death was far too convenient for everyone concerned.

Austria just needed an excuse to steamroller in. The Serbian government wanted a reason to fight." He opened his eyes a crack. "I don't know, boss. I'm sorry."

Sanders put a hand on his shoulder. "You did a good job," he said, his voice rough. "You got both of you back, and there's been no major damage done."

"Ha!" Janos snorted.

"Jan," Dieter murmured. "It's okay."

"No," Janos snapped. "It is not okay. It is bad. You are bad. You are hurt and all is bad." He glared accusingly across the bed at Sanders. "You say 'no major damage.' Do you not see him? Do you not see his hurt?"

Sanders gazed passively at him. "I do, and I'm sorry, but it had to be done."

Janos scowled at him. "You fuck off now, yes?"

Sanders nodded, rising. "We'll talk later, Dieter." Dieter waved wearily with his fingertips.

As soon as Sanders was gone, Janos rose and filled a glass of water. He slipped his arm under Dieter's shoulders and helped him to sit up enough to drink. The water was cool and sweet, and Dieter gulped it down greedily.

"You rest now," Janos said, laying him down against the pillows.

With effort, Dieter managed to move sideways and patted the bed beside him.

Janos hesitated. "Your ribs..."

"Fuck them," Dieter whispered. "I don't want to be on my own. Please."

Janos nodded. He kicked off his shoes and climbed up onto the bed, arranging himself on his side beside Dieter. He laid his arm across Dieter's hips. "This is good?"

Dieter covered Janos's hand with his. "Good," he whispered, not trusting his voice not to crack like fucking glass.

Janos nuzzled his brow. "Rest now."

"Mm." Dieter nodded, tracing circles on Janos's wrist. "Jan?"

"Hm?"

"What happened to Sanders's face?"

"Oh." Janos was silent for a moment and then said, "I did."

Dieter's eyes flew open. "What?" he demanded, tilting his head to stare at him.

Janos shrugged, gazing at him. "We check life signs," he said quietly. "They were bad. I want to come for you. He say no. I hit him."

Dieter stared at him. "Oh, you silly poof," he whispered, his vision blurring with stupid tears. "You shouldn't have done that."

"Hit him?"

Dieter nodded. "Or cared so much, you stupid fuck," he whispered. "Why do you care?"

Janos brushed the tears from Dieter's cheeks. "Because you do too."

"Sentimental arsehole," Dieter whispered.

"It is so." Janos kissed his temple gently. "Now, rest."

Chapter Thirty-Seven

Dieter was being checked by Doctor Bellevue.

Janos didn't dare stay in the room to see the mess of Dieter's body. Seeing him covered in blood and bruises was bad enough, but knowing there were scars and stitches beneath the bandages—caused by both friend and foe—was enough to make him angry, and he didn't want that.

He'd barely slept in the three days since Dieter's return. He couldn't sleep while Dieter was being operated on, and then, he couldn't sleep until Dieter woke up and he knew he would be all right.

It wasn't so simple though.

Dieter had seen many things in his modern world, but he had never been beaten so cruelly, or half starved by coarse food, or seen someone die before his eyes.

Even when he slept in Janos's embrace, he woke gasping and shaking. He'd been violently sick more than once. He was having trouble eating. Janos knew all those responses, and he knew it would be a long time until Dieter could be considered well again.

He remembered his own father when he returned from the war. He'd been bone-thin and sat staring into the fire, day after day, a bottle in one hand, the other clutching the arm of the chair. When he did speak, it was only to lash out, to hit someone or something, real or imagined, so they left him alone, and when he died, it was a mercy.

He would and could not let Dieter end up like that.

It was why he walked through the halls in silence and opened the door to Sanders's office without knocking.

Sanders raised his eyes. Like Dieter, he looked drawn and tired. "Janos."

"You will give Dieter time off," Janos said, shutting the door behind him. "He will need long time to be good again." He walked over and sat down at the desk. "When he can leave bed, I will take him home, and I will stay with him. No tracker."

Sanders nodded. "I was thinking the same thing."

Janos leaned forward and rested his elbows on his thighs. "You knew he would not come back good."

"I had to take the chance," Sanders agreed quietly. "He did the job he went to do, and I'm sorry for what happened to him, but I had no choice."

Janos ran his hand over the stump of his arm. "You broke rules first," he observed quietly. "Llewelyn sees me every day. If you break rules, he thinks he breaks rules too."

Sanders nodded. "You were an exception we can never allow again."

"Too late." Janos sighed, swiping his hand over his face. "What happens to him?"

Sanders shook his head. "We're not sure yet. He's not been speaking much since he came back. He'd put so much stock in saving the world from war, and now, I think he blames himself. If he hadn't listened to Potiorek, he might have succeeded."

"History is strong," Janos disagreed. "History will still happen."

"He was an optimist."

"He is asshole. He sees world as simple thing. He only sees one man. Save one man and make all things right." Janos shook his head. "One man is only small part of big broken machine. Fix one part, and machine still works for little while, but machine will still break. Dieter tells this to all of them, but they do not listen." He shrugged. "Now, maybe they listen. Now, maybe they see they cannot fix all things."

"That's a harsh way of looking at it," Sanders murmured, tapping the end of a pen on the desk.

Janos met his eyes. "You think same thing."

Sanders inclined his head. "I do. I didn't know if Llewelyn would come back, but he's come back a wreck. It's...useful."

Janos snorted. "You are sick bastard," he said, getting up and returning to the door. He paused there, glancing at him. "But not bad commander."

Sanders drummed the end of the pen on the desk. "We need to keep Dieter in confinement for at least a week. After, I'll sign him off for two months."

"Six. Nothing less. If you need him, he work from home. He does not need to come here. He work too much for too long. He does not have rest. Now, he will."

Sanders nodded curtly.

Janos headed out into the halls. He was prowling like an angry bear, but he didn't care. He headed down to the cafeteria. Ignoring the queue, he grabbed a tray and filled it with all the unhealthy crunchy fries and sticky sweet desserts Dieter liked best.

"Hey."

He swung around, glowering at the voice behind him. "What?"

"How is he?" Nicky Downie asked.

Other faces watched him too, waiting for an answer Sanders hadn't given them.

"Shit," Janos said. "He is shit." He glared along at the agents. Every one of them had come to him for advice. Any one of them could do exactly what Llewelyn had done. "If any of you do thing like this again, I fucking kill you, okay?"

He pushed through them without waiting for a response, balancing the tray against his torso as steadily as he could.

He was being unreasonable, but he was tired, and he was worried, and he was terrified of what had happened. He wasn't the strong one. He never had been. He'd spent his whole life hiding who and what he was. And now, Dieter, the person who helped him to be himself, needed him to be strong, and he didn't know how to do it.

Dieter was meant to be bold and happy and laughing, and all Janos saw was a lost little boy staring at him. He was going to find a way to make him happy again if it killed him, and if it meant being rude to some people, then so be it.

He made his way up through the building and knocked the door open with his elbow but hesitated in the doorway.

He wasn't surprised to see Sally sitting on the edge of the bed.

"I come again later?" he offered.

"Stop moving," Sally said to Dieter, sitting back a little. "Unless you want to look like some kind of deranged clown."

Janos approached, and at once, he wanted to hug Sally. She'd brought in a bag of make-up and was delicately painting around Dieter's eyes. Some colour had been brushed across his cheeks, and some of the tension in his body seemed to have faded.

"How do I look?" he asked, his fingers twisting together in his lap.

Janos set down the tray on the table behind Sally. "Less half-dead."

One of Dieter's eyes cracked open. "My boyfriend," he said with a mournful sigh, though there was a suggestion of a smile lurking around his lips. "King of compliments."

Janos patted his uninjured ankle, trying to keep the stupid, soft smile off his face. It felt strange to have people know about them, but good. It felt good. "If you want nice, polite boy, you look in wrong place." He fetched the fork and spoon from the cabinet beside Dieter's bed. "But I do bring food you like—to see if you can eat."

Dieter closed his eyes to let Sally finish her work. "I'll give it a try."

Janos hauled his chair alongside the bed. "Try is good." He settled in the seat, watching Sally add a last flourish of black liquid along Dieter's eyelids. She sat back, pleased.

"Not bad, even if I do say so myself," she said, screwing the lid on the bottle.

"Thanks," Dieter murmured, his eyes still closed.

Sally pecked him on the lips. "I'll come and visit later. You have my number if you need anything—a chat, a hug, my best eyeliner."

Dieter's lips twitched, and he opened his eyes. "Your best eyeliner?"

"Well, second best," Sally said, slipping down from the bed. "I don't love you that much." She didn't look at Janos, but she squeezed his shoulder in passing before heading out the door.

"Daft bird," Dieter murmured.

"Good woman," Janos said, pulling the table up the bed towards Dieter.

His lover eyed the plates and bowls. "I think you want me to get fat."

"Your ass is very small," Janos said solemnly.

"Dick."

"That is not."

Dieter rolled his eyes, picking up the fork and stabbing at the fries. Janos watched him as he nibbled them, then rose and went to refill the jug of water. When he came back, he sat on the edge of the bed and filled a glass on the table for Dieter.

"Did Bellevue say things?"

Dieter wrinkled his nose. "Fuck, yes," He set aside the fork and reached for one of the bowls of pudding. "You'd think I'd gone out and got the crap kicked out of me on purpose." He gingerly touched the bandages around his head. "She said it's healing, but she wants to keep an eye on me."

"People worry," Janos agreed, stealing a fry.

"Fuss," Dieter corrected, wincing as he shifted his weight. He took a couple spoonfuls of pudding and leaned against the pillow, closing his eyes with a grimace.

Silently, Janos got up and leaned closer to arrange the pillows better. His face was close to Dieter's when Dieter opened his eyes. He didn't say anything, just brushed his fingers against Janos's cheek.

Janos turned to kiss his fingertips. "You need to eat," he said quietly.

"I know," Dieter replied just as quietly. "Help me?"

Janos searched his face and then nodded. "I will promise you sexual favour for every mouthful," he said, schooling his expression into the most solemn one he could manage.

A flicker of a smile crossed Dieter's lips. "Yeah?"

"Mm." Janos set the bowl down to rest in Dieter's lap. "If you finish whole bowl, I promise very kinky fun."

"You're a bad influence," Dieter murmured, smiling tiredly. Janos picked up the spoon, but Dieter caught his hand before he could lift it from the bowl. "Jan, why are you still speaking English? We can speak Hungarian if you want."

Janos gazed at him. "When I was bad, you spoke my words to make things better for me. Now, I do same for you."

Dieter went all bright eyed again, and Janos cursed inward. Dieter's emotions were too fragile for silly, sentimental statements.

Janos sat up and added gruffly, "Anyway, my English is better than your Hungarian. Is kindness to my language to stop you using it."

To his relief and pleasure, Dieter actually laughed, his expression brightening. "Fucking arsehole."

"Only if you eat all pudding," Janos replied gravely, but couldn't stop himself from smiling too.

Chapter Thirty-Eight

It took four days for Bellevue to let Dieter get out of bed, even to walk only as far as the window, still limping on his aching ankle. It was another couple of days before the bandages were removed from his head for the last time.

They'd kept him away from mirrors, and it was only after his first shower on his own that he saw himself reflected in the misted glass.

He ran a hand—shaking like an old man's—over the glass and stared at the stranger there.

His trip to the past had only been ten days, but he looked like a shell of himself. Part of it was down to the nightmares that kept waking him, every fucking night without fail, and the fact that he was still throwing up every morning.

His face was chalk white, his eyes sunk in shadowed hollows. The bruises on his body were fading, but his chest still resembled a mess of rotting fruit. When they shaved off his beard, they shaved off his hair as well, and he tentatively traced his fingertips over the swollen lump on the back of his head. A jagged scar remained where the skin had split open, raised and uneven.

The door hissed opened, and he lowered his hand, gazing down at the sink.

"You are clean now?" Janos said.

Dieter nodded. "I look like shit."

Janos walked into the bathroom to stand beside him and slipped his arm around Dieter's bare waist. "Ha! This is nothing." he said, squeezing Dieter warmly. "You do not have arm cut off. I win this game."

Dieter leaned into him, light-headed. "You're a competitive asshole," he murmured.

"And you are stupid man who must go to bed." Janos shifted his arm around Dieter's waist and steered him towards the bedroom. Dieter's feet slipped on the smooth floor, but Janos's grip was gentle and firm, holding him upright.

Dieter sat on the edge of the bed, unresisting as Janos took the towel from around his waist and started gently drying his bruised body. He stared at his empty, open palms, lying limp in his lap.

"I'm being fucking useless, aren't I?" he said quietly.

Janos shook his head. "You have seen bad things. You have hurts. This makes any man feel bad." He knelt beside the bed and towelled his way up Dieter's legs one at a time. "It is not useless. It is human." He kissed Dieter's knee lightly. "You care. This is good thing."

Dieter reached out to touch Janos's hair. "Does it get easier?"

Janos nodded. "With help. You talk to Sally. You talk to me. This will be good." He rose to his feet and stooped to gently kiss Dieter. "Do not stay quiet or inside here." He tapped his finger to Dieter's chest, then his brow. "I have seen this before, all closed away. It is like poison. It makes worse."

Dieter pressed his palm to Janos's, their fingers folding together. "Who?" he asked quietly, watching the way their hands fitted together.

Janos was silent for a long while and then finally said, "My father. It is all bad for him. He come home from big war, and he is...not right."

Dieter shivered. "We might have changed it. If that bastard had done what he intended, the war might have been different. Your dad might have been different. You..."

"Would not have met you." Janos drew his hand free from Dieter's and cupped Dieter's face. "You must stop thinking of 'might.' Might did not happen." He kissed him hard, his hand sliding to cradle Dieter's head. "Now, we are here. Now is now."

Dieter nodded, tipping himself forward to knock his forehead on Janos's chest. Janos rubbed down the nape of his neck, down his back, in soothing circles.

"I need to speak to Llewelyn," Dieter said unhappily, his voice low. "I need..." He shook his head, his brow rubbing against Janos's shirt. "Shit." His voice broke. "I don't know, Jan. I don't know what I need."

Janos stepped between Dieter's knees and embraced him. "You need ending," he murmured as Dieter put his arms around him, clinging to him as tightly as he could, his fingers digging into Janos's back. "Like putting outside and closing door."

Dieter nodded again, closing his eyes.

He had to face the bastard.

The last two days, before the team came for them, were a blur of pain. Dieter remembered following the car containing the archduke towards the governor's home. He'd found Llewelyn there, covered in blood that wasn't his, blank-eyed, and Dieter mutely took him by the arm and made him rise.

He didn't remember much else, apart from the pain.

They'd walked.

They must have walked.

There was no other way they could have reached the rendezvous point.

He couldn't remember it.

All he remembered was the sound of the gun and the blood gouting from the archduke's mouth.

Beyond that, his only recollection was his own blood throbbing behind his eyes. The pain in his leg was unbearable, and all he could do was keep breathing. A day more, Bellevue had told him, and he could have died from blood poisoning from the head wound and the raw band of flesh carved from his swollen ankle by the chains.

He didn't know why Llewelyn had come with him. He didn't know why the man hadn't killed him and gone on the run. He didn't care either. But Llewelyn was the reason he'd been put in there in the first place. Dieter needed some kind of resolution, whether it was an apology or contempt or anything. Anything but the blankness he was drowning in.

He knew Janos would want to come with him, but it would be a bad idea.

Sanders's bruised face told of just how physical Janos could get when something he cared about was harmed. Llewelyn had pushed the situation and caused the mess Dieter was in. That would be provocation enough for Janos to beat the seven shades of shit out of the man, and Dieter was well aware that he would let him.

Dieter dressed himself as steadily as his hands would allow and let Janos try to tempt him with all kinds of titbits of food. He wasn't eating enough. He felt fucking shit, but every mouthful was an effort.

What surprised him was how patient Janos was.

During his own healing, Janos had always been sharp and curt, but to Dieter, he was nothing but gentle. His father, Dieter supposed. Seeing the damage trauma had done to someone else, he wanted to avoid it again. It wasn't to say Janos treated him like he was made of fucking glass. He was still being a sarcastic bugger, but he didn't try to guilt or bully Dieter into eating.

He just…distracted Dieter enough so forgot about having no appetite, and that was a start. It was why he managed half a bowl of some kind of noodles and shredded meat, instead of pushing it away after one bite.

"Do I have permission to leave the room yet?" Dieter asked, propping his hands on his thighs.

Janos searched his face. "You're ready?"

Dieter nodded. "If I don't do it as soon as I can, I won't do it at all," he said, releasing a shaky breath.

"We can get chair with wheels. So you do not need to walk?"

Dieter glanced down at his swollen ankle, still swathed in a healing seal. "Yeah. I think I might need it."

Less than half an hour later, he was in a chair pushed by Sanders. Janos wasn't happy about being left behind, but Sanders insisted limited access to Llewelyn was best. Dieter didn't care enough to ask why. He just fixed his eyes on his hands, clenched together in his lap to stop them from shaking.

"I don't know if he wants to see you," Sanders murmured once they were in the lift.

Dieter looked up at him wearily. "Well, I didn't want to go to the fucking past and have my life ruined," he said, "so he can fucking deal with it."

Sanders put a hand on Dieter's shoulder. "I know." He was silent for a moment and then said, "He's not in a good state. I don't know if you'll even get any sense out of him. You need to know that."

Dieter returned his gaze to the shiny door of the lift. "Blind leading the fucking blind," he whispered bitterly.

The rest of the journey was made in silence to the confinement wing on the tenth floor. They kept a series of rooms as something between a prison and protective custody of a kind. The rooms were secure and could only be opened by specific people. It had only been used once before: for Janos.

Sanders swiped his pass to get them through the first set of doors, and a tall, thin woman emerged from a side room. She checked them both on the staff records on her palmtop and then opened the next set of secure doors, letting them in. A man waited on the other side and led them to a final door with a small square window at eye level.

"You're sure you want to do this?"

Dieter nodded, staring straight ahead.

The door slid open, and Sanders wheeled him into a room much the same as his own, several levels away. Llewelyn sat beside the window, bent over a mess of papers, and he looked as wretched as Dieter felt.

Dieter watched him in silence for several minutes and then glanced up at Sanders. "Can you wait outside?"

"I don't think…"

"Sanders, I need to talk to him about things you can't hear," Dieter said quietly. "Please. Out. Now."

The door closed behind them, so Dieter could only assume he'd gone.

He didn't really care anymore, his eyes fixed on Llewelyn.

The man was watching him warily from beneath his lashes.

"Mike."

Llewelyn turned away, and his hand moved spasmodically on the paper in front of him. His fingernails were bitten down to the quick, crusted with blood along the edges. For a man who'd been military in his precision and control, he seemed like a stranger.

"I thought you'd come," he said in a low voice.

"You knew I would," Dieter replied, surprised how calm his voice was. His voice only though. He couldn't remember ever being more furious in his entire life.

"I'm sor—"

"Don't." Dieter snarled, gripping the handles of the wheelchair so hard it hurt. "Don't you even fucking try to apologise to me, you stupid, ignorant fuck." His breath shrilled between his teeth. "You knew the rules. You know why we can't change things back then, but you just had to fucking do it, didn't you? And now look what you've done. Now everyone knows, historically, Michael fucking Muller was the fucking driver who got Franz fucking Ferdinand assassinated."

Llewelyn flinched away. "I wanted to stop a war," he said, his voice hoarse with disuse. "Is it a crime?"

"Stop a war," Dieter echoed. "You are a fucking child if you think it's that easy. Someone was going to die to start this thing. If it wasn't him, it would have been someone else. What kind of hero complex do you have, to think saving one man is enough to stop a continent from imploding!"

"I had to try!"

"And you fucked up!" Dieter said savagely, struggling to his feet. He staggered closer and slammed his hand down on the table. "What did you think would happen? That you'd drive a bit faster and no one would try and get in the way? Did you think it was just one faction of assassins? Didn't you even fucking listen to a word I said about the fucking powder keg?"

Llewelyn stared blankly at Dieter's hand and then up at him. He'd lost weight, a lot of it, and he was gaunt. "I know," he said unsteadily. "And I remember the gun. I saw the gun. And I didn't stop it."

"No." Dieter's voice, now quieter, shook with suppressed rage. "You could have. All you had to do was keep going, but you didn't fucking think. You just saw an Austrian uniform and thought he was a friend, after everything I told you, you stupid fucking incompetent."

He leaned closer, snarling as Llewelyn shrank away, covering his face. "You killed him, as much as Princip did. You stopped the car. You could have saved him, and you didn't, and now you're whining because you're the one who let them light the fucking fuse when you could have stopped it." He pushed himself upright, one hand against the table. "Congratu-fucking-lations."

Llewelyn shook his head, fingers biting into his scalp. "I only wanted to stop it," he whispered, his voice breaking.

Dieter stared down at him. Ten days ago, he might have cared. A fortnight ago, he would have been the first person reassuring Llewelyn. Six months ago, he might've been guilty over upsetting someone who'd been traumatised by the past.

That was then.

Now, he was a man who would have fired the necessary shot to begin the war, because the past had happened and couldn't be changed. He would have killed, and he would have died there because the stupid idealistic bastard in front of him wanted to be a fucking hero. He had put aside his morals. He'd had the weight of a gun in his hand. He'd been sprayed with the blood of the man he would have killed and heard the rattle of fading breath in his throat. He'd seen Franz Ferdinand's face. He'd seen the man bleeding, staring, stunned, dying.

He turned away from Llewelyn, stumbled to the wall and pressed his hands to it, rested his forehead between them. His head ached, nausea and dizziness washing over him, and he should call Sanders, get out, leave.

He remembered the smell, the oil of the car, the gunpowder, the blood.

Worse than the pain, that. Knowing he would have killed if he had to.

"Dieter." Llewelyn's voice was a thin, frail thing. "I am sorry. I am."

Dieter shook his head. "Not yet," he whispered.

He didn't turn, bracing himself against the wall as he tried to get to the wheelchair. His ankle stabbed with pain. "When you think beyond the man, when you think about the trenches, the people, the children, who died, the starvation, the bombings, the disease." His voice trembled. "When you think your stupidity could have stopped it, but it didn't?" Dieter leaned on the chair and glanced over, hollowed out, exhausted, and weak. "That's when you're going to be fucking sorry."

He banged his hand on the door and fell into the chair as the door slid silently open.

Sanders took him back the way they had come. The hallways were too bright, and Dieter closed his hands over his eyes, pain lancing through his head. He heard voices, his name called, but shook his head, not willing, ready, to face anyone else. His eyes burned, and he tried to push away the thoughts crowding in on him.

It was only when the door of his room opened in front of him, only when he saw the familiar dimmed lights, that he lifted his head.

"Jan?" he whispered.

Janos was in front of him in a heartbeat, on his knees, and gathered Dieter in his arms.

Dieter clung to him, and shaking, silent, he wept.

Chapter Thirty-Nine

Dieter's recovery was slow.

As soon as he was permitted, Janos took him home from the institution. Sanders didn't even try to get Janos to put on the tracker cuff.

Dieter was still weak, even though a month had passed since his return. His wounds still bothered him, and his nightmares jolted him awake most nights, but Janos was there for every night in the medical wing. As soon as they were back in the apartment, he quietly installed his few possessions in the empty bedside cabinet.

He sat on the edge of the bed and offered his hand to Dieter, who was staring around the room as if he could barely remember it.

"You will be well," he said, as Dieter's cool fingertips brushed his.

"Wish I could believe you," Dieter murmured, watching the way their fingers interlaced.

Janos tugged him a step closer, and Dieter sank beside him on the bed. "I will help you. You helped me in new world. Frightening world." He gazed up at him. "I want to help you. You are my Dieter, and I am your Janos. We are one another's."

A ghost of a smile hovered around Dieter's lips. "Next thing I know," he murmured, "you'll be proposing marriage."

Janos put his head to one side. It was true, he could. In this world, in this time, there were no laws to stop them from being bound to one another. And maybe, one day, he would ask, and one day, maybe Dieter would answer yes. Maybe.

"Not now," he said, brushing his thumb along the side of Dieter's palm. "Now, I ask you to rest and grow strong and smile again."

Dieter leaned his shoulders against Janos's, still gazing at their joined hands. "I'll try," he said quietly. "I promise."

Janos drew his hand free and gently tilted Dieter's chin up. "Thank you." He didn't know what for. Nothing. Everything. For being with him. For supporting him. For just being Dieter. All of it. He leaned closer and kissed him gently, his lips skimming Dieter's.

Dieter's lips parted in a shivering sigh, and Janos drew back.

"Rest now," he murmured, dragging his knuckles gently down Dieter's cheek. "You have come a long way."

"You'll stay with me?" Dieter asked, quiet and small.

Janos nodded. "For as long as you need," he promised. He leaned closer and pressed a kiss tenderly to Dieter's brow. "Into bed. I will fetch you warm milk. I have honey now."

Dieter was almost smiling as he pushed himself onto the bed. "Fussy old woman," he whispered.

Janos paused in the doorway, gazing at him. "Sometimes," he agreed, then added with a touch of mischief, "but this time, honey is sticky, so no mouth job."

Behind him, as he turned towards the kitchen, Dieter laughed, and it was the sweetest sound he had ever heard.

Acknowledgements

Once more, the usual suspects, my motley crew, get all my thanks. Beth and Ash, who have been dealing with me flailing over this series since 2014. Look! It's almost done! And NineStar, for picking up my sprawling convoluted temporal baby and giving all of it a home.

About the Author

C.B. Lewis has been making up nonsense since she was able to talk. Now, she puts it into computers and turns it into books. She is chuffed to bits to officially be yet another one of the collective of authors from Edinburgh.

Facebook: www.facebook.com/CB-Lewis-369293759939573

Tumblr: www.tumblr.com/blog/cb-lewis

Website: www.cblewis.co.uk

Other books by this author

Out of Time Series

Time Lost (Coming Summer 2020)

Time Taken

Time Turns

Out of time

Coming Soon from C.B. Lewis

Time Lost
Out of Time. Book Two

At first, everyone assumed it was a burglary.

The postman was the first on the scene. He'd arrived early in the morning to make a delivery to the house in question and found the front door wedged open. No one answered when he rang the bell, so he called the police. The two constables arrived to investigate, and they were the ones who found the body.

It escalated after that.

Not even noon, Jacob thought grimly. Hell of a way to start a Monday.

His autopod shuttled along, arcing off from the main highway. As much as he missed manual controls of old-fashioned cars and early autocars, he appreciated the driverless function of the pod because it gave him time to skim through the images from the crime scene en route.

He wouldn't get a feel for the scene until he got there, but the images let him know what he was about to walk into. There were signs of a struggle in the room where the body was found, and plenty of blood, but the rest of the house seemed undisturbed.

"Control to Delta Seven. ETA to destination?"

Jacob leaned forward and cleared the images from the display on the windscreen, bringing up his location on the map. Beyond it, he could see the country roads through the glass.

"ETA fifteen minutes, Control," he replied, then muttered under his breath, "Into the backside of nowhere."

It was half an hour beyond the miles of sprawling suburbs of the city in the middle of green fields and close to a forest. The nearest amenities had to be at least four miles from the building. He shook his head. What kind of person chose to live all the way out there anymore? It wasn't as if there were a shortage of housing in the city.

A chime indicated another image had been received.

Jacob opened it up and leaned forward, frowning.

A door, just visible, blended into the pattern of the wall. No handle, no visible hinges.

"You seeing this, sir?" Constable Foley's voice rang through the speaker.

"I am indeed, Foley," he said, widening the image. "Is that a safe room?"

"Looks that way, sir," the constable replied. "The dust in front of it suggests a box was moved and recently. Looks like someone might be in there."

Smart girl, Jacob thought with approval.

"Any response?"

"Not yet, sir, but if they were attacked—"

"They might not be capable of replying," Jacob finished. "Keep trying." He minimised the image and looked out through the windscreen. "I have visual on you, Foley. Be with you soon."

Ahead of him, the house was visible between the trees. The red brick structure had to be at least two centuries old, but even from a distance, the modern touches were obvious. The windows were thick and secure. The roof had been replaced with faux slate.

The autopod purred to a halt beside the four other vehicles lining the gravel courtyard, and the door slid aside. Jacob stepped out and glanced at the other vehicles. He recognised the coroner's transport pod, and the standard blue-and-white patterned squad pod, but the other two were probably the homeowner's.

Foley opened the front door to greet him.

Half his age, she hadn't been with the force long enough to be as jaded as him yet. She smiled in greeting. "Morning, sir."

He winced. "Say afternoon. It makes it a little more bearable."

She laughed. "You want a summary, sir?"

"I read up on it on the way over. Any word on the owner?"

"Thomas Sanders," Foley said, leading him towards the house. "Forty-eight. Widower with one young son. He's a well-reputed scientist and engineer. High up in some kind of historical and scientific research program in the city, the Temporal Research Institution."

"Have you been able to make contact with him?"

Foley shook her head, her sandy ponytail swinging. She offered him overalls to cover his suit. "We've tried his business and private numbers. His colleagues said he's been on a leave of absence for health reasons for several weeks. Our best bet is the safe room."

"Any sign of the son?"

Foley shook her head. "We assume he's with his father."

"Do we have an ID for the body yet?"

She hesitated in the hallway. "That's the strange thing, sir. We can't find anything on him. His prints aren't in the system. No DNA trace either. We still need to run facial recognition, but so far, we've got nothing."

"That's not unusual."

Foley looked at him. "There's something off about it all. I'll show you."

The house was spacious inside. The lower level was split into four rooms, all branching off from a wide, sunlit hall. Foley led him down the hall and to one of the rooms at the back, her covered boots thumping on the wooden floors.

Jacob stopped in the doorway, taking a moment, then stepped across the threshold. The crime scene team was still at work.

The room appeared to be some kind of laboratory with workbenches running along one wall. Another wall was covered in old-fashioned whiteboards with all kinds of incomprehensible text and codes marked on them in half a dozen colours. Jacob studied it for a moment, but whatever Sanders was working on, it was far beyond Jacob's barely adequate physics A level.

There were little machines here and there, suspended from the boards by wires. Spools of wire and gears were scattered across the floor. Several boxes had been upended from shelves and lay on their sides.

In the middle of it all, the body lay face down on the floor, a bloodied hammer close at hand.

Danni Michaels was working on the body and glanced up with a nod. "Sir."

"Cause of death?" Jacob said, keeping his eyes off the dead man's face.

"Looks like blunt force trauma," Danni replied, nudging her magnifying glasses up her nose with her knuckles. "I don't think it's a wild guess to say the weapon was that hammer. It was a single blow, landed here."

Jacob gritted his teeth and looked. The left side of the man's forehead was ruptured. His eyes were open, and he had a look of surprise on his rigid, bloody face. He was young. Maybe thirties. Dark haired. His eyes were dark, the pupils flared wide open, but death sometimes did that. Blood had spread in a wide, sticky pool around his body. Jacob swallowed down the familiar rising acid.

Christ, he hated the messy ones.

He glanced around the room.

A pair of slippers, several steps away from the blood pool, had left bloody prints on the polished floor. The owner must have kicked them off, and they'd ended up at least three feet from each other. Not good shoes for running, slippers. If he—men's slippers, size nine approximately—had already knocked down the man on the floor, then there had to be another assailant whom he was running from.

"Any sign of this man's accomplice?"

"Accomplice?" Foley asked.

Jacob gestured to the slippers. It was easier than looking at the body. "You don't try and run from an unconscious, nearly dead man. There was someone else here."

"We haven't seen any sign of anyone else," Foley replied. "Sorry, sir. I didn't even notice that."

He offered her a brief smile. "That's why I'm a DI, Foley." He motioned back to the body. "You said there was something off?"

Foley nodded, crouching by the body. "Take a look at his right eye."

Jacob went down beside her, propping his forearms on his knees. It took him a moment, but then he saw what she was pointing out: The pupil wasn't just blown. There was no iris at all.

"What the hell..." He leaned closer. "Michaels, can I borrow your magnifiers?"

She handed them over and obligingly shone the torch over the man's eyes. "Clever, isn't it?"

Jacob stared at the man's eye and then looked up. "A synthetic bionic eyeball? Is that even possible?"

Michaels shook her head. "I've heard of people developing them, but I've never heard of any successful trials." She looked back down at the body and grinned. "I'm looking forward to getting it out and seeing what it's made of."

"And there's one of those images I just didn't need," Jacob murmured, peering through the magnifier again. The pupil was a focusing lens, from the looks of it. High-quality, high-end technology. "Foley, have you looked up anywhere that might carry tech this advanced?"

"We're putting together a list," she said. "But from what we're hearing back, this is off the charts, sir. No one has heard of technology like this before, or if they have, they're not telling us about it."

He straightened up. "You said this Sanders was a scientist?"

"Doctor in physics and engineering," she confirmed.

"Could he have made something like this?"

She hesitated. "From all accounts, he didn't deal in human biology or bio-artificing."

"Doesn't mean he couldn't." Jacob ran a hand over his face. "Well, if we can't find this man by standard identification, maybe we can find him by the eye he doesn't have. Danni, we need all the information you can get us as soon as possible."

"Sir," Danni said at once.

Jacob glanced at Foley. "Where's Singh?"

"Still trying to get into the safe room." She jerked her head. "This way."

The safe room was up the stairs in what appeared to be a playroom. One wall was all windows; another was covered in posters and drawings. Kid's toys and games were scattered all over the place. Singh was working his way along the one blank wall with a scanner.

Jacob glanced around. "You said Sanders has a son?"

"Ben," Foley confirmed.

"About eight?"

Foley looked at him in surprise. "Seven and a half. Is this another one of those detective things?"

Jacob chuckled. "This time, it's one of those dad things."

Singh looked over his shoulder at them, sighing in frustration. "Foley, I know you said to scan for a high intensity of fingerprints on the wall, but this whole wall is fingerprints." He nodded at Jacob. "Afternoon, sir."

"Singh." Jacob approached, looking the wall up and down. "It's very smoothly done, isn't it?" He rubbed his short beard thoughtfully with his fingertips. "No visible buttons or latches anywhere?"

"None we could find," Foley said. "I thought it might be a pressure-point system, but seems not. We requested an expert, but they've been delayed."

"I think we need to un-delay them," Jacob said, touching his earbud to activate it. "If Sanders is wounded and inside there, we need to get him out. If not, we need confirmation, because this could be an abduction."

It was close to an hour before the locksmith arrived. By the time he did, the body had been removed. The crime scene unit was working their way out from the house across the grounds, searching for trace evidence of the intruders.

While they waited, Jacob had gone down to the laboratory to take another look at the whiteboards. He didn't see what it had to do with Sanders's work at the Temporal Research Institution. A quick search suggested the institution specialised in identifying historical discrepancies and confirming historical events. It could be something to do with locating old records and creating algorithms, he supposed. You would need a specialised engineer to do that.

"Sir?"

Jacob turned. "Foley?"

"The smith is here. I thought you might want to be present if he can open the door."

They headed back up the stairs to the playroom. The locksmith was already working on the wall with a scanning device.

"Apparently," Singh said, joining them, "all safe room doors come installed with a registration chip, in case the mechanism needs to be deactivated in an emergency."

"Not unlike this," Jacob observed. "Useful."

The locksmith glanced over. "It's a recent make. Give me two minutes."

In the end, he took less than thirty seconds, and the door swung outward.

Inside, there was a room big enough for a family, but only one person was there. A small tawny-haired boy shrank back into the corner of the room, his arms wrapped around his legs, his face bone white.

Jacob motioned for the smith and the two constables to back off, and crouched a couple of feet away from the door.

"Hey," he murmured.

The boy was shivering and tears rolled down his face from swollen, red-rimmed eyes.

Jacob took out his badge, laid it on the floor, and slid it across to the boy. "It's okay. I'm a policeman. My name's Jacob." He watched as the boy tentatively leaned forward and looked at the badge. "Are you Ben?"

The boy nodded. "Where's my dad?" His voice shook as much as he was.

"We're trying to find him just now." Jacob offered a hand. "Do you want to come out? You don't need to stay in there."

"Dad told me to stay here." Ben wrapped his arms tighter around his legs. "He told me to, until he came to get me."

"I know." Jacob knelt and sat back on his heels. "We want him to come and get you, too, Ben, but right now, I think he'd want you to be safe, don't you? How about we keep you safe?"

"P-promise?"

Jacob nodded. "Promise."

Ben got unsteadily to his feet. His trousers were sodden, and there was vomit on the front of his shirt. The poor kid must have been terrified. Jacob knelt up, offering both his hands, and Ben's icy fingers wrapped around his.

"There you go," Jacob said as gently as he could, drawing Ben back out. "You're safe now."

The little boy gave a sob and stumbled forward and wrapped his arms around Jacob's neck, clinging to him. Jacob scooped him up and rose to his feet with the boy in his arms. He rubbed his hand in circles on Ben's back.

"You're okay," he murmured. "You're okay."

Also Available from NineStar Press

Connect with NineStar Press

Website: NineStarPress.com

Facebook: NineStarPress

Facebook Reader Group: NineStarNiche

Twitter: @ninestarpress

Tumblr: NineStarPress